# About the Authors

as far back as she can remember **Michelle Conder** ed of being a writer. She penned the first chapter omance novel just out of high school, but it took study, many (varied) jobs, one ultra-understanding nd and three gorgeous children before she finally wn to turn that dream into a reality.

helle lives in Australia, and when she isn't busy g she loves to read, ride horses, travel and practise Visit Michelle: www.michelleconder.com

& Boon novels were **Julia James'** first 'grown up' she read as a teenager, and she's been reading them ince. She adores the Mediterranean and the English ryside in all its seasons, and is fascinated by all historical, from castles to cottages. In between g she enjoys walking, gardening, needlework and g 'extremely gooey chocolate cakes' and trying to t! Julia lives in England with her family.

**erly Lang** is a Southern belle with a trouble-g streak and a great love of strong heroes and even r heroines. A former ballet dancer and English , she now does yoga and writes the kind of books ways loved to read. She's married to her college eart, is mum to the most amazing child on the , and shares her office space with a dog named . Visit her website at www.BooksByKimberly.com

# The Hidden
## COLLECTION

March 2020
**Hidden Desire**

May 2020
**Hidden Motives**

April 2020
**Hidden Past**

June 2020
**Hidden Passion**

# Hidden Passion

## MICHELLE CONDER

## JULIA JAMES

## KIMBERLY LANG

MIX
Paper from
responsible sources
FSC
FSC C007454

book is produced from independently certified FSC™ paper
to ensure responsible forest management.

or more information visit www.harpercollins.co.uk/green

Printed and bound in Spain
by CPI, Barcelona

# MILLS & BOON

First Published in Great Britain 2020
By Mills & Boon, an imprint of HarperCollins*Publishers*
1 London Bridge Street, London, SE1 9GF

HIDDEN PASSION © 2020 Harlequin Books S.A.

*Girl Behind the Scandalous Reputation* © 2012 Michelle Conder
*The Forbidden Touch of Sanguardo* © 2014 Julia James
*The Taming of a Wild Child* © 2013 Kimberly Kerr

ISBN: 978-0-263-28162-0

# GIRL BEHIND THE SCANDALOUS REPUTATION

## MICHELLE CONDER

For Paul who always takes the kids – even when it means missing a surf, for my kids who so graciously accept when mummy is busy, for Laurel who tirelessly reads my dodgy first drafts, and for mum who is always there when I need her most. And for Flo for her keen insights and endless encouragement. Thank you all.

# CHAPTER ONE

'Is THIS your idea of a joke, Jordana?' Tristan Garrett turned away from the view of the Thames outside his tenth-storey office window to stare incredulously at his baby sister. She sat in one of the navy tub chairs on the visitors' side of his desk, legs crossed, immaculately groomed, and looking not at all like a crazy person sailing three sheets to the wind—as she sounded.

'As if I would joke about something so serious!' Jordana exclaimed, gazing at him, her jade-green eyes, the exact shade of his own, wide and etched with worry. 'I know it sounds unbelievable but it's true, and we have to help her.'

Actually, her story didn't sound unbelievable at all, but Tristan knew his sanguine sister had a tendency to see goodness in people when there was none to see at all.

He turned back to stare at the pedestrians lining the Thames and better able to enjoy the September sunshine than he was. He couldn't stand seeing his sister so upset, and he cursed the so-called friend who was responsible for putting these fresh tears in her eyes.

When she came to stand beside him he slung his arm around her shoulders, drawing her close. What could he say to placate her? That the friend she wanted to help wasn't worth it? That anyone stupid enough to try and smuggle drugs out of Thailand deserved to get caught?

Normally he would help his sister in a heartbeat, but no way was he getting involved in this fiasco —and nor was she. He gave her an affectionate squeeze, but he didn't try to contain the edge of steel in his voice when he spoke. 'Jo, this is not your problem and you are not getting involved.'

'I—'

Tristan held up his hand to cut off her immediate objection, his solid-gold cufflinks glinting in the downlights. 'If what you say is true then the girl made her bed and she'll have to lie in it. And may I remind you that you're eight days away from the wedding of the year. Not only will Oliver not want you getting involved, but I doubt the Prince of Greece will want to sit beside a known drug-user—no matter how beautiful.'

Jordana's mouth tightened. 'Oliver will want me to do what's right,' she objected. 'And I don't care what my wedding guests think. I'm going to help Lily and that's that.'

Tristan shook his head. 'Why would you risk it?'

'She's my best friend and I promised I would.'

That surprised him. He'd thought their friendship had died down years ago. But if that was the case then why was Lily to be maid of honour at Jo's wedding? Maid of honour to *his* best man! And why hadn't he thought to ask that question two weeks earlier, when he'd found out Lily was coming to the wedding?

He frowned, but decided to push that issue aside for the more pressing problem at hand. 'When did you speak to her?'

'I didn't. A customs officer called on her behalf. Lily wanted to let me know why she couldn't meet me, and— Oh, Tristan, if we don't help her she'll probably go to jail.'

Tristan pushed back the thick lock of hair that had fallen over his forehead and made a mental note to book a haircut.

Much as he didn't want to, he could see that he needed to get tough with his sister. 'Which is probably the best place for her.' He scowled. 'She'll be able to get help there.'

'You don't mean that!'

Didn't he? He didn't know. But what he did know was that his morning had been a lot better before Jordana had rushed into his office, bringing to mind a girl he'd rather strip from it altogether.

Honey Blossom Lily Wild.

Currently voted one of the sexiest women on the planet, and a talented actress to boot. He didn't follow films but he'd seen her first one—some art-house twaddle made by a precocious upstart of a director about the end of the world. Tristan couldn't remember the plot. What man could? It had Lily naked, save for a white oversized singlet and a pair of cotton panties masquerading as shorts, in almost every scene. The movie had signified to him that as a culture they were heading backwards—and people like Lily Wild were half the reason for that.

He and his father had tolerated the girls' teenage friendship because it had made Jordana happy—and neither man would ever have jeopardised that—but Tristan had disliked Lily on sight when he'd first come across her as a gangly fourteen-year-old, hiding drugs under his sister's dormitory mattress. She'd been haughty beyond her years that day, and if he had his time again he'd suggest his sister be relocated to another boarding school quick-smart.

Tristan heaved a sigh and returned to the smooth curve of his walnut desk, stroking his computer mouse to get rid of the screen saver. 'Jo, I'm busy. I have an important meeting in half an hour. I'm sorry, but I can't help.'

'Tristan, I know you have a thing about drug-users, but Lily is innocent.'

'And you know this how, exactly?' he queried, deciding that humouring his sister might expedite her leaving.

'Because I know Lily, and I know she doesn't take drugs. She hates them.'

Tristan raised an eyebrow. Was his sister for real?

'Have you conveniently forgotten the fallout from your eighteenth birthday party? How I caught her hiding a joint when she was fourteen? Not to mention the various press photos of her completely wasted in between.'

Jordana frowned and shook her head. 'Most of those photos were fakes. Lily's been hounded by the press her whole life because of who her parents were—and, anyway, she's far too sensible and level-headed to get involved in something as destructive as drugs.'

'And that would be why there was the scandal at your eighteenth? Because Lily is *so* level-headed?'

Jordana glanced at the ceiling before returning resigned eyes to his. 'Tristan, that night was so not what it seemed. One dodgy photo—'

'One dodgy photo?' he all but shouted. 'One dodgy photo that could have destroyed your reputation if I hadn't intervened!'

'You mean if you hadn't made Lily take the blame!'

'Lily *was* to blame!' Tristan could feel the old anger of six years ago welling up inside him. But it wasn't like him to let his temper override common sense and he controlled it with effort. 'Maybe if I had contacted her stepfather when I caught her with marijuana the first time she wouldn't be in the colossal mess she is now.'

Jordana briefly lowered her eyes before meeting his again. 'Tristan, you've never let me properly explain about any of this. What if the marijuana you found Lily hiding when we were fourteen wasn't hers? Would you be so disappointed if it was mine?'

Tristan expelled a breath. He really didn't have time for this. He got up and rounded his desk to enfold Jordana in his arms. He knew what she was trying to do and he loved her for it—even if the little bimbo she was trying to protect didn't deserve her loyalty.

'I know you're trying to take the blame for her, Jo. You've always protected her. But the fact still remains that she's trouble. She always has been. Surely her stepfather or stepsisters can help her?'

Jordana sniffed against his chest and pushed away a little. 'They've never been very close, and anyway I think they're holidaying in France. Please, Tristan! The officer I spoke to this morning said she might be deported back to Thailand. And, no matter what you think, I can't let that happen.'

Tristan swore under his breath. He had to admit he didn't want to imagine the gorgeous Lily Wild wasting away in a Thai prison cell either. 'Jo, my specialty is corporate law, and this will fall under the criminal jurisdiction.'

'But surely you can do *something*!' she implored.

Tristan released his sister and stalked over to the floor-to-ceiling windows again.

Unwelcome images of Lily as he'd last seen her crowded in and he forcibly held them back. She had been intruding on his thoughts and dreams for years now, but more so of late. Ever since Jordana had mentioned she was coming to the wedding, in fact, and to say that he resented her for it was putting it mildly.

He closed his eyes, the better to control the physical reaction he always seemed to have when he pictured her, but that only made it worse. Now he could not only visualise her, he could almost scent her as well.

Jordana touched his arm, and for a split second he imagined it *was* Lily.

Tristan muttered another curse under his breath. 'Jo, forget Lily Wild and concentrate on your wedding,' he growled, feeling like a heel when his sister flinched back from him.

'If Lily's not going to be there I might not even *have* a wedding.'

'Now you're being melodramatic.'

'And you're being horrible. Lily's been unfairly targeted...'

'Jordana, the woman wasn't targeted. She was caught red-handed!'

Jordana looked at him with the kind of pain he hadn't seen in her eyes since the day they had buried their mother. He'd vowed then that he'd do anything to protect her in the future and safeguard her happiness, and wasn't what he was doing now the opposite?

But what she was asking was impossible...

'Tristan, I know you hate drugs because of Mum, but Lily

isn't like that. And you usually jump at the chance to help a worthy cause.'

Tristan stared at Jordana. Her words brought back memories of the past he'd much rather leave dead and buried. And maybe it was somewhat illogical but he blamed Lily for that as well—because without her latest antics he wouldn't be having this conversation with his sister at all!

He turned back to face Jo and unclenched his jaw. 'Jordana, the key word in this situation is *worthy*. And as far as I'm concerned a drug-addicted actress who has hit the skids does not a worthy cause make.'

Jordana stared at him as if he'd just kicked a dog, and in that instant Tristan knew he was defeated. No way could he let his sister think so badly of him—and on top of that an image of Lily in a Thai prison cell kept swimming into his consciousness and twisting his gut.

He shook his head. 'This is a big mistake,' he warned, ignoring the little glow of relief he felt when Jordana's face lit up with unconcealed gratitude. 'And don't look at me like that. I might not be able to do anything. It's not like she shoplifted a bar of soap from the local chemist.'

'Oh, Tristan, you are the best brother in the world. Shall I wait and come with you?' Jordana was so happy she was practically singing.

Tristan looked up blankly, his mind already turning over to how he would approach the problem. When her words sank in his eyebrows shot skywards. 'Absolutely not.' The last thing he needed was his interfering sister getting in the way. 'I'll call you when I know something. Now, go. Do wedding stuff, or something, and leave me to sort through this mess you're so determined to get us in the middle of.'

He barely registered it when she kissed his cheek and let herself out of his office, already issuing orders down the phone to his secretary. 'Kate, reschedule all my meetings for the afternoon and tell Stuart Macintyre I want him in my office five minutes ago.'

He eased back in his chair and blew out a breath.

Was he completely crazy to get involved with this?

Lily Wild was trouble, and if seeing her bent over his father's prized nineteenth-century Dickens desk snorting cocaine at Jo's eighteenth party wasn't proof enough of that, then surely her attempt to smuggle drugs through Heathrow today was.

Not that Lily had ever admitted to taking drugs the night of his sister's party. She'd just given him a phoney, imperious smile that had incited his temper to boiling and after that he hadn't wanted to hear any excuses. Why bother? In his experience all users were supposedly as innocent as Carmelite nuns.

And what had made him even more irate was that earlier that night Lily had looked at him with those violet-coloured doe eyes of hers as if he was the only man in the world for her. And, fool that he was, he'd very nearly bought it!

Up until that point she had been nothing more than an irritation, occasionally taking his sister to her stepfather's industry parties when they were too young, and running away from him whenever he had come across her at the family estate during school holidays.

But she hadn't run away from him at the party. Quite the opposite in fact.

*Forget it*, he told himself severely as his mind zeroed in on the potent memory of how he had danced with her that night. Touched her. Kissed her.

The realisation that he'd very nearly lost control with her still rankled. But she had tasted pure and sweet, and so hot and…

Tristan shook his head and swore violently. Instead of reliving a moment that should never have happened in the first place he should be remembering how he had come upon her in his father's private study with a group of social misfits, his beloved sister, and about half a kilo of cocaine.

It had taken ten minutes to have Security dispense with everyone but his sister, and twenty-four hours to shut down the internet photos of Jordana that had been taken on a guest's mobile phone.

The taste of Lily, unfortunately, had taken a little longer to shift.

Lily Wild squirmed uncomfortably on the hard metal chair she had been sitting in for the last four hours and seventeen minutes and wondered when this nightmare she was trapped in would end. She was presently alone in a small featureless room that would make any director on a cop show proud.

Earlier today she had been equal parts nervous and excited at the prospect of returning to England, her home, for the first time in six years.

She had been lined up at border control for ages, and had just made it to the passport-check booth when the official behind the partition had directed her to a row of officers with sniffer dogs. She hadn't been concerned as she'd seen she was just one of many being checked over. Instead her mind had been on Jordana, hoping she would like the wedding present she'd bought for her and Oliver in Thailand, and also on how much she was looking forward to her long-overdue break.

Then one of the attending officers had lifted a medium-sized plastic bag out of her tote and asked if it belonged to her. She honestly hadn't been able to remember.

'I don't know,' she'd answered.

'Then you'll have to step this way.' He'd indicated a long, over-bright hallway and sweat had immediately prickled on her palms—like the heat rash she'd once developed while filming in Brazil.

Now, looking around the small featureless room, she wondered where the two customs officials had gone. Not that she missed them—particularly the smarmy younger one, who spoke almost exclusively to her chest and threatened to deport her to Thailand if she didn't start co-operating.

Which was a laugh in itself, because all she had done since they'd detained her was co-operate!

Yes, the multicoloured tote bag was hers. No, she hadn't left it unattended at any time. Yes, a friend had been in her hotel room the night she'd packed. No, she didn't think he'd gone near her personal belongings. And doubly no, the small plastic vials filled with ecstasy and cocaine were not hers! She'd nearly had a heart attack at the question, sure they must have made a mistake.

'No mistake, ma'am,' the nicer of the two officials had said, and the prickle of sweat had made its way to her armpits and dripped down the back of her neck like a leaky tap.

They'd then questioned her for hours about her movements at Suvarnabhumi Airport and her reasons for being in Thailand until she was completely exhausted and couldn't remember what she'd told them. They'd left after that. No doubt to confer with those watching behind the two-way mirror.

Lily knew they suspected Jonah Loft, one of the guys working on the film she had just wrapped, but only because he had been in her room just before she had left for the airport. She felt terrible for him.

She had met Jonah at the New York rehabilitation centre she volunteered at, and it wouldn't take the authorities long to discover that he had once had a drug problem.

Fortunately he was over that now, but Lily knew from her work with addicts that if anything could set off a relapse it was people not believing in them. Which was why Lily had got him a job on the film in the first place. She had wanted to give him a second chance, but she supposed when they found out she had been the instigator of having him work on the film it would reflect badly on both of them.

And yet she knew he wouldn't have done this to her. He'd been too grateful—and hopeful of staying clean.

Lily sighed. Four hours and twenty-eight minutes.

Her bottom was numb and she stretched in the chair, wondering if she was allowed to get up and walk around. So far she hadn't, and her thigh muscles felt as if they had been petrified. She rubbed her temples to try and ease her aching head.

She hoped Jordana had been contacted so she wouldn't be concerned about why she hadn't made it through the arrival gate. Though, as to that, Jo would likely be more worried if she *did* know what was holding her up. Lily just prayed she didn't contact her overbearing brother for help.

The last thing she needed was the deliciously gorgeous but painfully autocratic Tristan Garrett finding out about her predicament. She knew he was supposed to be one of the best lawyers alive, but Lily had only ever had acrimonious dealings with Tristan—apart from ten unbelievably magic minutes on a dance floor at Jordana's eighteenth birthday party. Lily knew he hated the sight of her now.

He'd devastated her—first by kissing her in a way that had transported her to another world, and then by ignoring her for the rest of the night as if she hadn't even existed. As if they hadn't just kissed like soul mates…

And just when she'd thought her teenage heart couldn't break any more he'd come across her in his father's study trying to clean up a private party Jordana should never have been involved in, and jumped completely to the wrong conclusion.

He'd blamed Lily—and her 'kind'—and thrown her out of his home. In hindsight she supposed she should have been thankful that he'd taken the time to organise his chauffer to drive her the two hours back to London, but she hadn't been. She'd been crushed—and so had her stupid girlhood fantasy that he just might be the love of her life.

Looking back now, she couldn't imagine what had possessed her even to think that in the first place. They were from different worlds and she knew he had never approved of her. Had always been as disgusted as she was herself at her being the only offspring of two notoriously drugged-out hippy celebrities who had died—*in flagrante*—of a drug overdose.

Not that she'd ever let him see that. She did have some pride—not to mention her late father's wise words running through her head.

'Never let 'em know you care, Honeybee,' he'd always said.

Of course he'd been referring mostly to rock music reviews, but she had never forgotten. And it had held her in good stead when she'd had to face down more than her fair share of speculation and scandal, thanks to her parents and, sometimes, to her own actions.

The hard scrape of the metal door snapped Lily back to the present and she glanced up as the smarmy customs official swaggered back into the room, a condescending smile expanding his fleshy lips.

He sat opposite her and cocked an eyebrow. 'You are one lucky lady, Miss Wild,' he said in his heavy cockney brogue. 'It seems you're to be released.'

Lily stared at him impassively, blinking against the harsh fluorescent light and giving nothing away as to how she was feeling.

The official sprawled back in the chair and rhythmically tapped the table with what looked like a typed report, staring at her chest. Men like him—men who thought that because she was blonde and had a nice face and reasonable body shape she was easy—were a dime a dozen.

This guy was a marine wannabe, with a flat-top haircut that, instead of adding an air of menace, made him look as if he should be in the circus. But even if he'd had the polish of some latter-day Prince Charming, Lily wouldn't have been interested. She might make movies about love and happy-ever-after but she wasn't interested in the fairy tale for herself. Not after her mother's experiences with Johnny Wild, and the humiliating sting of Tristan's rejection of her all those years ago.

'That's right,' Marine-man finally sneered when she remained silent. 'You celebrities always seem to know someone who knows someone, and then it's all peaches an' cream again. Personally, I would 'ave sent you back to Thailand to face the music. But lucky for you it ain't up to me.'

And thank heavens for that, Lily thought, trying not to react to his leering scrutiny.

'Sign these.' He shoved the stapled document across the table at her, all business for once.

'What is it?'

'Conditions of your release.'

Release? She really was being released? Heart thudding, and as if in slow motion, Lily took the sheets of paper, not daring to believe it was true. She bent forward, letting her long wavy hair swing forward to shield her face from his prying eyes. She was shaking so badly the words appeared blurry on the page.

When the door scraped open a second time she didn't bother to look up, assuming it was the other official, returning to oversee her signature. Then a prickly sensation raised the hairs on the back of her neck, and a deeply masculine and very annoyed voice shattered her concentration and stole the breath from her lungs.

'You'll find it's all in order, Honey, so just sign the damned release so we can get out of here.'

Lily squeezed her eyes shut and felt the throbbing in her head escalate. She'd recognise that chocolate-covered voice anywhere, and waited for the dots to clear behind her eyes before peering up to confirm that not only was her nightmare of a day not over, but it had just taken a distinct turn for the worst.

Fortunately Jordana had received the message about her delay, but unfortunately she'd done exactly what Lily had feared: she'd gone to her big brother for help.

# CHAPTER TWO

LORD Garrett, Viscount Hadley, the future twelfth Duke of Greythorn, stood before her, with enough tension emanating from his body to fire a rocket to the moon.

'Tristan,' she breathed unnecessarily, her mind at once accepting that he was the most sublimely handsome male she had ever seen and rejecting that fact at the same time. He seemed taller and more powerful than she remembered, his lean, muscular physique highlighted by the precise cut of his tailor-made charcoal suit.

His chestnut hair was long, and lent him an untamed appeal he really didn't need, framing his olive complexion, flawlessly chiselled jaw and aristocratic nose to perfection. Her gaze skimmed up over the masculine curve of his lips and settled on cold, pale green eyes ringed with grey that were boldly assessing her in return.

His wide-legged no-nonsense stance set her heartbeat racing, and without thinking she snuck out her tongue to moisten lips that felt dryer than the paper she held between her fingers.

His eyes narrowed as they followed the movement, and Lily quickly cast her eyes downwards.

She pinched the bridge of her nose to ease the flash of pain that hammered behind her eyes, and blinked uncomprehendingly when a Mont Blanc pen was thrust in front of her face.

'Hurry up, Honey. I don't have all day.'

Lily wanted to remind him that she preferred Lily, but her throat was so tight she could barely swallow, let alone speak.

She grabbed the pen, flinching as her clumsy fingers collided with his, and scrawled her signature next to where he stabbed at the paper. Before she knew it the pages were whisked away, Tristan had grabbed her tote bag from Marine-man and he was ushering her out through the door with a firm guiding hand in the small of her back.

Lily stiffened away from the contact and rubbed her arms. He was well over six feet and seemed to dwarf her own five-foot-ten frame.

'If you're cold you should try wearing more clothing,' he snapped, hard eyes raking her body as if she were a foul piece of garbage.

Lily looked down at her white T-shirt, black leggings and black ballet flats.

'Ever heard of a bra, Honey?' His voice was silky, condescending, and Lily felt her breasts tighten as his gaze rested a little too long on her chest, her nipples firming against the fabric in a way she'd do anything to stop.

Lily was taken aback by his hostility, and it was all she could do not to cross her arms protectively over her body. She really wasn't up to dealing with any more animosity right now.

But she didn't say that. Instead she stared at the Windsor knot of his red tie and rubbed at the goosebumps that dotted her arms.

Tristan muttered something under his breath, shrugged out of his jacket, and draped it around her shoulders. She wanted to tell him she was fine, but before she could say anything he reached for her upper arm and propelled her down the long corridor, his clean, masculine scent blanketing her mind like a thick fog.

Tension bunched her stiff muscles, but she could hardly tell him to slow down when all she wanted to do was get as far away from the airport as possible. When he paused at the entrance to the duty-free hall Lily glanced up, feeling like an errant schoolgirl being dragged around by an enraged parent. She tried to loosen his grip, put some distance between them, but he ignored her attempt, tightening his hold before marching her through the throng of passengers. It reminded her of a couple of occasions in the past when he'd stormed into nightclubs and goose-stepped herself and Jordana out. It had been mostly at her stepfather Frank Murphy's parties, and in hindsight Tristan had done the right thing making them leave at their age, but at the time Lily had been hopping mad.

She noticed the large steel doors leading to the arrivals hall and breathed a sigh of relief. Hopefully Jordana was waiting on the other side, and once through Lily could thank Tristan for his help and bid him farewell until the wedding.

Her nerves were shot, but the relief that washed through her at the thought of freedom was suddenly cut short as Tristan veered left and led her into one of the small, dimly lit bars that lined the cavernous concourse.

The bar was long and narrow, with booths lining one wall and a polished wooden bar with red padded bar stools along the other. Except for two business types, deep in conversation, and an elderly gent who looked as if he might tumble into his early-afternoon schooner, the place was empty.

Lily waited to find out what they were doing, and was surprised when Tristan ordered two whiskys, watching as he glared at the bartender, whose eyes had lingered a little too long in her direction.

As soon as he'd moved off to get their drinks Tristan turned to her, and Lily nearly recoiled at the feral anger icing his eyes.

'What the hell are you doing back in my sister's life?' he demanded, his voice harsh as he lowered it so only she could hear.

Lily did recoil then and stared at him mutely.

Six years just seemed to evaporate before her eyes, and they might have been standing in his father's study again, where he'd accused her of something she hadn't done and called her a cheap slut.

Lily's eyes fell to his sensual mouth, now flattened into a thin line, and she quickly lowered them down the thick column of his tanned neck to rest once again on his silk tie. Looking at his mouth brought that devastating kiss to mind. She instantly reminded herself of his equally devastating rejection of her in an attempt to marshal her body's unexpected leap of excitement. How could she still feel so quivery over someone who had treated her so appallingly?

Tristan's tense silence seemed to envelop her, and she realised he was still waiting for her to respond to his rude question.

In all her mental imaginings of how this meeting between them would go this had not featured.

In one scenario she'd imagined they might be able to put the past behind them and become friends. Laugh over her silly teenage crush and his mistaken belief that she had set up the private party that had been splashed all over the internet. In that particular daydream she had raised her hand and said, *Please—don't give it another thought. It's over. It's in the past.*

But she didn't think that would play so well in this situation, and stupidly—so it now seemed—she had forgotten to prepare the whole busted-for-drugs-at-Heathrow scenario.

How remiss of her!

Now she had to ad lib, using a brain that wanted to drool over him like a beginner art student viewing her first Rodin nude.

Only she was no longer an impressionable girl caught in the throes of her first crush, Lily reminded herself firmly. She was a mature woman in charge of her own life. And wasn't one of her goals on this trip to meet Tristan as an equal? To look at him, talk to him, and put the juvenile attraction that had plagued her so often in the company of other men to bed? Metaphorically speaking, of course.

'I was invited to the wedding,' she said as politely as possible, given that his harsh question had evoked exactly the opposite response.

'And what an error of judgement *that* was,' he sneered, 'I can't imagine what my sister was thinking.'

Lily frowned and glanced at the bartender, pouring whisky into two glasses, so that she wouldn't have to look at Tristan. Perhaps the best thing at this point would be to apologise for inconveniencing him and leave quick-smart.

She watched as Tristan picked up his glass and swallowed down the contents with a slight flick of his wrist; his brows drawing together when she made no attempt to do the same.

'Drink it. You look like you need it.'

'What I need is a soft bed,' she murmured, only realising how he'd taken her innocent comment when his eyebrows arched.

'If that's an invitation you can forget it,' he dismissed.

Invitation!

Lily expelled a rushed breath, and then inhaled just as hastily, wishing she hadn't as Tristan's virile and somehow familiar scent wound its way into her sinuses. She felt the shock of it curl through her body and suddenly felt too warm.

Her heart rate picked up, and before she could change the direction of her thoughts she was back at the kiss she had been trying so hard not to think about.

He'd been lean and muscle-packed where she'd pressed against him, impossibly hard, and hot colour stole into her face as she remembered her youthful eagerness in his embrace. Lord, perhaps she had even instigated it! How mortifying... Especially in light of the fact that she couldn't recall any other man's kisses quite so readily.

Calling herself every type of fool for indulging in such useless memories, she swiftly removed his jacket and handed it back to him.

Then she sat her tote bag on the stool behind her and pulled out her favourite oversized black knit cardigan. She put it on. Found her black-and-white Yankees baseball cap and pulled that on too. Turning back, she couldn't see much beyond Tristan's broad shoulders, but the last thing she wanted was to be stopped on the way out by fans or—heaven forbid—any lurking paparazzi.

She noticed his condescending glance and decided to ignore it.

She was getting more and more agitated by her own memories and his snippy attitude. Logically she knew he had every reason to be put out, but she hadn't done anything wrong. Would it really hurt him to be civil? After all, it wasn't as if *he* had just been interrogated for hours on end over something he hadn't done!

Lily tried to smile as she hoisted her bag onto her shoulder. 'So, anyway, thanks for helping today. I can see that you didn't really want to, but I appreciate it all the same.'

'I don't give a toss what you appreciate,' he grated. 'I can't believe you would have the gall to try something like this, given your history. What were you thinking? That you could go braless and swish that golden mane around and no one would care what you had in your bag?'

Lily's eyes flew to his. Did he seriously think she was guilty?

'Of course I wasn't thinking that!'

'Well, whatever you *were* thinking it didn't work.'

'How dare you?' Lily felt angry tears spring into her eyes at the injustice of his comment and blinked them back. 'I didn't know that stuff was in my bag, and I've already told you these are my travel clothes and I look perfectly respectable.'

His eyebrows arched. 'That's debatable. But I suppose I should be thankful you're not displaying as much skin as you usually do on your billboards.'

Lily didn't pretend to misunderstand him. Movie billboards were often more provocative than they needed to be, and most of her fellow actresses found it just as frustrating as she did.

Not that Tristan would believe that. It was clear he still thought the worst of her, just as he always had, and the sooner she was on her way the better.

She looked up to suggest exactly that, but was startled when he leaned in close, invading her space.

'Tell me, little Honey Blossom, have you ever been in a movie that required you to actually keep your clothes *on*?'

Lily bristled. She hadn't been called Honey Blossom since she was seven, and she'd been fully clothed in all but her first film. 'My name is Lily, as you well know, and your comments are not only insulting and incorrect, but completely outrageous.'

He cast her a bored smile and Lily's blood boiled. Of all the rude, insensitive—

'Just finish the damned drink, would you? I have work to do.'

Lily felt so tense her toes curled into her boots until they hurt. Enough was enough. Thankful or not, she didn't have to put up with his offensive remarks.

'I don't want your *damned* drink,' she returned icily, angling her chin and readjusting her cap. 'And I don't need your odious presence in my life for a second longer. Thank you for your assistance with my…unfortunate incident, but don't bother coming to say hello at the wedding. I assure you I won't be in the least offended.'

Lily gripped her bag tightly, and would have marched out with her head held high if Tristan hadn't made a slight move to block her.

She hesitated and looked at him uneasily.

'Pretty speech,' he drawled, 'but your *unfortunate incident* has landed you in my custody, and I give the orders now—not you.'

Lily's eyebrows shot up. 'Your *custody*?' She nearly laughed at the thought.

He evidently didn't like her response, because he leaned in even closer, his voice deadly soft. 'What? Did you think I would just ignore the conditions of your release and let you waltz out of here by yourself? You don't know me very well if you did.'

Lily edged back and felt the bar stool behind her thighs, a tremor of unease bumping down her spine. She hadn't read the release form at all, and had a feeling she was about to regret that.

'I didn't read it,' she admitted, sucking on the soft flesh of her upper lip—a nervous childhood gesture she'd never been able to master.

Tristan frowned down at her, and then must have realised she was serious because he had the gall to laugh. 'You're kidding.'

'I'm glad you find it funny,' she snapped, staring him down when his grim smile turned into a snarl.

'Now, *funny* is probably the last thing I think about this situation—and here's why. You just signed documents that place you under my protective custody until you're either released—' his tone implied that was about as likely as buying property on another planet '—or charged with possession of narcotics.'

Lily felt dizzy and leaned heavily on the bar stool at her back. 'I don't understand…' She shook her head.

'What? You thought the evidence might up and magically disappear? I'm good, Honey, but I'm not that good.'

'No.' She waved her hand in front of her and briefly closed her eyes. 'The custody bit.'

'It's a form of house arrest.'

'I didn't know.'

'Now you do. And now I'm ready to leave.'

'No!' Her hand hovered between them and her voice quavered. 'Wait. Please. I… What does that mean, exactly?'

He looked at her as if she was a simpleton. 'It means that we're stuck with each other 24/7 for the foreseeable future, that's what it means.'

Lily blinked. 24/7 with this gorgeous, angry man…? No way. She pressed her fingertips to her aching forehead and ordered herself to think. Surely there was another solution.

'I can't stay with *you*!' She blurted out before her thoughts were properly in order.

His eyes sparkled into hers, as hard as polished gemstones. 'Believe me, the thought couldn't be more abhorrent to you than it is to me.'

'But you should have told me!'

'You should have read the paperwork,' he dismissed.

He was right, and she hated that. Only it was because of him that she hadn't read it in the first place.

'You crowded me and told me to hurry.'

'So now it's my fault?' he snapped.

'I wasn't blaming you.' She swiped a hand across her brow. This was terrible. 'But if you had warned me about what I was signing I wouldn't have done so!'

He went still, his over-long tawny mane and square jaw giving the impression of a fully grown male lion that had just scented danger.

'Warned you?'

Too late Lily realised he'd taken her comment as an insult.

'And what exactly would you have done, hmm? Do tell.'

Lily pressed her lips together at his snide tone and tried not to notice how imposing he was, with his hands on his hips drawing his shoulders even wider. If she'd thought he hated her six years ago it was nothing compared to the contempt he clearly felt for her now.

And she wasn't so much looking to put the past behind her any more as she was in burying it in a six-foot-deep hole! 'I—I would have looked for an alternative,' she stuttered. 'Brainstormed other options.'

*'Brainstormed other options?'* He snorted and shook his head, as if the very notion was ludicrous. 'We're not in a movie rehearsal now, Honey!'

Lily's heart thudded heavily in her chest. If he called her Honey one more time she might actually hit him. She took a deep, steadying breath and tried to remember that he felt he had a right to be angry, and that maybe, if their situations were reversed, she would feel the same way.

No, she wouldn't. She'd be too worried for the other person to treat them so—so...indignantly.

'Listen—' she began, only to have her words cut off when he pushed off his bar stool and crowded her back against her own.

'No. *You* listen,' he bit out softly. 'You don't have a choice here. You're no longer in charge. I am. And if you don't like it I'll give you another option. It's called a prison cell. You want it—it's back that way.' He jerked his chin towards the entrance of the bar, his eyes never leaving hers.

Lily blanched. Lord, he was arrogant.

'I didn't do it,' she enunciated, trying to keep her voice low.

'Tell it to the judge, sweetheart, because I'm not interested in hearing your protestations of innocence.'

'Don't patronise me, Tristan. I'm not a child.'

'Then stop acting like one.'

'Damn you, I have rights.'

'No, you *had* rights.' His tone was soft, but merciless. 'You gave up those rights the minute you waltzed through Heathrow carrying a bag full of narcotics. Your rights belong to me now, and when I say jump I expect you to ask how high.'

Lily froze. He had some nerve. 'In your dreams,' she scoffed, now just as angry as he was.

# CHAPTER THREE

No, TRISTAN thought disgustedly, when he dreamt of her she was not jumping up and down; she was usually naked, her lithe body spread out over his bed, and her soft mouth was begging him to take her. But this was no dream, and right now making love to her couldn't be further from his mind.

Kissing that insolent curl from her luscious mouth—now, *that* was closer. But completely giving in to the insane desire that still uncomfortably rode his back—no. Not in this lifetime.

Not that he was at all surprised to find himself still attracted to her. Hell, she looked even better now than she had six years ago—if that was actually possible.

Even the bartender was having trouble keeping his distance—and not just because he'd probably recognised her face. Tristan doubted he'd be ogling any other actress with his tongue hanging out of his mouth, and there were many far more worthy of a second glance than this sexy little troublemaker.

No, the bartender was staring because Lily Wild looked like every man's secret fantasy come to life—even with those dark smudges beneath those wide purple eyes. But she damned well wasn't his. Not this time.

He should have just said no to Jordana, he realised distractedly. Should have made up a story about how it couldn't be done.

But he had too much integrity to lie, and in the end a close friend who specialised in criminal law had pulled a rabbit from a hat and here they were. But only by the grace of some clapped-out piece of nineteenth-century legislation that he would recommend be amended at the next parliamentary sitting.

'Did you hear me, Tristan?' she prompted, her glorious eyes flashing with unconcealed irritation. 'I won't let you bully me like you did once before.'

Tristan cast her the withering glance that he usually reserved for the seediest of his courtroom opponents.

Oh, he'd heard her all right, but she had no choice in the matter, and the sooner she got that through her thick, beautiful skull the better.

'Don't push me, Lily,' he grated warningly, and saw her teeth clench.

Her hands were fisted by her sides and he knew she probably wanted to thump him. Despite himself he admired her temerity. Most women in her position—hell, most *men*—would be grovelling or backing away, or both. Instead this little spitfire was arguing the toss, as if she might actually choose jail over him.

'Then don't push *me*!' she returned hotly.

He looked at her and tried to remind himself that he was a first-rate lawyer who never let emotion govern his actions. 'You signed the contract. Deal with it,' he said curtly.

She slapped her hands on her hips, the movement dragging her oversized cardigan open and bringing his attention back to her full, unbound breasts. 'I told you—I didn't know what I was signing,' she declared, as if that might actually make a difference.

Yeah, yeah—just as she didn't know how the drugs ended up in her bag. He had yet to come across a criminal who actually admitted any form of guilt, and her vehement denial was boringly predictable.

He noticed that the two businessmen who earlier had been deep in conversation were now stealing surreptitious glances at her. Not that he couldn't appreciate what they were looking at: tousled pearl-blond hair, soft, kissable lips, a mouthwatering silhouette, and legs that went all the way into next week.

They'd looked even longer coming down his parents' staircase at Jo's eighteenth party, in a tiny dress and designer heels. And just like that he was back at Hillesden Abbey, the family estate, at the precise moment she had approached him.

'Hey, wanna dance?' she'd invited, standing before him in a silver mini-dress that clung in all the right places, hip cocked, bee-stung pout covered in war paint.

He'd declined, of course. Just looking at her had stirred up a dark lust inside him that, at seventeen, she had been way too young to handle.

'But you danced with Jordana,' she'd complained, fluttering ridiculously long eyelashes like a woman on the make. 'And the girl with the blue dress.'

'That's right.' His friend Gabriel had elbowed him. 'You did.'

'So? What about it?' Lily had shifted her weight to her other hip, her dress riding up just that tiny bit more, head tilted in artful provocation.

He'd been about to refuse again, but Gabriel had interrupted and said *he'd* dance with her if Tristan wouldn't, and for some reason that had got his back up.

He'd thrown his friend a baleful glare before focusing on Lily. 'Let's go.'

She'd smiled her now famous million dollar smile at Gabriel and Tristan had gritted his teeth and followed her onto the dance floor.

As if on cue the music had turned dreamy and he'd almost changed his mind. Then she'd turned that million dollar number his way, stepped into his arms, and he'd no longer had a mind to change.

'It's a great party, isn't it?' she'd murmured.

'Yes,' he'd agreed.

'This is nice,' she'd prompted.

'Yes,' he'd agreed.

'Are you having a good time?'

Not any more; not with his self-control unravelling with each breathy little question.

He remembered he'd been so focused on not pulling her in close that he failed to notice when *she* had moved in on *him*. Then he'd felt the slide of her bare thigh between his jean-clad legs and the thrust of her pert breasts against the wall of his chest and self-control had become a foreign concept.

His hand had tightened on her hip to push her back, but she'd gripped his shoulder and looked at him with such unguarded innocence his heart had skipped a beat, and almost of its own accord his hand had slid around to the sweet indentation at the small of her back.

Her breath had hitched and when she'd stumbled he'd caught her against him. Her body had instantly moulded to his as if she was unable to hold herself upright. And he'd been unable to hide his physical reaction from her. His body had been gripped in a fever of desire: heart pounding, body aching and warning bells clanging so loudly in his head it was a wonder he'd been able to think at all.

He'd stupidly danced her into a secluded corner, with every intention of reprimanding her and telling her he didn't *do* girls barely out of nappies, but she'd quivered in the circle of his arms, lips delicately parted, and he'd fused his mouth with hers before he'd even known what he was about.

The bolt of pure heat that had hit his groin at the contact had almost unmanned him.

Before he'd known it he'd had one hand tangled in her golden mane, the other curved over her bottom and his tongue deep in her mouth, his lips demanding a response she had been more than happy to give.

He'd completely lost all sense of where he was, and hours could have flown by before a hand had circumspectly tapped him on the shoulder.

Thomas, the family butler, had stood behind him, seemingly

mesmerised by the imported mirror balls suspended above the dance floor.

Apparently his father required his presence most urgently.

For a second Lily's dazed disappointment had only been outweighed by his own. Then he'd realised what he'd nearly done and been appalled at himself. She was his little sister's friend, and the erotic images playing through his mind were highly inappropriate.

He remembered he'd abruptly released her and curtly told her not to bother him again, that he wasn't interested in babies. And then she'd punished him by attaching herself to some Armani suit for the rest of the night like ivy on a brick wall.

One of the businessmen hooted a laugh, and the sound broke Tristan's unwanted reverie.

He closed his eyes briefly to recompose himself, and then made the mistake of glancing into the mirror behind the bar—where his gaze collided with Lily's.

For a split second something hot and primal arced between them, and then the pink tip of her tongue snuck out to douse her full lower lip and just like that he was hard again.

Damn. Had she done that on purpose? Had she known what he'd been thinking about?

He blinked slowly and turned his gaze as hard as his groin. He wasn't an idiot, and he wasn't going to let her use that come-hither look she'd probably learned in the cradle to manipulate him. The sooner she figured that out, the better for the both of them.

'I don't care what you did or didn't know. You signed the forms and now we're leaving.'

'Wait.' She put her hand out to touch him and then snatched it back just as quickly.

His jaw clenched. 'What now?'

'We need to sort this out.'

He picked his jacket up off the stool and shrugged into it. 'It's sorted. I'm in charge. You're not. So let's go.'

'Look, I know you're angry—'

'Is that what I am?' he mocked.

'But,' she continued determinedly, 'I didn't know I had that…stuff in my bag.' Her voice was barely above a whisper. 'And I'm not going with you until I know what happens next.'

Tristan glanced at the ceiling, hoping some divine force would penetrate it and put him out of his misery. He knew she had a headache. He'd known the minute he'd seen her. And now she was giving him one.

'You've got to be kidding me,' he groaned.

'No, I'm not. I mean it, Tristan; I won't let you push me around like you did six years ago. Back then—'

'Oh, cut the theatrics, Honey. There's no camera to turn it on for here.'

'Lily.'

He stared at her for a beat.

'And I'm not—'

Tristan glared at her and cut her off. 'You think I like this any more than you do? You think I didn't rack my brain to come up with an alternative? I have just involved a good friend of mine to get you out of this mess and all you can do is act the injured innocent. *You* broke the law, not me, so stop behaving like I'm the bad guy here.'

Lily seemed to lose a little steam over that. 'A friend?' she whispered.

'What? You thought I could just stroll up here myself and demand your release? I'm flattered you think I have that much power.'

Tristan glanced around the bar and saw that more passengers had entered. They were getting far more attention than he was comfortable with.

'He won't go to the press, will he?' she asked.

Tristan shook his head. 'So typical of you to be worried about yourself.'

'I wasn't worrying about myself,' she snapped. 'I was thinking about how this might impact Jordana's wedding if it gets out.'

'A bit late to think about that now. But, no, he won't say anything. He has discretion and integrity—words you'd need to look up in a dictionary to learn the meaning of.' He shook his head at the improbability of the whole situation. 'For God's sake, it's not as if you couldn't get a fix here if you were so desperate.'

She looked at him from under her cap. 'Whatever happened to being innocent in this country until proven guilty?'

'Being caught with drugs in your bag sort of makes that a moot point,' he scoffed.

Lily's chin jutted forward. 'Aren't lawyers supposed to be a little more objective with their clients?'

'I'm not your lawyer.'

'What are you, then? My white knight?'

A muscle ticked in his jaw. 'I'm doing Jordana a favour.'

'Ah, yes. The big brother routine,' she mocked. 'I seem to re-call you really enjoy that. It must have made you feel valued—rescuing Jordana from my disreputable company all those years ago.'

She wrapped her arms around her torso in a defensive ges-ture that pinched something inside him, but he refused to soften towards her. He had no respect for people who created a de-mand for drugs and hurt those around them by using, and all today had done was confirm his father's view that Lily Wild was bad news just waiting to happen.

'It's just a pity I didn't nip your friendship in the bud sooner. I could have saved my family a lot of embarrassment.'

That seemed to take the wind out of her sails and he almost felt bad when her shoulders slumped.

'So what happens now? Where will I be staying?' she asked.

Tristan pulled a wad of notes from his pocket and threw some on the bar. 'We'll discuss the ground rules later.'

'I'd like to talk about them now.'

He turned to her, what little patience he'd started with com-pletely gone. 'If I have to pick you up and cart you out of here I will,' he warned softly.

Her eyes widened. 'You wouldn't dare.'

Tristan crowded her back against the bar stool again. 'Try me.'

She inhaled a shaky breath and put her hand up between them. 'Don't touch me.'

Touch her? He hadn't really intended to, but now, as his gaze swept down her curvy body, he realised that he wanted to. Badly. He wanted to push aside that cardigan, slide his hand around her waist and pull her up against him until there was no sign of daylight between them. Until she melted into him as she had done six years ago.

'Then co-operate,' he snarled, crowding even closer and perversely enjoying her agitated backwards movement. It wouldn't hurt her to be a little afraid of him. Might make sure she kept her distance this time.

'I'm trying to.'

Her eyes flashed, and the leather creaked as she shifted as far back on the stool as she could, her monstrosity of a bag perched on her lap between them.

Tristan leaned forward and hooked his foot on her bar stool, jerking it forward so she was forced back into his space. He caught her off guard, and his bicep flexed as she threw her hand out to balance herself. Her breath caught and her eyes flew to his.

'No, you're not. You're trying to bug me.' He watched as colour winged into her face, his eyes narrowing as she snatched her hand back from his arm. 'And it's working.'

She raised her chin. 'I don't like your controlling attitude.'

He stilled, and their eyes locked in a battle of wills: hers bright and belligerent, his surprised but determined. His nostrils flared as he breathed her in deep. She smelled of roses and springtime and he had to fight the instinct to keep inhaling her.

They were so close he could see the flawless, luminescent quality of her skin—a gift from her Nordic heritage—and her thick, sooty lashes, as long as a spider's legs, nearly touching her arched brow. His eyes turned hot before he was able to blank them out, and her breath stalled as she caught the heat.

He stopped breathing himself and felt the blood throb powerfully through his body. For a split second he forgot what they were doing here. Time stood still. But before he could wrap his hand around her slender neck and bring her mouth to his she blinked and lowered her eyes.

Tristan exhaled, his anger all the stronger because of the unwanted sexual tension that lay between them like a living thing.

'Do you really think I care?' he snapped. 'When I first heard you were coming to Jo's wedding I didn't even intend to say hello. Now I find that hello is the least of my problems, and I can assure you I will *not* spend the next eight days arguing every single point with you. So if—'

'Fine.' She cupped her hand over her forehead and winced.

He knew what she meant, but he was insulted by her attitude and wanted to hear her say it.

'Fine what? Fine, you want to come with me? Or fine, you want me to take you back to Customs?'

She raised her head and he waited. The smudges under her eyes looked darker, and her skin had lost even more colour.

'Oh, to hell with it.' He straightened and held his hand out to her. She took it, without argument, and he realised that the shock of the morning was finally starting to set in—or maybe she'd been in shock the whole time.

Her fingers were icy in his, and he shrugged out of his jacket once again and pulled it around her. She squirmed as if to push it off, and her eyes jerked to his when he grabbed her upper arms and dragged her close.

'Co-operate,' he growled, pleased when she stilled.

'You never say please.' She sniffed.

Hell, she was still trying to call the shots. He kept his eyes locked on hers, because if they dropped to her mouth he knew he'd taste her. He was hard and he was angry, and the adrenaline pumping through his veins was pushing his self-control to its outer limits.

'Please,' he grated after a long, tense pause. 'Now, can you walk?'

'Of course.' She gripped her bag and swayed when he released his hold on her.

He knew it would be a mistake on so many levels, but before he could think twice he scooped her into his arms and strode out of the bar.

She started against him, but he'd had enough. 'Don't say a goddamned word and don't look around. The last thing I need is for someone else to recognise you.'

And just like that she relaxed and turned her head into his shoulder, her sweet scent filling his every breath.

The cool breeze was a welcome relief as he exited the terminal and headed down the rank of dark cars until he found Bert.

His chauffer nodded and held the rear door open, but just as Tristan was about to toss Lily inside she laid the flat of her hand against his chest and looked up through sleepy eyes.

'My luggage…' she murmured.

Tristan's chest contracted against the hot brand of her touch.

'Taken care of,' he growled, wishing the unbearable physical attraction he still felt for this woman could be just as easily dealt with.

# CHAPTER FOUR

LILY collapsed back against the luxuriant leather car seat and closed her eyes, trying to equalise her pounding heart rate. Her head hurt and she felt shivery all over. She didn't know if it was remembering her previous attraction to Tristan that had brought it screaming to the fore, or the man himself, but she was unable to deny the sweet feeling of desire that had pooled low in her pelvis when he'd held her in his arms and looked at her as if he wanted to kiss her.

Kiss her? *Ha!* Shake her, more like it. Especially given how much he still disliked her.

As she did him.

Actually, now that she thought about it, her physical response was probably due to emotional tiredness and stress making her super-sensitive to her surroundings and nothing to do with Tristan at all. How could it be when he immediately assumed that she was guilty? When he clearly thought she was lower than dirt?

His cold arrogance fired her blood and made her want to fall back on all her juvenile responses to criticism. Responses that had seen her play up to the negative attention her celebrity lineage provoked by flipping the press the bird, wearing either provocative or grungy clothing, depending on her mood, and pretending she was drunk when she wasn't.

Nowadays she preferred to ignore any bad press or unfair comparisons with her parents' hedonistic lifestyles, and just live her life according to her own expectations rather than other people's. It worked better, to a certain extent, although she knew she'd never truly be able to outrun the shadow of who her parents had been.

Hanny Forsberg, her mother, had arrived in England poor and beautiful and on Page Three before she had found a place to live, and Johnny Wild, her father, had been a rough Norfolk lad with a raw musical talent and a hunger for success and women in equal measure.

Both had thrived on their fame and the attention it engendered, and after Lily was born they had just added her to their lifestyle—palming her off on whichever one wasn't working and treating her like a fashion accessory long before it had become hip to do so.

The camera flashes and constant attention had scared her as a child, and even now Lily hated that she always felt as if she was living under the sullied banner of her parents' combined notoriety. But none of that had been enough to put her off when her own creativity and natural talent had led her down the acting career path. Lily just tried as best she could to take roles that didn't immediately provoke comparisons between herself and her parents—though as to that she could play a crossdressing homosexual male and probably still be compared to her mother!

Sighing heavily, and wishing that one of her directors was going to call 'cut' on a day from hell, Lily turned to stare out at the passing landscape she hadn't seen for so long.

Unfortunately the rows of shop fronts and Victorian terraces soon made her head throb, and she was forced to close her eyes and listen to the sound of Tristan texting on his smartphone instead. A thousand questions were winging through her mind—none of which, she knew, Tristan would feel inclined to answer.

For a moment she contemplated pulling the script she had promised to read from her bag, but that would no doubt make the headache worse so she left it there.

No great hardship, since she didn't want to read it anyway.

She had no interest in starring in a theatrical production about her parents, no matter how talented the writer-director was.

She'd nearly scoffed out loud at the notion.

As if she'd feed the gossipmongers and provoke more annoying comparisons to her mother by actually *playing* her in a drama. Lord, she'd never hear the end of it. The only reason she was pretending to consider the idea was a favour to a friend.

Her mouth twisted as she imagined the look on Tristan's face if he knew about the role. No doubt he'd think her perfect to play a lost, drug-addled model craving love and attention from a man who had probably put the word *playboy* in the dictionary.

In fact it was ironic, really, that the only man Lily had ever thought herself to be in love with was almost as big a playboy as her father! Not that she'd fully comprehended Tristan's reputation as a seventeen-year-old. Back then she'd known only that women fell for him like pebbles tossed into a pond, but she hadn't given it much thought.

Now she was almost glad that he'd rejected her gauche overtures, because if he hadn't she'd surely have become just another notch on his bedpost. And if she *was* anything like her mother that would have meant she'd have fallen for him all the harder.

Lily removed her cap and rubbed her forehead, glancing briefly at Tristan, slashing his red pen through a document he was reading. If she tried to interrupt him now to discuss her house arrest he'd no doubt bite her head off. Still...

'I take it you won't be put out if I don't feel up to making conversation right now?' she queried innocuously, smiling brightly when he looked at her as if she had two heads. 'Thought not,' she mumbled.

Suddenly she was feeling drained, and not up to fighting with him anyway, so it was a good thing he'd ignored her taunt. A taunt she shouldn't have made in the first place. Never prod a sleeping tiger...wasn't that the adage? Especially when you were in the same cage as him!

Lily leaned back against the plush leather headrest and closed her eyes. The manly scent from Tristan's jacket imbued her with a delicious and oddly peaceful lassitude, and she tried to pretend none of this was happening.

Cheeky minx! She knew he didn't want to talk. He couldn't have made it any plainer. He slashed another line through the report he was reading and realised he'd marked up the wrong section. Damn her.

She sighed, and he wondered if she knew the effect she was having on his concentration, but when he glanced up it was to find she'd fallen asleep.

She looked so fragile, swamped in his jacket, her blonde hair spilling over the dark fabric like a silvery web.

He knew when he got it back it would smell like something from his late mother's garden, and made a mental note to have his housekeeper immediately launder it. Then he realised the direction of his thoughts and frowned.

He was supposed to be focused on work. Not contemplating Lily and her hurt expression when he'd cut off her attempts to explain her situation earlier.

He didn't want to get caught up in her lies, and he had taken the view that the less she said the better for both of them. She had a way of getting under his skin, and for an insanely brief moment back in the bar, when her eyes had teared up, he'd wanted to reach out and tell her that everything would be all right. Which was ridiculous.

It wasn't his job to fix her situation. His job—if you could call it that—was to keep her out of trouble until Jordana's wedding and find out any relevant information that might lead to her—or someone else's—arrest.

It was not to make friends with her, or to make empty promises. And it certainly wasn't to kiss her as he had wanted to do. He shook his head. Maybe he really had taken leave of his senses getting involved with this. Stuart, the friend and colleague who had helped him find the loophole in the law that had placed her into his custody, had seemed to think so.

'Are you sure you know what you're doing, Chief?' he'd asked, after the deal had been sealed.

'When have you ever needed to ask me that?'

His friend had raised an eyebrow at his surly tone and Tristan had known what was coming.

'Never. But if she's guilty and people question your involvement it could ruin your legal career. Not to mention drag your family name through the mud again.'

'I know what I'm doing,' he'd said. But he didn't. Not really.

What he *did* know was that he was still as strongly attracted to her as he had been six years ago. Not that he was going to do anything about it. He would never get involved with a druguser.

His mother had been one—although not a recreational user, like Lily and her ilk. His mother had taken a plethora of prescription meds for everything from dieting to depression, but the effect was the same: personality changes, mood swings, and eventually death when she had driven her car into a tree.

She had never been an easy woman to love. A shop girl with her eye on the big prize, she had married his father for his title and, from what Tristan could tell, had spent most of their life together complaining on the one hand that he worked too hard and on the other that the Abbey was too old for her tastes. His father had done his best, but in the end it hadn't been enough, and she'd left after a blazing row Tristan still wished he hadn't overheard. His father had been gutted, and for a while lost to his children, and Tristan had vowed then that he would never fall that deeply under a woman's spell.

He expelled a harsh breath. He was thirty-two years old and in the prime of his life. He had an international law firm and a property portfolio that spanned four continents, good friends and enough money to last several lifetimes—even with the amount he gave away to charity. His personal life had become a little mundane lately, it was true, but he didn't really know what to do about that.

Jordana thought it was because he chose unsuitable women most of the time, and if he did date someone 'worthy' he ended the relationship before it began. Which was true enough. Experience had taught him that after a certain time a woman started expecting more from a man. Started wanting to talk about love and commitment. And after one particularly virulent model had sold her story to the tabloids he had made sure his affairs remained short and sweet. Very sweet and very short.

He knew he'd probably marry one day, because it was expected, but love wouldn't play a part in his choice of a wife. When he was ready—if he ever was—he'd choose someone from his world, who understood the demands of his lifestyle. Someone logical and pragmatic like he was.

Lily made a noise in her sleep and Tristan flicked a glance at her, wincing as her head dropped sideways and butted up against the glass window. Someone the opposite of this woman.

She whimpered and jerked upright in her sleep, but didn't waken, and Tristan watched the cycle start to repeat itself. That couldn't be good for her headache.

Not that he cared. He didn't. She was the reason memories from the past were crowding in and clouding his normally clear thinking, and he resented the hell out of her for it.

But just as her head was about to bump the window again he cursed and moved to her side, to move her along the seat. She flopped against his shoulder and snuggled into his arm, her silky hair brushing against his cheek, giving him pause. He felt the warmth of her breath through his shirt and went still when she made a soft, almost purring sound in the back of her throat; his traitorous body responded predictably.

If he were to move back to his side now she might wake up and, frankly, he could do without her peppering him with the questions he'd seen hovering on her lips while he'd been trying to work.

She made another pained whimper and he looked down to see a frown marring her pale forehead.

Oh, for the love of God.

He blew out a breath and lifted his free hand to her hairline, stroked her brow. The frown eased instantly from her forehead and transferred to his own. If he wasn't careful this whole situation could get seriously out of hand. He could just feel it.

Five minutes. He'd give her five minutes and then he'd move. Get back to the waiting e-mails on his smartphone.

Twenty minutes later, just as he was about to ease his fingers from her tangled tresses, his chauffeur announced that the car had stopped. Well, of course he'd noticed.

'Drive us to the rear entrance, Bert,' he said, trying to rouse Lily. She rubbed her soft cheek against his palm in such a trusting gesture his chest tightened.

God, she really was a stunning woman.

How could someone born looking like she did throw it all away on drugs? He knew she must have struggled, losing both her parents at a young age, but still—they all had their crosses to bear. What made some people rise above the cards life dealt them while others sank into the mire?

According to Jordana, Lily was sensible, reserved and down to earth. Yeah, and he was the Wizard of Oz.

'You okay, Boss?' Bert asked, concern shadowing his voice.

Great. He hadn't noticed the car had pulled up again. He had to stop thinking of Lily as a desirable woman before it was no longer important that he neither liked nor respected her.

'Never better.' He exhaled, manoeuvring himself out of the car and effortlessly lifting the comatose woman into his arms. She stirred, but instantly resettled against him. No doubt a combination of shock and jet lag was laying her out cold.

A security guard opened the glass-plated door to his building, looking for all the world as if there was nothing out of place in his boss carrying an unconscious woman towards the service lift.

'Nice afternoon, sir.'

Tristan grunted in return, flexing his arms under Lily's dead weight.

He exited the lift and strode towards his office throwing a 'don't ask' look at his ever-efficient secretary as she hurried around her desk to push his door open for him.

'Hold all my calls,' he instructed Kate, before kicking the door closed with his heel.

He tumbled Lily gently down onto the white leather sofa in his office and she immediately curled into a fetal position, pulling his jacket more tightly around her body while she slept.

*Scratch laundering it*, he thought. He'd just throw the bloody thing away.

# CHAPTER FIVE

LILY was hot. Too hot. And something was tugging on her. Pulling her down. Jonah?

She blinked and tried to focus, and found herself lying in an unfamiliar room.

'Missing your boyfriend already, Honey?' An aggravated male voice she instantly recognised drawled from far away.

Lily tentatively raised herself up on her elbow to find Tristan seated behind a large desk strewn with leatherbound books and reams of paper.

For a moment she just stared at him in a daze, unconsciously registering his dark frown. Then the events of the morning started replaying through her mind like a silent movie on fast forward.

The flight, the drugs, the interrogation, Tristan—

'You called his name,' he prompted. 'A number of times.'

Whose name?

Lily didn't know what he was talking about. She didn't have a lover and never had. She smoothed her fingers over her flushed face and wiped the edges of her mouth. It felt suspiciously as if she had drooled. *Urgh!* She was grimy and sweaty, as if she'd been asleep for days. Of course she hadn't been— had she?

Lily peered at Tristan more closely and noticed the same white shirt he'd worn earlier, the sleeves now rolled to reveal muscular bronzed forearms. The same red tie hanging loosely around his neck and the top button of his shirt was undone.

Okay, still Friday. Thank heavens. She glanced around his impressively large and impressively messy office.

For some reason she had expected someone so controlling to be a neat freak, but his desk was barely visible behind small towers of black, green and red legal tomes and spiral-bound notebooks. A set of inlaid bookcases lined half of one wall, with books stacked vertically and horizontally in a slapdash manner, and what looked like an original Klimt dominated another.

And that surprised her as well. Klimt had a soft, almost magical quality to his work, and that didn't fit her image of Tristan at all.

'It's an investment,' he said, as if he could read her mind. 'So who is he to you?' Tristan repeated, pulling her eyes back to his.

'Gustav Klimt?'

Tristan made an impatient sound. 'The loser whose name you were chanting in your sleep.'

Lily shook her head, realising one of the reasons she felt so hot was because she still wore Tristan's jacket. Removing it quickly, she placed it on the seat beside her and met his scornful gaze. 'I don't know who you're— Oh, Jonah!'

'He'd no doubt be upset to find himself so easily dismissed from your memory. But then with so many lovers on the go how can a modern girl be expected to keep up?'

Lily's brow pleated as she gazed at him. No improvement in his mood, then. Wonderful.

And as for his disparaging comments about her so-called lovers—the press reported she was in a relationship every time she so much as shared a taxi with a member of the opposite sex, so really he could be talking about any number of men.

She was just about to tell him she didn't appreciate his sarcasm when he held up a manila folder, a look of contempt crossing his face.

'I've had a report done on you.'

Of course he had.

'Ever considered going directly to the source?' she suggested sweetly. 'Probably save you a lot in investigators' fees.'

Tristan tapped his pen against his desk. 'I find investigators far more enlightening than "the source".'

'How nice for you.'

'For example, you're currently living with Cliff Harris...'

A dear friend who had moved into her spare room due to financial problems.

'A lovely man.' She smiled thinly.

'...while you've been photographed cosying up to that effeminate sculptor Piers Bond.'

Lily had been to a few gallery openings with Piers, and Tristan was right—he was effeminate.

'A very talented artist,' she commented.

'And presumably sleeping with that dolly boy in Thailand behind both their backs?'

Lily suppressed her usually slow to rise temper and threw him her best Mona Lisa smile. A smile she had perfected long ago that said everything and nothing all at the same time.

'Grip,' she corrected with forced pleasantness. 'He's called a dolly grip.'

'He's also called a junkie.'

'Jonah *once* had a drug problem; he doesn't any more.'

'Well, you should know. You've been photographed going in and out of that New York rehab clinic with him enough times.'

Also true. She volunteered there when she could, which was how she'd met Jonah. She just hoped Tristan didn't know about the director's marriage she was supposed to have broken up while working on a film the year before. But since it had been all through the papers...

'And Guy Jeffrey's marriage? Or is that so far back you can't remember your part in that particular melodrama?'

Great. He probably knew her shoe size as well.

'My, your man *is* thorough,' she complimented dryly. 'But do you think I might visit the bathroom before you remind me about the rest of my debauched lifestyle? I don't think I can hang on till tomorrow.'

Tristan scowled at her from beneath straight brows, and if the situation hadn't been so awful she might have laughed. Might have.

She picked up her tote bag from the floor and grimaced as she realised she felt as if she was requesting a permission slip from the school principal when she had to ask for directions to the bathroom.

Tristan nodded towards a door at the rear of his office. 'Leave the bag,' he ordered, returning his focus to his computer screen.

'Why?'

'Because I said so.'

Rude, horrible, insufferable... He raised his eyes and locked them with hers. His gave nothing away about how he was feeling while she knew hers were shooting daggers.

She suspected she knew why he wanted her to leave it. She suspected he was trying to show her who was boss. Either that or he thought she'd been able to magic some more drugs into her bag after it had been searched by Customs. But, whatever his reasoning, he'd now succeeded in making her angry again.

She planted her hands on her hips, prepared to stare him down. 'There's nothing in it.'

He leaned back in his chair and regarded her as a predator might regard lunch, and goosebumps rose up along her arms. 'Then you won't mind leaving it.'

Lily felt her mouth tighten. No, but she wouldn't mind braining him with it either—and damn him if he didn't know it.

She stalked towards him, her narrowed eyes holding his, and before she could think better of it upended the entire contents of her tote onto his desk. He couldn't hide his start of surprise, and Lily felt inordinately pleased at having knocked him off his arrogant perch.

'Careful.' She cast him her best Hollywood smile before

swinging round towards the bathroom. 'I left a King Cobra in there somewhere, and it's trained to attack obnoxious lawyers.'

As parting shots went she thought it was rather good, but his unexpected chuckle set her teeth on edge. And if she was honest she was a bit worried she'd never find her favourite lipstick again in amongst all the rubble on his desk.

His bathroom was state-of-the-art, with slate-grey tiles and an enormous plate-glass shower stall. Lily would almost kill for a shower, but the thought of putting on her smelly travel clothes afterwards was not appealing. Plus Tristan was in the other room, and she didn't want to risk that he might walk in on her. She didn't think she could cope.

A sudden image of him naked and soapy, with water streaming off the lean angles and hard planes of his body, crowding her back against the slippery tiles pervaded her senses and made her feel light-headed. She wondered if he had an all-over tan, and then pulled a face at the image of male perfection that bombarded her. He probably had a very small penis, she thought, grinning at her wan complexion. It would only be fair.

But then she recalled the feel of his hard body pressed into hers in the secluded corner of that long-ago dance floor and knew he wasn't small. Far from it.

She wouldn't ruin her mood by thinking about that. Somehow tipping her bag upside down on Tristan's desk had alleviated her anger and lifted her spirits considerably.

She splashed cold water on her cheeks and poked at the dark circles under her eyes. She looked a mess. And her hair was unusually knotty around her temples. A vague memory of soothing fingers stroking her scalp came to mind and she realised at the same time that her headache was gone. Had he stroked her? Soothed her?

The comforting gesture didn't fit his harsh attitude, but she was secretly thrilled that he might have done it.

Thrilled? No. She shook her head at her reflection. Thoughts like that led to nothing but trouble, and hadn't he already made it completely clear that he detested every minute he had to spend with her? And didn't she feel exactly the same way? The man was rude, arrogant and obnoxious, to say the least.

She blew out a noisy breath and pulled her hair into a rough ponytail, securing it with the band she kept around her wrist for just such purposes—a habit that made Jordana shudder. But Lily had never been one for fashion and clothing, like Jordana. Which was probably why Jordana was a buyer for women's wear at a leading department store and Lily wore just about anything she recommended.

Lily turned towards the door and paused with her hand on the brass knob. She was almost afraid to return to the lion's den.

Then she chastised herself for her feebleness.

No doubt Tristan was just planning to lay down the law. Tell her he wanted absolute silence and co-operation again. And if he did she wouldn't argue. The less they had to do with each other the better.

Sure, she had questions, but perhaps it was better to try and stifle them. She'd soon find out what was going to happen, and as much as the thought of being at his mercy made her skin crawl what choice did she really have right now?

Yes, that would be the approach to take. Polite, but aloof. Mind her own business and hope he minded his as well.

Tristan regarded Lily coolly as she walked back into his office. She'd put her hair up, which made her look more unkempt than when she'd first woken up—and incredibly cute. A fact he found hard to believe when he usually preferred women well-mannered, well-bred and well-groomed.

He was still smarting from having lowered himself to question her about her lovers before, like some jealous boyfriend, and wouldn't have minded if she'd spent the rest of the afternoon in the bathroom. All the better for him to get some actual work done.

But she hadn't, and now her eyes alighted on the refreshments his secretary had just placed on his desk. He knew she must be hungry, because he doubted the customs officers had made it a priority to feed her earlier today.

He suppressed a grin when he saw her glance surreptitiously around for her bag. Much as he hated to admit it, he admired her spunk.

'No, I didn't bin it,' he said conversationally. 'Although there wasn't much in there worth keeping apart from a miniature pair of black panties.'

Her eyes flew to his and he had to wonder why he'd said that. It had gone totally against his intention to direct her to the sofa and tell her to keep quiet.

Her mouth gaped with embarrassment and he almost felt sorry for her. She'd obviously forgotten they were in there.

Then she recovered and sauntered across the room. 'I'm not sure they're your size, but you're welcome to keep them.'

'I generally like to take them off women, not put them on,' he purred, enjoying the way her eyes widened before lancing him with a knowing look.

'So I've heard,' she rejoined. 'But I was referring to your personal use, not...' Her pouty lips tightened and she looked flustered, dropping her gaze to the assortment of cups in front of her. 'Never mind. I take it one of these is mine?'

'Yes. Take your pick. I didn't know if you preferred coffee or tea so I ordered both.'

She looked at him as if she thought such thoughtfulness was beyond him and his mouth compressed. He could be thoughtful when the moment called for it.

'And I know what you were referring to.'

She didn't respond but sipped pleasurably at the tea she'd just poured. He watched the way her mouth pursed daintily around the edge of the cup. It hadn't been quite so dainty when it had opened under his six years ago, and no matter how hard he tried he couldn't seem to stop thinking about that.

It had been six years, for heaven's sake. He couldn't even remember the colour of his last lover's hair let alone how she'd tasted, and yet just looking at Lily Wild brought her unique flavour to mind. Her generous curves. Her responsiveness... Ah, the sweetness of a response that had most likely been fuelled by chemical enhancers. Or had it? It was a question that had kept him up late on more than one occasion.

'I feel like I'm on an episode of *This is Your Life*.' She smiled from behind her cup, the incongruous comment thankfully pulling his attention away from her mouth. 'Only the host usually smiles, and I would have expected at least one or two guests to have turned up by now.'

Tristan scowled—both at the flippant remark and his unquestionable hunger for somebody he didn't even like.

'Okay.' She sighed, completely oblivious to the tumultuous thoughts playing out in his head. 'I'm presuming you don't want my shoe size, so why don't you tell me what happens next and—?'

'No, I don't want your shoe size,' he agreed, cutting her off mid-sentence and leaning back in his chair. Some devil on his shoulder wanted to throw her as off-balance as he felt. 'I already know it. Along with your jeans size, your bra size, and of course what type of panties you like to wear.'

'That's an invasion of privacy,' she snapped.

'So sue me,' he drawled, unaccountably pleased to see her affable expression fade and her eyes flash purple sparks. Her watery attempt at friendship had annoyed him. He didn't want that from her. In fact he didn't want anything at all from her!

Lily pressed her lips together and tried to hold on to her temper. How dared he? Lounging back in his executive chair like King Tut. She took a deep breath and willed herself to remain calm. Polite and aloof...

*Just imagine he's a difficult director you have to put up with for a short while. You've done that before.*

She was trying to think of some way to regain her equilibrium when Tristan's mobile rang and thankfully he picked it up. He didn't even acknowledge her as he pushed away from his desk and presented her with his back as he walked to stand in the vee of the floor to ceiling windows that partially lined two walls of his corner office.

Lily started reeling through every foul name she could think of to call him, and then her eyes wandered to the view outside his window. London only had a handful of luxury skyscrapers and Tristan owned one of them. It wasn't the tallest, from what she could see, but it was certainly located on prime real estate near the heart of the city. Lily could see Big Ben, Westminster Abbey and the London Eye, and she hadn't had to pay a penny for the privilege.

Without even being aware of it she shifted her gaze from outside the window to the man standing in front of it, legs apart and one hand in his trouser pocket, pulling the fabric of his trousers tight across his taut backside.

Her eyes drifted down over his long legs and up again to the wide sweep of his shoulders, to the ripple of muscle evident beneath his close-fitting shirt. He really was an impressive male and, given his sedentary job, he must work out all the time to stay as fit as he looked.

As if sensing her too-intimate regard, Tristan glanced over his shoulder and pierced her with his green eyes.

The air between them seemed to thicken. Lily's breath caught and her body hummed with a vibrant awareness. Then a dismissive expression flitted across his face, and Lily released a long, steadying breath when he swung his gaze back to the window.

She heard him speaking rapidly to the caller about some EU presentation, effortlessly switching between English and a language she couldn't place. His keen intelligence was evident in the incisive timbre of his voice.

Lily's stomach growled, and she picked up a sandwich from the plate and forced herself to chew it. It was beyond her that she should feel such a strong physical reaction to someone who clearly couldn't stand the sight of her. And it was getting a bit hard to put it down to stress and anxiety. But surely the brain had some input when it came to sexual attraction?

Tristan ended his call, dropped the phone into his pocket and stalked to his desk, gripping the high back of his chair as he studied her with relentless intensity.

'I must say you seem remarkably composed for a woman who's potentially facing at least twenty years in the slammer,' he scorned, leaving Lily stunned by his coldness when minutes earlier there had been such heat.

'I trust the universe will work everything out.' She said, wincing inwardly at her prim tone and refusing to react as he raised a condescending eyebrow.

'The universe? As in the moon, the stars and Mother Earth?'

'No.' Lily tried not to roll her eyes. 'At least not in the way you mean. The universe is like a forcefield—an energy that we create for ourselves and others. Sort of like if we all think positive thoughts then good will always prevail.'

Tristan cocked his head as if he was seriously considering her view, but of course that was a fool's notion. 'Well, I'd say your universe was either out for lunch when you tried walking through Customs today, or it's working perfectly and you're as guilty as hell.'

Lily folded her arms and bit into her top lip.

How was it possible for someone to be so devastatingly attractive one minute and so perversely irritating the next?

'I also have great faith that the authorities know what they're doing,' she said waspishly.

'The authorities want someone to put behind bars.'

Lily angled her chin. 'Are you trying to frighten me?'

'I'm not even sure the Grim Reaper knocking on your door could do that. Perhaps you're not smart enough to see the danger.'

'You're very good with the lofty insults, Lord Garrett, but I believe that right *will* win out in the end.'

Tristan shook his head. 'I'm sure if some of those corpses

buried at Tower Hill could speak they'd suggest that was a little whimsical.'

Lily was sure that if some of those corpses could talk they'd tell him they were relatives of hers—and not the blue-blooded ones!

'Are you implying that I'm being unrealistic?'

'Actually, I thought I was doing more than *implying* it.'

Lily sniffed. 'I wouldn't expect someone like you to understand.'

'Someone like me?'

'Someone who thinks everything is either black or white. Someone who requires tangible proof before they'll believe anything.'

'It's called dealing in the real world,' he jibed.

'But sometimes the real world isn't always as it seems.'

Tristan made a scoffing sound. 'I thought I told you I didn't want to hear any of your protestations of innocence.'

Lily's eyes narrowed at his bored tone, and she breathed in deeply through her nose.

*Never let 'em know you care, Honeybee.*

She exhaled slowly. This would all be a lot easier if he'd just talk to her, instead of snapping off pithy comments here and there.

'And, as *pleasant* as this conversation is,' he continued, 'I have work to do. So I'd prefer you finish your tea and sandwiches over on the sofa.' He sat down and turned to his computer, dismissing her like some servant girl.

Oh, she'd just bet he'd prefer that. And she would have happily done so if he'd been a little nicer, but now...

'Actually, accusations and criticisms do not add up to a conversation. And would it really hurt you to be a little more civil?' she demanded, throwing the whole idea of polite and aloof out of one of his ultra-clean windows.

'To what end?'

He didn't bother looking up from his computer screen and that incensed her. 'To...to... I don't know. Just to be *nice*.'

'I don't do nice.'

Lily nearly laughed.

As if she hadn't worked that one out for herself! 'You know, for someone whose job it is to communicate with others you're not very good at it.'

That got his attention. 'My job is about justice, not communication. And you better be careful because I'm really good at it.'

Lily shook her head. The man needed to learn some home truths. 'You might be hot stuff in the courtroom, Lord Garrett, but personally you're an avoider. You'd rather shut me up than try to have a constructive conversation with me.'

'That's because I don't *want* to have a conversation with you—constructive or otherwise.'

Lily raised her eyebrows. 'That's a fine way to solve a problem.'

'I don't have… No—wait.' He tapped his pen impatiently on his desk. 'I *do* have a problem. She's blonde, five-foot-ten and won't stop jabbering on at me as if I care.'

Lily's mouth gaped, and she stuck her tongue against the back of her front teeth to prevent herself from telling him just what she thought of his rude comments and hurtful attitude.

'You really think you've got me all sussed out, don't you, Tristan?' Her voice was husky with raw emotion. 'I'm just some no-good dumb celebrity who takes drugs and uses the casting couch to get her roles as far as you're concerned.'

'Well, not if you're screwing the dolly boy. I can't imagine *he* can win you too many roles.' He leaned back in his chair and folded his arms behind his head.

Arrogant jerk.

Lily narrowed her eyes and stabbed her finger in his direction. 'You might have some two-bit report on your desk, but let me tell you—you know nothing about me. Absolutely nothing.'

'I know all I need to know,' he confirmed.

Lily shook her head. She was wasting her breath trying to

talk to him. He'd made up his mind about her a long time ago and there was nothing she could do to sway it. In fact, when the police found out who the real drug smuggler was he'd probably accuse her of sleeping with the whole police force to get the result.

She gave a slight shake of her head. When she'd left England six years ago she'd instigated a policy never to rise to people's bad opinion of her again, but for some reason she couldn't seem to help herself with Tristan. For some reason his condescending attitude hurt more than everybody else's put together—and she hated that.

Lily folded her arms across her chest and decided to give up all attempts to change his opinion. Let him think what he wanted.

'You know it's a good thing you're not my lawyer because I'd fire you.'

'Fire me?' He gave a harsh burst of laughter. 'Sweetheart, I wouldn't touch this case if it came gold-plated.' He sat straighter and looked down his aristocratic nose at her. 'Because I know what you are, Honey Blossom Lily Wild—or have you conveniently forgotten what happened at Jordana's eighteenth?'

Lily stiffened at the ominously quiet question. Here was the basis of his true hatred of her. The presumed ruination of his little sister because of her association with big, bad Lily Wild. He'd judged her on circumstantial evidence at least twice before, and she hated that he had never once given her the benefit of the doubt.

'You know—you know,' she spat, ignoring the inner voice that told her to calm down. 'I could make a movie about what you *don't* know, you ignorant jerk, and it would be an instant classic.'

'Ignorant jerk?'

That seemed to rile him, and it startled her when his chair shot back, nearly tipping over with the force of his movement. He circled his desk, a predatory intent in every silent step, and

Lily's heart bumped behind her ribs. She didn't think he'd hurt her, but still, the instinct to run was nearly overwhelming.

He stopped just in front of her, his hands balled on his hips, his green eyes ablaze with suppressed emotion.

'Let's see,' he snarled, leaning over her and caging her in with his hands on the armrests of her chair. 'You tried to hide a joint under my sister's mattress when you were fourteen, you took her to sleazy parties in the city—*underage*—you caused an outrageous scandal the night of her eighteenth, snorting cocaine from the glass front of my father's *seven-hundred-year-old* Giotto painting, and today you cart a truckload of charlie and disco biscuits into Heathrow.' He leaned in closer. The pronounced muscles in his forearms bunched. 'Tell me, Honey, how am I doing so far with what I *don't* know about you?'

Lily felt the back of the chair hard against her spine and ran her tongue over her dry lips. She could explain every one of those things—but he wasn't looking for an explanation, and frankly she was getting so sick of his rudeness she almost wanted him to dig a hole so she could bury him in it.

She remained tight-lipped, and his mocking expression said it all.

'What? No comment all of a sudden? No further explanation as to why I walked into my father's study and found a group of wasted idiots—my sister being one of them—and you leaning over the desk holding a rolled fifty-pound note, with some Armani-clad idiot standing behind you like he was getting ready to take you? What a surprise.'

Lily blushed profusely at his bluntness. That wasn't how it had been at all—but had it really looked like that? And how could he think she'd even been interested in that guy after the kisses they had shared?

'For heaven's sake, why would I kiss you if I—? Oh.' She stopped abruptly and nodded. 'You think I just went from you to him. Hence the cheap slut reference.' She shook her head as if she was truly stupid. 'Sorry, I'm a slow learner. Maybe you can add dumb blonde to my list of credentials? That's if you haven't done it already, of course.'

Tristan moved as quickly as a striking snake and reached down to pull her to her feet. 'Stop. Trying. To. Garner. My. Sympathies. You took a chance. It didn't come off. Now, deal with it.'

Lily tried to pull her hands free, and then stopped when she realised it was a futile waste of energy. Her eyes blazed into his. 'I don't know what ever made me think I could reason with you,' she bit out, adrenaline coursing through her veins. 'You know what? Go to hell. All you do is judge me and I've had it. You've never wanted the truth where I'm concerned and—oof!'

The air left her body as Tristan pulled her hard up against him and covered her mouth with his own. She tasted anger and frustration—and something else. Something that called to her. Something that left her mind reeling. After a token struggle she felt her resistance ebb away. Her brain simply shut down, leaving her body and her heart firmly in charge, and both, it seemed, craved his touch more than air.

Tristan knew it was a mistake as soon as he did it—but, seriously, just how much self-control did she think he possessed? Did she never give up? Standing there, glorious in her anger, her eyes sparkling like cabochon amethysts.

She shoved against him and tried to twist her mouth away, but Tristan wound her ponytail around his fist and held her head fast. Some distant part of his brain tried reminding him that he didn't behave like this. That he didn't shut women up with his mouth like some Neolithic cave dweller.

But it was too late. He'd been hungry for the taste of her all day, and something far more primitive than logic and civility was riding him now.

She moaned, her hands pushing against his shoulders, and he immediately gentled the pressure of his mouth. A voice in his head was telling him to stop. That now he was behaving like a jerk. That he hated this woman whose mouth felt like hot velvet under his.

She represented everything wrong with mankind. She took drugs, she partied hard, she was self-centered, self-absorbed—like his mother. Just when he might have had a chance of pulling away her fingernails curled into his shoulders, no longer pushing him away but drawing him closer, and he was lost.

He eased the hand in her hair and pressed his other one to her lower back, to bring her into firmer contact with his body, and delighted in her responsive quiver.

Right now he didn't give a damn about parties and drugs. Right now he was satisfying an urge that had started six years ago and got a whole lot worse today. He felt a groan rise up from his chest as her lips moved almost shyly beneath his. He wanted her. Hell, his body was aching with it. And he knew by the way her fingers clutched at his shirt that she felt the feral chemistry between them as intensely as he did.

He softened his lips even more and felt hers cling.

'Open your mouth, Honey,' he urged. 'I need to taste you.'

She obeyed instantly, and his tongue slid home and drank from her as if she was the finest wine. Only she tasted better. Sweeter than he remembered. He nearly expired at the shocking pleasure that jack-knifed through his body. She was like ambrosia to his senses, and he was once again reminded how men could start wars over a woman. And then he lost the ability to think at all as her tongue snuck into his mouth and she raised herself onto her toes to deepen the contact between them.

It was all the encouragement Tristan needed, and he widened his stance to take more of her weight, burning up when she rubbed her full breasts against his chest. Her soft, breathy whimpers incited him never to stop this crazy dance. His hands were unsteady as they skimmed down her torso, skating over her breasts and pulling her restless hips more firmly against his almost painful arousal.

She gasped and pressed even closer, buried her hands in his over-long hair.

Tristan couldn't contain another groan, and his hands rose up to push her cumbersome cardigan aside so that he could palm her breasts with both hands. She arched into him and his thumbs flicked over her peaked nipples. His senses revelled in her soft cries of pleasure. His lips drifted down over her neck as he dragged oxygen into his starved lungs, and he slid one hand down to delve underneath the elastic waistband of her tight leggings to cup her bottom. Her skin felt gloriously smooth and hot, and there was no thought of stopping now. He'd wanted this for too long, and he knew when he touched between her legs she'd be wet and wanting...

The strident buzz of his intercom resounded through the room like a death knell, and Tristan sprang back from Lily as if he'd been kicked.

'Tristan, I know you said no interruptions, but Jordana is on line one and threatening legal action if you don't take her call.' His secretary's humorous voice rang out clear, despite the blood roaring in his ears.

Hell. Everyone was a comedian all of a sudden.

'Tristan?'

'Fine,' he snapped. 'Tell her I'll be a minute.'

He watched Lily blink a couple of times, her hands on her heaving chest, her eyes hidden as she contemplated the foot of black carpet between them as if it was a seething pit of snakes. Her lips were deeply pink and swollen from his kisses.

He shook his head at his own stupidity.

He wasn't some hotheaded youth at the mercy of his untried hormones. What had he been thinking?

He noted the rise of hot colour that started at her neck and swept into her face. He didn't know if it was from embarrassment or desire.

'Hell,' he seethed, stalking back round to his side of the desk, raking his fingers through his hair. He willed his body to calm down. 'We are *not* going to do this. You are *not* going to look at me with that come-hither sexiness. You want to know what happens next? I'll tell you. You sit over there on that sofa and you don't move. You don't talk and you don't whine. The only thing you're allowed to do without me is go to the bathroom, and if I think you're up to no good in there you'll lose that privilege as well. Is that clear enough for you?'

'Crystal,' she snapped, straightening her clothing and pulling her cardigan tightly around her body.

She touched her tongue to her lips and another shaft of desire shot into his aching groin. Then she raised her chin and looked at him with over-bright eyes, and once again he felt like the jerk she'd called him earlier.

'You know,' she began softly, 'Jordana thinks you're one of the good guys. Boy, does she have *that* wrong.'

# CHAPTER SIX

TRISTAN sat opposite his sister at one of London's most exclusive eateries and tried not to brood over Lily's earlier comment. Because Jordana was right, damn it. He *was* one of the good guys, and he didn't know why he was letting the two-bit actress beside him, laughing over Oliver's unfunny jokes, make him question that.

Maybe because he'd kissed her the way a man kissed a woman he planned to sleep with and then blamed her for it. As if this maddening desire he felt for her was a deliberate spell she had cast over him... Which, come to think of it, was a much better explanation than the alternative—that he just couldn't keep his hands off her.

Which was not the case at all. What had happened in his office earlier was the result of extreme stress boiling over. Nothing more, nothing less.

Tristan prided himself on his emotional objectivity when it came to the fairer sex, and really this constant analysis of what had happened earlier was ludicrous. Yes, he was a man who liked his '*i*'s' dotted and his '*t*'s' crossed, but Lily was just an anomaly. An outlier on an otherwise predictable curve.

So what if his reaction to her was at the extreme end of the scale? It happened. Not often to *him* before, granted, but...once she was gone and his world had returned to normal he'd forget about her—as he had done the last time.

As he had done every other woman who had graced his bed. Only Lily hadn't graced his bed, and maybe that went some way to explaining his almost obsessive thoughts about her. He'd never had her. Had, in fact, made her off-limits to himself. And he wanted her. No point denying the obvious. Maybe if he had her—*no!* Forget it. Not going to happen.

But that didn't change the fact that now that his ferocious anger at being caught up in her situation had abated, and now he'd had a chance to observe her with Oliver and his sister all night, he had to admit he was starting to question his earlier assessment of her.

There was something so earthy and genuine about her. Something so lacking in artifice. He'd noticed it when she had engaged in a conversation with his PA and three of his paralegal secretaries.

She hadn't tried to brush them off, or spoken down to them. She'd been warm and friendly and called them by name. Something he would not have expected a drug-addicted diva to remember, let alone do.

He couldn't comprehend that he might have been wrong about her—but nor could he ignore the sixth sense that told him that something didn't add up.

Especially since the police believed that the haul found in Lily's bag, although small, had been intended for resale purposes. Lily just didn't strike him as the type who worked for a drug cartel, and nor did she appear to need money. Which left the possibility that she was innocent, had been framed, or had been an unknowing drug mule.

Or she'd brought the drugs in for a lover.

In his business Tristan had come across people who did far worse things for love, and he told himself the only reason he cared about this possibility was because he felt sorry for her. If she was so in love with some jerk she'd committed a crime for him she would definitely do jail-time. Lots of jail-time.

As if all that wasn't bad enough, the langoustines poached in miso—Élan's signature dish, which he had enjoyed many times before—had failed to get the taste of her out of his mouth. And that was just damned annoying.

Lily shifted on the black leather bench seat beside him and for the millionth time he wished she'd just sit still. They had been given a corner booth, overlooking Hyde Park, and whenever she so much as blinked, or turned to take in the view, his mind thought it was a good idea to let him know about it.

He glanced around at the *über*-modern, low-lit interior and recognised some of the more celebrated restaurant clientele, who all seemed to be having a better time of it than him. Laughter and perfume wafted through the air, along with the sound of flatware on Limoges china, but none of it could distract him from his unhealthy awareness of her.

He reached for his glass and took a long pull of classic 1956 Mouton Rothschild Medoc, forcing his attention from the spoon Lily was trying to lick the last morsel of ice cream from, as if it was thousand-pound-an-ounce caviar, and back to Oliver's discourse about his barbaric Scottish ancestors and some battle he'd no doubt claim they had won against the English.

God, his friend could talk. Had he known that about him?

Lily leaned forward and laughed, and Tristan refused to look at the way her low-cut silk blouse dipped invitingly, wondering where her tent-like cardigan had disappeared to.

When they had arrived at Jordana's prior to dinner the two girls had cried and hugged for an eternity. Then Jordana had whisked Lily away to shower and change, berating him for not thinking of it himself. Tristan hadn't told her that the last thing he needed was to have Lily Wild naked in his shower!

Now she was dressed in a red gypsy blouse, fitted denims and ankle boots, all provided by his sister. Her hair was brushed and fell in shiny waves down her back and she'd put on a bra. Pink. Demi-cup. Though he'd be a lot happier not knowing that. Because she had fabulous breasts and he couldn't help wondering what they would look like naked.

'It was love at first sight.'

Jordana's words sounded overly loud to his ears, and brought his awareness sharply back to the conversation.

What was?

Tristan looked at his sister, who was thankfully gazing at her fiancé and not at him, and released a breath he hadn't even realised he was holding.

'That's rubbish,' Oliver grouched. 'It took a month of haranguing you to help me find the perfect anniversary present for my parents before you even agreed to a real date.'

'I wasn't talking about me!' Jordana giggled pointedly, and then squealed when Oliver grabbed her leg under the table.

Lily laughed at their antics—a soft, musical sound that curled through Tristan's abdomen like a witch's spell.

'Steady on,' he said, as much to himself as to Oliver. 'She's still my baby sister, you know.'

'Stop your whining, you great plonker,' Oliver retorted. 'You're just jealous because you can't find someone who'll have you.'

'Ah, but haven't you heard, my good friend?' Tristan drawled. 'A man doesn't know what real happiness is until he's married. And by then it's too late!'

Jordana pulled a face. 'Oh, ha-ha. You'll fall in love one day. Once you get your head out of those legal bibles and stop dating women who are entirely unsuitable.'

'That swimwear model didn't look too unsuitable to me.' Oliver grinned.

'That swimwear model looked like a bobby pin.' Jordana said archly. 'Or should I say *booby* pin?'

'Lady Sutton, then?' Oliver offered.

'Hmmm, right pedigree, but—'

'I *am* still here, you know,' Tristan grumbled, 'and I'll thank you both for staying out of my personal affairs. There's nothing worse than two people who think love conquers all trying to talk perfectly happy singles into jumping off the same cliff.'

Not to mention the fact that he had no plans to relinquish his freedom to such a fickle and painful emotion as love.

But that reminded him that now would be a good time to find out who Lily could be so in love with she'd risk everything to please him.

And he had a right to know. He'd stuck his neck out for her, and he'd be damned if he'd risk getting it cut off because she'd done some idiot's bidding.

'What about you, Lily? Ever been in love?' he asked, smiling benignly as she shot him a look that would have felled a tree.

Now, what on earth had made Tristan ask her that? He'd ignored her all night, and when he did speak to her it was to ask something she had no intention of answering. Not seriously anyway...

'Oh, gosh, how long have you got?' Lily jested lightly, trying to think of a feasible way to change the subject. She'd rather talk about money than love!

'As long as it takes,' Tristan replied amiably.

She cast him a frosty look and murmured her thanks as a waiter discreetly refilled her water glass just before she picked it up.

Tristan scowled at him, but Lily appreciated his attentiveness. As she did the 'no cameras' policy the restaurant insisted on. No doubt the main reason the place was so well-attended by the super rich. Although, as to that, this restaurant exuded a class all of its own.

Eating out had been the last thing Lily had felt like doing, especially after the incident in Tristan's office, but she'd have done anything not to be alone with him. Which she would be once they left the restaurant.

And now he wanted to discuss her love-life as if they were best friends!

She didn't think so.

There was no way she would tell him that, yes, she had thought herself silly enough to be in love once.

With *him*!

Especially not when she had returned those kisses in his office a few hours earlier as if she still *was* in love with him.

Unbelievably, her body had gone off on a tangent completely at odds with her mind, and she was still shocked by her behaviour.

And his.

Although she shouldn't be. Tristan had been angry and had shut her up in the most primitive way possible. It didn't make it right—in fact it was downright wrong—but then so had been her response. She should have slapped him, not kissed him back. All she'd done was confirm his view that she was easy. A view she already knew would be impossible to reverse, so why even try? It wasn't as if he would believe the truth anyway.

'Well, let's see...' Lily paused, avoiding Jordana's interested gaze and counting on her fingers. 'First there was Clem Watkins, and then Joel Meaghan. Then—'

'Joel Major, you mean? And Clem? The guy from the gym squad?' Jordana scoffed. 'He had a nose that looked like he'd gone ten rounds with a hockey stick and he thought the ozone layer was a computer game.'

Lily pasted on a smile. 'He had good teeth, and he realised his mistake about the ozone layer almost straight away.'

'After everyone laughed. How could you have been in love with them? You didn't date either one.'

And that, Lily thought as she tried to ignore Jordana's frowning visage, was one of the problems with ad-libbing. Or telling white lies. You made mistakes.

Like forgetting that your closest friend was also at the dinner table and knew almost all of your teenage secrets.

'I'm not interested in your high-school dalliances, Lily.' Tristan cut in scathingly, his voice rising over the sounds of laughter in the background. 'I do want to get home tonight. Let's talk about *men* you've been in love with.'

*Ha!*

'Let's not,' Lily said, dismissing him with one of her enigmatic smiles. 'You'd be bored silly.'

'Humour me,' he insisted, his tone intimate as he shifted

his hand along the back of the velvet seat. 'Who's the current love of your life?'

His thumb grazed one of her shoulderblades and the heat of his touch burned through her thin blouse like dry ice.

Lily jerked forward and pretended she had been about to place her water glass back on the table.

He had done that deliberately, and if she hadn't agreed to put on a united front for Jordana and Oliver she'd happily tell him where to go.

Looking at the sexy little smile curving his lips, she knew he knew it. Which only fuelled her ire. If he thought he had the upper hand in this situation he had another thing coming.

'Oh, don't be silly,' she cooed, reaching across and placing her hand a little too high on his thigh, and patting him as one might a family pet. 'You already know everything there is to know about me. Remember?'

She felt a spurt of pleasure when Tristan looked taken aback by her action.

'I thought it was your contention that I didn't?' He replied lazily, smiling a devil's smile and clamping his larger hand over hers, effectively imprisoning her palm against his muscular thigh. 'I've always believed it's better to go directly to the source when you want to find something out.'

Lily's smile froze as his steely thigh muscles contracted beneath her palm. Her fingernails automatically curled into his trousers and she gave serious consideration to piercing through the heavy fabric to the flesh beneath.

Heat surged through her body as he squeezed her hand and locked his darkly amused eyes with hers. Lily shifted her gaze to the twinkling lights of the park through the unadorned windows before managing to recover her equilibrium enough to flick her dismissive gaze back over him.

'How very open-minded of you,' she purred pointedly, digging her nails into his thigh once more before dragging her hand away.

Lily had wanted to put Tristan in his place, but instead he

threw his head back and laughed—a delightfully masculine sound that was like fingernails down a chalkboard to her highly strung emotions.

She could see Jordana and Oliver looking perplexed, and then Tristan smiled at her. 'That's just the kind of guy I am,' he said, picking up his wine glass and holding her gaze as he stroked his thumb over the stem.

'I take it that was an in-joke?' Jordana offered, jolting Lily's attention away from Tristan.

'I don't know.' Lily sniffed. 'I didn't find it funny at all.'

'Well, regardless, now I'm even more confused.' Jordana tilted her head. 'Are you seeing someone, Lil, or not?'

Lily saw the open curiosity in her friend's face and wished she could rewind the last few minutes—because Jordana was far too nosy and would no doubt start hassling her about how hard she worked and how she needed to get out more.

'No.' She sighed, and then, feeling herself observed by Tristan's sceptical gaze, added, 'No one of any importance, that is.'

Let him make of that what he would!

'Well, good,' Jordana surprised her by saying. 'Because like Tristan, you've gone for completely the wrong partners so far. But—' she raised her index finger as Lily was about to intercede '—as you're my best friend I've decided to help you out.'

'How?' There was nothing scarier than Jordana on a love mission.

'Ah, not telling. Let's just say I have a little surprise for you during the wedding celebrations.' Jordana cast Oliver a conspiratorial glance from behind her crystal wine glass.

Lily didn't even try to smile.

'Jordana, what are you up to?'

'Now, don't be like that,' Jordana admonished her. 'I know how hard you've worked the past couple of years and it's time you cut loose a little bit. Look around, Lil.' She waved her glass towards the row of white tabletops. 'Have some fun, like your peers.'

Lily gave her friend what she hoped was a good-natured grimace. Jordana was sounding more and more like her old therapist, and that was just plain scary. 'Jordana, you're starting to scare me, and—much as I hate to agree with Tristan—I think you're so loved-up at the minute you're blinkered. I'm very happy as I am. I don't want a relationship. I like being single.'

'I'm just loading the gun, Lil, you don't have to fire the bullets,' Jordana returned innocently. 'Now, how about a pot of tea to finish off?'

'We really should be going,' Tristan said. 'Lily's tired.'

Lily looked at him, surprised he'd noticed. She *was* tired, but she'd do anything to prolong the time before being alone with him.

'No, I'm not.' She smiled brightly. 'And I never finish a meal without a cup of peppermint tea.'

'I'll have one too,' Jordana said.

Tristan and Oliver both raised their hands to signal the waiter at the same time, and Lily couldn't help laughing. Clearly Jordana had found herself an alpha male top dog to stand up to her overbearing brother.

The waiter took their order and Lily excused herself to use the bathroom.

Tristan frowned at her as she stood up, and she knew exactly what he was thinking. 'Be a dear and mind my handbag, would you?' she said to him, tilting the smaller satchel she had brought along in place of her tote precariously towards him and enjoying the way his eyes flared at her provocative move.

Serve him right for asking her such a personal question before, and trapping her hand against his thigh.

'Lily! Hi.'

Lily looked up into the mirror above the handbasin into the gorgeous face of a previous co-star she had shot a film with two years ago.

'I thought it was you. Summer Berkley—we worked together on *Honeymooner*.'

'Yes, I remember.' Lily wiped her hands.

Summer was a quintessential LA actress, with the tan, the boobs, no hips whatsoever and the hair just so. But she had a good heart, and a genuine talent which would eventually take her further than all the rest combined.

They swapped stories for a few minutes, and when Lily couldn't stall in the bathroom any more without drawing attention to the fact that she was doing so, she reluctantly preceded Summer into the dimly lit corridor—and almost straight into Tristan, leaning indolently against the opposite wall, arms folded, legs crossed at the ankles.

'Oh, *hello*,' Summer breathed behind her, and Lily mentally rolled her eyes. 'Are you waiting for us?'

'In a manner of speaking.' Tristan smiled at the redheaded Summer with bemused interest.

Lily decided there was no way she was standing around to watch Tristan hit on another woman, but when she moved to sidestep him he deliberately snagged his hand around her waist to waylay her.

Lily stiffened, and couldn't miss Summer's disappointed pout before she strutted suggestively past Tristan, who looked designer casual with the top buttons of his shirt undone and a five o'clock shadow darkening his chiselled jaw.

'I'm sorry, Lord Garrett. Did I take more than my allotted thirty seconds?' Lily murmured, stepping away from his touch.

Tristan let her go and held up his mobile phone. 'I had to take a call. But, yes, as a matter of fact, you did. And deliberately, I have no doubt.'

'Now, why would I do that?'

'Oh, I don't know.' His smile didn't reach his eyes. 'Because you like bugging me?'

'Hardly,' Lily denied, looking down her nose at him. 'Do you mind?' She looked pointedly towards the restaurant's dining room.

'Why don't you want me to know who your current lover is?' he asked.

Lily stared at the stubble on his chin and wondered absurdly if it was hard or soft. 'If I ignore you will you go away?' she queried hopefully.

'Nope.'

She sighed. 'How about because it's none of your business, then?'

'Is he famous?'

'No.'

She had to step closer to Tristan to allow two women to walk past, but quickly stepped back again.

'Married?'

'No!'

'Do I know him?'

Lily let out a breath. She couldn't understand why he was pushing this. He was starting to sound like a jealous beau. But that was ridiculous. He didn't even *like* her, did he?

'I don't see that it's any of your business,' she said again with icy politeness, folding her hands across her chest.

'Unfortunately for you everything about you right now is very much my business.'

Lily shook her head. 'I don't see how. You're not my lawyer, and the question is irrele—'

She broke off with a squeak as Tristan grabbed her elbow again, to avoid more diners heading to the bathroom and marched her around a short corner, stopping in front of a closed door.

They were close enough now that Lily could feel heat—and anger—emanating from his muscular frame.

'If you brought those drugs into the country for someone else,' he began scathingly, 'and you get approached by the moron while you're in my custody I could be implicated. Not only could my reputation and legal practice go down the drain but, depending on how it played out, I could be charged along with you.' His voice never lost its tenor, and the message was clear. 'So, whether you think my questions are relevant or not is completely *irrelevant* to me.'

Lily's heart beat heavily in her chest. So that was what was behind his earlier probing. She had been right. He wasn't interested in her as a person. She hated the fact that for a brief moment she had toyed with the idea that he might actually like her. Talk about living in a dream world.

She swallowed, not wanting to dwell on the way that made her feel—because she couldn't—wouldn't—continue to be disappointed by his low opinion of her.

She looked furtively around the small space and realised she was trapped between some sort of cupboard and Tristan and would need to push past him to return to the dining room.

For a minute she considered ignoring him, but she knew how well that would go down. And nobody had ever benefited from pulling a tiger's tail that she knew of…

'I wasn't anyone's drug mule and I don't know who the drugs belong to or how they ended up in my bag. And, contrary to *popular* belief, I don't have a lover right now. Sorry to disappoint you on that score.'

His brooding gaze held hers, and Lily resisted the urge to slick her tongue across her lips. He looked annoyed and intimidating, and a lot like he had when he'd thrown her out of his family home six years ago.

'What happened in my father's study six years ago?' he asked suddenly, and Lily wondered if maybe he really was a mind reader!

'You threw me out of your home and told me not to contact Jo again,' she said immediately.

'Which you ignored.'

Her eyes widened. 'Did you really expect me to cut myself off from her?'

His lips curved up slightly, as if he found the question amusing, but his eyes remained hard. 'Of course I expected it. But there's nothing I can do about that now. And that's not what I was asking about and you know it.'

If he was asking about the private party he had interrupted at Jo's eighteenth that was his problem. If Jordana hadn't already told him that *she* had instigated the party then Lily wouldn't do it either. It wouldn't serve any purpose but to make him think poorly of Jo, and Lily had no intention of ruining relations between them so close to the wedding by being some sort of tattle-tale after the event.

'I see no point in rehashing the past,' she said.

'Well, that's too bad, because I do.'

Lily unconsciously squared her shoulders. 'Actually, it's too bad for you, because I don't.'

Tristan's eyes narrowed dangerously. 'You were keen enough to talk earlier.'

'And you pointed out what a terrible idea that was, and now I'm agreeing with you.'

'Careful, Lily. That's twice you've agreed with me... Don't want to make a habit of it.'

Lily leaned forward and balled her hands on her hips. 'Well, here's something else I agree with you about—we need to set some ground rules before we go any further, and your macho "I'm in charge" routine just isn't going to cut it. Especially in public.'

'Really?'

'Yes, really.' Lily angled her chin up, ignoring the mocking glint in his eyes. 'And the first rule is that what happened back in your office is never to be repeated.'

'Now, how did I know you were going to say that?' he murmured silkily.

'I don't know. Putting that off-the-scale IQ of yours to good use for once?' she quipped, a sense of her own control making her reckless.

'Don't pretend you didn't want it,' he grated. 'You've been eating me up with your eyes ever since I picked you up today.'

'Oh!' Lily forgot about the fact that they were in a public space. 'You are something else!'

'So I've been told.'

'I just bet you have. You have quite the reputation as a ladies' man, but if you think I want to join their lowly ranks you can think again.'

'That's not how you played it six years ago,' he sneered.

'Six years ago I was too young to know any better—and don't forget I was high as a kite,' she lied. Why not *really* play up to his nasty opinion of her? Answering honestly before hadn't done much to change his opinion of her.

'Well, that might be.' His eyes flashed in response to her taunt. 'But you weren't high back in my office, and the way you tried to crawl up my body you wouldn't have stopped until I was deep inside you and you were completely sated.'

Lily gasped. His words conjured up a sensual image that caused her pelvis to clench alarmingly. 'You're delusional if you think that,' Lily spat breathlessly.

The cupboard's doorknob poked into her back as she instinctively moved back when Tristan closed the small space between them.

His eyes glittered dangerously into hers. 'A challenge, Honey?'

'No!'

'Oh, yes.'

He placed a hand either side of her head and leaned in, his mouth so close she could feel his warm breath on her lips, smell the coffee and wine he'd consumed.

Lily's heart sounded as loud as a road train in her ears, and her pelvis continued to clench in wicked anticipation of his kiss. Try as she might, she couldn't seem to find the will to resist his animal magnetism that was pulling her under.

Tristan's gaze held hers for a lifetime. 'Oh, yes,' he whispered again. 'Definitely a challenge.' He straightened away from her and dropped his arms, his expression closed. 'But, as gorgeous as you undoubtedly are, I'm not interested—so go play your games somewhere else.'

# CHAPTER SEVEN

THE ride to Tristan's home was tense, to say the least. Lily was still fuming over the humiliation of nearly embarrassing herself before, when she had almost reached up and pulled Tristan's taunting mouth to hers. Something she hadn't even been aware she was about to do until he'd pulled back.

Until *he'd* pulled back.

She swallowed a moan of distress and watched one neon sign become another as Tristan steered his silver Mercedes through the streets from Park Lane to Hampstead Heath—one of London's most prestigious addresses.

How dared he tell her that he wasn't interested in her? As if she would care! How about the fact that *she* wasn't interested in *him*?

And he'd certainly been a little more than interested back in his office. Interested in sex, anyway. Not that she would have let it get that far. But deep down she knew what he was trying to say. She wasn't his type. He thought her attractive, but nothing more.

Frank Murphy, her stepfather, had warned her about men like Tristan. 'They'll take one look at that face and figure and, believe me, they won't care about your personality. You give them what they want and you'll get a reputation for being easy.' *Like your mother.* The unspoken words had hung between them and Lily shifted uncomfortably at the memory.

Her mother had been ruled by her desires. Or, more specifically, her desire for Johnny Wild, but Lily wasn't like that.

Which was one of the reasons she resented this attraction she still felt for Tristan. She'd sworn never to fall for an unattainable man, and here she was all but salivating over one.

Dammit, Tristan was right. She had wanted him earlier in his office. Had, in fact, been completely enthralled by the sensations and emotions his touch had evoked.

The memory made her cheeks heat with shame. Hadn't she learned anything from his first rejection of her? Was she just a glutton for punishment?

Lily sighed and leaned her head back against the butter-soft leather seat, wishing she hadn't decided to come back to England after all this time. She should never have told Jordana she could make her wedding. Would be *in* her wedding!

It seemed that the stars had aligned and no matter which way she looked she was being sent a message that she wasn't as ready to come home as she had thought. And maybe she never would be.

Thankfully her morose thoughts halted when Tristan's powerful car pulled up and waited for the ten-metre-high wrought-iron gates to open. Lily glanced at the towering stone mansion softly lit by discreet exterior lights that made it seem as if it touched the skyline.

The car inched forward and down into an underground car park that held a motorbike, a four-wheel drive, and a gleaming red sports car.

A sense of entrapment suffused her, and Lily felt so tense she jumped out of the car before it had come to a complete stop. Then wished she hadn't as she swayed and had to grab hold of the roof to steady herself.

Tristan's mouth tightened, but he didn't say anything as she followed him to a lift.

A *lift*!

'The house belonged to an elderly couple before I bought it,' he said, noticing her surprised reaction.

Lily didn't respond; emotional exhaustion and jet lag were weighing her down as effectively as a giant bag of sand. She calculated that it was about 5:00 a.m. in Bangkok, which meant that she'd been up all night, and the effort it took to work that out made her nearly trip over her own feet when the lift doors opened.

Tristan cursed and reached for her, and cursed again when she stumbled trying to avoid him.

'Don't be a fool,' he ground out as she wrenched her elbow out of his reach.

'I don't want you touching me,' she snapped, wedging herself into the far corner of the panelled lift and staring at his shoes.

'Fine—fall over, then,' he mocked, moving to the opposite side of the small space.

Tristan had briefly considered arguing with her, but if she wanted to deny the sexual chemistry between them then that was her prerogative. He should probably take a leaf out of her book and do the same thing. It had been silly, goading her in the restaurant, rising to her challenge. A challenge, he'd sensed from her awkwardness afterwards, that had been more innocent than intentional.

And maybe he'd have more success ignoring the chemistry between them if she'd stop flinching every time he came within spitting distance of her? Because that just made a primitive part of him want to pursue her even more.

'You need to stop doing that,' he said.

She raised her eyes from his feet all the way up his body and looked at him from under pitch-black lashes. 'Breathing?' she quipped, folding her arms across her chest as he mimicked her leisurely scrutiny.

He barely resisted the urge to smile. *Yeah, that would help.*

She glanced away and worried her top lip and he wished she'd stop doing that as well.

The lift doors opened and Tristan strode out and dumped his keys on the small hallway table, walking through the vast foyer and up the marble staircase. He noticed her glance around at the pristine surroundings and the priceless artwork on the walls as she trailed behind.

His home was modern and elegant, with eclectic pieces he'd picked up from his travels here and there, and he wondered what she thought of it. And then wondered why he cared.

He stopped outside the room he'd asked his housekeeper to allocate to her. 'This is your room. Mine's at the end of the hall.'

He opened the door and stood back to let her precede him inside. When her scent hit him between the eyes he steeled himself against what he was about to do.

'As you can see, your suitcases are already inside the dressing room and the *en suite* bathroom is through there.' He flicked open another door and hit the light switch. 'My housekeeper was instructed to make the room ready, so you should have everything you need.'

She didn't say anything, just stood beside the silk-covered queen-sized bed clutching her bag.

'I'll need to see the bag before I go,' he said evenly.

'What for?' She snapped her eyes to his.

Because after she had spent so long in the bathroom at the restaurant with that redhead with the fake lips he had wondered if she hadn't slipped Lily a little something. Of course Lily might have already taken it, but he hadn't seen any evidence of that when he'd backed her up against the cupboard in the restaurant. All he'd seen then was a heady desire that matched his own.

He knew the chances of the woman giving Lily something were slim to none, but with a Scotland Yard detective due to interview her in the morning he wasn't prepared to take that chance.

'The bag.'

She narrowed her eyes. 'You already know what's in it. Remember?'

'That was before you visited with your friend in the restaurant bathroom.'

'Oh, come on. It's not like I planned to run into her.' Lily's tone was incredulous.

Tristan held out his hand and Lily lobbed her bag at him as if it was a missile. 'Have it—and good luck to you.'

Tristan walked closer to her and upended the contents onto the bed. There wasn't much to see but cosmetics and a purse. He checked the purse and then dropped it back on the bed.

'Now you.'

She didn't move, and he clenched his jaw when he saw understanding dawn across her stunning face.

'Tell me you're kidding.'

He sincerely wished he could. 'The way I see it we can do this one of two ways. Either I search you or you strip.'

She made a small sound and then slapped her hands on her hips. Her eyes, when they met his, were glacial. 'Is this how you get your kicks? Trying to frighten innocent women into doing what you want?'

'I didn't ask for this,' he grated, his eyes drawn to the little gap at the centre of her blouse where the red ribbon tied in a bow. 'But it's my house. My rules. So—arms out.'

He stepped towards her and she stepped backwards—and came up against the bedside table.

Her gaze flitted between him and the bedroom door, as if she was contemplating making a run for it. 'I'm clean. I promise you I am.'

'Don't make this harder than it has to be.' He stopped just in front of her.

The colour was high on her cheekbones and the pulse-point in her neck looked as if it was trying to break free. Just when he thought he'd have to consider force she surprised him by suddenly opening her arms wide.

'Go ahead. You don't scare me.'

Tristan stepped forward. Impudent witch. He might be as hard as stone at the thought of touching her but he actually resented having to touch her like this. No matter how much he tried to deny it to himself, he knew that he would much prefer her willing and wanting. And he'd lied to her before. He *was* interested. Too interested.

Wanting to get this over with as quickly as possible Tristan circled her tiny wrists and ran both his hands up the long sleeves of her blouse at the same time.

'My stepfather warned me about men like you,' she said, her voice a breathy caress in the otherwise silent room.

'Is that right?' His hands rounded her shoulders and then ran lightly under the heavy cascade of her hair and across her back. He felt her shiver and swallowed hard.

'That's right—*oh*!' She gasped as his hands skimmed around her ribcage and rose to cup her breasts. Her nipples peaked against his palms and made it nearly impossible for him to leave that tiny bow done up.

'Keep talking,' he growled, his hands skimming back down over her torso. It was easier to ignore the feel of her if she kept annoying him. 'You were saying something about men like me?'

He knelt at her feet and unzipped one of her boots.

'Yes,' she said, and her voice was only a touch uneven. 'Men who only want one thing from a woman and then discard them when they're finished.'

'That "one thing" being sex, I take it?' He put the boot aside and set to work on the other one.

'Yes, I'm sure you do,' she bit out scornfully. 'Take it, that is.'

He looked up to find her studying the ceiling. 'This is hardly *taking it*, Lily,' he retorted gruffly. 'And let's just say I'm not enjoying this either—but I don't usually entertain possible drug felons, so you'll have to excuse my current *modus operandi*.'

'I'll excuse nothing,' she spat.

'And—' he stopped, completely losing his train of thought when he found his face on a level with that part of her body he'd love to touch. To taste.

Was she as aroused as he was? Wet even?

*Hell, don't go there. Just don't go there.*

He blanked his mind as much as possible as he ran both hands up over one long, lean leg, finally remembering what he was about to say. 'And I've never had a woman complain.'

'That's not true.'

He stopped and looked at her.

'I remember reading about that girl. A model who said that you tricked her into thinking you cared. That you wouldn't know love if it...if it hit—no, knocked you on the head.'

Tristan paused. 'She's entitled to her opinion, but it wasn't my fault she fell in love with me. She knew exactly what type of relationship she was getting into, and love was never part of the deal.'

'Silly girl.' Lily folded her arms across her chest and stared anywhere but at him. 'She doesn't know how lucky she was. Personally, I don't know any woman in her right mind who could ever imagine being in love with you.'

He shifted to her other leg.

'Unfortunately it happens. But women fall in love with many things, and it's rarely the man they see in front of them.' And in him, he knew, they saw a title and a life of privilege. Like his mother had with his father. *Shopping, champagne and chauffeurs,* he'd heard her brag to more than one friend.

'You should be thankful they want something at all. It's not like you can rely on your charming personality,' she scorned.

Tristan laughed—a hard sound in the deathly silent room. 'I'm not looking for love.' He rose and reached around to cup her bottom, closing his eyes as he slid both hands into her deep back pockets.

Lily's hands flew to his chest, as if to hold him back, but how easy would it be just to tug her forward and let her feel how much she aroused him?

'What happened?' She gasped breathlessly. 'Did a woman scorn you, Tristan?'

He knew she was deliberately trying to distract him, and that she was right to do so.

'No woman's ever got close enough to scorn me, Honey,' he

sneered, skating his hands along the inside of her waistband and then finally cupping between her legs.

'You bastard!' she seethed, her hand rising to slap his face.

He stopped her, but deep down he knew he deserved it. He let her go so she could stalk to the opposite side of the bed.

'I hope you're satisfied.'

*Not by a long shot, sweetheart.*

'That was necessary. Nothing else,' he said evenly.

'Keep telling yourself that. It might make you sleep better tonight,' she spat.

'I'll sleep just fine,' he lied.

'Well, you shouldn't. But I'm curious—is it just me you don't trust, or all women?'

'Don't go there.'

'Why not? Your attitude is abysmal for someone whose parents were happily married—'

'Actually, my parents weren't happily married.'

'They weren't?' She blinked in surprise.

'No. I don't think my mother ever really loved my father and he refused to see it. Which was to his detriment in the end, because as soon as she got a better offer she took off.'

'Oh, that's terrible.' Her automatic compassion was like a fist to his stomach.

'Yeah, well, that wasn't the worst of it. Love has a way of making fools of us all. Something to remember.'

He turned sharply on his heel and strode from her room before he did something stupid. Like throw her on the bed and give her what he knew they both wanted—no matter how much she tried to deny it.

Once in his room, Tristan shed his clothes and jumped into the shower, turning the mixer all the way to cold and dousing his head as if it was on fire. He let the freezing water wash over him for a minute and then reset the temperature to hot. God, that search... He blew out a breath. The more he tried to control his physical reaction to her the more out of control it seemed to become.

This situation was seriously driving him crazy. *She* was seriously driving him crazy. And, worse, the memory of the day his mother had walked out on them wouldn't leave him alone.

Tristan had overheard his parents arguing. Overheard his mother telling his father that he had nothing she wanted. That her son, Tristan, had nothing she wanted either. And that had bitten deep, because every time she had spiralled downwards Tristan had always been there to try and help her. Tried to be there for her. So to have her only want Jordana...

The memory still chilled his blood. It had taken him a long time to realise that no one was good enough for her and that all those years of trying to win her love and approval had been for nothing.

He scrubbed his hand over his face and shut the mixer off. He pulled on silk boxer shorts and walked up the outdoor circular staircase to his rooftop balcony.

The night was cool, and he enjoyed the sting of air on his skin as he leaned on the wrought-iron railing and looked out over the dark mass that was the Heath and the twinkling coloured lights of London beyond. The cumulus clouds that hung over the city had a faint pinkish tinge due to the light pollution, but he barely noticed. His mind was focused on replaying the day's events in his head.

Which wasn't a good thing—because his head was full of more questions than answers.

He didn't know whether to believe Lily about her not having a current lover, but he was beginning to suspect that she was telling the truth about not knowing she'd had drugs in her bag. That was disconcerting, because it meant he'd been wrong about her. He couldn't remember the last time he'd been wrong about a person. Hated to think that he was now. Because if he was he owed her an apology.

Could she really be as genuine, as *untouched,* as she appeared? Or was he just a fool, being taken in by a beautiful and duplicitous woman? One whose job it was to pretend to be someone she wasn't.

Whatever she was, he desired her more than he'd desired any woman before—and that wasn't good.

He gripped the balustrade so tightly his palms hurt. He needed an outlet for all the pent-up energy whizzing through his blood, and the only thing he could think of to assuage his physical ache was totally off-limits.

Straightening, he clasped his hands behind his neck, twisting his body from side to side to ease the kinks in his back. A run usually helped clear the cobwebs away. And if he didn't have a suspect movie star sleeping next door he'd put on his joggers and do exactly that. But then, if he *didn't* have a suspect movie star sleeping next door he probably wouldn't need to go for a run at—he glanced at his watch—one in the morning.

Grimacing, he strode inside and flopped face down on his bed.

Given that he couldn't get rid of her in the short term, the only way he could think of to deal with this situation was with the detached professionalism he would offer any client and ignore the attraction between them.

He'd told her more than once today that he was in charge, and damn it if he wasn't going to start behaving as if he was tomorrow.

# CHAPTER EIGHT

'A MOVIE premiere? Is this your idea of a joke?'

Tristan's PA flinched as she stood on the other side of his desk, and he realised he'd said almost those exact words to his sister at almost this exact time yesterday.

Again he'd been having a great morning, and again it was shot to—

Okay, so it hadn't been *that* great a morning, what with Lily waking up late and a police detective waiting around in his home until she did so, but it was definitely ruined now. He cut a hard look to Lily, who stared back impassively at him from the white sofa.

'Uh, n-no,' Kate stuttered.

He glanced back at his computer screen, at the images Kate had brought up of the legions of fans who had camped out overnight in Leicester Square to get a glimpse of Lily Wild at some premiere to be held that evening.

'Lily, tell me this is a joke.'

He watched Lily's throat work as she swallowed, and then he returned his eyes to his surprised PA, who didn't seem to know what to do with her hands. She'd never seen him on the verge of losing his temper before and she was clearly daunted.

'I wasn't going to say anything,' Lily informed him coolly, standing to walk over to his desk.

Only she wasn't so cool deep down, because she didn't seem to know what to do with her hands either, and nervously pleated the loose folds of her peasant skirt.

His eyes swept upwards over her clinging purple shirt and then into eyes almost the same shade. 'I'm sure you weren't,' he mocked.

'Only because I was going to cancel my attendance—not because I didn't want you to know about it.'

Cancel it? He doubted that very much. She'd set up her attendance long before now, and while she might be feeling apprehensive about her drug bust he doubted she seriously wanted to miss an opportunity in the limelight. She'd chosen that life, after all.

'Oh, you can't cancel!' Kate cried, trying very hard not to appear starstruck. 'The premiere was delayed until today so you could make it, and there are people who have camped out in the cold night to see you. They'll be so disappointed. Look.'

She pointed to the computer screen, but Tristan's eyes stayed locked on Lily's face.

Just as they did later that night, when he found himself in the back of his limousine being whisked through central London on his way to Leicester Square.

It wasn't quite sunset, but the sky was filled with leaden clouds that blocked the setting sun from view and made it darker than it otherwise would be. Light rain splattered the windows, and Tristan wondered if Lily looked so nervous because she was worried that the rain would ruin the look she and Jordana had come up with in his bathroom or something else.

Because she certainly looked nervous.

Her chest was rising and falling with each deep, almost meditative breath she took. Her hands were locked together in her lap, and with her eyes closed she looked like Marie Antoinette must have before being dragged to the guillotine. But he didn't think Marie Antoinette could have looked anywhere near as beautiful as Lily Wild did at this minute. As she did every damned minute.

Then the car rounded the final bend and he suspected he knew why she might be nervous.

The car pulled up kerbside, and the door was immediately opened by a burly security guard wearing a glow-in-the-dark red-and-yellow bomber jacket. A wide red carpet extended in front of them for miles, dividing the screaming mass of fans barely constrained behind waist-high barricades.

Men and women in suits trawled the carpet, and the fans went from wild to berserk, waving books and posters around like flags, as Lily alighted from the car into a pool of spotlights.

The stage lighting on nearby buildings and trees was no match for the sea of camera flashes that blinded Lily, and then himself, on both sides as Tristan followed Lily out of the car.

An official photographer rushed up and started snapping Lily from every angle, while a woman in a dark suit and clipboard motioned her along the carpet to sign autographs for the waiting fans.

Tristan felt as if he'd stepped into an alternative universe, and wasn't wholly comfortable when Lily approached one of the barricades and the fans surged forward as one, making the beefy security guards who could have moonlighted as linebackers for the New Zealand All Blacks square off menacingly.

Tristan felt sure the fans were about to break through the barricades, and his own muscles bunched in readiness to grab Lily and haul her behind him if that should happen.

In the surrounding sea of multiple colours and broad black umbrellas held aloft to ward off the fine rain falling from the sky Lily stood out with her cream-coloured dress, lightly golden skin and upswept silvery-blond hair.

When he had first seen her in the dress Jordana had produced earlier—a knee-length clinging sheath with a high neck—he'd known he was in trouble. Then she had turned to reveal that it had no back, and he'd nearly told her to go back and put on her blouse and peasant skirt. But then he'd have had to explain why, and he didn't like admitting why to himself let alone anyone else.

Now he could appreciate that Jordana had wrought a small miracle, and had made Lily look like a golden angel amid a sea of darkness.

Which, aesthetically, was wonderful, but was not so great for his personal comfort level—nor, he could safely say, that of any other man who happened to look upon her that night!

He watched her now, doing her thing with the fans, and thought back over the interminable day.

All day she had been a paragon of virtue. She'd done exactly as he wanted—sat on the white sofa in his office and acted as if she wasn't there. Which should have made it easier to ignore her but hadn't. Because while she had immersed herself in a script with all the verve of someone preparing to sit a final exam he had struggled to find one case that held his attention long enough for him to forget she was in the room.

When he'd tried to engage her in a conversation about what had happened the night of Jo's eighteenth birthday party she had clammed up, and he had to wonder why. Jordana had implied that he'd been wrong about Lily's involvement, but if so why would Lily remain tight-lipped and only throw him that phony smile of hers when he broached the topic?

A roar from the crowd snapped his head around as a tall, buff Latino heart-throb dressed in torn jeans and a crumpled shirt swaggered towards Lily, raising both hands to wave at the near-hysterical crowd as he went. Lily turned and swatted the man with her million-dollar smile and Tristan felt his insides clench. That smile was like the midday sun coming out from behind heavy clouds—bright and instantly warming. Seductive and impossible to ignore. And so genuine it made his jaw harden. She had yet to turn it his way again, and he realised that he wanted her to. Badly.

The heart-throb draped his arm around Lily's waist and leaned in to kiss her, smiling at her like some long-lost lover.

They looked good together, his dark hair a perfect foil for her blondeness, and Tristan's eyes narrowed as he watched them work the crowd. His initial instinct to leap forward and rip the actor's arm from its socket slowly abated as he calmed his senses and realised that the actor's light touches here and there were too tentative to be that of a lover.

If the guy had known her intimately he wouldn't be just placing his hand on her hip now and then for a photo. He'd be subtly spreading his fingers wide over the small of her back, which Tristan already knew was sensitive to a man's touch. He'd let his fingers trail the naked baby-soft skin there and smile into her eyes when she delicately shuddered in response. Maybe he'd even press lightly on her flesh to have her arch ever so slightly towards him. Maybe exert just enough pressure so that he could hear that soft hitch in her breath as her mouth parted—

*Hell.*

Tristan pulled his thoughts back from the brink and dug his hands into his pockets, calling himself an idiot and wondering how long he could continue like this.

The crowd gave a howl of complaint as Lily and the heart-throb walked back towards the red carpet. The actor's hand hovered behind her protectively, and even though Tristan knew they weren't lovers he could tell by the expression on the Latino's face that he'd probably give up that arm to become so.

He was immensely irritated by the man's proprietorial air—and by his own desire to possess her. Especially when she had done little to incite his attention. And why hadn't she?

Lily Wild was turning out to be an enigma, and he was not at all happy to find that he might have been guilty of stereotyping her just as much as the next person.

'I have to do the red carpet thing and answer a few questions from the press and then we can go in,' she murmured over the noise of the crowd.

He nodded, but his eyes were on the actor, and Tristan found himself deliberately stepping into Lily's personal space to let the heart-throb know she was off-limits.

Lily's eyes widened quizzically, but the actor got the message, throwing his chest forward in a display of machismo.

They took each other's measure for a beat, and then the actor gave a typically Mediterranean shrug.

'Hey, man, don't sweat it.' He laughed, backing down when it became obvious that Tristan wouldn't. 'I was just helping Angel, here. You know how she gets in crowds.'

Tristan didn't, but he nodded anyway and watched the heart-throb amble further along the line.

He put his hand on Lily's arm to stop her following. 'What was he talking about?'

Lily sniffed, and raised a hand to wave at her fans. 'Nothing.'

He tightened his grip as she made to shrug him off. 'How was he helping you?'

'Not by feeding me drugs, if that's what you're thinking.'

He hadn't been thinking that, and her comment ticked him off. 'Then tell me what he was talking about.'

'I can't explain here.' She nodded to a fellow actor who blew a hello kiss. 'I don't have time.'

'Make time.'

'Oh!' She huffed, and then leaned closer to him, her delicate perfume wafting into his sinuses. 'I used to have agoraphobia. Now can we go?'

Tristan frowned. 'Fear of open spaces?'

'Do you even know *how* to whisper?' she complained, clearly uncomfortable with the subject matter. 'Most people think of it as that, but in my case it's a fear of crowds and being trapped in a situation I can't control.'

'That's what the therapy was about?' he said.

She glanced at him sharply. 'How do you know…? Oh, your special investigator's report. Well, it's nice to know he got some things right.'

'How do you know it was a he?'

'Because from the little I know of what's in it he's made snap judgements on very little evidence at all—just like a man.'

Tristan bit back a response and refocused. 'How bad is your phobia?'

Lily sighed. 'It's not bad at all. Jordi Mantuso and I swapped stories on set and he was just being kind.'

Tristan was shocked by her revelation. 'And are you okay? Right now?'

She looked taken aback by the question and he gritted his teeth, realising that his behaviour towards her had given her a very negative impression of who he was.

'Y-yes. I'm okay. It's not like I can't go out in a crowd—it's more a fear of being trapped by them.'

'Like when you were a child and surrounded with your parents' crowds of fans?'

The softness that had come over her face at his concern disappeared, and she looked away before glancing back. 'Yes. They think that's where it started. But I haven't had an attack in years.'

One of the female minders approached, to find out what was delaying them, and Tristan watched Lily paste on a smile that didn't reach her eyes as she walked towards the rows of paparazzi.

She answered questions and posed for photographs like the professional she was, and he couldn't help respecting the adversity she had learned to overcome in order to work in her chosen profession.

He could see her making moves to finish up, and then her body stiffened. Something was wrong. Was she having a panic attack?

'I don't do theatre,' she was saying firmly.

'But why not, Lily? You've been offered the role of a lifetime, playing your mum. Are you not even considering it?'

'No.' Polite, but definite.

'What's wrong with the U.K., Lily? Don't you like us?'

'Of course.' Another pretty smile that didn't quite reach her eyes. 'My schedule hasn't allowed me to return to England before now.'

'The roles you choose...' an oily voice spoke up from the rear and paused for effect '...they're very different women from your mother. Is that a deliberate decision on your part? Is that why you won't take the West End gig?'

Lily felt Tristan step closer, and the warmth from his body momentarily distracted her from the reporter's question. She hated this part of the proceedings. And she wouldn't take the part playing her mother if it was the last known acting role on the planet.

'I choose my roles according to what interests me. My current film, *Carried Away,* is a romantic comedy, and…I like happy endings…what else can I say?' Lily smiled and turned to answer another question about location, before the same reporter who had been taking potshots at her from the get-go piped up again.

'Do you ever worry about being thought of as like your mother?'

'No.' Lily's smile felt as if it was made of cardboard and she thought about making an exit.

'What's it like kissing Jordi Mantuso?'

'Divine.' Lily's smile was genuine, and the fans who had caught her words whooped.

But the oily guy was back. 'Miss Wild, I'm still not clear about the West End gig. We've heard the director is holding off signing another female lead, so is the reason you won't do it because you're worried about the theatre aspect or…something else?'

Oh, this guy was good. He was a top-of-the-line paparazzo with a nose for a juicy story, and Lily could feel some of that old panic from years ago—the panic she had just told Tristan was firmly under control—well up inside her.

It was being back in London that was doing it. The whole stigma of who her parents had been. And the paps here were relentless. She rarely had to face such insolence in other parts of the world.

The reporter's question had become jumbled in her head and she was struggling to swallow when she felt Tristan's hand snake around her lower back and rest possessively over her hip-bone; his fingers spread wide, almost stroking her through her the delicate fabric of her dress.

She felt a flush heat her face as her stomach muscles trembled, and fervently hoped he wouldn't notice either response.

She tried to turn and silently berate him, but his fingers held her in place. His breath stirred the wisps of hair coiling around her temple as he leaned in closer and stole the breath from her lungs.

'You've forgotten he's a slimeball and you're taking his question seriously. Just look up at me as if I've said something incredibly funny and ignore him.'

He let her half turn in the circle of his arms, but she couldn't force the response he'd suggested.

Her hand automatically came up between them and flattened against the black designer shirt Jordana had provided him with. Her fingers curled into the fabric. She didn't know if she was trying to hold him back or draw him closer, because her brain had frozen at the open hunger banked in his direct gaze.

The noise of the crowd, the cameras, the lights…everything faded as Lily felt suffused with warmth and a sexual need that was as debilitating as it was exciting.

She felt his swift indrawn breath as she held his gaze, and was powerless to look away when his eyes dropped to her mouth.

Dimly she became aware of the crowd chanting, 'Kiss! Kiss!' and as if in slow motion a soft smile curved Tristan's firm mouth.

He leaned in and gently touched his lips to hers. The soft contact was fleeting, but still her lips clung, and as he pulled back and looked at her she knew he'd felt her unbidden response. He stared at her as if he wanted more—and if he didn't the screaming fans certainly did.

Lily's fingernails flexed, and somehow she found the wherewithal to pull back, once again becoming aware of the whistles and wild catcalls of 'Who is he?' and 'Is that Lord Garrett?' from the press.

The camera flashes were relentless, and Lily knew that while Tristan's actions had been motivated purely to help her out of an awkward moment, hers had not.

And wishing it was otherwise wouldn't make it so.

# CHAPTER NINE

'I ENJOYED the film,' Tristan said, breaking the heavy silence between them. Lily didn't look at him but continued to stare out of the window as his chauffeur drove them through the glistening London streets.

It was late, and after two hours of sitting beside Tristan in a darkened movie theatre she felt uptight and edgy. The awareness she had been trying to keep at bay by pretending to read that hateful play for most of the day had exploded the minute his lips had touched hers on the red carpet.

No doubt he'd felt sorry for her after her earlier disclosure, but that didn't stop her from wanting him to touch her because he wanted to, not out of some misplaced duty to look out for her.

And she didn't want to make polite small talk with him now. She just wanted to get to the safety of her room and go to bed. To sleep.

In hindsight she should have been more prepared for the intrusive questions of the U.K. press, and probably would have been if worry over her case and the tension between herself and Tristan wasn't taking up so much head space.

Of course that brief kiss would be headline news in the papers tomorrow. Would be on the internet right now in this era of instantaneous news reports!

She knew she shouldn't be angry about what he'd done. He'd only been trying to help. But her own response to his sensitivity both now and this morning, when he'd made a Scotland Yard detective wait two hours until she woke from an exhausted sleep, and yesterday when he'd eased her headache while she slept in the car, made it harder for her to keep ignoring her feelings for him.

Especially after his disclosure about his parents and the pain in his voice when he had referred to his mother. The knowledge that he'd been hurt as a child made Lily feel differently towards him. Made her want to soothe him. To find out what had been worse than his mother leaving. Feeling this way about him wasn't clever. It could only lead to heartache—her own!

She sighed heavily and felt his gaze linger on her. She really didn't want to have any reason to lessen the animosity between them. Without that it would be far too easy to fall back into her adolescent fantasy that he was her dream man. What she needed to remember was that deep down he was essentially a good person, but any solicitude he extended towards her didn't automatically cancel out what he really thought of her.

'No comment, Lily?'

And he was calling her Lily now, instead of Honey. Oh, she *really* didn't want him being nice to her.

'You shouldn't have done that before,' she berated him, letting her embarrassment and uncertainty at this whole situation between them take centre stage.

He glanced at her briefly. 'Tell you I enjoyed your film?'

'Divert attention away from that reporter on the red carpet by kissing me.'

His direct gaze made her nervous, so she focused on the darkened buildings as the big car sped along Finchley Road.

'You looked like you needed it,' he said softly.

'I didn't.' Lily knew she was being argumentative, but she couldn't seem to stop herself. 'And now your picture—*our* picture—is going to be splashed all over the papers tomorrow. They'll think we're lovers.'

The car pulled up outside his exclusive mansion and he turned to her before opening the door. 'They'd probably have assumed that anyway given that I accompanied you.'

Bert opened the door and Lily smiled her thanks to him before stalking after Tristan, annoyance at his cavalier attitude radiating through her. 'Assuming and confirming isn't the same thing,' she retorted. Realizing too late what her words implied, she hoped he wouldn't pick up on it.

Movement further up the street alerted them to a lurking photographer, and Lily allowed Tristan to usher her up the short walkway to the black double front doors that looked as if they shone with boot polish.

He pushed one open and she preceded him into the marble foyer, and then followed him through to the large dining room where he turned to face her.

'Interesting phrasing. But I'm not sure how I could have confirmed something that's not true?' he drawled, a dangerous gleam lighting his eyes.

'Oh, you know what I mean,' she said, flustered by the strength of her confusing emotions. 'I'm tired.'

'Is that your way of defending your Freudian slip?'

'It wasn't…' She noted his raised eyebrow and swore. 'Oh, go to hell,' Lily fired at him, walking ahead of him through to the vast sitting room, dominated by a king-sized sofa that faced plate-glass windows overlooking the city.

'You know, all this outraged indignation over my attempt to help you before seems a little excessive to me,' Tristan said from behind her.

Lily turned, her eyes drawn to his lean, muscular elegance as he propped up the doorway even though she was determined not to be drawn in by his brooding masculinity. 'Oh, really?'

Tristan leant against the doorjamb and studied Lily's defiant posture. Her face was flushed, and more wisps of hair had escaped her bun and were kissing her neck. Her lips were pouting, and he'd bet his life savings that she'd crossed her arms over her chest to hide her arousal from him. He knew why she was so angry. He knew she felt the sexual pull between them and was as enthralled by it as he was.

And, while she might be upset with the media fall-out from his actions on the red carpet, he hadn't missed the way her lips had clung to his and how her violet eyes had blazed with instantaneous desire when he'd kissed her.

'Yes, really. Want me to tell you what I think is behind it?' he asked benignly.

'Pure, unadulterated hatred.' She faked a yawn and he laughed.

'You know what they say about hatred, Lily.' Tristan stalked over to the drinks cabinet and threw a measure of whisky into a glass. Two days with her and he was beginning to feel like an alcoholic!

'Yes, it means you don't like someone. And my reaction to your behaviour is not excessive in the slightest. All you've done tonight is give the tabloids more fodder—and for your information I could have handled that reporter by myself.'

Tristan raised his glass and swallowed the fiery liquid in one go, welcoming the sharp bite of distraction from the turn the conversation had taken. All he'd done was compliment her performance!

'Was that before or after you had the panic attack?' he asked silkily.

'It wasn't a panic attack! And just because I tell you something personal it doesn't mean you get to take over. You're not God's gift—even though you clearly think you are.'

Tristan turned slowly and stared at her. He'd heard the clear note of challenge in her voice and he knew the reason for it. And, by God, if he didn't want to do something about it— regardless of everything that lay between them.

He wanted her, and he knew for damned sure she wanted him, and looking at her right now, with her legs slightly apart and her hands fisted on her hips, her chin thrust out, he knew she wanted him to do something about it too.

Not that she would admit it.

He let his eyes slide slowly down her body and then just as slowly all the way back up. The pulse-point in her throat leapt to life, but she made no attempt to run from the hunger he knew was burning holes in his retinas.

There was something interminably innocent about her provocative stance, almost as if she didn't know what she was about, and it pulled him up for a minute. But then he discounted the notion. She might not be the Jezebel he thought she was, but women like Lily Wild always knew what they were about. He'd had enough of the simmering tension between them, and knew just how to kill it dead.

'Okay, that's it,' he said softly, placing his empty glass on the antique sideboard with deliberate care. 'I'm giving you fair warning. I'm sick of the tension between us—and the reason for it. You've got exactly three seconds to get moving before I take up from what we started six years ago. But this time there'll be no stopping. You're not seventeen any more, and there's no secretary to interrupt us like yesterday. This time we're on our own, and I'm not in the mind to stop at one kiss. Neither, I suspect, are you.'

Lily didn't know what thrilled her more—his blunt words or the starkly masculine arousal stamped across his handsome face. Her heart took off at full gallop and her stomach pitched alarmingly.

Six years ago she had wanted him with the desperate yearning of a teenager in the throes of a first crush. The night of Jo's party she had dressed for him, watched him, noticed him watching her—and then, on the back of a couple of fortifying glasses of vintage champagne, she had asked him to dance... and melted into him. Loved the feel of his strong arms around her, the sense of rightness that would have led her to do anything with him that night. And right now she felt exactly the same way. Which just didn't make sense. None of this made sense.

*Does it have to?*

'Onc.'

She shook her head. 'Tristan, don't be ridiculous. There's no point to this.'

'I couldn't agree more, but we have unfinished business between us and denying it hasn't made it go away. Nor has trying to ignore it. In fact, I think that's only made the problem worse.'

'And you think acting on it will solve it?'

He raised that arrogant eyebrow. 'Got a better idea?'

No, she didn't, and right now her body yearned for his with a desperation that was all-consuming. Yearned to experience more of the pleasure he'd wrought on her body yesterday. Yearned for a completion that Lily was starting to suspect only this man could fulfil.

Jordana's provocative suggestion that she cut loose and have some fun returned to mock her.

Could she?

Would having sex with Tristan fall under that banner? It wasn't as if she was holding out for a marriage proposal or anything. The only reason she hadn't had sex before was because of the lack of opportunity and…enticement. She'd never felt the way Tristan made her feel just by looking at him. Why keep denying it?

And then there was the notion she'd had to meet him this trip as an equal. To put the attraction she had always felt for him to bed…

'Two.'

His soft voice cut through her ruminations and she realised her heart was pounding behind her ribcage.

She swallowed. He hadn't moved, and yet the room seemed smaller; he seemed closer. Her senses were entirely focused on him.

His hair had flopped forward and she could see he was breathing as unevenly as she was. She found it almost shockingly exciting to think she could arouse a man like him to such a state. Because he *was* aroused. She could see the unchecked desire glittering in his darkened eyes and feel the dangerous intensity of his tautly held body.

Her stomach clenched and she felt an answering hunger in herself at the thought of finally being able to touch all that roughly hewn muscle. So what was she waiting for? Armageddon?

Lily slicked her tongue over her arid lips, a nascent sense of her own feminine power heating her insides and making her breasts feel firmer, fuller.

He must have sensed her silent capitulation because he moved then, pacing towards her with the latent grace of a man who knew exactly what he was about, and any notions Lily had had of taking charge of their lovemaking flew out of the window. She felt like that inexperienced seventeen-year-old again in comparison to him and his wealth of sexual experience.

He stopped just short of touching her and Lily gazed into his face with nervous anticipation.

'Tristan…' Her voice was a whisper of uncertainty and for a second her inner voice told her she was mad. She couldn't possibly give this giant of a man what he needed.

Tristan reached out and curled his hand around the nape of her neck, angling her face to his. He stared at her for what felt like ages. 'Tell me you want this.'

His warm fingers sent shock waves of energy up and down her spine and Lily was breathing so hard she was almost hyperventilating.

Want it? Need it sounded closer to the mark.

'I do.' She ran her tongue over her dry lips. 'I do want this. You.'

She heard an almost pained sound come from Tristan's throat as he lifted her face to his and took her mouth in a searing kiss. No preliminaries required.

Both his hands spread wide either side of her face as he held her still beneath his plundering lips and tongue.

Lily felt a sob of pure need rise up in her throat and reached up to grip his broad shoulders, to hang on as she gave herself over to the sensation of his masterful kiss.

He tasted of whisky and heaven, and for a moment Lily's senses nearly shut down with the overload of sensation rioting through her.

She pulled back, gasping for breath as she realised the dizziness was from a lack of oxygen, hyperventilating for real now as he angled her head back and skated his lips across her jaw and down the smooth column of her neck.

'Oh, Lord…' Lily whimpered, her face nuzzling his to bring his mouth back to her own.

He gave a husky chuckle and acquiesced, kissing her with such unrestrained passion she thought she might faint. His big body moved in, pressing her into the wall behind her.

His kiss claimed her. Branded her. The hard wall was flat against her back as his equally hard chest moulded to her front.

She moved her hands into his hair and lifted herself to try and assuage the ache that had grown to almost painful proportions between her thighs.

One of his hands disentangled from her hair and found the naked skin at small of her back as he stumbled back slightly at her eager movements.

'Oh, Lily, you're killing me,' he groaned into her mouth, his hands not quite steady as he held her in place against him.

His touch seemed as if it was everywhere and nowhere, and Lily could feel all her old emotions for this man welling up inside her. She couldn't have stopped what was happening now even if she'd wanted to.

She shivered and arched into his caresses, moving restlessly against him as wanton pleasure consumed her. His touch was electric, but it wasn't enough. She wanted to feel him all around her, and inside that part of her that somehow felt soft and hollow and unbearably empty.

'Tristan, please…' Lily implored, her hands kneading the hard ridges of his upper back. He seemed to know what she needed because he brought his mouth back to hers, his tongue plunging inside as his leg pressed firmly between her thighs.

She felt a moment's relief—but her dress hampered him from putting more pressure where she wanted it most and she squirmed in frustration.

Keeping her upright with his thigh, Tristan brought both hands up to cup her breasts, and then higher to drag the shoulders of her dress down her arms, baring her to the waist. Lily held her breath as he pulled back an inch and looked at her with such heated desire she could have wept.

For the first time ever she truly felt like a goddess, and when his eyes met hers they were dark with barely checked need.

'Honey, I want to go slow, but...' His eyes dropped back to her breasts and he placed his hands either side of her ribcage, lifted her body to meet his mouth. 'You're exquisite,' he whispered, his hot breath skating across an aroused nipple just before his mouth opened and sucked her flesh into its moist cavern.

Her legs gave out and Tristan had to tighten the arm around her waist to hold her up. Damp heat flooded between her thighs and she could dimly hear someone panting Tristan's name in a litany. She realised it was her.

She stopped, tried to centre herself, and then he grazed her with his teeth and she felt her insides convulse.

'Don't stop,' he breathed urgently against her flesh. 'Say my name. Tell me what you like.'

Lily didn't know what she liked, except for everything he was doing to her, and she gave herself over to him as he shifted his attention to her other breast, digging her nails into her palms. Wanting, needing to touch him as he was touching her.

She tried to move her arms and gave a mew of frustration when she found they were trapped by the tight band of his arms and her dress.

'Help me...' she began, but he already was, pressing his thigh firmly against her and moving his arms so she could disentangle her hands.

Once free, she immediately set to work on the buttons of his dark shirt.

He was breathing just as hard as she was, and a fine sheen had broken out over the skin her jittery hands were having trouble exposing. Then he raised both hands to her breasts to tug at her nipples and Lily's fingers fumbled to a stop.

'That's not helping,' she groaned, involuntarily arching into his caress.

'Then allow me.' Tristan grabbed hold of his shirt and tore the rest of the buttons free, leaning in close before she was able to look her fill of his sculptured chest, his ridged abdomen. Then his chest hair scraped her sensitised nipples, and she forgot about looking as feeling took precedence.

'Oh, God…' Lily swayed and rocked against the rigid length of him pressed into her belly.

'Easy, Honey,' Tristan soothed, but Lily was beyond easy. She needed him to touch her between her legs. The ache there was now unbearable.

She groaned with relief when she felt his hands smooth over her thighs and ruch her dress up around her waist, her legs automatically widening to accommodate his seeking hand.

His movements seemed as unsteady as she felt, and it imbued her with a sense of power.

Unable to keep her mouth off him, she bent her head and licked along his neck, breathing in his earthy masculinity.

'Tristan, please, I need you,' Lily begged, her voice sounding hoarse. Another saner voice was telling her that later she'd be embarrassed by such uninhibited pleading. But her body couldn't care less about later on.

It was caught up in the most delicious lassitude and straining for something that seemed just out of reach.

Then his fingers whispered over the very tops of her upper thigh and the feeling came closer. A lot closer.

Lily's breath stalled and her body stilled, and when finally he slipped his fingers beneath the lacy edge of her barely there panties and stroked through the curls that guarded her femininity she nearly died, clinging to his broad shoulders. Her body was his to do with as he willed.

And he did. His fingers slipped easily over her flesh, unerringly finding the tight bud of her clitoris before pressing deeper. Stretching her with first one and then two fingers.

A groan that seemed to come from the very centre of his body tore from his mouth. 'Honey, you're so wet. So tight.' He seemed lost for a second, and then established a rhythm within her that created a rush of heat to the centre of her body. But suddenly he stopped.

'No, I want to be inside you when you come.' He pulled his hand free and Lily's nails dug into his shoulders in protest.

She heard the metallic sound of his belt buckle and the slide of his zipper and in seconds he was back.

Only her panties were in the way, and with a decisive movement they went the way of his shirt.

Lily followed an age-old instinct and rocked against him, her mouth on his neck, her hands in the thick lusciousness of his hair.

'Honey, you keep that up and this will be over before I'm even inside you,' he said hoarsely, stroking his tongue into her open mouth. He eased back, seeming to remember where they were. 'Not here though.'

'Yes, here.' Lily demanded against his mouth, an urgent excitement driving her beyond the edge of reason.

Her lower body felt as if it was contracting around thin air and she needed him inside her. Filling her.

Tristan sucked in an uneven breath and lowered both hands to cup her bottom, lifting her into him. 'Put your legs around my waist,' he instructed gruffly, and Lily blindly obeyed as the velveteen tip of his body nudged against the very centre of hers.

The back of his neck was taut and sweaty and Lily's head fell forward and she nipped at his salty skin. He must have liked it, because with a sound that was part pain, part pleasure, he tilted her body towards him and surged into her in one single, powerful thrust.

For a second the world stopped, and then Lily registered a harsh cry and realised she must have bitten down on Tristan's neck—hard—as her body initially resisted his vigorous invasion.

He swore viciously and instantly stilled, reefing his head back and cupping her face in one hand to pull her eyes to his.

'Honey, please tell me this isn't your first time.'

Lily felt the momentary sting pass as her body stretched to accommodate his fullness, and wrapped her arms tightly around his neck.

'Don't stop,' she breathed as her body completely surrendered to his and tiny sparks of pleasure returned between her thighs.

She shifted to try and elevate the feeling, but Tristan's fingers dug into her hips to keep her still. 'Wait. Let your body adjust to me.'

'It has,' she insisted, and felt his slightly damp hair brush her face as he shook his head.

'Please, Tristan, I need to—'

He rocked against her and Lily moaned the word *move* as if it had six syllables.

Tristan eased in and out of her body gently, and then with more urgency, and Lily's brain shut down. All she could do was feel as a thrilling tightness swept through her and urged her on. Then Tristan moved one hand up between their bodies and lightly stroked his thumb over her nipple, and Lily's world splintered apart as pleasure clamped her body to his.

Tristan swore again, and thrust into her with such force all Lily could do was wrap her arms around his neck and hang on as he claimed her body with his and reached his own nirvana.

After what felt like an hour Lily became conscious of how her uneven breathing was pressing her newly sensitised breasts into the soft hair on Tristan's chest, and also of how hard the wall was behind her—despite the fact that Tristan had curled his arm around her back to take the brunt of the pressure.

She was also conscious that Tristan still had his mouth buried against her neck, his lips pressed lightly against her skin as he tried to regulate his own breathing.

Her arms were slung laxly over his shoulders and a feeling of utter contentment enveloped her. A sense of euphoria was curling through her insides like warm chocolate syrup.

It was madness. This inexplicable feeling of completeness that swelled in her chest. But maybe it was because she'd had a life-changing experience. And she had. Nothing had prepared her for what had just happened. No song. No movie. No book. And she knew she'd remember this moment for ever.

But even through her high she could discern that Tristan wasn't feeling the same way. He was unnaturally still, his breathing too laboured, as if he was having trouble composing himself. She shifted then, and the hardness of the wall scraped her skin. The air was slightly chilly now, as the sweat started to dry on her body. She shivered, still supported by his strong arms. Muscles she'd never felt before contracted around his hardness, still buried deep inside her, and she flinched as he cursed.

He pulled out of her, gently lowering her to the parquetry floor, stepping back. A look of abject disgust lined his face.

The shock of it made Lily recoil, and she quickly dropped her eyes and dragged her crumpled dress into place.

She heard him readjust his own clothing, and a primeval survival instinct she had honed as a child took root inside as she blanked out the feeling of utter desolation that threatened to overwhelm her for the first time in years.

'Don't say anything,' she ordered, knowing that the best form of defence was attack, and was mildly surprised when shock replaced the revulsion she had seen on his face.

Good. She might not be as practised as he was in these post-sex matters, but pride demanded that she did not behave like the bumbling fool she now felt.

For him this was just run of the mill but for her it was—

*'Don't say anything?'* he all but bellowed. 'You should have told me you were a virgin.'

*Never let 'em know you care, Honeybee.*

She looked at him levelly. 'It slipped my mind.' In truth she had hoped he wouldn't notice. But that seemed like a stupid notion in hindsight, given his size. 'And you wouldn't have believed me anyway, would you?'

He glanced to the side and it was all the answer Lily needed. Of course he wouldn't have—when had he ever believed her? Something tight clutched in her chest and she toed on the shoe that had fallen off when her legs had been wrapped around his lean hips.

'I didn't use a condom,' he said, the bald statement bringing her eyes back to his.

She wasn't on the pill. Why would she be?

'I think it's a safe time,' she murmured automatically, trying to quell a sense of panic so she could think about when her last period had been.

He groaned and paced away from her, one hand raking the gleaming chestnut waves back from his head as if he might tear it out.

'Look, Tristan, this was a mistake,' she said with an airiness she didn't feel. 'But it's done now so there's no point moaning about it.'

He stopped pacing. 'And if you're pregnant?'

She turned from her study of an ancient Japanese wall hanging and wet her lips. 'I'll let you know.'

He placed his hands on his hips and she tried really hard not to stare at his muscular torso.

'Look, if it's all the same to you,' she continued casting around the floor for her discarded underwear, 'I could do without a post-mortem.'

She didn't look at his face but she heard his sharp inhalation.

'It's next to the cabinet,' he bit out, and Lily followed his line of vision to where her tiny nude-coloured thong lay crumpled in a corner. She marched over and snatched it up, balling it into her fist. No way was she going to inspect the state of it while he stood there towering over her like some Machiavellian warlord.

'Well, I'm going to bed,' she stated boldly, turning towards the back staircase and heading for the relative safety of her room.

He snagged her arm as she moved past him. 'Did I hurt you?' His voice low and rough, as if the concept was anathema to him.

Lily cleared her throat. 'Uh, no. It was… I'm fine.'

# CHAPTER TEN

FINE.

She had been going to say *it* was fine, Tristan thought moodily the next morning as he stared out of his kitchen window at the grey London skyline. The colour reflected his dismal mood perfectly.

But last night hadn't been fine. It had been amazing, sensational, mind-blowing. The most intensely involved sexual experience of his life, in fact. And he hated that. Hated that he hadn't had the wherewithal to go slow, and hated that he hadn't been able to take her into his arms afterwards and carry her up to his bed. Make love to her again. Slowly this time. More carefully...

He released a pent-up breath and scrubbed his hand over his face, remembering how she had looked afterwards. Gloriously dishevelled. Her dress creased, her hair half up and half down where his hands had mussed it, her lips swollen from his kisses.

He could recall with bruising clarity the moment her body had sheathed his, her shocked stillness. And she had bitten him—marked him—because even though she had denied it he *had* hurt her. The thought made him feel sick. He should have been more gentle. *Would* have been if he'd known.

A virgin!

She had been a virgin, and afterwards he had been disgusted with himself for taking her with all the finesse of a rutting animal against a wall.

Damn.

If there had ever been a time he'd felt this badly he couldn't remember it. Maybe when he'd come across her in his father's study doing cocaine—or so he had thought at the time—with some loser she had just had sex with.

Correction: *hadn't* had sex with.

Damn.

His head was a mess, and last night, after the deed was done, he'd stood in front of her like some gauche schoolboy with no idea how to fix what had just happened. Which was a first. But what could he have said? *Hey, thanks. How about we use a bed next time?*

And what about her response? *Don't say anything,* she'd said, and, *I could do without a post-mortem.*

Damn.

He couldn't have been any more shocked by her off-handedness if she'd hit him over the head with a block of wood. On some level he knew it was a defence mechanism, but it was clear she also regretted what they'd done together and that had made him feel doubly guilty.

Not that it should. She was an adult and had wanted it just as much. Things had just come to a natural head with two people available and finding themselves attracted to each other.

So he would have gone about things a little differently if he'd guessed the extent of her inexperience? If she'd told him! But that hadn't happened, and he didn't do regrets.

Tristan rubbed at a spot between his brows.

He might not do regret, but he owed her one hell of an apology for his condescending behaviour of the last two days. As well as his readiness to accept all the garbage that was written about her.

But hadn't it been easier to accept she was an outrageous attention-seeker like his mother so he didn't have to face how she made him feel?

Which was what, exactly?

Confused? Off-balance?

He took a swill of his coffee and grimaced as cold liquid pooled in his mouth.

He put his cup in the sink and stopped to look again at the morning papers on his kitchen table.

An earlier perusal of the headlines on the internet had confirmed that Lily's concerns the previous night had been well founded. A photo of their kiss was plastered over every two-bit tabloid and interested blog in the Western world.

On top of that someone had snapped their photo at the airport right before he had put her in the back of his limousine that first day. She'd had her hand on his chest and the caption in that particular paper had read 'Lord Garrett picks up something Wild at Heathrow'.

Cute.

So what to do about her? Try and play it cool? Pretend he wasn't still burning up for her? And *why* was he? Once was often more than enough with a woman, because for him sex was just sex no matter which way you spun it.

But it hadn't felt like just sex with Lily, and that was one more reason to stay away from her.

The thought that this was more than just an attraction chilled him. He didn't do love either.

Damn. Who'd mentioned anything about love?

He blew out a breath and snatched the papers off the bench. One good deed. That was all he'd tried to do. And now his life was more complicated than a world-class Sudoku.

When Lily woke that morning she remembered everything that had happened the night before in minute detail. Every single thing. Every touch, every kiss, the scent of him, the feel of him...

She rolled onto her back and stared at the crystal chandelier above her bed. She loved that these perfect antiques were woven into the ultra-modern décor of his amazing home.

Part of her wanted to regret last night. The part that had been hurt by his obvious rejection straight afterwards. But another part told her to get over it. She'd had sex. Big deal. People did it every day. Granted, it probably wasn't the smartest thing to have sex with a playboy type who thought she belonged in a sewer...but at least she hadn't made her mother's grave error and fallen in love with him.

And in a way it had been necessary. Tristan had been right when he'd said there was unfinished business between them. As much as she'd tried to deny it there had been, and now it was gone. Finished—as it were.

It wasn't as if Tristan had promised her a happy-ever-after. And even if he had she didn't want one. So what was there to regret? Except having to face him again. That could be awkward. Oh, and the small matter of an unplanned pregnancy. She didn't know how that had slipped her mind. Not that she was worried. She trusted the universe too much to believe that was a possibility, and she was still in the early part of her cycle so that was safe—wasn't it? She'd never had to consider it before, and those sketchy high school lessons on the birds and bees weren't holding up very well ten years down the track.

Pushing aside her thoughts, she glanced around the elegant, tastefully decorated room. His whole house was like that. State-of-the-art and hideously expensive. Lots of wide open spaces, acres of polished surfaces, toe-curlingly soft carpets against contrasting art and antiquities. And it was neat. Super neat. But that was most likely his housekeeper's doing, because his office was another story altogether.

It made her wonder at the person he was. Because as much as she wanted to hate him she knew she didn't. Most of his actions, she knew, were driven by a deep-seated sense of responsibility and a desire to look out for his sister, and even though he had been harsh with her he'd also been incredibly tender. If she was being completely honest with herself, his sharp intellect and take-no-prisoners attitude had always excited her.

Lily felt herself soften, and swung her legs onto the boldly striped Tai Ping carpet and headed for the shower, her body tender from his powerful lovemaking.

She showered quickly and smoothed rosehip oil all over her face and arms, running a critical eye over herself. She knew her face was much lauded, but like anyone she had her problems. A tendency for her skin to look sallow, and dark circles that materialised under her eyes as soon as she even thought about not getting eight hours sleep a night. Right now they looked like bottomless craters, and she reached for her magic concealer pen to hide the damage of another night with very little sleep.

Discarding the towel she had wrapped around her body, she donned her silk robe and felt the flow of the fabric across her sensitised skin. Her breasts firmed and peaked, and just like that she was back in Tristan's living room with his mouth sweetly tugging on her flesh.

*Stop thinking about it*, she berated herself. She was an intelligent woman who paid her own bills and made her own bed, and yet the only bed she could think of at the minute was Tristan's—with both of them in it! And since he wasn't thinking the same thing why torture herself with fantasies? She should be thinking about how she was going to face him still feeling so…so aroused!

A knock on the outer door brought her head around and she turned sharply towards the bedroom. It would be Tristan because she knew it was still too early for his housekeeper to have arrived, and she berated herself for dithering in front of the mirror for so long. It would have been more prudent to meet him downstairs, fully clothed.

'Come in,' she called reluctantly, tightening the sash around her robe and crossing her arms over her chest.

He did. And he looked gorgeous and refreshed. Just how she wanted to feel.

He walked over and dropped a couple of newspapers on her bed, and then stood regarding her, his hands buried in his pockets. His hair, still damp, curled enticingly around the nape of his neck and his olive skin gleamed darkly against his pale blue shirt. But it was his guarded expression that eventually held her attention. A level of awkwardness about his stance that gave her pause.

'I owe you an apology.'

'For last night?' Her voice was sharp and she moistened her lips. 'That's not necessary.'

'Yes, it is.' His voice was that of a polite stranger. 'If I had known it was your first time I never would have let things go so far.'

Lily sighed. She had been trying not to feel bad about what had happened last night but his open regret wasn't helping. Nor was the way he paced back and forth. 'I think we should just forget it ever happened,' she said, not quite able to meet his eyes. Lord, was this worse than his rejection of her six years ago? 'As you already said, we had unfinished business—and now…now we don't.'

He stopped pacing. 'And you're okay with that?'

'Of course. Aren't you?'

'Of course.'

Lily nodded. Of course. What had she expected? A declaration of love? Even the thought was ludicrous, because she absolutely didn't want that.

'So…'

'I also want to apologise for my attitude towards you when I picked you up. For accusing you of using drugs and knowingly bringing them into the country,' he said.

Lily's eyebrows shot skyward. 'So because I was a virgin I'm innocent of drug smuggling as well? Gosh, if only I'd thought to tell the customs official it would have saved all this hassle.'

Tristan threw her a baleful look. 'Your virginity has nothing to do with my reasoning.'

'No?'

'No,' he said irritably. 'I had already worked out you weren't a user before then. And you'll be pleased to know I've fired my investigator.'

'Shooting the messenger you mean?' she jeered.

'His work was substandard—even with the limited time

frame he had to collate the information. Hell, I thought you'd be happy to hear that.'

'Happy that a man lost his job because he confirmed your view of me? He probably just gave you what you wanted, like everybody else does,' she said caustically.

'Don't push it, Lily. You weren't exactly forthcoming with the truth when I questioned you.'

'That's because I don't find it beneficial to bash my head against a brick wall.'

She saw a muscle tick in his jaw as he regarded her from under hooded eyes.

'Tell me why I found you hiding a joint under Jo's mattress when you were fourteen.'

'I thought you were apologizing?' she countered.

'I did.'

'It could use some work.'

Tristan said nothing, his expression coolly assessing. It was a look Lily had come to recognise. It meant that he fully intended to get his own way.

'Don't use your courtroom tactics with me, Tristan,' she said frostily. 'They won't work.'

'Would it help if I tell you Jordana has already admitted that it was hers?'

Lily tried to keep her surprise from showing. 'When?'

'The day of your apprehension at Heathrow. I didn't believe her at the time.'

Lily placed her hand against her chest with a flourish. 'Oh, and for a minute there I felt so special.'

She could see her sarcasm had irritated him, but he rubbed a hand across his eyes before piercing her with his gaze again.

'It's confession time, Lily. I know my sister hasn't been the saint I've wanted her to be, and I'm tired of the misunderstandings between us.'

Lily thought about arguing—but what was the point? He'd only get his own way in the end.

'If you remember, you visited our boarding school on a surprise birthday visit for Jo—only she saw you from the rec room. She called me on the internal phone and asked me to hide it. I hadn't expected you would walk in without knocking.'

'And the night of Jo's eighteenth? In my father's study? No evading the answer this time.'

'You should ask Jordana.'

'I'm asking *you*.'

Lily crossed the floor and sat on the striped Rein occasional chair in the corner. 'I don't know how the party in your dad's study got started. I was tipped off by a mutual friend, and by the time I got there it was in full swing. I felt responsible, because the guy who'd brought the drugs worked for my stepfather's company, but no one listened when I told them to clean it up. So I decided to step in and do it myself and—'

'I walked in, put two and two together, and came up with several hundred.'

'Something like that.'

'And you didn't think to defend yourself?' His tone was accusatory.

'You didn't exactly give me much of a chance, remember?' she felt stung into retorting.

Tristan shook his head and strode over to the window, pushing the heavy curtain aside to stare outside.

Lily shifted and tucked her legs under her on the chair, absently noting how the light from the incoming sun picked up the bronzed highlights in his hair.

Then he turned back, his expression guarded. 'I'm sorry.'

Did he *have* to look quite so good-looking?

She cleared her throat and shifted uncomfortably on her seat. If he was apologising why did she suddenly feel so nervous? 'It's fine; I shouldn't have invited that guy in the first place.'

He shrugged as if that were inconsequential. 'I shouldn't have jumped to conclusions. I…I wasn't quite myself that night.'

Lily's mind immediately spun back to the dance floor. The kiss. Had he not been himself then either? How embarrassing.

'Me either,' she lied.

He nodded, as if that solved everything, and Lily's heart sank a little. 'Was there something else?'

He shook his head and then glanced towards her bed.

'Actually, yes.' He pointed to the bed. 'I'm sorry to say that your premonition about the photos has come true.'

Lily rose and walked over to the bed. 'Oh.'

'I said a little more than that myself,' he acknowledged ruefully.

'I did too.' She glanced up briefly. 'Internally...'

She thought a momentary smile curved his mouth, but it might easily have been a trick of the light given how stiff and remote he seemed.

'I should go.'

'Yes,' Lily agreed, following him with her eyes as he walked to the door. Then he stopped abruptly.

'Are you...okay this morning?' His voice was rough and slightly aggressive and she knew what he was asking.

'I thought we'd just agreed to forget last night?'

'I'm allowed to check how you are, dammit. And don't say *fine.*'

She arched an eyebrow. 'Will great do?' she asked lightly.

His nostrils flared and she thought that maybe now was not a good time to aggravate him.

Tristan's mouth tightened. This situation was intolerable. He couldn't be in the same room with her and not want to touch her, but it was obvious by the proud tilt of her head that she wouldn't welcome his advances. He didn't know what he had expected from her this morning, but her suggestion that they forget last night had surprised him. And annoyed him. Because he wasn't sure he *could* forget it!

The phone in his pocket rang and he checked the caller ID before answering. Bert had been caught in a six-car pile-up on Rosslyn Hill. He didn't want another car. He'd call a cab—it would be quicker.

'What happened?'

'Bert's been caught in an accident.'

'Is he okay?' Her concern was genuine, and he was reminded of how yesterday she had given Bert unsolicited signed promotional pictures of herself when she found out his daughters were fans.

'It was minor, but he's wedged between two other cars. I'll arrange someone to help him out and call a cab.'

'I'll get dressed.'

Tristan's eyes drifted down over the dove-grey silk wrap she wore and he noted the delicate pink that swept into her face. Even with the shadows beneath her eyes she was quite simply the most beautiful woman he had ever seen.

'Good idea.'

Twenty minutes later Lily joined Tristan on a rear terrace that looked out over a sizable manicured garden flanked by a glassed-in pool and gymnasium, absently noting that it was hard to believe she was in the middle of one of the busiest cities in the world.

Tristan wore his suit jacket now, and she felt like a tourist in her simple jeans, white T-shirt and faithful black cardigan. She noticed him glance at her cardigan as he watched her approach, a bemused expression flitting across his face.

'What?'

'Nothing.' He shook his head. 'I would offer you tea, but I'd like to get going and check that Bert is okay.'

'Sure.' Lily followed him back through the house towards the front door.

'It seems traffic is particularly bad this morning. The cab driver has had to park up the road a way.'

'That's okay.' Lily smiled. 'I like walking. It's a New York pastime.'

'I suppose it is,' Tristan agreed, feeling awkward and out of sorts after her disclosures in her bedroom. His instincts warned him to keep his distance from her. After last night she was more dangerous to his emotional well-being than she had ever been, and in hindsight having sex with her had been a terrible idea.

Lily waited for him to open the front door and stepped out ahead of him—straight into the view of at least twenty members of the press, who had breached his security gates and were filling the normally pristine space of his forecourt, trampling grass and flowerbeds as they jostled for position.

They shouted an endless list of questions as camera flashes momentarily blinded them both.

It was like a scene from a bad movie, and after a split second of shocked inertia Tristan grabbed Lily around the waist and hauled her back inside.

'Oh, my gosh!'

'I'll call the police,' he stated grimly, slamming the door shut before he turned to her and grabbed her chin between his thumb and forefinger. 'Are you okay?' His eyes scanned her face for signs of distress, wondering if perhaps she might have a panic attack.

'I'm fine,' she confirmed. 'I told you, I rarely have attacks any more—and, anyway, you grabbed me so quickly I barely had time to register they were even there.'

She smiled and he trailed a finger down her cheek, noting the way her eyes widened and darkened. Tristan felt his body harden and tamped down on the response. He was supposed to be forgetting last night and keeping his distance.

He dropped his hand and stalked through the house until he reached the kitchen.

'I'm sorry. I should have expected this...' she said.

Tristan shook his head. Not sure if he was more agitated at himself, her, or the hyenas filling his front garden. 'I don't know how you live like this.'

She swallowed. 'It's not normally this bad. In New York you get followed sometimes, but it's different here.'

'It's disgusting.'

'I'm sorry.'

He swore, and Lily flinched.

'Stop apologising. It's not your fault,' he bit out. 'If anything it's mine.' He raked a hand through his hair and pulled his mobile out of his pocket. 'Make a coffee, or something. We might be a while.'

'Do you want one?'

'No, thanks.'

After a brief interlude in his study, Tristan strode out into his rear garden and found Lily sipping tea on a stone bench, studying one of the statues that dotted his garden.

'Plans have changed,' he said brusquely, not enjoying the way she seemed to fit so seamlessly into his home.

'Oh?' Lily replied, confused.

'We leave for Hillesden Abbey in an hour.'

'How?'

'Helicopter.'

'Helicop...? But I have a dress fitting today with Jo.'

'You *had* a dress fitting. The seamstress will travel to the Abbey during the week to meet with you.'

'But surely Chanel don't...?'

'Yeah, they do. Now, stop arguing. A car will be pulling up in ten minutes to take us onto the Heath.'

'Helicopters leave from the Heath?'

'Not as a general rule.'

Ten minutes later two police motorcycles escorted a stretch limousine along Hampstead Lane and pulled up near Kenwood House, where a bright red helicopter was waiting. A few curious onlookers watched as they alighted from the car—but no paparazzi, Tristan was pleased to note.

'Are you okay to fly in one of these?' Tristan raised his voice above the whir of the rotors.

'I don't know,' Lily yelled back. 'I never have.'

He helped her secure the safety harness and stowed their overnight bags behind her seat.

'I'm co-piloting today, but let me know if you feel sick.'

'I'll be fine.' She smiled tentatively and he realised she probably would be. She was a survivor, and quick to adapt to the circumstances around her.

He handed her a set of headphones and took his seat beside the pilot, not wanting to think about how that was just one more thing to admire about her.

He was looking forward to going home. His father was away on business until Friday, when Jordana would arrive to commence her wedding activities, but Tristan always felt rejuvenated in the country. And most importantly of all, the Abbey was *huge*. It had two hundred and twenty rooms, which should be more than enough space to put some physical distance between himself and Lily and still remain within the constraints of the custody order. He felt sure that if he didn't have her underfoot the chemistry between them would abate. Normalise. She'd just be another pretty face in a cast of thousands.

His chest felt tight as the ground fell away, and he berated himself for not thinking of the Abbey sooner.

# CHAPTER ELEVEN

LILY closed the last page of the play and stared vacantly into the open fire Thomas, the family butler, had lit for her earlier that night. The writer had captured a side of her parents she hadn't known about. He had focused on their struggles and their hunger for fame and what had driven it, rather than just the consequence of it.

The result was an aspect of their lives Lily knew about from her mother's diaries but which the press rarely focused on. It was an aspect that always caused Lily to regret who they had become. She had expected that reading the play would imbue her with a renewed sense of disgust at their wasted lives—and it had, sort of—but what she hadn't expected was that it would fill her with a sense of yearning for them still to be around. For a chance to get to know them.

A log split in the grate and Lily rose to her feet and prodded at it with the cast-iron poker. Then she turned and wandered over to the carved wooden bookcases that lined the Abbey's vast library.

She had been in Tristan's ancestral home—a palatial three-storey stone Palladian mansion set amidst eleven thousand acres of parkland resplendent with manicured gardens, a deer forest, a polo field and a lake with swans and other birdlife—for four days now.

She'd taken long walks every day, as she and Jordana had done as teens, petted the horses in the stables, helped Jamie the gardener tend the manicured roses along the canopied stone arbour, and caught up with Mrs Cole, the housekeeper, who looked as if she'd stepped straight out of a Jane Austen novel.

In fact the whole experience of wandering around on her own and not being bothered by the busyness of her everyday life was like stepping back into another era, and the only thing that would have made her stay here better was if she'd been able to see Tristan more than just at the evening meal, where he was always unfailingly polite, and nothing more. It was as if they were complete strangers.

For four days he had studiously locked himself away in his study and, from what Lily could tell, rarely ventured out.

Lily paused beside the antique chessboard that was always set up in the library and sank into one of the bottle-green club chairs worn from years of use.

At first she had thought Tristan had flown them to the Abbey to avoid the constant threat of paparazzi, but it had soon become depressingly apparent that he'd relocated them so that he could avoid *her* as well!

And she couldn't deny that hurt. After his apology back in his London home she had thought maybe they could build a friendship, but clearly he didn't feel the same way. Clearly the chemistry he had felt for her had been laid to rest after just one time together. She only wished she felt the same way.

Unfortunately, consummating her desire for him that night had resurrected an inner sexuality only he seemed to bring out in her. And now that she had experienced the full force of his possession she craved it even more.

'Want a game?' a deep voice said softly from behind her chair, and Lily swung around to find Tristan regarding her from just inside the doorway. She'd been so deep in thought she hadn't heard him come in.

Her heart kicked against her ribs at the sight of him in black jeans and a pale green cashmere sweater the exact shade of his eyes. He looked casually elegant, while she was conscious that she had changed into old sweatpants and a top before coming downstairs to read.

'I… If you like,' Lily found herself answering, not sure that saying yes was the sanest answer, all things considered. The man hadn't said boo to her for four days and now he wanted to play chess…?

'Can I fix you a drink?'

'Sure,' she said, not sure that was the sanest idea either.

'I know you're not fond of Scotch, but my father has an excellent sherry.'

'Sure,' she parroted, ordering her brain to come online. Her body quickened as he walked slowly towards her, and she straightened the pawns on their squares to avoid having him see how pathetic she was.

'You start,' he offered.

Lily tilted her head. 'Is that because you're so sure you can win?'

He smiled a wolfish grin. 'Visitor's rules.'

'Oh.'

'But, yes, I'm sure I can win.' He flopped into a chair and chuckled at her sharp look.

*He had no idea.*

She regarded him with a poker face. 'Is that a challenge, Lord Garrett?'

'It certainly is, Miss Wild.'

'Then prepare to be defeated.' She smiled, knowing that she was actually a pretty good chess-player. It was one of the things she liked to do while sitting around waiting for scenes to be set up on location.

She leaned forward, her ponytail swinging over one shoulder, and rested her hands on her knees, concentrating on the chess instead of on him. Given his overriding confidence she guessed he'd be a master player—and she'd need all her wits about her.

'You're good,' Tristan complimented her an hour later, as she chewed on her lip and considered her next move.

So far he had countered every one of her attacks and she was fast running out of manoeuvres.

'Did you enjoy your swim this morning?' he asked, leaning back in his chair, his long legs sprawled out on either side of the low table.

His question made her glance at him sharply. 'How do you know I went swimming this morning?'

'I saw you.'

'But you weren't there.'

'Yes, I was.'

Something heavy curled between them and Lily cleared her throat. 'So why didn't you swim?'

'It's your move.'

Lily looked down at the board. Had he really been at the pool? And if so why hadn't he joined her? Mulling it over, she carefully moved her bishop across the board—and then watched as Tristan immediately confiscated it with his marauding rook.

'Oh!' Lily looked up to see a wicked glint in his eyes. 'Not fair! You were trying to distract me!'

'It worked.'

'That's cheating.'

'Not really. I did turn up for a swim.' His voice was low, deep, and an unexpected burst of warmth stole through her.

'Then I repeat: Why didn't you have one?' She lifted her chin challengingly, sure that he was just playing with her.

'Because I didn't trust myself to join you,' he said dulcetly.

Was he flirting with her?

Lily's heart raced and she quickly averted her eyes, not sure she wanted an answer. Her stomach fluttered alarmingly and she looked at the chessboard without really seeing it.

'Aren't you going to ask me why?' he murmured.

Lily looked up and, seeing the competitive glint in his eyes, realised what he was doing. 'No,' she said a little crossly, 'because you're only trying to put me off my game.' And she *wasn't* going to be disappointed by that.

He laughed softly and the deep sound trickled through her like melted chocolate.

They played for a short time more, and finally Lily threw up her hands when he cornered her king.

'Okay, you win.' She smiled, not totally surprised at the outcome. After the swimming comment she'd lost all concentration.

She wondered if now wouldn't be a good time to go to bed. A cosy ambience seemed to have descended, and with the crackling fire behind them it would be all too easy to forget that he was here, with her, under duress.

Tristan tried to ignore the heat in his groin as his eyes automatically dropped to that lethal smile of hers, before sliding lower to the tempting swell of her pert breasts beneath the loose T-shirt. Did the woman even *own* a bra?

Oh yeah, he remembered. A pink one... He felt his body grow even harder at the image of her standing before him in matching delicate lace underwear. He loved the thought of her in matching underwear—not that she was wearing any at the moment...

He got up to top up his drink and give his hands something to do.

He'd been avoiding her all week, only seeing her at mealtimes, where she'd been so coolly remote they'd barely spoken to each other.

But he'd seen her. Watched her take long walks in the park, listened to her musical laugh as she'd helped Jamie choose which roses would be cut for the house in preparation for Jordana's wedding in two days' time.

Before, he'd been honest about not trusting himself to join her in the pool that morning, but he could see she hadn't believed him. Which was probably just as well.

Because distance had not done a damn thing to dampen the need he had to touch her, or just to be with her—which in some ways was scarier than the other.

Emotions he'd never had any trouble keeping at bay threatened to take him by the bit and make him forget all his good intentions to avoid relationships of any sort. She was dangerous, he knew it, but he couldn't deny he was drawn to her flame. Some primal desire was overriding his superficial instincts to keep away.

And now, against his better judgement, he returned to her side, holding the decanter of sherry in his hand. 'Here, let me pour you another drink.'

'No, I should…go to bed.'

The words hung between them but he ignored her hesitancy until she raised her near-empty glass.

'One more won't hurt.'

He replaced the stopper and sat the decanter beside his chair. He wasn't sure what he was doing; he only knew he didn't want her to go yet.

'Mmmm, this is nice,' she murmured, sipping at her glass.

He leaned back and studied her. She looked beautiful, with her hair in a messy ponytail, no make-up and her legs tucked up under her. The space between them crackled like the logs in the fireplace and he knew from the high colour on her cheeks that she felt it too. At this moment she had never seemed more beautiful to him. Or more nervous. He wondered whether she would bolt if he described the scene playing out in his mind.

'I've noticed you going for walks every day,' he said, in an attempt to distract himself.

'Oh, yes.' Lily's enthusiasm lit up her face. 'It's such a beautiful space here. You're so lucky to have it.'

'What do you like about it?' he asked, curious despite himself.

'It's rejuvenating, peaceful—and so quiet. And I love that your family has left the forest untouched.'

All the things *he* loved!

'They used to hunt there, that's why.'

'Oh, don't spoil it.' Her mouth made a moue of disappointment and he laughed.

'Never fear, Bambi is safe from this generation of Garretts.'

She smiled and the almost shy look she cast from under her lashes caught him in the solar plexus.

'That's nice.'

'That's only because I'm not here all that often,' he teased.

'I don't believe you. And you're spoiling it again,' she scolded, picking up on the falseness behind his words.

'Come over by the fire?' he murmured, mentally rolling his eyes at the stupidity of that suggestion.

But she did, and he poked at the fire while she found a comfortable position on the Persian rug.

'What was it like growing up in your world?' she asked, watching him carefully as he sat down opposite her, his drink dangled over one knee.

Tristan didn't like talking about himself as a general rule, but he'd invited her to sit by the fire and couldn't very well ignore her question.

'Privileged. Boring at times. Not that much different from any other life, I expect, apart from the opportunities that come with the title—although that also comes with a duty of care.'

'What do you mean?'

He glanced at her, and then back at the fire. 'I take the view that being born into the nobility is about being a custodian of history. All this is grand and awe-inspiring, but it's not mine and it never will be. I'm fortunate enough to look after it, yes, but this house is a part of something much bigger and it belongs to everyone, really.'

'Is that why you open your home to the public?'

'Partly. People are naturally curious about the country's history, and my ancestors have accumulated a lot of important artefacts that deserve to be viewed by more than just a privileged few. Especially if those privileged few don't understand the importance of what they have.'

'Do you mean people who don't care about their heritage?'

Her softly voiced question brought his attention back to her, and he wondered at the looseness of his tongue and the need he suddenly felt to unburden himself of the weight of the less salubrious aspects of his history. He suspected, given Lily's dislike of the press, that she wouldn't run off and disclose his secrets—and really they weren't all that secret anyway.

'My grandfather was a heavy drinker and gambler, and he ran the property into quite a severe state of disrepair. My father had to work two jobs for a while to try and rebuild it, and while he was off working my mother thought a good little money-earner might be to sell off some of my father's most prized heirlooms.' He couldn't stop the note of bitterness from creeping into his voice.

'Oh, how terrible!' Lily cried. 'She must have been so unhappy to try and reach out that way.'

Tristan cut her a hard glance. 'Reach out?'

'Yes. My mother did terrible things to get my father's attention, and—'

'My mother wasn't trying to get my father's attention,' he bit out. 'She was trying to get more money to fund her lifestyle.'

Something she'd talked about endlessly.

'I'm sorry.' Lily touched his arm and then drew her hand back when he looked at her sharply. 'And was your father able to recover them? The heirlooms?'

'No.' His tone was brittle even to his own ears. 'But I did.'

Lily paused and then said softly. 'You don't like her very much, do you?'

Tristan put another log on the fire and ran an agitated hand through his hair, realising too late that he'd said too much. How should he respond to that? Tell her that he would probably have forgiven his mother anything if she'd shown him a modicum of genuine affection as he'd been growing up? But she had, hadn't she? Sometimes.

'My mother wasn't the most maternal creature in the world, and as I matured I lost a lot of respect for her.' He spied the bound folio next to the stone hearth and realised it was the play Lily had been carrying around with her. 'What are you reading?' he asked, reaching for it.

Lily made a scoffing noise. 'Not a very subtle conversation

change, My Lord. And not a very good one either. It's a play about my parents.'

'The one that slimeball reporter asked you about?'

She shifted uncomfortably and he wondered about that.

'Yes.'

'But you don't want to do it?'

'No.'

He watched the way the firelight warmed her angelic features and wondered what was behind her reticence to do the play. 'Tell me about your life,' he surprised them both by saying.

She shook her head. '*Quid pro quo*, you mean.'

'Why do you call yourself Lily instead of Honey?' he queried, warming to the new topic but sensing her cool at the same time.

For a minute he didn't think she was going to answer and then she threw him one of those enigmatic smiles that told him she was avoiding something. 'My stepfather thought it would be a good idea for me to change it. You know—reinvent myself. Make a fresh start.' She laughed, as if it was funny, but the lightness in her tone was undermined by the sudden tautness of her shoulders.

'How old were you?'

'Seven.'

'Seven!'

'I was a bit traumatised at the time—wouldn't speak to anyone for six months after my parents died. Plus my parents weren't the most conventional creatures, so it was a good idea, really.'

'Jordana said you were named after your mother?'

'Sort of. She was Swedish and her name was Hanna— Hanny. When she moved to England her accent made it sound like she was saying honey—so everyone called her that. I guess my parents liked the name. Which was why it was such a good idea when Frank suggested I change it. It set me free to become my own person.' She stopped, more colour highlighting her cheeks.

Tristan didn't agree. He knew of Frank Murphy. His office had handled a complaint against the man some years back, and he had a reputation for being an egotistical schmuck.

Tristan knew the story about how Hanny Forsberg had married him in a whirlwind romance and then returned to her one true love a week later. Only to die in said lover's arms that very night. Tristan couldn't imagine Frank Murphy taking her defection well, and wondered if he had taken his anger out on Lily.

'I'm not sure that would have been his only motivation,' he commented darkly, swilling the last of his Scotch and placing his empty glass behind him.

'What do you mean?'

'I mean Frank Murphy is a self-interested swine who would have been looking out for his own interests before yours.'

'Frank's not like that,' she defended.

'Come on, Lily. Frank Murphy is a user. Everyone knows that. And the accolades he got from taking in Hanny's orphan were huge.'

'Maybe.'

Tristan hadn't missed the flash of pain in her eyes before she shifted position and moved closer to the fire, her hands outstretched towards the leaping flames. He wondered what was going through her mind and then shook his head.

'I've upset you.'

'No.'

'Yes. I didn't mean to imply that Frank didn't care for you. I'm sure he did.'

'No. He didn't. Not really.'

'Lily, it's a big responsibility to look after a child that's not your own. I'm sure—'

'There was no one else.'

'Sorry?'

'Nobody else wanted me.' She shrugged as if they were discussing nothing more important than the weather. 'When my parents died I had nowhere to go. I would have become a ward of the state if he hadn't stepped in.'

'What about your grandparents?'

'Johnny's had died and my mother's were old, and they'd disowned her after her first Page Three spread.'

'But Johnny had a brother, I recall.'

'Unfortunately he used to get more wasted than Johnny and looking after a seven-year-old was not high on his list of things to accomplish.'

'Your mother—'

'There was no one, okay? It's no big deal. I think I'll go to bed.'

'Wait!'

'For what?'

'You're upset,' he said gently.

Lily shivered as if a draught of cold air had caught her unawares, and for a minute she seemed lost.

'Did you know I found them?' She held her hands out to the fire again, as if seeking comfort. 'The police kept it quiet, to preserve my "delicate psychological state", but I found my parents' bodies. It was Sunday morning and they were supposed to make me blueberry pancakes and take me to the park. Johnny had promised it would be a family day. Instead I woke up and found my mother lying on the sofa with vomit pooled in her hair and my father slumped on the floor at her feet. It was like some sort of Greek tragedy. If my mother could have looked down on the scene she might have enjoyed the irony of finally having my father in such a supplicating pose.'

Lily gave a half laugh and for a minute he thought she had finished speaking, but then she continued.

'At first I tried to wake them, but even then I knew.' She shook her head at the pointlessness of such a gesture. 'There's something about the utter stillness of a dead body that even a small child can understand. I knew—I knew even though I didn't know what was wrong—I knew I would never see them again.'

She stared into the fire for a long moment and Tristan thought it was lucky her parents weren't here right now or he'd kill them all over again. Then Lily gave an exaggerated shiver and smiled brightly at him.

'Gosh, I haven't thought of that for years.'

Something of the anxiety he felt must have shown in his face because she turned back to the fire and sipped at the sherry she had barely touched. She was obviously upset and embarrassed, and Tristan felt heaviness lodge in his chest. He'd had no idea she'd suffered such a huge trauma at such a young age.

As if sensing his overwhelming need to comfort her she shot him a quelling look he'd seen before, but his mind couldn't place.

'I'm fine now,' she dismissed, but Tristan could see it was an effort for her to force her wide, shining eyes to his. 'Completely over it.'

No, she wasn't. Any fool could see that, and he didn't like that she was trying to make light of it with him. 'No, you're not. I think you hide behind your parents' controversial personas— the controversial persona you've also cultivated with the press. Almost as if you use your past as a shield so people don't get to see the real you.'

Lily stiffened, shock etched on her features, and then Tristan remembered where he'd seen that haughty look before. Right after they'd had sex that first time.

# CHAPTER TWELVE

LILY stared at Tristan and willed the ground to open up and devour one of them. She'd been having such a nice time and now he'd gone and ruined it.

'You don't know what you're talking about,' she whispered, placing her glass carefully on the hearth and willing the lump in her throat to subside. She stared at the inlaid stonework around the fireplace and realised she was about to cry. Cry! She never cried, and she wasn't about to start in Tristan's presence.

'Lily…'

Lily quickly scrambled to her feet, holding her hands out in front of her as Tristan made to do the same. 'I'm…'

The words wouldn't come and she turned to flee, making it only as far as the upholstered French settee before Tristan caught her.

'I can't let you leave like this.' He spoke gruffly, swinging her around to face him and Lily promptly burst into tears.

She tried to push him away but he was like an immovable force and she pounded his chest instead. 'Let me go. Let me—' A sob cut off her distressed plea and Tristan gathered her closer.

'Lily, I'm sorry. I really am an insensitive fool, and you were right the other day. I don't know anything.'

Rather than making her feel better that only made it worse and she buried her face in her hands, unable to hold back her tears any more.

'Shh, Lily, shh,' Tristan urged, holding her tighter. 'Let me soothe you,' he husked, his voice thick with emotion.

Lily tried to resist, but somehow all the events of the week converged and rendered her a sobbing mess, unable to put up any resistance when Tristan sank down onto the settee and pulled her into his lap.

He continued to stroke her even after her tears had abated and Lily rested against him, her mind spinning.

Tristan was wrong when he said she hid behind her public image. It was just easier to let people think what they wanted. They would anyway, and really she didn't care a jot what anyone thought.

But if that were true then why had she turned her back on the country she loved and set herself up in America, where people judged her more on her actions than on her past? Why had she always tried to do what Frank expected of her? And why had Tristan's rejection of her hurt so much six years ago?

Lily drew in a long, shuddering breath and then released it, her body slowly relaxing in Tristan's warm embrace. Try as she might she couldn't find valid reasons for her actions. Valid reasons for why she let the press write what they wanted about her. It was easy to say that no one would believe her if she corrected them. But why not?

An image of her mother, wretched and crying, came to mind, and Lily squeezed her eyes against the devastating image.

But then other images crowded in. Happier ones. Her mother singing to her and towelling her off after a bath. Her father putting her on his shoulders as they strolled through Borough Market eating falafels and brownies. Visiting her mother's photo shoots and putting on make-up with her in front of her dressing-table mirror. Curling up with her father while he played around with his guitar.

Lily gulped in air and her heart caught. More unprecedented memories of her parents stumbled through her mind and she felt breathless with surprise.

She felt Tristan's arms tighten around her, one of his hands stroking from the top of her head to the base of her spine as one might soothe an upset child. As her mother had once soothed her.

Her father's mantra came to mind, trying to rescue her. But for once it didn't work. Because Tristan was right. She *did* care what people thought about her.

Slowly she lifted her head and peered up at him. She knew she must look an absolute fright, and was shocked when Tristan pulled the sleeve of his expensive cashmere sweater over his hand and wiped her eyes and nose.

'That's gross,' she grumbled, ducking her head self-consciously.

She felt him shrug. 'That's all I had.'

He chuckled, and Lily smiled into the curve of his neck. Being in his arms gave her a sense of security she hadn't felt since before her parents had died, and although part of her, the self-preservation part, told her to pull away, that she had embarrassed herself enough, that she was better off handling this alone, she couldn't get her limbs to obey. He was just so big and warm, and his rich scent was extraordinarily comforting.

*But none of this is real*, she reminded herself glumly.

'You can let me up now,' she said quietly, pushing back from him as those disturbing thoughts stole through her mind.

When Tristan made no move to release her completely she looked up at him. 'I said you can let me go now,' she repeated, in case he hadn't heard her.

'I heard.' He nodded, but didn't move.

'I think...I think I should go to my room and be alone with my misery.'

'Now, I was always told that misery preferred company,' Tristan jested.

'Tristan, please...' Embarrassment was overriding pain and Lily couldn't smile at his teasing words. 'I can't do this. You were right. I *am* a coward. I...I need time alone to think.'

Tristan curled his arm around her shoulders, preventing her from pulling further away.

'Thinking is probably the worst thing you can do right now. And I never said you were a coward.' He feathered her ponytail through his fingers as if learning its silky texture. 'You're one of the bravest people I know. And you're loyal and warm and smart. You've faced false drug allegations with dignity and you have a generous spirit. It's why people are so drawn to you.'

'People are drawn to me because of the way I look and because of who my parents were,' she argued.

He tapped her on the end of her shiny nose and she squirmed. 'You're too young to be cynical. And you're more than the sum of your parts, Lily Wild.'

Lily felt more tears well up at his kind words and buried her face against his shoulder again. 'You're a nice person. How come you don't show that side of yourself more often?'

He tensed momentarily. 'I already told you I'm not nice,' he said, his voice gruff. 'I'm just saying all this to make you feel better.'

'Oh.' Lily laughed as she was meant to. But he didn't fool her. He *was* nice. Too nice.

She shifted off his lap so she was sitting beside him, wanting to tell him what was going through her mind even though she'd revealed more about herself tonight than she had to anyone else.

'You were right before,' she began haltingly. 'I *have* used my past as a type of shield.'

'That's perfectly understandable, given your experiences.'

Lily paused. 'Maybe. But it's also helped me avoid recognising things like…like the fact that for years I've been so ashamed of who my parents were and how they died that I hated them. And I've let their destructive love for each other cloud the way I relate to people. You see, my mother kept diaries for years. Basically she and Johnny would binge on each other and then he'd go off with his groupies and my mother would cry and rail and swear off him—until he came back and the whole cycle would start over again.'

Tristan was quiet, and Lily's fingers absently pleated the soft wool of his sweater as she leaned against him and soaked up his strength and sureness.

'That sounds like the problem was less about how they felt about each other and more about how they felt about themselves.'

'What do you mean?' she queried, leaning back a little to look up at him, her eyes drinking in the patrician beauty of his face in the soft light.

He shrugged. 'I'm guessing Johnny Wild loved himself a little too much and your mother didn't love herself nearly enough.'

Lily digested his words and then blew out a noisy breath. 'Of course. Why did I never see that?'

'Too close to the trees, perhaps?'

She shook her head. 'You're really smart—you know that?'

No, if he was smart he'd get up and go to bed right now, instead of wondering what she would do if he reached up and released her silky mass of hair from the confines of her hair tie. If he was smart he'd be questioning this need to comfort her and touch her rather than just going along with it as if he had a right to do those things.

'Not always,' he acknowledged, feeling the air between them thicken as he tried to ignore her soft hands on his chest. 'You need to stop doing that.'

He heard the hitch in her breathing at his growled words and the sound sent a jolt of lust to his already hardened groin.

'Or...?'

He clenched his teeth against the invitation apparent in that one tiny word. 'There is no "or".'

'Why not?'

'Lily, your emotions are running high.'

She looked him square in the eye, her purple gaze luminous despite her reddened eyelids. 'And yours aren't running at all?'

He needed her to stop looking at him as if he was better than he was. 'That's not emotion, sweetheart—that's sex. And the two should never be confused.'

'Believe me, I know that.' She expelled a shaky breath but didn't remove her hand. Instead she slid it further up his chest and ran the tip of her finger underneath the crew neck of his sweater, along his clavicle.

'Lily—'

'I want to make love with you.'

Tristan wanted that too—but could he risk it?

She'd noticed his hesitation and her eyes had clouded over. 'Sorry. I— Look, if you don't want to I'll understand…'

'Don't want to!' His hands felt unsteady as they automatically reached out to stop her from getting up. 'Lily, you drive me crazy.'

She shot him a surprised look and he nearly laughed. Didn't she know the effect she had on him? Didn't she *know* why he had stayed away from her for four days? Why he should have stayed away tonight as well…?

'I do?'

'Oh, yeah.' His hot gaze swept down over her tear-smudged face, baggy T-shirt and worn sweatpants. 'Stir crazy…' he whispered.

He felt her tentative hands creep into his hair, and groaned when she leaned in and placed her soft, full mouth against his own. Oh, God, this was heaven—and he couldn't fight both of them.

He cupped her face briefly, deepening the kiss and sealing his mouth to hers. He flipped her over on the settee and shoved his hands under her T-shirt. She moaned and arched into his hands, and Tristan felt like a starving man being offered a king's dinner. He yanked her T-shirt up and fastened his lips on one pert breast, tugging at her sweet flesh, licking, sucking, drowning in the aroused perfume of her body.

'Tristan!'

Her loud gasp and uncontrolled writhing fed his urgent need, and he attacked her sweatpants and panties and drew them down her legs, frustrated when they became tangled.

He sat up and pulled them all the way off, and then knelt on the floor in front of her, not even caring that the floorboards were hard on his knees. He parted her thighs so that he could feast on her in a way that had kept him hard for more nights than he cared to count, but he stopped when he felt her stiffen.

'Tristan…'

Her voice was uncertain, and he remembered that she had been a virgin until a few nights ago and that maybe no one had ever done this for her before.

His hands instantly gentled on her inner thighs, and his fingers massaged her silken skin until he felt her muscles lose their rigidity.

'Take down your hair,' he whispered softly, gazing at her breasts rising beneath her T-shirt with her movement. A soft cloud of pure gold swirled around her shoulders and he inhaled deeply. 'Now the T-shirt.'

His thumbs kept stroking her inner thighs, slowly drawing them further apart, and he could feel tiny shivers of anticipation running along the surface of her skin. His own skin felt hot and tight, and it got even worse when she swept the grey T-shirt up over her head. Her breasts were standing proudly for his inspection, her nipples hardening into tight pink buds. Saliva pooled in his mouth at the thought of reaching up and capturing one, but he had other endeavours on his mind.

He glanced down at the soft nest of golden curls at the apex of her body, and then back up to her face.

'Let me,' he husked, desire beating like a fever in his blood. 'I've wanted you like this for ever.'

She wet her lips and arched involuntarily as his sure fingers moved higher up her softened thighs, bringing her closer to the edge of the settee as he delved between her damp curls.

She was slick and ready, and Tristan lowered his head and devoured her with his lips, his tongue, his fingers. She made the sexiest noises he'd ever heard, and when she came he thought he might too, lapping at her until he had fully sated himself with her taste. Then he rose, and felt like an emperor as he looked down upon her pliant flushed nudity.

His heart lurched, and desperation and need grabbed him

by the throat as he quickly divested himself of his clothing and rolled a condom over his now painful erection.

She sat up and reached for him, but Tristan shook his head. He'd wanted to take things slowly this time, and already slow had gone the way of the birds. If she touched him he doubted he'd even make it inside her body.

'Next time,' he promised hoarsely, picking her up and carrying her back in front of the fire. 'I need to be inside you now.'

'Oh, yes.' She held her hands out to him, and Tristan settled over her and drove deeply inside her body on one long, powerful thrust. Her body accepted him more easily this time, but still she was tight and he tried to give her a minute to adjust.

Only she didn't want that and immediately wrapped her legs around his hips. 'More,' she pleaded, trying to move under him.

Tristan couldn't resist the urgent request and drove into her over and over, while he brought them both to a shattering climax that took him to the stars and beyond.

# CHAPTER THIRTEEN

'I'LL be back,' he murmured against her mouth, and Lily flopped back against her pillows as Tristan quietly closed the bedroom door behind him.

She'd almost felt sick earlier, when she'd woken in the early-morning light to find Tristan trying to slip out of her bed without waking her. He'd pulled on his jeans, a frown marring his perfect features, and then he'd noticed her watching him. He'd looked remote, but then his eyes had devoured her and he'd walked over and let his lips follow suit.

'I'm going to make you a cup of tea,' he'd whispered, and she'd smiled and trailed her hand down his naked chest.

She didn't really want tea, just him, but she was glad now of the momentary reprieve as she stared at the ceiling and memories of last night swept blissfully into her consciousness.

Last night he'd told her she drove him crazy, and a slow grin spread across her face as she recalled the tortured way he had gasped her name when he climaxed. She liked the idea of driving him crazy. She liked it a lot. Because she felt the same way. She only had to think of him walking into a room for her hormones to sit up and beg.

Last night he had made love to her in front of the open fire and afterwards carried her to bed, where she had promptly curled against him and fallen into the deepest sleep she'd had since arriving back in the country.

He'd promised her slow, but she had no complaints about their lovemaking. In fact she'd loved it! The urgency, the excitement...the way he'd touched her, cared for her. In fact she loved everything about him.

Lily put her fingers over her face.

She loved him.

Oh, Lord. Did she?

She tested the words out silently in her head. And her heart swelled to bursting.

No. She couldn't. But she did. Completely and utterly.

And it had been there all along. It was the reason she'd been so nervous about seeing him again. It was the reason she had been so upset when he'd thought she was guilty of carrying drugs into Heathrow. That he'd thought her guilty of being a drug addict.

It was the reason she had been so morose these last few days, and the reason she had allowed herself to be swept away in the library last night. No, had *wanted* to be swept away—by him.

Lily swallowed, her heart pounding. They had made love so reverently, and she had given everything to him and he had seemed to do the same back.

He'd told her she drove him crazy with desire, and although he hadn't said he loved her she couldn't believe he didn't have any feelings for her.

But even if he did what did that mean?

Nothing. Because he didn't do love. He'd made that clear enough. And he wouldn't want her to love him either. Only... what if he felt differently with *her*?

*Right. And how many other women haven't wanted that to be true?*

Oh, Lord, she was starting to go back and forth like an entry in her mother's diary. He loves me. He loves me not.

The man had just spent four days avoiding her—he was hardly likely to go down on bended knee after one night in bed with her.

Something she couldn't deny that she now wanted. Lily blew out a breath.

In admitting that she had fallen in love with Tristan it was as if a wall against all her secret hopes and dreams had come down. She wanted what Jo and Oliver had. She wanted somewhere to belong, someone to love her. She wanted something lasting.

She groaned audibly and rolled onto her stomach and grabbed her pillow. What did she do now?

Seriously she didn't expect him to declare his undying love for her, but she couldn't stop herself from wanting that. Yearning for it. But he hadn't looked pleased to see her this morning, had he? No. He'd seemed distracted. Troubled. She'd dismissed it after his ferocious kiss, but…

*Enough!* She raised a big red stop sign in her head. She wouldn't do this. Play mental ping-pong over a man. The best thing to do would be to wait. Because really she had no idea how Tristan was feeling, and until she asked him she was just making up stories in her head. Lovely, sugar-coated romantic stories. But stories nonetheless.

Deciding to stop mooching around, she checked the bedside clock and was shocked to see that it was already nine-thirty. And, even worse, it was Friday. Jordana was due at the Abbey this morning to start all her pre-wedding pampering treatments, followed by lunch with a couple of girlfriends, and then a rehearsal dinner for close family and friends!

Maybe she should have a quick shower before Tristan got back? Or maybe she should go and find him and remind him that Jordana was due.

But then her phone rang and took the dilemma of what to do next out of her hands.

Pushing the tangled sheet aside, she jumped out of bed and reached for her tote bag beside the dressing table. Fumbling around inside, she finally located her mobile and quickly checked the caller ID. It was the detective working on her case.

*Her case!* Somehow she'd forgotten all about it with thoughts of Tristan swamping her mind.

'Good morning, Detective.'

'Miss Wild.' His polite, modulated tones echoed down the

line. 'I apologise for not delivering this news in person, but due to workload issues I'm unable to travel to Hillesden Abbey today, and Lord Garrett was adamant that we inform you of any breakthrough in your case as soon as it came to light.'

Lily swallowed, her palms sweaty around the silver phone. 'And…have you had a breakthrough?' she asked breathlessly.

'Not just a breakthrough, Miss Wild. We've solved the case. Or should I say Lord Garrett has solved the case.'

'Tristan?' Lily shook her head.

'Lord Garrett contacted us two days ago, after finding a discrepancy between the personnel records we initially received from the airline and the records that had been e-mailed to him.'

Lily plopped down on the velvet ottoman in front of the dressing table and stared at a baroque wall plaque. 'I don't understand.'

'One of the attendants who worked on your flight was not on the personnel list we were given, and was therefore not interviewed and fingerprinted. We were unaware of the last-minute replacement because the person who dealt with the staff-change had forgotten to send the information through to payroll. As we were given the original payroll records the replacement flight attendant did not appear on our list and was therefore not part of our initial investigation.'

He went on to explain that when Tristan had started looking into the case he'd picked up on the discrepancy and immediately informed the police.

'But why did she do it?' Lily asked.

'The flight attendant was bringing a small amount of narcotics into the country to earn a few extra quid on the side. When she learned that sniffer dogs would be going through not only the passengers' belongings but also the flight crew's she panicked, and you were an easy target. She was aware of your parents' notoriety and hoped that would be enough to prevent her own capture.'

Lily remained silent, struggling to process the information. 'So what happens now?'

'You're free to go, Miss Wild.'

'And the custody order?'

'Will be repealed by the courts some time today.'

Lily thanked the detective and sat for a few moments, completely stunned.

She was free.

She clasped her phone to her chest, trying to make some sense of it all. The whole sordid mess seemed surreal, and what stood out for Lily now was how sorry she was that her parents were still mainly remembered for their drug-taking rather than their artistic talents. Previously she would have felt suffocated by that. Tainted by it. But after her conversation with Tristan last night she saw that her parents had been only human. They'd made mistakes, yes, and paid the ultimate price for those mistakes. But they had tried.

It didn't mean she had to agree with their lifestyle choices, but nor did it mean she had a right to condemn them either—as many had condemned her. Except the author of the play hadn't judged them. He'd written a funny, informative and ultimately tragic account of their lives in a beautiful and heartfelt manner. And if she were to play her mother it could be her gift to them. Her gift to herself.

Lily felt short of breath at the surge of emotion that swept through her body.

Tristan. She wanted to talk to him. Share this with him because she knew he would understand.

She was free! And he had believed in her. Had helped her.

Lily sprang off the ottoman and grabbed the first items of clothing she found on the floor.

She wanted to feel Tristan's arms around her as he held her to him while she told him her news. Or did he already know?

She didn't care. She wanted to drag him back upstairs and make love with him. Run her fingers over his morning stubble—run her hands over his chest and take him into her hands as he had stopped her from doing last night.

Her body quickened, clearly agreeing with the direction of her thoughts and—

*What if he's been working on your case just so that he can be rid of you?*

The ugly thought weaved through her mind like an evil spell but she immediately pushed it aside. No stories any more. Just facing her fears head-on.

'I couldn't believe it when Mrs Cole told me you were in the kitchen making a cup of tea. And why are you only half-dressed at nine-thirty? You're usually up with the birds.'

Tristan turned at the sound of his sister's voice. He was half-naked because he'd needed to get out of Lily's bedroom fast and had forgotten his sweater.

'What are you doing here?' he asked, a little more harshly than he'd intended.

'I have a little thing called a wedding at the local manor house tomorrow. Remember?'

Tristan rubbed his belly. 'I meant in the kitchen.'

'You didn't respond to Oliver's text last night about meeting him at the polo field at half-eleven, so when Mrs Cole mentioned you were in here I thought I'd remind you. What *are* you doing in here?'

'Fixing tea. What does it look like?'

He glanced away from his sister's too interested gaze and willed the kettle to boil.

'Who for?'

'Didn't you say you had somewhere to be?'

Jordana tilted her head, her eyes narrowed. 'Why is your hair all over the place? And what's that mark on your shoul—? Oh, God.' She clapped her hand over her mouth in a melodramatic show. 'You've got someone stashed upstairs!'

Tristan followed Jordana's gaze to his right shoulder and saw the imprint of Lily's fingernails from their lovemaking last night.

He'd woken this morning to find her curved in his arms,

his upper arm numb from where she had used it as a pillow all night and a boulder the size of Mount Kilimanjaro lodged in his chest. He'd never woken up having held a woman all night before. In fact he usually tried to find a plausible excuse not to wake up with one at all, and he didn't mind admitting that having Lily snuggled against him like a warm, sleepy kitten had scared the hell out of him.

As had the feeling of well-being he'd been unable to dislodge alongside the boulder. If he'd thought the first experience with her mind-blowing then last night had been indescribable. She'd been completely abandoned in his arms and he... Suffice it to say it had been the most complete, the most intimate experience he'd ever had with a woman—even more unsettling than making love to her five nights ago.

He'd tried to sneak out of bed, but she'd woken when he was halfway into his jeans. He'd turned when he heard the bedcovers rustling to find her leaning up on one elbow, the linen sheet clutched to her chest and her golden mane spilling over one shoulder.

Her soft smile had slipped when he'd hovered over the idea of just walking out, but he hadn't been able to. Not after all they'd shared last night. He wasn't that big a heel. So he'd kissed her. Devoured her. Sucked her tongue into his mouth and very nearly forgotten why he had to get away.

'So?' Jordana prompted, bringing his eyes back to hers.

'None of your business. And keep your voice down.' The kitchen staff weren't close, but still he didn't want them overhearing. He turned back to the boiled kettle and filled the teapot, wishing that he hadn't sent Mrs Cole off when she'd offered to make the tea for him.

'I'll find out. I mean, she has to come downstairs some time...'

Tristan scowled at her too happy face. He'd be glad when this damned wedding was over and his loved up sister would go back to normal. 'Leave it alone, Jo.'

'Why? She must be important. Someone special?'

He put the kettle back on the hob and ignored her.

'Maybe it's a guy?'

'Jordana!'

'Just joking, big brother. Jeez, Louise, where's your sense of humour?'

Tristan turned away and asked himself the same question. But her next inane remark sent him into panic mode.

'That's okay.' Jo leaned against the bench. 'I'll ask Lily. She'll know.'

Tristan banged a lone mug on the tray. No way would he be having tea in Lily's room with his sister on the warpath.

'You won't ask Lily anything. You'll keep your nose out of my private life.'

'Why so tetchy? I'm only teasing you.'

'I'm not in the mood.'

'Well, that's obvious. Where is Lily anyway?'

'In her room.'

'Really?' She raised her brows at him. 'How can you be so sure? And isn't that peppermint tea? Lily's favourite?'

'I said leave it alone, Jordana,' Tristan growled.

'Oh. My. God. It's *Lily*.' Both hands were clapped over Jordana's cheeks. 'You're sleeping with my best friend!'

'Jo—'

'I'm so excited. I told Oliver I thought there was something between the two of you at the restaurant. I knew it. This is great.'

'Jordana, it's not great.'

'It is. I think you love her. The way you were looking at her that night at dinner… I told Oliver I thought it was fated. Lily getting into trouble and you bailing her out. It was as if it was meant to be.'

Tristan recoiled as if she'd slapped him. He was *not* in love with Lily Wild.

'Jordana, you're a dreamer. If I did care for Lily Wild it would never be serious, so you can forget about taking your romantic fantasy to the next level.'

'Why?'

'Because I'm not ready to get married, and even if I was Lily is not one of *us*. Now, if you don't mind, I have to start my day.'

Jordana didn't move from where she'd stood in front of him. 'That's very snobbish of you.'

'You can look at it any way you want, but I have responsibilities to uphold—and if there's one thing I've learned from our parents it's that love fades. You might want to believe in for ever after but believe me that's the exception, not the rule. I have no intention of falling into Father's trap and marrying a woman who might or might not be looking for an entrance into our society. One who will run away when she finds out there's a lot more to the title of Duchess than champagne and shopping.'

'Lily's not like that,' Jordana protested.

Yeah, he knew that. But he needed to tell his sister something to get her off his back, and if he told her that what he felt for Lily scared the life out of him she'd want to wrap her arms around him and kiss him better.

Anyway, he enjoyed his freedom. He liked having sex with a variety of women and he liked his life the way it was. Didn't he?

Tristan shook away the disquieting question. 'I don't care. I don't need love and I don't love Lily Wild. She's special to you—not to me. Personally, I can't wait until this damn drug case is over and I can get on with my life again. And the sooner you get that through your head the happier I'll be. Here.' The tea tray clattered as he shoved it at Jordana's chest. 'Take this to her, will you? And tell her—tell her…' He shook his head. 'Tell her whatever you like.'

'Can I tell her I think you're afraid and letting the mistakes of our parents get in the way of your own happiness?' she asked softly.

Tristan cut her a withering glance and stalked out of the room. His sister had always been a child with stars in her eyes.

It was why he and his father had protected her so much after their mother had died. She was too dreamy and too easily led. He remembered how he and his father had thought Lily would lead her astray.

Only she hadn't. Lily had actually tried to protect her.

He gritted his teeth. Lily hadn't turned out to be at all what he had expected.

He marched out of the kitchen and took the stairs two at a time as he sought refuge in his own suite of rooms.

Lily wasn't trouble waiting to happen. She was beautiful inside and out. He should never have slept with her again last night. It had been hard enough getting her out of his head six years ago, after one innocent kiss, and he doubted he'd be able to get her out of his mind as quickly this time when she left the Abbey.

Left the Abbey? He braced his hands against the sink in his bathroom and stared at his dishevelled reflection, wondering why that thought filled him with dread.

Because he wasn't finished with her, that was why. And by the look in her eyes this morning she wasn't finished with him either. They had started something last night—nothing permanent, but something definitely worth pursuing for as long as it lasted.

Jo had just panicked him before. Made him think this was more than it really was. But Lily herself wasn't interested in relationships and for ever after. Hadn't she said as much at Élan the other night? So what was he so het-up about? He didn't have to end things so abruptly; he could just let them run their natural course.

Lily pressed herself back against the hallway wall as Tristan stormed out of the kitchen, her hands against her chest as if that would make her thin enough to be invisible.

But he didn't see her anyway. He was in too much of a rage.

She let her head gently fall back against the wall.

It wasn't a cliché that eavesdroppers rarely heard anything

good about themselves, and Lily was still trying to register exactly what she *had* heard. Something about her not being special. Not being one of them. That he didn't love her and couldn't wait for her case to be over so he could get his life back.

Jordana had said something after that, but her softer tones hadn't carried quite so clearly.

Lily felt the methodical beat of her heart as her thoughts coalesced.

She supposed she now wasn't left in any doubt as to how he had felt this morning. That frown had been real and the kiss he'd given her had not. What had it been, then? Pity?

Lily reeled sideways and then righted herself. She wished she could go back ten minutes and reverse her decision to come downstairs looking for him.

Or did she? Wasn't she better off knowing how he really felt? Better off knowing that if she'd jumped into his arms as she'd wanted to do she would have just embarrassed them both? Wasn't this part of facing her fears?

A shiver of misery snaked down her spine and she blinked to clear her vision. She heard a rattling sound from the kitchen, and then voices, and quickly turned to sprint up the staircase before Jordana headed out to deliver her tea.

She made it to her room unseen and leaned back against the door, her breathing laboured and her stomach churning. Tristan's angry words were parroting through her brain like a DVD on repeat mode. He didn't love her. Didn't want to love her and never would love her. And, worst of all, she wasn't good enough for him.

She blinked. The shower. She would jump in the shower so that Jordana didn't see how upset she was.

In all honesty she hadn't expected that Tristan would wake up in love with her, but did he seriously think she was interested in his *title*?

Right now she'd like to tell him where he could stick it—only then she'd have to admit she'd overheard his conversation with Jo and she couldn't go there. Not without breaking down altogether.

Like her mother used to do over Johnny. Her mother had always turned to alcohol when Johnny had turned to his groupies, and where once Lily had looked back in anger at her mother she now looked back in pity. Because finally she truly understood what it felt like to fall in love with a man who didn't love you in return.

Lily felt as if she had a claw stuck in her throat as she let the hot water beat down over her face. As much as she might understand her mother a little better now, she also realised that she truly wasn't anything like her. She was her own person, and she wouldn't cling to Tristan, or rant or beg. She'd hold her head up high, tell him it had been great, and walk away.

Oh, Lord. She sucked in a deep breath and felt tears form behind her eyes. She remembered the moment she'd found her parents had died, the moment her uncle had said he couldn't take her, the moment her mother's best friend said she couldn't take her, the moment Frank had sent her to boarding school because she didn't want to appear on his TV show any more, and the moment six years ago when Tristan had sent her away.

But none of that had felt anywhere near as painful as hearing Tristan say he didn't love her, and it was only Jordana calling her name from the other room that prevented her from sliding to the floor and dissolving into a puddle of misery.

# CHAPTER FOURTEEN

WHERE the hell was she?

Tristan scowled as he leaned against one of the ornate oak sideboards in the main drawing room, sipping an aperitif and talking with one of Oliver's cousins while awaiting the remaining guests for the rehearsal dinner.

A waiter discreetly circulated amongst those already present, and Tristan glanced through the open double doors to where a lavish dining setting, resplendent with antique crystalware, awaited twenty-four of Jordana and Oliver's close friends and family for the rehearsal dinner.

From what he could tell the room was empty of everyone other than waiting staff. Which meant that Lily wasn't down yet.

Tristan knew he should have been in a better mood, given that his baby sister was marrying one of his oldest friends the following day, but he wasn't. After his run in with Jordana this morning his day had gone from bad to worse.

He'd been off his game during polo from the start, and then Oliver had informed him that Jordana's 'surprise' for Lily was to set her up with all three of his single cousins!

Tristan had left the field immediately after that and discreetly cornered Jordana, telling her in no uncertain terms to rearrange the evening's place settings so that Lily sat beside him. Only she'd floored him by telling him that Lily had already asked that the place settings remain as they were.

Then she'd apologised for her earlier behaviour. 'Lily set me straight this morning,' she'd said. 'She told me she was just taking my advice and "cutting loose" by having a harmless fling with you, and that it was now well and truly finished.' Which had been news to him. 'I was just a bit carried away by the excitement of my wedding. I'm truly sorry to have teased you the way I did.'

Tristan had reassured her it was fine, but really he hadn't heard much after 'harmless fling' and 'cutting loose'. His memories of last night certainly did not fit under either one of those banners! And as for things being finished...

Did that mean Lily actually *wanted* to be set up with one of Oliver's cousins? This mountain of a man he was currently attempting to converse with, perhaps? Tristan hoped not, because objectively speaking he was an attractive devil. If Lily went for brawny males—and she had certainly been admiring his own muscles last night—then Hamish Blackstone would be right up her alley.

He scoured the room again for Lily and tried to clear the scowl off his face. Where was she? Avoiding him?

He'd deliberately stayed away from her all day to give her a chance to do girlie stuff with Jordana, convincing himself that the last thing either woman wanted was a male hanging around. But really, if he was honest, he'd been upset to find Lily constantly in his thoughts, and after their unbelievable lovemaking last night he'd needed time to think.

And what he'd thought was that there was no way she was getting it on with one of Oliver's cousins this weekend. Or the next, for that matter, and... Where on earth *was* she?

He was just about to go in search of her when the hair stood up on the back of his neck and he knew she'd arrived.

He turned to see her poised to enter the room from the single side door leading in from the south corridor and his heart stopped. For maybe a minute.

Not enough time to kill him, but long enough that it had to beat triple time to oxygenate his brain again.

George Bernard Shaw was meant to have said, 'Beauty is

all very well at first sight; but who ever looks at it when it has been in the house three days?' Tristan could safely answer that he did! If anything, as he looked at her standing in the doorway wearing a powder-blue Grecian-style gown that left her arms and décolletage bare, with her glorious hair upswept, he didn't think he'd ever seen a more divine creature. And by the intake of breath of his drinking companion *he* hadn't either.

'That's Lily Wild,' Hamish Blackstone announced under his breath.

Tristan grunted and waited for Lily to make eye contact with him. But she didn't. Instead she stepped straight up to a group of women that included the bridesmaids and Oliver's mother, looking relaxed and composed and every inch the movie star that she was.

'She's taken,' he found himself telling Hamish.

'You're joshing me?' the Scot spluttered. 'Jordana said she was single. Who's the lucky guy? I'll deck him.'

Tristan looked him up and down and thought he just might with those tree trunk arms. 'Excuse me. I need to mingle.'

He needed to talk to her, that was what he needed to do, and he didn't care who knew it. She couldn't just ignore him after last night.

'Cutting loose' be damned!

Lily smiled politely and answered questions about acting and America and everything else in between.

When she had first walked into the drawing room she'd sensed Tristan's presence and deliberately hadn't looked for him. She didn't want to see him. She had her pride, and she'd decided earlier that she wasn't going to collapse as she had wanted to do in the shower. That had been shock, and she'd had all day to steel herself against seeing him again.

Maybe it wouldn't be so hard.

He hadn't tried to see her once throughout the day, and since Jordana had set up a mini-beauty salon upstairs in her wing of the house she hadn't had time to see him either. Not that she'd wanted to.

What she was secretly hoping was that he would be glad she was keeping her distance and not make a big deal of it. He might even be happy about it. The last thing a man like Tristan Garrett wanted was a woman to go all starry-eyed over him. Or, even worse, over his precious title!

Which reminded her of how Jordana had said that Tristan was to be partnered with Lady Amanda Sutton at the wedding. A woman Lily had met at lunch earlier that day, who was charming, titled, and completely enamoured of Jordana's brother. Something Tristan hadn't told her about last night while he'd been making love to *her*!

'What was that, dear?'

'Nothing.' Lily smiled pleasantly at Oliver's mother from behind her champagne flute.

Lily let her anger at Tristan's subterfuge course through her. Maybe it was illogical, and maybe even a little unfair seeing as how he wasn't actually dating Amanda Sutton but Lily didn't care. She didn't feel logical right now. Or fair. She felt hurt and stupid and…empty.

Tristan had been magnificent last night. Strong, gentle, masterful, funny—every woman's ideal man come to life. Only he wasn't…or at least he wasn't *her* ideal man. Not that her body seemed to be getting that message. Even now it yearned for her to turn, seek him out, as if he was truly hers to touch and talk with. To laugh with and…

*Oh, stop mooning, Lily!*

It was time to smile and behave like the perfect maid of honour during the evening's festivities, and to do that she'd clearly have to make sure that any interactions she had with Tristan were later rather than sooner.

Which, okay, wasn't exactly facing her fears head-on—but one step at a time. Come Sunday she'd fly home and lick her wounds. Regroup. Forget Tristan Garrett.

'Lady Grove, Sarah, Talia.' Tristan's deep voice resonated

directly behind her. 'Do you mind if I borrow the maid of honour for a moment?'

'Of course not,' Lady Grove murmured. 'I'm sure you both have final touches to go over before tomorrow.'

'Absolutely.' Tristan smiled. 'Lily?'

Okay, so sooner was probably a good thing. It would mean she could relax for the rest of the night. Or not, she thought as she turned towards Tristan and saw him dressed in a black tuxedo.

Oh, Lord, but he was sublime. And he'd had his hair cut. The mid-length layers framed his masculine features to perfection.

Lily couldn't suppress a shiver of awareness as he took her arm and led her across the polished marble floor to a far corner of the room. Fixing a pleasant smile on her face, she subtly broke free of his hold.

At least this was one scenario she'd had time to plan for. *No tears, no tantrums*, she reminded herself. No matter how much she felt as if she was falling apart inside.

She lifted her glass to her lips and glanced around the room at the other guests, as if she didn't have a care in the world. But Tristan squared off in front of her, his broad shoulders effectively blocking her view and giving her nowhere else to look but directly at him.

'If you think you're sitting next to Hamish Blackstone tonight you've got another thing coming,' he ground out between clenched teeth.

Lily blinked, wide-eyed at his fervent tone. She had no idea what he was talking about.

Tristan knew he had surprised Lily with the dark vehemence in his voice. Hell, he'd shocked himself.

He'd known as soon as he'd laid eyes on her that she was miffed, and he planned to find out what was bothering her and fix it.

He'd thought maybe she was upset that he hadn't brought her

tea up this morning. Or hadn't sought her out during the day. Both theories he'd have put money on, but now he knew she'd taken umbrage at his tone as well, and logically he couldn't blame her.

'Excuse me?' she said with icy disdain.

Yep, she was definitely annoyed with him.

'You heard.' No way was he backing down now. She had to know she wasn't sitting next to anyone but him tonight.

'But maybe *you* didn't,' she said stiffly. 'I'm no longer under your protective custody any more. You're free to get on with your own life. Get on with Lady Sutton.'

Tristan's eyes narrowed. 'What does Amanda have to do with this?'

'She's your guest at the wedding.'

Tristan shoved his hands in his pockets and relaxed back on his heels. She was jealous. Hell, he hadn't even come up with that one. He'd quite forgotten he'd agreed to partner Amanda at the wedding.

'She's no threat to you. She's just a family friend, and she isn't really my guest.'

Lily gave a derisive laugh. 'I'm not threatened.' She tilted her champagne flute towards the light and watched the bubbles fizz. 'But the local grapevine says she wants to be a lot *more* than just a family friend, and she does have the correct *lineage*.'

Tristan frowned. As if he cared about Amanda's lineage… 'Forget Amanda. She's irrelevant.'

'She'd no doubt be upset to hear you say that.'

Tristan frowned. This conversation was not going at all as he'd planned. He declined a glass of champagne as a passing waiter stopped, and determinedly turned his back on an Italian count he'd befriended at Harvard.

'I'd like to thank you for your help in solving my case,' she said politely.

'It was nothing.' Tristan waved away her gratitude.

'Still, I'd like to pay you for your services and—'

'*Pay* me!' Tristan thundered, halting her mid-sentence. 'Don't be absurd, Lily.'

She didn't seem pleased with his response, but no way was she paying him for something he'd wanted to do for her—had *needed* to do for her.

His narrowed eyes lingered on her face. 'Is this because I didn't bring you your tea this morning?'

'I beg your pardon?'

'Don't play games, Lily. You know what I'm talking about.'

She raked him with her gaze and he felt as if she'd actually touched him.

'Or are you upset because I didn't try to see you today?'

'Didn't you? I didn't notice.' She smiled, her wide kohl-rimmed eyes staring at him as if she'd like to slice him in half, her glossy peach-coloured lips clamped together tightly.

He wondered incongruously how the gloss tasted and felt an overpowering need to prise those lips apart and sweep his tongue inside the warm haven of her mouth. At least then they'd be communicating a little better than they were now.

'Look, I'm sorry. I would have but I thought you'd be— Damn, did I mark you?' His eyes had drifted down over her neck to where a slight shadow marred her golden skin.

'Er…no.' She automatically lifted her hand to the exact spot he had been talking about. 'I…scratched myself with the hairbrush.'

He didn't even try to curb the grin that spread across his face. *Hairbrush, my foot.*

'What's wrong?' he murmured softly, deciding it was time to cut to the chase.

She shrugged and glanced over his shoulder at the nearby guests. 'Wrong? What could be wrong?'

'I don't know. That's why I'm asking. But I'm not going to keep at it all night.'

That brought her eyes back to his. 'Is that supposed to be a threat?'

Why couldn't she just be happy he was willing to ask about

her feelings? He knew plenty of his friends who wouldn't have been. Hell, *he* would never have even considered having this type of conversation before Lily. He would have moved on long ago.

*So what's different this time?*

He couldn't answer his own question and so pushed it aside.

He ran a hand through his hair and shifted the weight on his feet. 'Lily, we had wild, uninhibited sex last night and now you can barely look at me. What's wrong?'

She smoothed at an invisible smudge on her cheek. 'I hardly think this is the place for that type of discussion.'

Tristan let out a frustrated breath. 'I couldn't agree more.' He grabbed hold of her elbow and all but frog-marched her across the room, smiling pleasantly at the familiar faces milling around but avoiding all eye contact.

He reached the side door and drew Lily out into the family's private corridor. She hadn't made a fuss, but then he'd been counting on the fact that she wouldn't.

He stopped beside a spindly hall table that was probably a thousand years old and turned, hands on hips, legs apart. 'Now talk.'

Lily folded her arms across her chest. 'Is this your usual approach after a night with a woman?'

'Don't push me, Lily.'

'Ah—your favourite expression comes out to say hello.'

Tristan's patience was wearing thin, and he knew she knew it. 'What. Is. Wrong?'

'What's wrong? You're behaving like an ape is what's wrong. We had sex. What do you want—a reference?'

'It wasn't just sex,' he denied.

'What was it, then?'

'Great sex.' He smiled—a slow, sensual smile that was meant to cajole her out of her mood. Unfortunately it backfired.

'Oh, well, pardon me. We had *great* sex. What more do you want? It's not like it was anything *special*, was it? I thought you'd be pleased to be able to get on with your life and...' Her voice trailed off and she clamped her lips closed, as if she didn't want to reveal too much of herself or her intentions.

'And what? Now you want to play the field? Get every other man's attention?' That had been his mother's area of expertise. 'You want to get it on with one of Oliver's cousins now that I've broken you in?'

Her shocked gasp reverberated off the vaulted ceiling and he knew his comment had been a low blow. But, dammit, he'd wanted to hear her deny any interest in other men. And now he wished she'd slap him. Anything was better than being stared down by this icy creature who just wanted to get away from him.

'I'm going back in.' She moved towards the door and his hand shot out to stop her.

Something wasn't right. She wasn't anything like his mother and he knew that.

'I'm sorry. That was uncalled for.' His gaze fastened on her face and she stared back at him, her eyes glittering with barely veiled pain.

Then the way she'd spat the word *special* at him, and *get on with your life* registered in the thinking part of his brain.

'You overheard me talking to Jordana this morning.' His tone was accusatory when he hadn't meant it to be, and her eyebrows hit her hairline.

'I wasn't going to embarrass you by mentioning it.'

'I'm not embarrassed.' Actually, he was still trying to recall exactly what he had said. He'd spent most of the day trying not to remember that particular conversation.

He tried to clear his head and think on his feet—something he was usually exceptionally good at, but which was eluding him tonight.

'You weren't meant to hear any of that.'

Lily shrugged as if it didn't matter. 'I'm sure you didn't say anything to Jordana that you wouldn't have said to me if I'd asked.'

Possibly. But hadn't he said he was sick of her case? And

that she wasn't special? And something about his future title? Had he really said she was after that?

Okay, he could understand why she had her back up. He probably would have too if their situations had been reversed.

He shoved his hair from his forehead and smiled at her. 'I know you're not after my title.'

She looked at him as someone might regard a mutant rodent. 'What a relief.'

'And after last night you must *know* I think you're special.'

'How am I special?' she asked immediately.

How was she special? What kind of a question was that?

Tristan tugged at his shirt collar, annoyed when she held her hand up.

'Don't bother answering that. I think I know.' Her voice was full of scorn, and that got *his* back up.

Why the hell did he feel guilty all of a sudden? They were both consenting adults, and she had asked *him* to make love to *her*!

'I didn't hear you complaining last night.'

'That's because I wasn't,' she agreed.

'Then what's the problem?' he asked aggressively.

'There *is* no problem. We had a good time and now it's over.'

'Just like that?'

'You want flowers?'

'Lily—'

She threw her hands up. 'Tristan, I can't do this.'

'Then how about we do this instead?' he murmured throatily, crowding her back against the hallway table, quickly reaching around her to snatch at a teetering vase that was probably two thousand years old.

He righted the vase, coiled his arm around Lily's waist and did what he'd wanted to do all day. Pulled her in close and sealed his lips to hers.

She resisted for maybe half a heartbeat, and then her mouth opened and his tongue swept inside. He groaned at the sheer heaven of her wildfire response and swept his hands down over the gauzy fabric of her dress. She gripped his shoulders and pressed her breasts into his chest. He wished he'd removed his jacket. And his shirt.

'Hmmm, nice gloss.' He licked his lips, tasting…cherries? And then nearly fell over the table himself when she let out a sharp cry and pushed him away from her.

'You *ever* kiss me against my will again and I'll slap you,' she said breathlessly.

'You wanted it,' he said definitely.

'No. *You* wanted it. I'm over it. And get that smug look off your face. Physically you're one heck of a package, but when it comes down to it you've got nothing I want.'

Tristan felt as if a bomb had just gone off in his head. His mind reeled, memories of his mother's words from over a decade ago dragging him under, but he shoved them away with steely determination, blanking the pain that threatened to tear him in half.

What was going on here? Was he actually about to beg? And for what? One more round in the ring? Not even his father had been that stupid. And Tristan could have any number of women. Didn't she know that?

He smiled—a true predator's smile. He'd nearly lost it over this woman and for what? Sex?

Forget it.

'Good to know,' he murmured evenly. 'Because unless you're willing to put out, *Honey Blossom*, you have nothing I want either.'

Lily's chin jerked up and she covered her mouth with the back of her hand and slowly wiped his kiss off before striding down the hallway. It was a good move. An admirable one. And he would have applauded her if she'd hung around.

Thank God he hadn't offered her anything more. Not that he'd been going to. He'd never offered a woman anything more than a good time between the sheets, or on some other serviceable surface, and Lily Wild was no exception.

He swore viciously. He hated her. God, how he hated her.

Making him remember his mother, engaging his emotions like she had. Like some courtesan deliberately setting out to trap him. To make a fool of him.

He glanced down at the antique vase and nearly picked it up and hurled it down the long corridor.

He was happy she was gone because his instincts about her had been right all along: she was nothing but trouble.

# CHAPTER FIFTEEN

TROUBLE with a capital *T,* Tristan reminded himself the following morning as he stood beside Oliver in morning suit and top hat at the entrance to the Gothic cathedral, making small talk with yet another expensively dressed wedding guest.

It was a splendid day—except the sun had come out to grace Jordana's big day and brought half the paparazzi in the Western world along with it. No doubt the combined news of Lily's near-arrest and subsequent release and the many royal attendants at Jordana's wedding was causing them to swarm like coachroaches. The local constabulary was also out in force, to keep intruders at bay, as well as a top London security firm that looked as if it employed some of the men from Lily's premiere.

And if Tristan was feeling slightly seedy—well, that was just the Scotch he'd consumed last night, after a dinner that would surely go down as the worst ever. Having to sit next to Amanda Sutton and feign a civility he didn't feel while Lily made eyes at one of the Blackstone boys hadn't exactly put him in the best mood.

'Smile, you great idiot,' Oliver grumbled into his ear. 'It's my wedding day.'

Tristan cut him a dark look and then gracefully bowed over some old dowager's gloved hand.

'And *why* is it, exactly?' he drawled.

'What?'

He waited for Oliver to agree on the splendid weather they were having with the dowager's daughter.

'Your wedding day?'

Oliver looked flummoxed. 'Is that a trick question?'

'You said you'd never give up your freedom for anyone.'

'That was before I fell for your sister.'

'You could have just lived with her.'

Oliver shook his head. 'And have someone steal her away at the first opportunity? I don't think so. Anyway, I want the world to know that she's mine. That we belong together. She's my soul mate, and I can't imagine a life without her in it.'

Tristan fidgeted with the wedding rings in his pocket. 'If that's not already a Hallmark card you could probably sell it to them for a few quid. Carlo!' Tristan shook hands with the Italian count he'd stayed up drinking with last night. 'Good to see you up in time for the ceremony.'

'You didn't tell me there was alcohol in that Scotch last night, Garrett.'

'Hundred-year-old.'

'That's the last of the wedding guests.' The wedding planner stopped in front of them and gave the Count a scathing once-over. 'So,' she spoke to Oliver and Tristan, 'if you'd both like to make your way down to the altar?'

Oliver led the way, and when they finally reached the front of the church straightened Tristan's tie.

'Leave my bloody tie alone.'

Oliver grinned. 'You could just tell her and get it over with,' he whispered.

Tristan scowled. 'Tell who what?'

The harpist started up, and Oliver dashed a hand across his forehead. 'Stop being a coward, Garrett. It's obvious you're in love with her. Just *tell* her.'

Tristan swallowed. Hard. 'Am I supposed to know who you're talking about?'

Oliver threw him a dour look. 'Unfortunately ignoring it or denying it doesn't make it go away. Believe me, I did try.'

Tristan scowled.

'Now, shut up and do your job, would you?' Oliver growled. 'And for God's sake smile—or your sister is likely to make us do this all over again.'

A look of utter joy swept over Oliver's face as he did the non-traditional thing of turning to watch his bride walk down the aisle, and Tristan swallowed heavily as he too turned, his vision immediately filled with Lily walking behind Jordana in a flowing coffee silk and tulle creation that curved around her sublime figure like whipped cream. All the other women decked out in their wedding finery, including Jordana in her delicate couture gown, couldn't hold a torch to his Lily. She was so refined, so poised, and yet so vibrantly alive—and then he knew.

Oliver was right. He loved her. Maybe he'd always loved her. The words slotted into his head like the final piece in a puzzle. Actually, the second to last piece of a puzzle. The final piece was how she felt about *him*…and by the way she avoided eye contact with him as she moved closer he could see that wasn't looking good.

Lily gazed around at the grand ballroom of the manor house Jordana had chosen for her wedding reception. It was filled with circular tables, each with an enormous central flower arrangement and ringed with white cloth-covered chairs tied with bows at the back.

Jordana and Oliver's wedding day had been picture-perfect and she'd never seen her friend happier. Jordana's beautiful face was still aglow as she chatted and smiled contentedly with her wedding guests.

'I wanted to thank you for being such a good friend to my daughter, Miss Wild.' The eleventh Duke of Greythorn surprised her as he stopped beside Lily's chair.

'Actually, Your Grace, it is I who feels blessed to have Jordana's friendship.' Lily smiled, completely thrown by the

Duke's open warmth when previously, she knew, he hadn't approved of her at all.

'Tristan has informed me of all that you have done for Jordana over the years, and I know that if your parents were alive today they would be very proud of the person you have become.'

Lily felt tears prick behind her eyes, and if she'd been standing she would have dropped into a curtsey in front of this stately gentleman. He seemed to sense her overpowering emotions and patted her hand, telling her to enjoy her evening, and Lily watched slightly dumbstruck as he returned to his seat at the head of the table.

'Ladies and gentlemen.' The MC spoke over the top of the band members tuning their instruments and drew her attention away from the Duke. 'If I could please ask Earl and Countess Blackstone and their attendants Lord Tristan Garrett and Miss Lily Wild to take to the floor for the bridal waltz?'

The bridal waltz? Already?

Lily glanced around the room and noticed that Tristan had stopped conversing at a table in the opposite corner and was staring at her intently.

No way. She couldn't dance with him. She smiled serenely as she quickly threaded a path through the cluster of guests milling around on her pre-planned escape to the toilets.

She had managed to avoid being alone with Tristan the whole day, and had already decided that there was no way she could dance with him tonight without giving away just how broken-hearted she felt.

The band struck up a quintessential love song and Lily fairly flew out of the room—and right into Tristan's arms.

'Going somewhere?' he mocked.

Lily tried to steady her runaway heartbeat. 'The bathroom.'

'During the bridal waltz? I don't think so.'

'You can't dictate to me any more, remember?'

'No, but it's your last official obligation for the day, and I didn't take you for a shirker.'

Lily huffed out a breath and noticed the interested glances from the guests around them. 'I'll do it because it's expected,' she stated under her breath. 'Not because you challenged me.'

Tristan smiled. 'That's my girl.'

Lily was about to correct him and say that she wasn't his girl, but they were on the dance floor and he had already swept her into his arms.

She held herself so stiffly she felt like a mechanised doll, but there was nothing she could do about that. She couldn't relax, couldn't look at him. Then she remembered an old childhood trick she'd used to employ when she was in an uncomfortable situation. Counting. Once, she remembered, she'd counted so high she'd made it to seven hundred and thirty-five!

'You look exquisite today.' Tristan's eyes glittered down into hers and Lily quickly planted her gaze at a spot over his shoulder. One, two, three...

'But then you look exquisite all the time.'

Nine, ten...

He swirled her suddenly, and she frowned as she had to grip him tighter to stop herself from falling. He was wearing a new cologne tonight and the hint of spice was doing horrible things to her equilibrium. Nineteen, twenty...

'How's Hamish?'

Lily looked at him. She knew why he was asking that. She had found out from Jordana in a fit of giggles last night that her 'surprise' was to be set up with any of Oliver's three single cousins. Which was what Tristan had been so angrily referring to when they'd talked prior to dinner last night.

She hadn't known about Jordana's cunning plan then, and she knew Tristan's ego had been bruised when Jordana had fooled him into believing that Lily had welcomed her attempts at matchmaking. Which she hadn't. And she had apologised profusely to each of the men when she'd told them that actually she wasn't available.

They'd been completely charming, and she'd wished things were different so she might have been in a better position to invite their interest. But of course she wasn't. Her feelings for Tristan were too real and too raw for her to even attempt friendship with another man at this point.

Clearly Tristan's ego was still affected, if the way he was studying her was any indication.

'Fine, I expect,' she answered.

Tristan scowled and brought her hand in tightly against his chest. His other hand was spread wide against that sensitive spot in the small of her back. He was holding her so closely now Lily could hear the brush of her tulle skirt against his trousers.

Lily swallowed and concentrated on holding in the quiver that zipped up her spine, completely forgetting what number she was up to. *Damn.* One, two...

'Are you counting?' Tristan's deep voice was incredulous.

'Would you stop talking?' she whispered furiously, trying hard to ignore the growing tension in his big body.

Then he stopped dancing altogether, and Lily became acutely aware of the murmur of voices and the soft sway of Jordana's silk gown as she moved in time with the music. Lily stood in the circle of Tristan's arms, glancing around nervously at the interested faces of the wedding guests circling the dance floor.

She was just about to ask him what he was doing when he made a low sound in the back of his throat. 'Oh, to hell with it,' he muttered, deftly hoisting her and her close-fitted tulle skirts into his arms. 'Excuse us,' he threw at a surprised Oliver and Jordana as he strode past.

'What are you doing?' Lily squeaked, smiling tremulously as if nothing untoward was going on when it definitely was.

'Keep still,' he ordered, and Lily, not wishing to make any more of a scene, ducked her head into his neck just as she had done at the airport a little over a week ago, to hide her face from the amused glances of the wedding guests who were parting like the Red Sea to let Tristan through.

'Oh, I hate to imagine what everyone is going to think!' she fumed, scowling at the smiling waiter who had *kindly* held open the door to a smaller, private dining room and who was now in the process of closing it behind them.

She glared at Tristan, her heart beating a mile a minute, as he let her down, and stalked to the other side of the room, feeling marginally calmer with a two-metre-long mahogany dining table between them.

Tristan stood with his hands in his pockets and stared at her. 'They'll think I'm in love, I expect. Either that…' He paused as if to gauge her reaction. 'Or they'll think I've lost my mind.'

'Well, we both know the former isn't the truth,' she snapped. 'Don't play games with me, Tristan. I don't like them.'

Tristan blew out a breath. 'Lily, I need to talk to you, and this seemed the only way to achieve that objective.' He circled the table towards her, and stopped when he realised she was moving as well—but in the opposite direction. 'Would you stop that? I'm not going to bite you.'

Lily stared at him. He was so rakishly appealing with his ruffled hair and formal wedding attire it made her heart feel as if it was enclosed in a giant fist. She felt her old survival instincts rise up and did her best to blank out the pain of being so close to him and yet so far away.

'I'm getting a little tired of you thinking you can pick me up and carry me wherever you want. Next time it happens I won't be so concerned about creating a scene,' she warned with haughty disdain.

'Would you have come if I'd asked?'

His voice was soft, almost like a caress, and it confused her senses. Made her body soften. Lily did her best to clamp down on the rioting emotions running through her and focused on his question.

She lifted her chin and tried to stop her lips from trembling. Of course she wouldn't have come with him. She had nothing to say to him that wouldn't involve making a complete fool of herself.

'Say what you have to say so we can get out of here. I

don't have much time left,' she added, thankful that her voice sounded steadier than she felt.

'Time left for what?'

Lily noted Tristan's sharp tone and decided now was not the time to tell him she was booked on the red-eye back to New York this very evening. After enduring the rehearsal dinner and feeling so tense a slight breeze might have snapped her in half she had changed her travel plans so she could head back to London and fly home to New York early.

Being around Tristan and watching him smoulder with Lady Sutton last night had nearly done her in. She loved him too much to imagine him with another woman, so seeing him with one who could offer him everything she couldn't was just unendurable. Better that she start her life again without him as soon as possible. Facing her fears head-on…or perhaps just running away. She didn't care which at this point. Her only criteria was that when she finally broke down she did so in private.

Lily steeled herself to look at him and lifted her gaze once more to his. He stood across the table from her, his expression as fierce as an angry warlord facing down a known enemy. She had no idea why. Had something happened earlier that she didn't know about and for which she was about to get the blame again?

'Are you going to answer my question?' he asked, almost too politely.

'Are you going to answer mine?' she parried.

Tristan exhaled and ran an agitated hand through his hair. He looked tired and strung out—very unlike his usually composed self.

'Lily this doesn't have to end.'

Lily, stared at him, not sure what he was referring to.

'*We* don't have to end,' he clarified, a strange, shadowed look settling on his face.

Lily wet her dry mouth. All she could think about was how last night he had confirmed that he really didn't want her. That she had just been an itch he had wanted to scratch. 'Last night you said…'

'Please forget what I said last night. I was hurt and angry.'

'Hurt?'

Tristan gripped the back of the upholstered dining chair in front of him. This conversation was not going at all the way he had hoped. Lily was supposed to have picked up on his lame declaration of love and thrown herself into his arms. Instead she was spitting at him and looking much the same way she had when she'd felt she had to defend her honour after they had made love that first time.

Okay, so maybe he wasn't going about this very well. But he'd never told a woman he loved her before. Had never *wanted* to love a woman before. Opening up about his emotions wasn't exactly his strong suit after years of holding them at bay.

He cleared his throat, more nervous now than he had been during his first courtroom appearance—which, come to think of it, he hadn't been nervous about at all…'Lily, I'd like to say something to you and if you still want to leave after that then I won't try and stop you.'

Lily stared at him, seemingly transfixed, as he walked slowly around the table and pulled out one of the dining chairs for her to sit down in.

She slid into it, almost with relief, and Tristan paced a short way away and then stopped, turning to face her.

'I told you the other night that my mother left my father, but what I haven't told you is that on the day she left, when I was fifteen, I overheard my parents arguing. During the argument my mother told my father she hated him and that he had nothing she wanted—that I also had nothing she wanted and that she was taking Jordana with her and not me.'

'Oh, Tristan.'

He held up his hand gently and shook his head. 'I'm not telling you this so you'll feel sorry for me. It has no doubt coloured my past relationships, as your parents have coloured yours, but I need you to understand something. My mother was not an easy woman to love but God knows I tried. There was a big age gap between myself and Jordana and for a while I was my mother's saviour. Her little hero. Then Jordana arrived, my father started working more, and I became relegated to the sidelines. I never understood why, and slowly, over the years, I learned to protect myself by switching my feelings off. I became angry with my mother and blamed myself. Two nights ago you inadvertently helped me see that what I hadn't understood was that my parents just had an unhappy marriage and I was one of the victims of that.'

'Parents often don't see the impact they have on their children when they aren't happy within themselves.' Lily offered softly.

'No.' Tristan shook his head. 'And it certainly put me off wanting to risk my heart with another person, but…' He looked down at Lily's small hand enfolded in his, not even having realised that he had reached out to her. 'Lily, the other night I accused you of using your past as a shield, and I've only just come to realise that I do the same thing. I've put up barriers to my emotions my whole life because my mother's love was so unpredictable and my parents' relationship was so unstable and I don't want to do that any more. Actually, that's not completely true.' He looked up sheepishly. 'If I could still do that I probably would. But if I do I'll lose you, and after you walked away last night I realised that's more painful than everything else put together.'

Lily swallowed and looked down at their enclosed hands, then slowly back up to reconnect with his eyes. 'Why?'

Tristan leaned forward and kissed her. A kiss filled with all the love and tenderness he had been afraid to show her until now. He pulled back and waited for her eyes to flutter open. 'Because I love you, Lily. I think I always have.'

Lily shook her head, her expression dazed. 'You love me?'

'With all my heart. And the more I say it, the more I want to say it.'

'But you never approved of me...'

'Partly true. I disliked your lifestyle because I was always worried that Jordana would go the way my mother had, but really what I resented about you the most was how protective I felt towards you. Whenever I heard you were at one of your stepfather's parties, and I was in the country, I always came and got you out. I even did it once when Jordana wasn't with you. Remember?'

'I assumed you thought she *was* with me.'

'No. I knew she was home safe—and that's just where I wanted you to be. But it wasn't until Jo's eighteenth that my feelings for you changed. As soon as I saw you in that silver mini-dress I knew I couldn't deny that my feelings for you were more than just protective. I wanted you so much that night it hurt. But you were too young, and I was too closed to my emotions, and then when I came across that private party it was easy to blame you. It gave me an excuse to turn my back on the way you made me feel. But you changed me that night. I haven't been able to look at a woman since, be with a woman, without imagining she was you. Crazy, I know...'

'Not so crazy.' Lily reached up and almost reverently cupped his face. 'I fell so deeply in love with you that night I've compared every other man I've ever met to you and found him lacking.'

'Lily, does that mean what I think it means?'

Lily smiled and blinked back the tears blurring her vision. 'That I love you? Totally. Completely. How could you not know?'

Tristan felt such a deep surge of joy well up inside him he thought it would burst out. He grabbed Lily off the chair and hauled her onto his lap, crushed her mouth beneath his.

When he finally let her up for air he felt a sense of rightness with the world, but he could see by the way she gnawed her top lip that she still had questions.

'What is it?'

'I was just remembering yesterday morning, when you came

out of the bathroom. You looked…you looked unhappy…and then you told Jordana—'

'Oh, Lily,' Tristan said on a groan. 'Please forget that. I woke up that morning with such a sense of well-being it scared the hell out of me. Honestly, I just wanted to get away from you. I've never woken up with a woman before and—'

'Never?'

He shook his head. 'Never. And then Jordana cornered me and guessed how I felt before I did and it drove me deeper into denial. I didn't want to let you in, Lily, but of course you were already there, and I was fighting a losing battle. It wasn't until Oliver told me how he felt about Jordana and the reasons he was marrying her that I finally realised I felt the same way about you. And I didn't want to fight it—you—any more. I'd do anything for you, Lily, and after we're married we'll—'

'Married!'

'Of course married. Where did you think this was headed, sweetheart? A picnic in the park?'

'I…I didn't think that far ahead. I'm still reeling from the fact that you love me.'

'I know neither of us has had the best role models when it comes to marriage—'

'Well, my father never actually asked my mother to marry him,' Lily said.

Tristan nodded and cupped her face between his hands. 'I'm not your father, Lily. I'll never cheat on you or leave you. And I don't believe a marriage has to be full of conflict if a couple are equally committed and willing to work through any issues together.'

Lily's smile was tremulous. 'You really love me?'

'Haven't I just said that?'

'It just seems like a dream.'

'It's not. At least I hope it's not.'

Lily sighed and let Tristan gather her close, revelling in the feel of his hands moulding to her torso and fitting her against him. She could hardly believe this was happening, and knew Jordana would be ecstatic when she found out.

Then a thought struck, and she pulled back a little to look up into his beautiful face. 'You know I knew nothing about Jordana setting me up with Oliver's cousins last night?'

Tristan smiled. 'I know. I figured that out some time between the first and second bottle of Scotch I consumed last night.'

'Oh.' Lily laughed.

'It's not funny.' He grinned back at her. 'You were the reason I saw the bottom of both of those bottles. But I have a feeling that my sister has been playing a little reverse matchmaking between us.'

'I did wonder about that myself...'

'And it worked. I nearly locked you in a tower last night after she said you'd told her you were just cutting loose with me.'

'I *did* say that.'

'What?' he asked, stunned.

'I didn't want her to know how deeply I had fallen for you and after overhearing how you felt. I...I have my pride, you know.'

'I know you do.'

'And, anyway, you don't have a tower.'

'I'd have built one for just that purpose,' he growled, his hands exploring the fitted bodice of her gown with increasing fervour.

'I love you,' Lily sighed.

'I never knew those three little words could sound so delicious.'

'Oh, I've just remembered. I'm supposed to be flying to New York tonight. I'll have to cancel the flight.'

'Damned straight. But when *do* you have to return to New York? For work?'

'I don't have any films lined up until next year. I was planning to take some time off.'

'Perfect.'

'Although...'

'Although?'

'I'm thinking of taking the role of my mother in that play I was telling you about.'

Tristan kissed her. 'I think that's a wonderful idea. You'll slay them. As you do me. Now, let's go upstairs.'

'Upstairs?'

'I organised a room.'

'But the Abbey is only two miles away.'

'That's two miles too far if I'm going to be able to make love to you with any level of skill and control.'

'I'm quite partial to what we've done so far,' Lily whispered, feathering the silky hair at his nape between her fingers.

'And I'm quite partial to you, my darling Honey Blossom Lily Wild.'

He bent to kiss her again but Lily dodged him. 'We have your sister's wedding to finish first.'

'Believe me, after the way we exited the dance floor nobody is expecting to see us back any time soon.'

'But I need to catch the bridal bouquet,' Lily protested as Tristan gathered her up in his arms and strode for the door.

'Why do you need a bouquet when you've got your groom right here?'

'I hadn't thought of that,' she admitted provocatively. 'Good thing you're here.'

Tristan stopped and caught her chin between his thumb and forefinger, raising her eyes to his. 'I'll always be here for you,' he said, capturing her lips in a sweet, searing kiss.

Lily's mouth trembled with emotion as she stared into Tristan's loving green gaze, happier than she had ever been in her whole life. 'And I you.'

\* \* \* \* \*

# THE FORBIDDEN TOUCH OF SANGUARDO

**JULIA JAMES**

To the utterly unforgettable holidays I've been privileged to have in Hawaii which inspired the romantic setting for Celeste and Rafael (and yes, I did go on a star-gazing expedition just like they did!!!!)

# CHAPTER ONE

CELESTE STOOD POISED at the head of the long curving flight of marble stairs that led down into the great hall below. It was already crowded with people in black tie and evening clothes, and servers were circulating with trays of champagne and canapés. Her fellow models for the evening were mingling in evening dress, prior to the charity fashion show that was about to start. She had arrived slightly late at the stately home in Oxfordshire that was the evening's venue, but had seized the last-minute opportunity to be here tonight, well away from London—and from Karl Reiner.

Celeste's expression tautened even just from her thinking about the man. She had known when she became the new face of Blonde Visage, one of the skincare ranges belonging to Reiner Visage—one for each complexion type—that Karl Reiner liked to have a more than professional relationship with the Reiner Visage models, but because he had been preoccupied with another 'face'—Monique Silva—Celeste had felt it safe to allow herself to be tempted by the lucrative contract. Making good, regular money was, even after years in the fickle and intensely competitive modelling business, not something to turn down lightly.

A bleak expression lit the back of her eyes.

There was never, *ever,* any such thing as easy money— She of all people should know that...

For now Karl had tired of Monique and was turning his

attention to Celeste—and he assumed she would be as willing as Monique had been.

Celeste's expression hardened. Karl Reiner could assume what he liked, but he would not get what he was after from her. Not even now he had flown in from New York this weekend specifically to pressure her to extend her contract—and pay the price he wanted her to pay for it.

Well, she would not be extending it. Yes, the money had been good, but these days making money was not the be all and end all of her preoccupations. A cold miasma seemed to touch at her skin. Not any more...

Her refusal was a message Karl Reiner didn't want to hear, and he had demanded she make herself available to have dinner with him in London tonight. To evade him Celeste had been obliged to volunteer at a late hour for the charity fashion show that was shortly to take place in the grand salon.

Just thinking about Karl Reiner and what he wanted of her—what he thought she would provide—intensified the feeling of a cold miasma on her skin. It was penetrating into her like a toxic memory, fetid and foul...

With effort, she pushed it from her mind.

*No!* She would not think—would not remember.

She had dealt with those memories long ago! Paid the price for dealing with them—a price she was still paying, must always pay—and it was a price she paid because there was no alternative. Could never be.

All she could do was what she had done for years now—build her career, focus only on that. Be dedicated, hardworking.

On her own.

Always on her own.

For a last fleeting moment the bleakness showed in her eyes again. She knew far too well the price she was paying for those memories whose dank tendrils dragged across her flesh.

A stab of self-revulsion jabbed at her. Once she had lacerated herself with such stabs, but she gave herself a mental shake. She would not let anything drag her mind down such dark pathways. She was here tonight to do a job. One she had done a hundred times before.

Yet as she gathered her long skirts gracefully, preparing to descend into the thronged hall below, something stayed her for one last moment. She felt as if something *were* different tonight. As if she were poised on the edge of her familiar world. On the threshold of a new one.

Then, with a sharp, dismissive intake of breath, she took a step forward and started to move down the staircase. There was no new world awaiting her. There could not be.

She did not need the echo of that trailing miasma across her skin to tell her that…

Rafael Sanguardo stood, empty champagne glass loosely held in long fingers, and let his dark gaze rest on his opulently baroque surroundings, painted and gilded to profusion. It was an irony not lost on him that, as one of the sponsors of the charity, he should be a guest here—considering that it had been the exploited wealth of the Americas that had built this eighteenth-century splendour and that it had been the labour of his *peon* ancestors, albeit under Spanish colonial masters and not British ones, who had so signally contributed to this display of old-world wealth.

But now history had turned its wheel of fortune. In the global village of the twenty-first century it was the industrious entrepreneurship of former colonials who generated much of the world's wealth—and Rafael Sanguardo knew he could count himself one of their number.

Thanks to his own intelligence, determination and drive, he had transformed himself in little more than a dozen years from an orphaned teenager living in one of the smallest of the string of countries stretching from Mexico to Colombia, via a philanthropic scholarship to a prestigious North American university, into a serial entrepreneur who had backed a succession of highly successful companies and who could now, had he so wished, have made his home in just such a palatial pile as the one he was tonight a guest in.

That was not his preference, however. He was footloose, preferring to rent apartments in London and New York and stay in hotels in whichever other countries he did business in. 'Settling down' was not on his agenda.

Not any more.

Madeline had seen to that.

Into his head stabbed the last words she had thrown at him. Mocking. Furious. Thwarted.

*'Why, Rafe, darling, what a puritan you are!'*

But her taunting had masked anger, lashing out at him. Repelling him as much as what she had disclosed to him had repelled him.

Repelled him still…

He pulled his thoughts away. Madeline was history. Out of his life. And she should be out of his head, too. She was not worth even the memory…

There was only one thing Madeline was worth—had only ever been worth—and that was what was most precious to her.

*Money.*

Rafael's mouth tightened. His eyes darkened. Well, now Madeline had all the money she craved—but money was all she had. Even though she had once craved more. Memory darkened his expression again. She had once craved *him*—craved everything that had once been between them.

Their affair had lit up like a torch between them. It had been a match that had seemed to be ideally cast. He the self-made, darkly handsome Latino multimillionaire, she the British flame-haired British beauty whose business abilities had made her as rich as him. They had been a wealthy, glamorous couple, cutting a swathe wherever they went.

Then it had ended.

Like an unwelcome replay, he saw the scene inside his head yet again.

*Madeline was looking at him. Looking at him with her almond-shaped emerald eyes from where she lay on the bed, her fabulous auburn hair tumbling sensuously around her naked shoulders. Her lush, peaked breasts were on show for him. So was the rest of her curved, enticing body. She lay, lounging back on the pillows. Alluring. Seductive.*

*'Now tell me you don't want me, Rafe, darling,' she purred.*

*She let her thighs slacken, easing her hand sensually along the divide between her legs.*

*He walked to the bedroom door. Turned to look at her. Still repelled.*

*'Be gone by the time I get back,' he told her.*

*Then he left.*

*He heard her laughter—that rich, mocking laughter— infused with what he knew was a jibing anger at him for his rejection of her, following him as he shut the front door of his apartment behind him.*

It tried to follow him still, that mocking, jibing, angry laughter, as he knew she wanted it to.

But its power was gone.

Just as Madeline had gone. Out of his life—totally.

Now even the thought of Madeline repelled him. As did everything about her…her looks, her attitude, her ambition, her values. *Everything*.

A hovering waiter pulled him back to where he was, and with a slight smile of thanks Rafael placed his glass on the extended tray. As he turned back, something caught his eye.

Some*one*.

Walking down the sweeping staircase with an aura about her that made his gaze focus piercingly. Taking in every-thing about her.

*Pale beauty. Hair caught in a chignon the colour of cham-pagne at the nape of her swan-like neck. Her face was in profile. Perfect profile. As perfect as her tall, slender body, sheathed in a single-shouldered ecru gown that moulded slight breasts, draped slender hips and dropped down long, long legs to skim slim ankles, revealed by the draping of her skirts, around which snaked the clasp of her heeled evening shoes.*

She must surely be one of the models, he realised. Her height, her slenderness, the way she held herself, the way she wore her clearly couture gown—all indicated that. As she reached the foot of the stairs she blended into the throng and was lost to his view. He craned his head a moment, seeking her, but could not see her.

A sense of frustration at her disappearance caught at him. Then he stilled, frowning for a quite different reason. A jolt of realisation.

This was the first woman who had caught his attention since he had severed all links with Madeline—

Oh, plenty of women had sought his attention—he was well used to that—but in the grim aftermath of Madeline none had been of any interest to him.

*So what is it about this one?*

Yet even as the question formed he knew it was redundant. He could answer it immediately.

*She is nothing at all like Madeline!*

Madeline's richly hued flashy beauty and her egoistic temperament had demanded that everyone look at her. The pale girl descending the staircase had looked as cool as Madeline had been fiery.

But there was more to the difference than looks, he sensed. Madeline would have descended the grand staircase like a drama queen, wanting everyone to gaze at her. To admire and envy her. To desire her.

This pale blonde girl had slipped down the steps as quietly as a ghost—as if she were not quite part of this world, as if she wanted no eyes drawn to her. Odd, he mused, in someone who was a model. If, of course, she *was* one.

Well, he thought, impatient to see her again, if she were, he had better go and take his seat and find out.

One thing he knew with certainty: whoever the pale, elusive blonde was, he wanted to see her again. His dark eyes glinted. Finally he'd seen a woman to spark his interest—an interest he definitely wanted to pursue. Would that interest survive acquaintance with her? Or would getting to know her put him off, despite that incredible pale beauty of hers?

*Will she prove as flawed as Madeline?*

That was the question that haunted him.

# CHAPTER TWO

THE MUSIC WAS starting up—glitteringly baroque Vivaldi to suit the era of the house—and in well-practised order the models issued out onto the runway constructed down the centre of the long salon.

The first gown was the same one the models had worn while mingling with the guests, and Celeste was glad of it. It was exactly the kind of gown she would have chosen for herself, had she been a guest. Flattering, but revealing nothing more than a bare shoulder, and in one of the pale colours that she liked. Another model had once told her she must like disappearing into the background. Celeste had only smiled slightly. But the girl had been right, for all that.

Muted, understated, discreet—those were the fashion watchwords she adhered to. And one more, too.

Modest.

Not for her, in her own clothes, plunging necklines or thigh-skimming hemlines. Even on the beach she preferred a one-piece.

Now, as she swished along the runway, she felt the tension that had assailed her as she'd stood at the top of the stairs evaporate. Years of experience as a model made this kind of tightly choreographed display second nature to her, and she walked with assurance and poise until, at the foot of the runway, she paused to reverse her direction.

And froze.

*Dark, long-lashed eyes, focussed on her. A shadowed face with lean cheeks, incised features. A mouth with deep lines around it. A sculpted jawline. Night-dark hair.*

For a timeless moment the impression carved itself into her vision. Then, with a jolt, she knew she must start walking again. Jerkily, she paced back up to the head of the runway and was swept offstage into the melee of the changing area, to emerge minutes later in a vivid scarlet evening gown. All the way down the runway she was conscious of the man sitting at the far end. Wondering whether he'd be watching her.

Hectically, her thoughts tumbled inside her head. She'd been eyed up often enough in her time as a model—and even though she didn't like it she never let it affect her.

So why had this man's regard so affected her? Why had it impacted on her in the few seconds she'd had to register it? What was so different about it? About him…?

As she neared the end of the runway she steeled herself for that dark, penetrating gaze—which didn't come. As she glanced briefly in his direction she saw that his attention was on his mobile phone. He was tapping in a text, long legs extended, completely ignoring her.

Immediately she felt her tension drop. She turned, skilfully manoeuvring her skirts, and plunged back up the runway. *So much for that!* she thought, with a wry dart of self-mockery.

Had she turned her head again, however, she might have felt differently.

Rafael's eyes had lifted from his phone and were settled, instead, on her retreating form. They went on watching until she disappeared. Then, and only then, did he resume his tapping.

He found, however, that his mind was not on his emails.

The show was over, the applause was dying away and guests were heading off for the buffet supper awaiting them in the dining room across the entrance hall.

Rafael got to his feet. There was a sense of purpose about him. The models would be mingling with the guests again and he wanted to find her—stake his claim before anyone else could be as drawn to her pale, haunting beauty as he was.

But as his eyes searched the crowded dining room it came to him that she simply was not there. The other models were—but not the one he wanted to see. He frowned. So where was she? He crossed the hallway back into the salon, where the runway was being dismantled by workmen. Still no sign of her.

He saw that a glass door to the side was open, and slipped through on impulse. He found himself out on a terrace and walked down it to the end. Turning the corner, he saw gardens stretching out before him. Steps swept down to the level of the lawns.

A figure had paused at the edge. A female figure, her evening gown pale in the dim light, craning her neck upwards. But she wasn't looking back at the mansion. She was looking up at the night sky.

Rafael's dark eyes glinted in the starlight and he started to walk down the steps towards her.

Celeste was gazing upwards, rapt. It was a glorious starry night! In London stars were, at best, dim and hazy. But here in the countryside they were bright and vivid, the mighty sweep of the Milky Way clear in the heavens. So unimaginably distant...

Once she had wanted only to be taken up amongst them, leaving the earth far, far behind...

'The ancient Chinese believed that the Milky Way was the source of the Yellow River.'

The voice came from behind her.

Celeste swirled round. There was little light, but she did not need light to tell her who this was. It was the man who had been looking at her as she'd walked along the runway.

The man who had made her aware of him as no man ever had...

He was heading towards her. She could not see his features, only his height, his strolling elegance as he came to stand beside her. She heard the deep, accented timbre of his voice as he spoke again. Felt her nerve-endings start to send messages to her she did *not* want to feel!

'They have a legend,' he went on, 'that says two lovers were cruelly parted by their parents and placed on either side of the Milky Way—the galactic river. We see them as stars, forever gazing at each other.'

He was looking at her as he spoke. Taking in her frozen stance, the sudden tension in her face. She looked, he thought, as if she was going to bolt—a reaction he found unusual in a woman. Long experience had taught him that women welcomed his attentions.

Madeline certainly had.

*But she is not Madeline.*

And that was what he wanted, he reminded himself. For her to be utterly different. So it was good that she was reacting as she was, wasn't it? But whatever the reason for her radiating wariness on all frequencies he wanted to dispel it.

'It's incredible, isn't it?' he said, keeping his tone conversational. 'To think of the vast distances of the heavens. Our galaxy is just one of billions, each with billions of stars.' He frowned slightly. 'Some of the stars we think of as stars are galaxies themselves. Andromeda is our closest, and it is...' He searched the sky with his eyes.

'It's there,' Celeste heard herself saying. 'In the Andromeda constellation, between Pegasus and Cassiopeia. The galaxy is M31—Messier body thirty-one—but it's not actually the closest galaxy to us, only to the Milky Way overall. It's going to merge with the Milky Way eventually, and form a giant elliptical galaxy in a few billion years.'

She pointed jerkily upwards, mentally castigating herself

for gabbling about galaxies and constellations, but other than marching away it had seemed the safest thing to do.

Though 'safe' was the very last thing she felt...

Her nerve-endings were firing in a way that she had never before experienced.

Rafael followed her gaze, then glanced across at her. Wanting to look at her. Wanting her to look at him. Wanting her to speak again.

He smiled appreciatively. 'You're very knowledgeable,' he remarked.

'I like stars,' she answered, in the same abrupt, jerky manner. 'They're very far away.'

Even as she spoke she started. *Why did I say that? Why am I standing here talking to him—letting him talk to me?*

And why was the deep, accented timbre of his voice reaching into her? Disturbing her...firing all her nerves at high pitch...

'Is that a commendation?' he asked dryly.

'Yes,' she answered.

As if she'd realised it was a strange thing to say, he saw her give a tiny shake of her head. As she did so, he saw her change. She dipped her head, tightened her grip on her skirts. Getting a grip, belatedly, on the situation. A situation she was going to terminate right now. Because she did not let situations like this arise.

*But there's never been a situation like this...no man has ever made me react like this!*

Which made it all the more imperative that she get away from him—right now! Stop this before it started.

'Excuse me,' she said. 'I must go back inside.'

Her voice had changed, too. It was clipped now, and quite impersonal.

Distant.

'Permit me to escort you.' Rafael's voice was smooth.

She did not hesitate. 'Thank you—no.'

Her tone was decisive, and before his eyes she turned and walked back up the steps. He looked after her.

From chatting about stars to cutting him dead—all in under a minute.

No, nothing like Madeline at all…

Celeste gained the salon and walked rapidly across it. Her heart-rate was up, and it was not because of her rapid ascent of the exterior steps. What on earth had she just gone and done? Standing there with that man, talking about astronomy! She'd gone out to the gardens for two reasons—to take advantage of the clear night sky and to delay having to mix socially. Because over supper she would inevitably see that man again.

The man who had come in search of her.

Because of course that was what he'd been doing! She wasn't an idiot—no one struck up a conversation about galaxies with a lone female if they weren't trying to chat her up! Then, to make her heart-rate race even more, a mortifying thought struck her. Had he thought she was standing out there stargazing in order to deliberately invite him to talk to her?

She felt her cheeks flush. Well, it didn't matter. It didn't matter either way. Because from now on she was going to avoid him totally until she could decently get away back to Oxford and the hotel room she'd booked. Staying well out of London and away from Karl Reiner for as long as possible.

But she didn't want to think about the repulsive Karl Reiner. And she didn't want to think about the man who had set her nerve-endings firing, elevated her heart-rate. A man who did not repel her.

Who attracted her—

*No!* A little twist of bitterness clenched inside her. What did it matter if, however inexplicably, he attracted her? It didn't matter! It *couldn't* matter.

*It could never matter…*

A dull, familiar stab jabbed at her.

*I am what my past has made me and nothing can change that—nothing!*

And men—all men—could be nothing of her present now.

Face set, she gained the dining room, forcing herself to take a breath—to assume the appearance, if nothing else, of calm. She made her way to one of the buffet tables around the edge, glad to see Zoe, a fellow model, there. They helped themselves to some undressed salad and a slice of chicken each.

'So,' said Zoe invitingly as they started to eat their meagre portions, 'what are you going to do about the guy who couldn't take his eyes off you? Has he made a move on you already?'

Celeste tensed. 'No,' she lied, trying to sound nonchalant.

'Shame,' said the other girl. '*I'd* go for him. Looks *and* dosh! Rafael Sanguardo. South American. He's a zillionaire investor. Used to hang out with that glitzy redhead on the *Top Ten Rich Women* list—Madeline Walters. Hotshot and hot totty! She made a fortune for herself and headed for the States to make another pile of dough. Of course…' she threw a sly glance at Celeste '…*you've* got Karl Reiner panting around after you, haven't you? Now he's through with Monique Silva. Mind you,' she added, 'I know which man *I'd* rather have in bed beside me! Señor Tall, Dark and *Very* Handsome Sanguardo! Creepy Karl wouldn't get a look-in!' She drew breath. 'Well, I'd better network. Plenty of useful contacts out there—and loads of loaded guys! And standing here by all this food is torture. See you!'

She sauntered off, leaving Celeste to her supper and her thoughts.

Rafael Sanguardo…

The name glided through her head. She'd never heard of him, but from the way Zoe had talked about him it sounded as if he was on the 'Mr Available and Rich' list that a lot of models made it their business to know about. She speared a sliver of chicken with decided resolve. Rafael Sanguardo was none of *her* business, and he would stay that way.

'May I help you to something more from the buffet?'

The deep, faintly accented voice addressing her was familiar.

And very unwelcome.

She turned. It was Rafael Sanguardo.

Celeste felt herself tense automatically. But not just because he was the one person here she wanted to avoid. For the first time she was seeing him in full light, rather than dim glimpses. And everything she'd glimpsed about him was overwhelmingly reinforced. He was, just as Zoe had flippantly called him, Mr Tall, Dark and *Very* Handsome! But it was not smooth, playboy-style looks that he possessed. His face was lean, with a tough-looking jawline, high cheekbones and a strong nose. But it wasn't those features that held her. It was the eyes.

They were dark—incredibly dark—with a hawkish look to them, and they were resting on her with an expression in them that instantly made her breathless.

*How? How is this happening?* she thought with a hollowing of her stomach. It *never* happened! Men could look her over and she'd be immune to it! Immune the way she *had* to be. But this man—*somehow*—was having this extraordinary effect on her, and she didn't know why.

All she knew, with a surge of intense self-preserving urgency, was that she had to stop it happening. Had to stop looking at him—stop looking at the way his long, lean body, darkly clad in what she knew must be a hand-tailored tuxedo, easily topped six feet, the way his DJ moulded his shoulders. His gleaming white dress shirt performed the same office for his torso, telling her that his physique was as honed as the planes of his face.

He was addressing her again, in that deep, accented voice that did things to her she did not want it to do! What had he just said? She had to reply—say something, anything—then walk away! *Food—he asked you about food! Do you want any? That was it.*

With effort, she found a brief reply. 'Thank you, but this is enough,' she managed to say.

An eyebrow quirked over the incredibly dark eyes that looked as if they were hewn from some ancient, volcanic rock. *Basalt,* she thought, *or obsidian...darker than slate.*

'It doesn't look enough for a sparrow,' he murmured. The dark eyes glanced at her. 'Fortunately you don't appear to have the starved, size-zero look about you that so many models have.'

Celeste could hear condemnation of excessive thinness in his voice. 'Models *have* to be thin!' she was stung into retorting. She was not objecting to his criticism of size-zero models, but to the way his eyes had washed over her. The effect that slow wash had had on her...

'It's shamefully perverse for women in the developed world to ape those who go hungry from necessity, not fashion!' he returned sharply.

She took a breath, making herself answer honestly. 'You are right,' she admitted.

For a moment she let her eyes meet his in acknowledgement of the truth of what he had just said. It was a mistake. For one endless moment she had the strangest sensation that she was drowning—drowning in a deep, fathomless ocean. Then, with an effort, she pulled her gaze away. Found that she was trembling with the effort.

'I'm sorry—that was very blunt of me,' she heard him respond. 'Though it is a pity that you will not try some of these richer foods.' He indicated the lavish spread in front of them.

Celeste glanced at them, and then back at the man who was so disturbing her. 'They do look delicious,' she allowed. 'But I mustn't.'

'You won't be tempted?' he said.

There was a trace of humour now in his accented voice. A trace that did yet more disturbing things to her. As did the glint in his eyes that told her it was more than food he wanted her to be tempted by.

She gave a decisive shake of her head. Time to stop this—right now.

'No,' she replied. Her voice was polite, but firm. She put down her now empty plate. Looked back at him. Made herself look at him but not react to him. Made herself say in a polite, social voice, using just the sort of tone she might use to anyone at all, 'Do please excuse me, but I have to circulate and show off this dress.'

She gave a smile—brief, polite, perfunctory. But this time she did not meet his eyes. Instead, she turned away, tall and graceful, and threaded her way into the throng.

Behind her, Rafael watched her disappear. Her second disappearing act of the evening.

*Why? Why does she run from me?*

That was the question uppermost in his mind—except for his overwhelming consciousness that in this second all too brief encounter his interest in her had not diminished, but intensified.

*There is something about her that is drawing me to her—something powerful, irresistible, overwhelming.*

Something that was sending a pulse through him. Something that was engendered by that extraordinary pale, pure beauty she possessed—the turn of her head, the flawless translucence of her alabaster skin, the perfect features of her face, delicate and exquisitely cut, the clear, luminous grey-blue of her eyes.

He knew with absolute certainty that he had felt something when she had turned that gaze on him, fully meeting his own—it was a gaze whose very brevity had told him that whatever the cause of her insistence on walking away from him, which she had now exhibited twice—it was not because she was irresponsive to him.

*It is the same for her as it is for me! I know it. The stillness, the betraying dilation of her pupils, the sudden intake of breath, the collision of her eyes with mine—acknowledges, confirms her reaction to me—*

It had told him all he needed to know...

Whatever had made her walk away, it was not because she was immune to him. So why had she? An unwelcome explanation intruded. Was it because she was already involved elsewhere? A burning urge to find out consumed him. Yet he did not even know her name.

He inhaled sharply, pulling himself together. It would be easy enough to find out everything he needed to know about her. She was a model, she worked for an agency, and that meant the information was out there. And if the answer was the one he realised he wanted it to be more with every passing moment, then he would set out to woo her—woo her and win her.

His imagination raced ahead, vivid and eager.

In his mind's eye he saw himself gazing into her eyes, clasping her hand, drawing her towards him, taking her slender, pliant body into his arms and lowering his mouth to her tremulous, tender lips, tasting their sweetness, seeking the nectar within, feeling her respond to his embrace, her body contouring against his with soft sensuousness, glowing with honeyed desire as her breasts peaked against him...

But imagination was not enough! He wanted the reality.

The reality of her pale, pure beauty, which was calling to him with a subtly compelling, insistent power that was impossible to deny.

# CHAPTER THREE

'YOU WANT MORE money to renew your contract. That's it, isn't it?' Karl Reiner's voice grated.

Celeste kept her expression fixed. Karl Reiner had demanded her presence at a dinner in a West End hotel hosted by a fashion magazine keen on retaining its share of the lavish Reiner Visage advertising budget. Since she was still—just—under contract, it had been impossible for her to decline.

She deeply wished she had. Wished she could just walk off the way she had when Rafael Sanguardo had made a move on her at the charity event the previous weekend.

Not, she found herself thinking, that anyone in their right mind would put Karl Reiner and Rafael Sanguardo in the same class. The difference was total. Karl's stocky stature and slack belly were the complete opposite of Rafael Sanguardo's tall, lean, honed physique—just as Karl's pouched, close-set eyes were a million miles from the dark, hawkish eyes that had rested so disturbingly on her. And Karl's receding dyed hair, swept back into a ponytail that he mistakenly seemed to think made him look creative and bohemian, had nothing of the feathered sable of the South American's.

Yet again Celeste felt the disquieting quickening of her pulse as an image of Rafael Sanguardo took shape in her mind. It had been doing so repeatedly ever since the weekend. She had tried desperately hard to put him out of her

mind but it had been impossible—just impossible! She could
bewail it all she liked, try as hard as she could, but it was no
good. That encounter, however brief, had imprinted itself on
her. Why, she did not know—could not understand. Could
not understand why her habitual immunity to men was failing her so pitiably when it came to Rafael Sanguardo.

But if she couldn't understand it at least she could do her
determined best to ignore it. Suppress it and crush it out of
her consciousness—out of her life. There was no point—
none whatsoever!—in thinking about him.

What Rafael Sanguardo wanted was not what she was
free to want...

An old, familiar ripple of revulsion went through her.
Those slimy trails across her skin—fetid memory made tangible.

And with Karl Reiner pressingly at her side tonight, making her skin crawl, revulsion came afresh. Recrimination
came in its wake. Why, oh, why had she ever got involved
with Reiner Visage?

But she knew the reason now—just as she had long ago.
Rejection seared within her.

*This is different! Entirely different! Karl Reiner can as-
sume what he likes. I will never go along with it!*

Nor was there anything he could say that would make her
sign a new contract. She would simply go on stonewalling
him, staying as composed and as civil as she could, until she
was free in a few weeks' time.

But his persistent unwanted attentions were becoming
even harder than ever to endure. He was badgering her repeatedly to renew her contract, and this evening he had
drunk freely, and she could see his temper mounting at her
continued refusal. Now, dinner over and guests dispersing,
he'd renewed the subject in the middle of the hotel lobby.

'No,' she said carefully, 'it's nothing to do with more
money. I simply don't wish to extend my contract any further. I've been very appreciative of it, naturally—'

'That's not the message you're giving out.' Karl cut across her brusquely.

Tight-lipped, Celeste refused to react. She knew very well that the cause of his pique was nothing to do with her not renewing her contract—it was because she wasn't going to do what Monique Silva had done: show her 'appreciation' in bed.

Anger flashed across Karl's face. 'Who the hell do you think you are?' he demanded. 'Models are ten cents a dozen!'

'As I say,' she repeated tightly, 'I've been very appreciative of the opportunity to represent the Blonde range of Reiner Visage, but—'

'But nothing!' He cut across her again. His face was set petulantly. 'I've done you favours! Now it's payback time! You damn well *know* what I want!'

He grabbed at her arm, closing his fingers around it. She halted, turning an icy gaze on him.

'Take your hand off me,' she bit out, jaw clenched. When he made no move to do so, she simply lifted his hand off her and stepped away. 'Good*night,* Mr Rainer,' she said decisively, and turned to go.

Infuriated, and despite the presence of other people in the lobby, he lurched at her, grabbing at her wrist again, yanking her round forcibly. His face was contorted in fury.

'Don't walk off, you stuck-up little bitch! Who the hell do you think you are? Behaving like a goddamn nun!' he snarled at her.

The alcoholic fumes of his breath reached her. His voice was loud and carrying.

'I can pick and choose any model I want—you hear me? And they'll be *grateful!* Girls like you put out for anyone who'll hire you! And since I've hired you you'll damn well put out for *me!* You're no different! You're just a two-bit whore like every other model!'

Celeste gasped in shock. For a second she could not move. Then, behind her, a voice cut through.

'Let her go,' it said. It was arctic. 'Let her go and get out of here before I throw you out onto the pavement.'

Karl's head swivelled. 'Who the hell are *you?*' he snarled slurringly.

Rafael did not answer him. He simply yanked Karl's hand away, then took his shoulder and elbow in a punishing grip and frogmarched him to the door, ejecting him onto the pavement.

'If you try and come back in,' he said pleasantly, 'I will pulverise you. Do you understand me?'

He didn't bother to wait for a reply, just went back into the lobby. His eyes went immediately to the frozen figure standing there, her ashen pallor registering her shock. He went up to her.

'Brandy,' he said. 'Don't argue. Then I'll see you home—and don't argue about that either. That charmless jerk is out on the pavement.'

She couldn't respond. Couldn't do anything except stand there, the vile echo of Karl's accusation slicing through her head.

*'You're just a two-bit whore like every other model!'*

Her face contorted and she felt nausea rise in her throat, foul and choking. Then, from nowhere, her elbow was being taken—not tightly, but firmly—and she was being guided across the lobby and into the hotel bar. Her steps were halting, but she went all the same. Numbness filled her.

Then, as she was helped up onto a bar stool, the numbness was suddenly pierced. Karl Reiner and his vile words disappeared from her consciousness. Replaced, totally, by the realisation of just who it was that was at her side now.

Her eyes flew to the man, tall and lean in a charcoal tailored lounge suit that only emphasised his naturally tanned complexion, who was taking his seat beside her.

Dear God—it was Rafael Sanguardo!

Shock ravined through her. Shock and something much more. Instant awareness, instant consciousness of everything about him that she had sought to suppress these past few days. To force down out of her memory.

Yet he was here now, in all his overwhelming, potent physical presence. Sitting beside her and looking at her with an expression of concern on his face, his dark eyes resting on her.

She hauled her gaze away. She could not cope with this—not now. Not after Karl Reiner's vile outburst. She could feel herself start to shake.

Immediately she heard Rafael Sanguardo speak. 'It's all right. He's gone. And he won't be coming back.'

He spoke with certainty, and an underlying grimness. Her eyes lifted to him again.

But he was not looking at her. He had turned his head to address the barman. 'Two brandies, please.'

As he gave his order he made a notable effort to control his emotions. They were surging strongly. One was an impulse to stride right out onto the pavement, seize hold of the jerk who had said what he had to the ashen-faced, shaken figure beside him and slam his fist into his foul-mouthed face. It took him aback, just how strong that urge was. A wave of protectiveness swept over him.

*No one's going to hurl that kind of abuse at her!*

The protectiveness he was feeling was almost overpowering... But him slamming his fist into her abuser was not what she needed right now! What she needed was to stop shaking, to pull out of the shocked state she was clearly in after that vicious little scene back there with Karl Reiner.

He knew who the man was, all right. Just as he now knew the name of the woman who had been dominating his thoughts ever since he'd laid eyes on her.

Celeste Philips—that was her name. It had taken little effort to discover it, courtesy of the organisers of the charity fashion show, simply by describing her. After that her professional bio had been easy to find via her agency. She was currently contracted to Reiner Visage—of which cosmetics company the unlovely Karl Reiner was President. Nor had it taken much digging to uncover Karl Reiner's even more unlovely reputation for pursuing the models he contracted.

A reputation that the ugly incident just now more than amply confirmed.

The two glasses of brandy were placed in front of him and he slid one towards Celeste.

'Drink it down,' he instructed. 'You're in shock.'

But Celeste gave a quick, jerky shake of her head. 'No—no brandy.' Her voice was slightly high-pitched. In her head she could hear Karl's foul words snarling at her again. Hear his vile accusation…

She fought to stay calm, at least on the surface. Inside was different…

'Coffee, then—you need something. You're white as a sheet.'

She lifted her face, made herself look at the man who had rescued her. The man she couldn't get out of her head. Who was now here, beside her, dominating her consciousness. 'I'm fine. It was just—' She stopped. Swallowed painfully.

'Damn,' said Rafael feelingly. 'I should have hit him. Trouble is…' his voice was deadpan '…I might have spoilt his looks.'

For a moment Celeste was on a knife-edge. Then the balance tipped, giving her a safety net, letting her pull herself together. The laconically uttered insult to the drunken, obnoxious Karl had retrieved her sufficiently for her to manage to find the darkly wry humour clearly intended in the remark.

She bit her lip. 'That's a low blow,' she heard herself murmur.

'The lower the better,' Rafael agreed. 'Low enough to… ah…quell his unwanted ardour.'

She gave a shaky smile, not quite meeting his eyes. She might be pulling out of the shock of what Karl had snarled at her, but that only meant she was now having to cope with this completely unanticipated encounter with Rafael Sanguardo. And cope she must—somehow.

And she must start with the most important priority. Gratitude.

She lifted her eyes again. 'Thank you,' she said. 'Thank you for what you did back there.'

For just a moment, as her eyes met his, she felt weak—as weak as a kitten. The blood seemed to be flooding back into her ashen cheeks, heating them. She could not drag her gaze away—his eyes were holding her...holding her as if there was a physical link between them...as if they were bound together...

She saw something shift at the back of his eyes—his dark, basalt-black eyes. Something that seemed to set every nerve-ending in her body jangling.

Then, with a quick movement of his head, he broke the moment. *'De nada,'* he said lightly. His tone of voice changed. 'So, coffee?' he said enquiringly. 'Or tea, maybe? Isn't that what the English drink to settle their nerves?'

'China tea would be lovely, thank you,' she assented, grateful for something so normal. She needed to feel normal again—needed it badly.

As Rafael Sanguardo relayed her request to the barman she felt the backwash of what Karl had said to her start to fade. Her state of shock was ebbing, and so, too, finally, was the sense of incessant strain she'd been under all evening. But even as it ebbed a new emotion replaced it—the shimmering awareness of the man beside her.

Who had appeared out of nowhere to wrest Karl Reiner off her—

'I don't understand,' she heard herself say. 'How did you come to be here like this?'

There was bewilderment in her voice.

'I've been meeting one of my UK CEOs for dinner,' Rafael replied. 'But I have to say...' His tone of voice changed again, and his gaze rested on her. 'I now understand the meaning of that English proverb that it is an ill wind that blows no one any good.'

He looked at her, but Celeste was blank. Rafael enlightened her.

'Even though I would not wish Karl Reiner on anyone, at least he has given me the opportunity not only to be of some small service to you—he has also provided exactly the opportunity I have been wanting to take since the weekend.' He paused deliberately, still looking at her. 'To see you again,' he said.

A troubled expression lit her face.

He saw it and said, his voice low, 'Would that be so very unwelcome to you?'

She bit her lip. She wanted to find some way—a polite, considerate way, especially after his rescuing her from Karl—of telling him that what he wanted was impossible... just impossible!

Rafael saw her silence, needed to know if there was one reason that would be an immovable obstacle for him.

'Is there someone else in your life right now?'

She swallowed, her expression still troubled. 'No, but—' She halted, not knowing what to say. How to say it.

Her hesitation was visible. A hideous thought speared Rafael's head. His expression darkened. 'Karl Reiner,' he began, his voice harsh, 'is he—?'

'No! Dear God, *no!*'

Her rebuff was so instant, so vehement, that it could only be true. Relief flooded through Rafael. If for a moment he'd thought that that despicable piece of ordure had any kind of *anything* with her—

'*Gracias a Dios!*' he said feelingly.

'How could you think—?' She broke off, shuddering.

Of course she had nothing to do with Karl Reiner in that way! Someone like her would never, *never* think of such a liaison! Hadn't she reacted strongly enough back there in the lobby to convince him of that? Her shock and disgust had been palpable.

He reached for his brandy, and as he took a mouthful an image formed in his mind. Madeline—Madeline being on the receiving end of what Karl Reiner had thrown at Celeste.

She'd have laughed. Laughed in his face, told him, 'In your dreams!' and walked off. Then she'd have regaled Rafael with it in bed. She'd have been totally unfazed by it, totally unaffected—she would have thought Reiner merely physically repellent, not repulsively offensive!

But Madeline was cut from completely different material from the woman at his side now. The woman who was cupping one slender hand around a teacup from which a delicate oriental fragrance was coiling upwards, stirring it with a silver teaspoon, focussed only on her task. He watched her for a moment, all thought of Madeline deleted as Celeste stirred her tea, inhaling the scent, and seemed visibly to calm herself.

'Better?' he asked quietly.

She nodded, lifting the cup to her lips to take a tiny sip of the hot liquid.

He let her be, contenting himself with looking at her. Her beauty, seen again after a space of days, was etching itself on his retinas. Tonight she was wearing a knee-length cocktail dress in eau de Nil, high cut at the neckline, with short cap sleeves. A jade necklace and earrings were her jewellery. Her hair was dressed differently, in a more complex style with braids and loops, but still worn up. An impulse went through him—a longing to see that incredible pale hair loosed from its confines, flowing like a silvery river over her naked alabaster shoulders...

He pulled his mind back from such impulses, focussing now on her features. Her perfect beauty was just the same as it had been when he'd seen her walking down the stairs at that charity event. A beauty that moved him so strangely—so strongly.

And so, too, did the other quality that had made him watch her then, as it did now.

That sense of aloneness—apartness. As if she moved in the world but was not fully part of it. As if it could not touch her.

What had she said about the stars? That they were very far away...

*As she is.*

His expression changed. *But I will get close to her. With me she will not be alone, apart. I will draw her to me! Woo her and win her!*

And he must make the most of this opportunity to begin his journey to that destination. She was here, beside him, and that, surely, was a start.

'Tell me,' he said, his voice holding in it nothing but quiet concern, 'how is it that you were with Karl Reiner tonight if he is so repugnant to you? I know that you are the face of Blonde Visage, but—'

She lifted her face sharply. 'How do you know that?'

He gave a half laugh. 'I could say that your face is your giveaway,' he said lightly, 'but I have to confess that, since fashion magazines are not my usual reading matter, I found it out from your agency.'

Her face worked. 'Why were you asking?' she demanded. But there was no need to ask. She knew. Rafael Sanguardo had shown his interest in her—she had been naive to think that just because she had walked away from him the other evening it would not be possible for a man of his means to find out a great deal about her!

His expression was deliberately transparent. 'I make no secret of the fact that I want to get to know you better, Celeste.'

It was strange to hear her name on his lips—a name she hadn't told him. She would have preferred him never to know, so that she could slip back into the shadows of life where she dwelt. But it was too late for that. All she could do now was hold him at bay, make it clear to him that whatever he was hoping for could not be.

'So why did you have to be in Reiner's unpalatable company?' Rafael pursued.

She made herself give a slight shrug. 'I'm still under contract, so it's unavoidable. Tonight he was a guest of one of the fashion magazines he places a great deal of advertising with—that was his excuse for me having to be here.'

'Excuse?'

She gave another shrug, not meeting his eyes, focussing only on the cup in front of her. 'You heard what he wants. He made it plain enough.' A sudden thought struck her, and without realising it she lifted her face to look at him.

'What you did—back there—will he make trouble for you?' There was concern in her voice. 'He could do you for assault—'

'He can try,' said Rafael.

And there was something about the way he said it that made Celeste realise that Karl—or anyone—would be very, very foolish to attempt to make trouble for Rafael Sanguardo. There was a toughness about him that was unmistakable.

But there was chivalry, too, she acknowledged. Even if his intervention *had* proved opportune for him, allowing him to do what he was doing now. Getting to know her—

*But it's no use—no use at all. Nothing can come of it— nothing!*

That was all she had to remember. And she should act on it right now. She should get to her feet, thank him once again and then go home—home to her little flat in Notting Hill: the fruit of her years of modelling, her quiet haven, where she could be apart from the hectic round of her career. Apart and alone.

The way she had to be.

Because nothing else was possible…would ever be possible…

She was condemned to the solitary life she led.

But Rafael Sanguardo was speaking again, interrupting her troubled thoughts. 'What about for you?' he was asking, that note of concern still evident in his deep, accented voice. 'Will it make things difficult?'

She gave another shrug. 'I've only got a few weeks left to run on my contract, and there's little he can do in real terms. I most definitely will *not* be resigning! Oh, there'll probably be some gossip—I dare say some of the people I work with will hear about it. But he has a reputation already, so it will hardly be a surprise.'

Rafael frowned. 'If you had warning of his reputation, why did you take the contract?'

She gave yet another shrug. 'He was involved with one of the other models under contract, so I thought he would leave me alone—which he did, by and large, until now. And the reason I wanted the contract in the first place was simple.' She looked straight at him, giving him the courtesy of an honest answer, for surely he deserved no less after his rescue of her. 'It paid well,' she said.

She lifted up her cup, took a mouthful of tea, breaking her gaze. Then she set down her cup again, looked at him once more. She swallowed, then spoke.

'Modelling is a crowded profession. Often poorly paid. Only a few make it to the very top. I won't be one of them, I know, but I've not done badly—for which I'm grateful,' she allowed. 'Anyway, it's the only way I know of to make money—'

She stopped, and for a moment—just a moment—there was an emptiness in her gaze. As if she had been scoured hollow.

Then it was gone.

Yet in its aftermath there seemed to Rafael to be the residue of something lingering. Unsettling. He wanted to banish it.

He took another mouthful of his brandy, feeling its

warmth filling him. 'It seems to me you know about astronomy,' he said.

He'd lightened his tone deliberately. Yet his attempt to lighten the atmosphere seemed to have failed. Her throat tensed; a shadow occluded her eyes. Memory oozed within her of the way she had first gazed desperately up at the heavens, wanting only to be part of them. Incorporeal. Free from her body...

Then she forced the memory from her. He'd obviously only made the remark as a conversational gambit—she must treat it as such.

'Hard to make a living at that,' she answered. 'And I am the rankest amateur!' she added lightly.

Rafael smiled across at her. 'Yet your name is ideally suited for a career in astronomy, no?' She looked blank, and he enlightened her. 'Celeste—celestial?' he said.

His eyes rested on her, drinking her in.

*And that is her aura, too—celestial. As if the impurities and imperfections of the world below the stars are nothing to do with her! As if she moves through this world apart from everyone else, everything else, untouched by anything that seeks to stain her...*

In his head he heard Karl Reiner's sordid accusation. If ever there was a woman who was an unlikely target for such foul names it was this one!

She was looking at him, a slight expression of surprise in her clear grey-blue eyes. 'Do you know, that's never struck me?' she said. 'Celeste and celestial...'

His own smile deepened. Absently she noticed how it curved the lines around his mouth, made his basalt-black eyes lighten. Noticed even more the way it seemed to make her breath catch. Made her want to do nothing more than go on sitting here, beside him, being with him—

No! She mustn't! It was pointless—useless! Talking to him about anything—anything at all—had no purpose! She was calmer now, recovered from that horrible scene out in the lobby, and so she must go—leave—go home to the life she had. A life that had no place for Rafael Sanguardo in it. No place for any kind of relationship with anyone.

She nerved herself to take her leave. To terminate this conversation that could go nowhere—nowhere at all! But he was speaking to her yet again, clearly intent on keeping her in conversation.

'So what first got you interested in astronomy?' Rafael asked.

Deliberately he kept his question casual—nothing more than the kind of enquiry anyone might make in social conversation. A safe topic under whose aegis to do what he most wanted to do—set her at her ease. Stop her tensing all the time. Make her comfortable talking with him. Make the most of the opportunity this evening had presented so that he could move on to inviting her out to dinner, and then from there to where he wanted to be—making love to her.

*Her arms around me, clinging to me, her mouth opening to mine, my hands curving around the bare column of her back, her hair loosened, streaming like a silver banner across the pillows, her body warm and yielding to desire...*

He felt the power of his own imagination, his own desire, kick through him. Surely she must feel it, too? Surely she must? Wasn't she starting to thaw to him, little by little? Slowly—oh, so slowly—but it was starting to happen, he was sure of it.

Then, as he finished his question, before his eyes he saw her face change. Closed.

Closed completely, as if a shutter had come down.

'I don't remember,' she said. Her voice was quelling. This time there could be no allowances for his simply making conversation. This was a subject that she must terminate— now. Just as she must terminate this encounter. She must go home right now.

Rafael's eyes narrowed minutely at her stony reaction. What had just happened? The change was total. He saw her reach for her teacup, lift it with a jerking movement and take a mouthful of the pale green fragrant liquid. Then she set the cup down with another jolt. Her eyes swivelled to his.

'Thank you so much for the tea, Señor Sanguardo. And thank you for intervening back there. It was very good of you.' She spoke rapidly, in clipped tones. Clipped, impersonal tones that went with the totally closed expression on her face.

He could see her total withdrawal happening in front of his eyes.

*She's gone away again—back into that separate space she lives in. The one she uses to keep the rest of the world at bay.*

She was getting to her feet, slipping gracefully off the high bar stool.

'Thank you so much,' she said again, her tone formal. She picked up her clutch bag from the bar surface and bestowed a tight, perfunctory smile on him again.

Rafael got to his feet as she did. 'I will see you home,' he announced.

Again, that look of immediate wariness—more than wariness...alarm—flared in her eyes.

'Purely and solely,' he continued, 'for the purposes of ensuring that you do not risk any further unwanted attention from the uncharming Mr Reiner. My car is outside, and it is no trouble, I assure you.' He looked down at her. His eyes were steady, their message clear. 'I will see you safely to your home and then leave you. Does that meet with your agreement?'

Celeste opened her mouth. She wanted to say, *No, it can't possibly meet with my agreement! I can't want to spend the slightest further amount of time with you because there is no point—absolutely and totally no point! I am not going to let you get to know me better and I am not going to have anything more to do with you and that is all there is to it!*

But she didn't say it. A sudden vision of Karl Reiner waiting outside her flat assailed her. However reluctant she might be to allow this magnetic, disturbing man who had behaved so chivalrously to drive her home, it was preferable to encountering Karl Reiner again—drunken and angry and still trying to press his hateful attentions on her.

Then, without any answer from her at all, she felt Rafael Sanguardo's strong hand cup lightly around her elbow and guide her out of the bar. It was only a light, courteous touch, but she was vividly aware of it. He dropped his hand the moment she seemed to be going the way he wanted her to—which was across the lobby and out onto the pavement. A hovering car glided to the kerb, and then a chauffeur was opening the passenger door for her and she was getting in.

'Where to?' Rafael asked her as he took his place beside her.

With a flurry of consternation Celeste realised she was going to have to tell him where she lived. Well, if he'd found out who she was, then he'd be perfectly capable of finding out where she lived as well. So she gave her address, and the car started to make its way westward out of Mayfair towards Park Lane.

It would take a good fifteen minutes at least to reach Notting Hill, Celeste knew, and in the meantime she had better make anodyne conversation to prevent Rafael Sanguardo getting any other ideas about how to pass the time in the back of his car...

'What part of South America do you come from, Mr Sanguardo?' she heard herself asking. Her tone was no more than politely interested.

He glanced at her. There was amusement in his eyes. 'Am I to take it that you've been making enquiries about me in return?' he asked.

*Damn,* she thought, *I walked into that one!*

'One of my fellow models the other evening at the charity show mentioned it,' she replied, making her voice as unconcerned as she could.

*Did she, now?* Rafael thought. *And does that mean that*

*you'd asked her?* A ripple of satisfaction went through him. She was not as studiedly indifferent to him as she was trying to make out. How long, he wondered, before she finally admitted that? Before she finally started to lower her guard to him?

But whenever that happened—and it *would* happen; he had set his mind to it, and nothing in the intervening days since seeing her walk down that marble staircase, captivating him with her opalescent beauty, had changed his mind on that—it was not happening now.

Her guard was sky-high. A guard consisting of polite attentiveness and the kind of impersonal conversation she could have with anyone at all. Well, he reminded himself, it was better than her doing her disappearing act again, and he would make the most of it.

'She was a little out,' he answered. 'My country of origin is Maragua, which is in Central America.'

He could see her give a little frown in the passing street lights as the car drew out into Park Lane.

'I thought Managua was the capital of Nicaragua?' she commented.

'It is. Which is why my country, *Maragua,* is so often overlooked. It's very small—hardly larger than El Salvador—and similarly has only a Pacific coastline.'

'I don't think I've really ever heard of it,' Celeste said apologetically.

'*De nada*—not many Europeans have,' he said. 'Which, overall, is probably a good thing.' His voice was edged. 'After all, the reason most developing countries are known about in the Western world is their wars and disasters! Fortunately we have few—though like all Pacific Rim countries we are subject to earthquakes.'

'Because the Pacific Ocean's floor is moving under the continental plates,' she acknowledged. 'Does that mean you have volcanoes, too?'

He nodded his head. 'One or two—fortunately inactive.'

He paused. 'Your geology is as good as your astronomy, it seems.'

His eyes rested on her expectantly. He felt another ripple of satisfaction. Beauty, even so notable as hers, was one thing, but it was inadequate on its own. Her stargazing had told him that she was informed and intelligent, and here was further proof.

'I like plate tectonics,' she answered. 'It makes sense of so much.'

'The whole planet earth is a living jigsaw—endlessly changing, endlessly renewing itself.' Rafael paused. 'I find that quite encouraging. If even the ground beneath our feet can change, then so can we. We can make ourselves anew.'

She looked at him. Her eyes flickered. His words echoed in her head. *We can make ourselves anew.*

For just a second she could feel something flare inside her—then it died. Crushed by the weight of the past. The past that was always her present. And her future…the only future possible for her.

Feeling a stone suddenly in her chest, she turned her head to look out of the car window. They had reached Hyde Park Corner and were turning into the park now.

Rafael indicated with his hand. 'What is that enormous house there, do you know?' he asked. He wanted her to keep talking to him—not slip away into that separate world she inhabited, shutting him out.

But she answered readily enough. 'Oh, that's Apsley House,' she said. 'It's the London home of the Duke of Wellington—you know, the Battle of Waterloo. Well, his descendants anyway. It's always known as Number One, London. I suppose it's because it's the premier private residence in London.'

If she was gabbling, she didn't care. This kind of innocuous exchange was all she could cope with. It blocked those tormenting words he'd said—*We can make ourselves anew.*

Anguish gripped her. *But I can't—I can't make myself anew! It's impossible—impossible!*

His voice relieved her. 'Is that the Serpentine?' he asked, glimpsing a dark mass of water to one side of the car as they cut across the park.

'Yes,' she answered. The stone was back in her chest. She launched into relating everything she knew about the Serpentine, then moved on to Rotten Row as they crossed it.

'It's still a bridle path,' she said. 'In the nineteenth century it was very fashionable for the upper classes to ride their horses there.'

Somehow she managed to make the subject of Victorian high society last till they reached her flat, and as the car pulled up along the quiet kerbside she turned to Rafael.

'Thank you so much,' she said brightly. 'It really is very kind of you.'

The chauffeur was holding the door open for her and she climbed out gracefully. The night air seemed cool after the interior of the car. Or perhaps it was just because she felt heated in her blood.

'Please don't get out,' she told Rafael.

'Which is your flat?' he asked, ignoring her and stepping out onto the pavement.

'Um...second floor,' she said. She was fumbling for her keys in her clutch.

She'd coped with the car ride, sounding like a tour guide to London, but her nerves were at breaking point. She had to get in. Get away from him.

'I'll wait until I see your light come on,' said Rafael.

Relief flooded through her. 'Thank you,' she said. She hurried up the steps to the front door, opening it with her key. She turned. He was still standing there. 'Goodnight, Mr Sanguardo,' she said, her smile flickering uncertainly.

For a moment she just went on standing there, looking at him. Letting the impact he made on her retinas be absorbed into her.

'Goodnight, Celeste,' he answered. He gave her a brief nod of farewell and got back into the car. The chauffeur slammed the door and went to the driver's seat.

Celeste went indoors, walking swiftly up to her flat. As she turned the light on and went to the living room windows to see the car pulling away she could feel her heart's hectic beating.

And she knew exactly what had caused it.

*Rafael Sanguardo...*

His name echoed in her head. Not letting her go.

Later, as she lay in bed, she knew she should get to sleep. She had an early start tomorrow and looking haggard was not acceptable for a model—yet she lay sleepless all the same.

Memories from the evening circled in her mind. Not the stressful dinner with Karl Reiner, but the time she had spent with Rafael Sanguardo. It was his words that kept playing in her head.

*We can make ourselves anew...*

Her eyes stared out into the darkness of her bedroom.

*Can we? Can we make ourselves anew?*

But the question was hollow. Its flavour bitter. And into her head came more words. Karl Reiner's...

Anguish gripped her.

# CHAPTER FOUR

CELESTE WONDERED THE next day whether Rafael Sanguardo would try to get in touch, but there was nothing from him. She told herself she was glad—must be glad—for there could be no future for her with him in it.

So why, then, did she keep thinking about him, replaying her time with him? There was no point! Yet, berate herself as she might, she could not get him out of her head. Even when she was enduring the final photographic sessions under her Reiner Visage contract he was there, dominating her consciousness, her thoughts. Vivid and potent. And as disturbing as ever. As tormenting as ever.

*His sculpted features, the mobile mouth, the sable hair, the dark obsidian eyes, the deep, accented voice...*

And then she was back to the beginning again, trying to get those images out of her mind. Trying to move on beyond the completely pointless question of what it was about him that was getting to her.

*Because it doesn't matter why! It's irrelevant—totally irrelevant! It changes nothing! Nothing at all! If he tries to get in touch with me again I'll just say no, that's all. The way I always do. Always... Because nothing else is possible. Nothing.*

In her eyes a shadow passed. An old, familiar shadow... And with it came the clenching of her stomach, the crawling of her skin.

* * *

Rafael relaxed back in the first-class seat on the plane, a pleasant sense of satisfaction filling him. And anticipation. He'd been in Geneva, raising finance for his latest ventures; with his track record, banks were always eager to meet with him. But his thoughts were not on business now.

An image floated tantalisingly in his mind. Pale, beautiful...*celestial*...

He'd given Celeste time and space since delivering her to her flat, but now he was going to make his next move. Would she respond? he wondered. Or would she try and evade him? His mind flickered over the situation. She was not immune to him—he could tell that with every male molecule in his body—yet she was holding him at bay. Why, since she had admitted she was not involved with anyone else, he could not fathom. She gave no impression of trying to play him, and her evasiveness seemed totally genuine. But why be evasive in the first place?

His eyes narrowed as he thought it through. Maybe it was because of men like Karl Reiner. If he was the norm for men in the world of fashion and modelling she moved in, he could understand Celeste's evasiveness. To be treated as that all-time prime jerk had treated her would make anyone cautious about accepting attentions from men.

Well, he was no Karl Reiner, and he would win her confidence and make her realise he was nothing like that! Soon—very soon now—he would convince her that all he wanted from her was what he knew with every instinct she wanted, too...

Time together—with him.

His pleasant sense of anticipation intensified.

Celeste's phone was ringing. It was Sunday evening and she was ironing. She was keeping busy—deliberately so. Anything to keep Rafael Sanguardo out of her head! Her work with Reiner Visage had finally ended, to her relief, and since then she'd thrown herself into a round of activity while waiting for another modelling assignment to come up.

So far she'd given herself a whole set of beauty treatments and set a challenging exercise schedule—runs in Holland Park, yoga, Pilates and dance classes. And she had a full medical assessment booked for a few days' time as well, with blood tests and body scans.

It was not just for the sake of her modelling career that she paid such attention to herself. A shadow dimmed her eyes. She needed not only to stay beautiful but to stay fit and healthy. She would not go the way of her poor, stricken mother...

A familiar sadness filled her, squeezing her heart. She had promised her mother she would not suffer the same terrible fate that had befallen her—forewarned was forearmed, and regular check-ups were routine for her.

Now, as she folded a pillowcase and reached for the next one to iron, she let the phone go to the answer machine. As the caller started speaking she froze.

She did not need to ask whose was the distinctive accented voice.

*How did he get my phone number?* was her first thought, swiftly discarded. He knew her name and address—easy enough to find her landline number! At least, she thought with a sense of relief, he hadn't phoned her mobile, so hopefully he didn't have that number.

She listened to him speak, the iron poised in her hand. The deep tones wove into her senses almost before she caught the gist of what he was saying.

'I was wondering whether you might like to have dinner with me some time. I'm in the UK this coming week—let me know what evening would suit you. You can reach me on the following number.'

He gave the number—a London landline—and hung up. He didn't bother, she noticed, saying who he was.

*He knows I know...*

As the phone went quiet again she stared out across her living room. The TV was on in one corner, playing an old black-and-white movie. She did not see the images—only the inner image in her head. Rafael Sanguardo in all his disturbing, unsettling, lean good looks.

*Why is he getting to me?*

The question formed again, as it had been doing since she had first seen him watching her. And it was just as unanswered. As unanswerable.

And all the more disturbing for it.

The following day she was booked for a catalogue shoot—it wasn't the most glamorous of modelling work, but it paid solidly and Celeste welcomed it now she was without the Reiner contract. When she got back to her flat the entrance hall contained a vase with a huge bouquet of white lilies in it, their scent filling the small space. A gilt-edged card with her name on it was attached to the lavish wrapping.

Upstairs, she opened the envelope. The card said simply 'Rafael'. Nothing more than that. Her face set, she put the extravagant bouquet on the dining table. Behind her set expression, though, her thoughts were tumbling around.

They resolved into a single question.

*What am I going to do about him?*

The question stayed with her all the evening.

So did the scent of the lilies, pervading the living room, the whole flat. It was a scent she could not avoid, nor ignore. Just like the single, simple question hovering in her head. She knew perfectly well what answer was required. Go on ignoring Rafael Sanguardo, whatever he did.

It got increasingly hard during the rest of the week. He phoned again, leaving another message—more or less a repetition of the first—and the following day yet another bouquet of flowers arrived. These were quite different from the exotic, opulent lilies—just a slender posy of freesias in delicate pastel colours, with a sweet, fresh scent. The card held just a question: 'Perhaps you prefer these flowers?'

She put them in a vase on her dressing table in her bedroom, so their delicate scent would not be drowned by the heady lilies. But it meant that wherever she was in her flat there was a reminder of Rafael Sanguardo.

At least her days were very busy with the catalogue shoot, and she was glad of that. Less glad, though, to return home and find yet another floral tribute had arrived from Rafael Sanguardo. This time it was a cluster of tiny rosebuds in the palest blush-pink. She put them beside the freesias. If he kept going like this she could open a flower shop, she thought.

But his phone call that evening told her she was going to have a respite. He simply left a message saying that he was flying to the Far East for a week, but would be back in London thereafter.

'Perhaps your schedule will allow you some evenings out then,' he said. 'I'll phone you.'

He seemed totally unperturbed by her persistent lack of reply to him. Yet the deep, accented tones of his voice seemed to linger in her consciousness long after she'd deleted the message.

She eyed the phone warily. Maybe she should simply call him and tell him that he was wasting his time. But even that seemed an ordeal. *Why can't he just take the hint—get the message from the fact I'm not phoning him back? Why can't he just disappear out of my life?*

But even as she thought that she felt a strange little pang go through her. A pang that was the most disturbing reaction of all…

Thoughts and emotions crowded into her head. If Rafael Sanguardo was going to be abroad, then maybe she should plan to do likewise. Go somewhere different from where he was going to be—somewhere she could try and get him out of her mind.

Resolved, the next morning she went to her agency with a request for a foreign location shoot.

Her booker looked put out. 'Just because you ditched

Reiner Visage, it doesn't mean you can get the work you want at the drop of a hat!' he pointed out tartly. Then he relented. 'OK, OK—I know. Creepy Karl's enough to make anyone run a mile! Hmm…let's see. Hang on for a mo—I'll put some calls in.'

He picked up his phone and Celeste wandered off to sit on one of the group of white leather chairs nearby. She'd just sat down when the door from the street was pushed open and someone came in. It was a model Celeste didn't recognise. She was very fair-skinned, with hair as blonde as her own. She looked young, still in her teens, and unsure what to do. One of the bookers greeted her, and she went up to him eagerly, sitting herself down, her long, thin legs splaying like a newborn foal's.

Celeste looked at her. The girl could have been herself all those years ago. Memory pierced. Sharp—like a needle under the skin. Finding the nerve beneath. She picked up a magazine and busied herself with its contents. A few moments later her own booker called her across.

'Can you do Hawaii? Five days, end of next week? One of the models booked for it has just discovered she's pregnant and wants out!'

Celeste nodded. Hawaii was definitely far enough away to get some perspective and would suit her very well.

Her booker finished telling her the details and she got up to go. As she did so the very young new model got up as well. Her face was shining.

'Oh, that's brilliant! Thank you!' she said excitedly to her booker.

She got to the door just before Celeste, and held it open for her. As they stepped out onto the pavement Celeste said in a friendly voice, 'Got a casting?'

The girl beamed. 'My first one! Tomorrow! It's for skincare. I'm just terrified I'll wake up tomorrow with a zit!'

Celeste laughed. 'Drink nothing but water for the rest of

the day,' she advised, half joking. 'Who's the client?' she asked, just to be friendly.

But when the girl answered Celeste's expression changed.

'Reiner Visage,' breathed the girl. 'They're ever so posh! I can't afford any of their stuff myself! Do you think I can get some free samples?' she asked ingenuously.

Celeste didn't answer. Her face was grave. The girl looked so young— *Young and naive and vulnerable...*

Memory's needle went under her skin again.

'Listen,' she said, sounding serious, 'if you do get picked, please be careful. Karl Reiner's nickname is Creepy Karl, and he's earned it!'

She debated whether to tell the girl about the hassle she herself had had, then decided not to. The odds were against her getting a Reiner contract at her very first casting, and she was obviously so thrilled right now that Celeste didn't want to spoil the moment with an unnecessary warning.

She fished in her bag for a scrap of paper, scrawled her name and mobile number on it and gave it to the girl. 'I'm Celeste Philips. Let's have a coffee some time,' she said, her voice friendly again.

The girl's eyes shone. 'Oh, that would be brill—thanks! I don't know any other models yet. My flatmates all work in offices. I'm Louise, by the way—Louise Foreman,' she said.

'Well, good luck, Louise,' Celeste said, refraining from adding, *But not tomorrow.*

'I'll put your name and number in my phone right away,' Louise said happily. 'Thank you ever so much! I can't wait to tell my mates I've got a casting!'

She trotted off, busy with her phone. Celeste watched her go. *Was I really ever that young?* she thought. *That eager?*

But she had been. Of course she had. After all, modelling had been going to make her fortune. The fortune she'd wanted so much...

Like a guillotine, she sliced down the steel door in her

head that she kept forever locked. Seeing that young girl, so like herself once, had let it start to open.

But it wasn't just the young model who had turned the key in that door. Like an unwelcome intruder, Rafael Sanguardo's image formed in her mind, as disturbing now as it had been from the start.

*What power does he have to do that? Why does he get to me the way he does? Why can't I just delete him and never think about him again?*

The answer was as disturbing as the man himself.

And one thing was for sure: Rafael Sanguardo's image did not come with a delete button...

Rafael's brow was furrowed in concentration as he focussed on the figures his laptop screen was displaying. Calculations ran rapidly through his head.

'Sorry to disturb you, but Miss Philips has just turned the corner.'

His driver's voice interrupted his concentration, but he looked up at once.

'Thank you,' he said crisply, shutting his laptop lid. He twisted his head very slightly to look out of the window of his parked car. He saw her at once.

She was wearing jeans, a grey sweater and sneakers. Her hair was in a long plait to one side, and she had a capacious leather bag on her shoulder. She looked fresh and fit, her face without a trace of make-up, clean and clear, her figure slender and long-legged.

Rafael watched her a moment, analysing his feelings. They had not changed. Even casually dressed, as she was now, she had an impact on him that went straight to the same place as when she was dressed to the nines. Holding his gaze totally. Filling his vision.

He got out of the car, watching her register his presence. Watching her stop dead.

Casually, he walked up to her. 'You really do take evasion to the limits, don't you?' he said pleasantly.

Celeste glared at him. 'What are you doing here?' Her heart had started to slug, and she hated him for it. Hated herself.

'Asking you to dinner,' Rafael answered, unconcerned by her aggrieved tone.

The grey-blue eyes flashed. 'Thank you—but no, thank you,' she said. Then she frowned. 'I thought you were in the Far East?'

'I came back early,' Rafael said smoothly. His voice changed. 'I found I didn't want to be away.' He paused. 'From you,' he finished.

His eyes were resting on her. She was flustered, he could see. More than flustered. Her skin had flushed—that pale, translucent, flawless skin that he wanted to reach out a hand and smooth with the tips of his fingers...

*Her skin betrays her—her own body betrays her...*

Celeste Philips could stonewall him all she liked. She could ignore his calls—ignore *him*—but what she could not do was hide her response to him.

'So,' he went on, his voice still smooth, his eyes still resting on her, 'are you busy tonight?'

He saw her square her shoulders.

'Look,' she began, 'I really don't think—'

'Then don't,' he interrupted.

His voice wasn't smooth any more. Something had changed within it—something that reached into her, past all her defences.

'Don't think, Celeste. Just smile and say, *That would be lovely!* And then I will smile, too, and we'll agree what time I'll send the car for you, and then you'll go up to your flat and spend the next couple of hours making yourself even more beautiful than you look right now. And I will drive off and bury myself in work, the way I've been doing since I last saw you, because that's the only way I've kept functioning.' He drew breath, his eyes never leaving hers. 'So, that's all agreed, then. The car will be here for you at eight.'

She opened her mouth again. He laid a single long finger against it, silencing her. He felt her lips tremble beneath his touch.

'Dinner,' he said, holding her gaze with his—a troubled gaze that told him of her wariness, her mixed emotions. 'Just dinner, Celeste. Simple, pleasant, undemanding. You can get to know me a little more, and I you. And if we agree that, yes, we enjoy each other's company—after all...' the slightest tug pulled at his mouth '...we share a fondness for astronomy and geology, and who knows how many other ologies, hmm?—then, and only then, we can decide whether we would like to enjoy more of each other's company. There—is that really so very onerous?'

He dropped his hand. This time she did not open her mouth to speak. She just looked at him, an almost helpless look on her face now, as if she had finally run out of ways to gainsay him.

He took a breath. 'One evening of your life, Celeste. That's all.' He held her eyes, then veiled his own with a dipping of his long black lashes. He turned away, reached for the handle of the car door. 'Eight o'clock, Celeste,' he reminded her.

Then he lowered himself into the rear passenger seat and pulled the door shut. A moment later the car had moved off into the road, leaving Celeste behind, standing motionless on the pavement.

But with a heart-rate that felt as if she'd just sprinted five hundred metres.

Slowly, very slowly, she raised the tips of her fingers to her lips. It seemed to her they could still feel Rafael Sanguardo's cool touch...

# CHAPTER FIVE

THE CAR CAME at eight. Celeste could see it from her living room window, pulled over by the kerb. She stared down at it. Was she mad to be doing this?

She knew she was. Mad even to think of doing what she was going to do. Have dinner with Rafael Sanguardo.

*But it's only dinner! And I need to do this! I need to use it to tell him that what he wants isn't going to happen! It just isn't!*

She picked up her evening bag, headed downstairs to the waiting car. Tension pulled at her as she walked out onto the pavement. Deliberately she had chosen a dove-grey dress with a high neckline and a modest knee-length hem. Her make-up was subdued and her hair was in a neat French pleat.

All the way to the restaurant she strove for calm composure. Tonight she would tell Rafael Sanguardo that his efforts were in vain—that there could be nothing between them.

The restaurant—a double-fronted white stucco house in Knightsbridge—was not one she knew. She was shown into the dining salon and instantly her eyes went to the man who dominated her thoughts…her senses. As she was shown to his table, Rafael got to his feet.

'You came,' he said.

His voice was warm. His gaze warmer. It did things to her that it shouldn't. That she must not allow.

She looked very slightly taken aback at his greeting. 'Did you think I wouldn't?'

He quirked an eyebrow. 'Would it have been so surprising? Given your reluctance?'

She said nothing, only took her place as the chair was drawn out for her. She settled into her seat, accepting the napkin unfurled for her and the pouring of water for her. A pair of menus was discreetly placed on the table, and then they were left alone.

The restaurant was almost full, she could see that instantly, although the tables were skilfully arranged such that none was too close to another and each seemed to have a circle of privacy around it, helped by the copious greenery that adorned the room. The decor was late Victorian, with a lot of dark red.

Rafael saw her looking around. 'A little florid, I agree,' he murmured. 'But the food is outstanding, and I don't think this restaurant features on the fashionista circuit.'

'No,' Celeste said. 'I've not been here before.'

'Good,' said Rafael. 'I'm pleased to be able to offer you a new experience.' He picked up his glass of water. 'To new experiences,' he said.

There was a glint of mordant humour in his dark eyes.

Celeste bit her lip, but did not reply. Rafael reached for the menus, opening one and offering it to Celeste, who took it and busied herself studying it.

It saved her from studying him instead. Which, she knew with a little plunge of her stomach, was what she badly wanted to do. She wanted to study him—take in every one of his features and understand, finally, what it was about him that had such an effect on her. Why him? Why this man?

Why, why, why…?

'Will you eat as little as you did at the charity show?' he asked, making her lift her head from the blurring words on the menu.

She frowned slightly. 'Oh, no—I skipped lunch today, as I was working, so I have a full calorie allowance tonight.'

He nodded. 'So you'll go for the baked Camembert, followed by *confit* of duck, and a very large chocolate mousse with cream to finish—is that it?'

He said it straight-faced, and just for a moment Celeste thought he meant it. Then she saw the glint of humour in his eyes.

'I wish…' she said. She looked quickly at the menu again. 'Undressed prawns, and sole with green vegetables—no sauce.'

'Hmm…really splashing out, I see,' Rafael murmured. 'Do you have any calories to spare for wine?'

'Dry white,' she answered, then promptly wished she hadn't. Rafael Sanguardo was disturbing enough to her without the aid of alcohol…

But he was beckoning the wine waiter and going through the wine list with him in a knowledgeable fashion. Then, their dinner order given and the ritual of the arrival of the wine performed, she was left facing him with no other distractions.

'What do you think of the wine?' Rafael was asking, and she took a grateful sip—that would occupy a few moments of time.

'Very good,' she said, for it was crisp and tart and perfectly chilled.

'I'm glad,' he said. Then, glancing at her, he said, 'I'm saving the champagne for our breakfast in bed tomorrow morning.'

She choked, clunking her wine glass down on the table. As she recovered, her eyes flew to his face. It was completely deadpan. Then, a second later, that glint in his eyes came again.

'It's what you think of me, though, isn't it?' Rafael said. He took a breath, his expression changing. 'You know,' he said slowly, 'I've never met anyone as…as *wary*…as you are.

I'm truly astonished that I've actually finally got you sitting here, of your own free will, having dinner with me.' His eyes rested on her. 'Can it be that you've finally decided I'm safe?'

Celeste blinked, her eyes flaring. *Safe?* Rafael Sanguardo sat there and called himself *safe?* A man who was getting past every defence she possessed? Defences she had never even needed till now!

She pulled herself together. He was giving her the perfect opportunity she was looking for. To inform him, as clearly as was needed, that this was not the start of something—it was the end of it.

'Mr Sanguardo—' she began.

'Rafael,' he corrected.

She couldn't bring herself to say his given name. It would create a level of familiarity that was exactly what she was trying to distance herself from.

'I really do have to make something clear to you,' she went on. She fiddled with the stem of her wine glass, steeling herself. Why was it so hard to say what she had to say? It wouldn't be the first time. Usually it never came to this, because men who were keen on her had backed off long before now—frozen out by her lack of response to their overtures—but from time to time she'd had to spell it out with capital letters. This was definitely one of them.

But it wasn't like any of the earlier times. Because then, she knew, with a hollowing of her insides, it had been no effort at all to say no to what was on offer. Whereas now...

*I don't want to say no to him...*

The words were in her head before she could stop them, forcing themselves into her consciousness. For the first time she had finally encountered a man to whom her customary rejection to all males was not easy and effortless to make. For the first time she had encountered a man to whom she did not want to say no.

She wanted to give a completely different answer...an answer that was singing in her blood, that had leapt in her eyes the very first moment she had seen him, that was making her want to do nothing more than let her eyes gaze at him, soak him up. Her nerves were tingling in every limb, her heart was beating that much faster, her breathing was unsteady…

Then harsh reality sounded in her head.

*But it's no good! I have to say no! I have to say no to Rafael Sanguardo. Because I always have to say no.*

How could she ever say anything else when that clinging trail of slime still left its fetid trace across her skin…would always do so…?

*I can't escape the past—what I did. And I can never be free of it—never! So what else can I say to any man except no…*

And that was exactly what she was going to do now. *Make* herself do.

'I have to be completely honest with you,' she ploughed on. She was looking at him full in the face and he sat back, a veiled look in his eyes. 'This isn't personal, I assure you, but it wouldn't be fair of me to let you think that having dinner like this is in any way…um…well, a date—because it isn't.'

'Why not?' The question cut across her hesitant explication. It was asked with an air of casual curiosity. The veiled look was still in his eyes.

'Well, because—' She stopped.

'Yes?' One dark eyebrow quirked. He picked up his wine glass, holding it in long fingers but not drinking from it. He looked relaxed, unfazed by what she was saying.

'Because I just don't *do* this stuff, that's why,' she said bluntly.

'Ah, "stuff",' he repeated with an air of discovery. 'That's very enlightening. Do, please, elaborate.'

She took a breath. 'Like I said, it isn't personal, but I've made it a rule not to…to… Well, to do what I'm doing now, I guess. Or,' she added pointedly, 'anything else!'

'Such as champagne breakfasts in bed?'

*'Yes!'*

Rafael responded ruminatively. 'Well, I can understand why, if you move in a world populated by the likes of Karl Reiner, you have that rule, and I regard it as entirely sensible. But, Celeste…'

Now his eyes were unveiled, and she reeled from the expression in them that blazed like a searing fire.

'I am *not* cut from that cloth, and therefore you have absolutely nothing to be wary of in that respect. I had hoped you'd realised that already, but if I have to make it even clearer then I shall!'

'It isn't that. I don't think you're anything like Creepy Karl. It's just—'

'Yes?'

He was back to veiling his gaze again, waiting to hear what she said next. She looked away a moment. Only a glance into the restaurant beyond her. But it went a lot further than that.

Back through time…

Then, slowly, she brought her gaze back to his face.

'I don't date,' she said. 'I don't date and I don't have relationships. Or romances. Or affairs. Or whatever you want to call them. I just…*don't.*'

She could hear the silence. Hear it stretching between them. Keeping them apart.

She saw him set down his wine glass, straighten in his seat, lean towards her. He reached a hand out and covered one of hers, still lying palm-down on the tablecloth. His hand felt warm and strong. He held it for a few seconds only, then released it. It felt cold, suddenly, without his there.

'We'll take it very slowly,' he said.

She shook her head. She felt a heavy weight in it. Yet with a flicker of her mind she knew she did not sense the weight as crushing.

*Comforting…*

The word formed in her mind and she tried to shake it loose. She must not think that—*must not.*

She heard his voice continue. 'As slowly as continental drift,' he said.

And now his eyes were resting on her, and the expression in them was one she had not seen. It did strange things to her, tightening her throat as if she were about to cry, which made no sense at all.

'Will that be slowly enough for you?' he asked.

She felt her head incline, for the weight it was bearing was too great. Continental drift… A pull of desolation went through her. She had her own version of continental drift.

*An island of my own, cut off from the rest of the land— drifting ever further away, taking me with it, taking me away from everything like this. Everything that goes with a man like Rafael Sanguardo…*

She wanted to tell him so—tell him that even geological time would not be enough to accomplish what he wanted. But she kept silent.

'Good,' he said. His voice was quiet. Then, in a different tone, he said, 'Ah, I believe this is our food arriving.'

It was, and she was glad. It gave her the chance to pull herself together, to shake loose the weight in her head. What had happened just then she did not know—only that she was glad she was past it. She'd said what she had to say—that his attempt to persuade her into dating him, romancing him, having an affair with him, was not going to work and could not work—and that was the important thing. At least his words had indicated that he wasn't going to try and hustle her, pressurise her or hurry her. And that meant, she realised with a little ripple of relief that carried agitations of its own, that she didn't have to keep her guard sky-high this evening. That she could afford to lower it a little—just a little.

*The way I want to…*

The realisation was impossible to suppress. And that in itself was disturbing, too. But she was here now. To stand up and leave would be rude, and churlish, and he did not de-

serve that. It was not his fault that she could not do what he
had so openly stated he wanted to do.

*He's done nothing wrong—he has not behaved badly.
When he intervened over Karl Reiner he was chivalrous
and protective. Now he is only being attentive, as he said
he wanted to be. There is nothing to fault him.*

No, the fault was not in Rafael Sanguardo…

She felt them again—those trailing tendrils that dragged
across her skin, the miasma of the mind that she could never
banish. Never free herself from. That barred her for ever
from what Rafael Sanguardo was offering her.

*All I can have of him is this—this brief time with him.*

And she must make the most of it! Take what little she
could. Put aside, just for now, her endless reserve, for she
had made it as clear as she could that there could be nothing between them—nothing more than this.

So slowly, very slowly, she started to feel the tension
around her begin to ebb a little. She would have this evening and then go home. Home to her solitary life. The only
life she could have.

But until that moment she was here, with Rafael Sanguardo, making conversation with him, safe and innocuous.

'Apparently,' he said, 'this house was owned by a Victorian banker who bankrupted himself aspiring to impress
the aristocracy—doubtless those who went riding in Rotten
Row, as you described the other evening—but they regarded
him as a *parvenu.*'

'You were only supposed to inherit money then,' Celeste
commented, 'not make it yourself.'

'That rules me out, then,' Rafael replied, that mordant
glint in his eyes again.

'I think,' she answered with a slight frown, 'that if you
were foreign it was actually a bit easier to get into high society. No one knew who you were, you see.'

One dark, arched eyebrow quirked. 'Wouldn't I have been

regarded as one up—if that—from a savage native escaped from the jungle?'

'I think you would have been considered exotic,' she said. 'And mysterious.'

*And you'd have had Victorian maidens swooning by the dozen...*

Rafael gave a laugh, the lines around his mouth deepening.

*Make that by the hundreds...*

Celeste dragged her mind away. She'd set him clear on what she was not going to do—get involved with him in any way—so she had to stop, *right now,* thinking any thoughts at all that countered that.

But it was hard to sit here, only a few feet away from him, and not think such thoughts. Not to feel again the confusion, the incomprehension, about just why it was that he could make her think such things. Feel such things...

'You make me sound like a character in Dickens,' he replied.

'More like Joseph Conrad, I think. You know—*Nostromo,*' she went on. 'It's a novel set in your part of the world. About a town that has vast mountains of silver and how that wealth tempts everyone. Corrupts many.'

'There was such a mountain,' he told her. 'In Peru. And it tempted and corrupted, and in the end caused the death of many. Including the wretched miners forced to mine it for their masters.' His expression changed. 'It may sound ironic, but it's actually been a blessing that Maragua has very little mineral wealth to exploit, since such exploitation has so seldom been for the benefit of the mass of inhabitants of the countries.'

She looked across at him. 'Is there great poverty still in Maragua?'

'Substantial—but it is diminishing. There was a change in government in Maragua a few years ago,' he continued, clearly approvingly, 'to one that is more moderate, less extreme. It has helped considerably. It understands that prosperity is built on investment—investment in infrastructure, the environment, education, entrepreneurship—and a lot of hard work by everyone, not just the *peones*.'

She looked at him curiously. 'But you live and work in Europe and the USA, don't you?'

'It's where I made my money, yes,' Rafael allowed. 'But the habit of sending remittances home by those working abroad has a long tradition in Latin America and it actually contributes signally to the economy of the region *en masse*. However, at my level those remittances can take the form of specific investments in targeted projects for long-term national benefit. I work closely with several other Maraguans who, like myself, have "made good", and we now intend to grow our native economy and welfare for the benefit of all our fellow citizens.'

'That sounds very…admirable…' Celeste sought for the right word.

He gave a dismissive shrug. 'It makes sound economic sense. Wealth begets wealth—as the Western world learned last century. If the masses become prosperous they drive the economy further upwards in a virtuous circle.'

Celeste frowned. 'But isn't there a danger of pollution and environmental degradation as living standards rise with consumer demand?'

'Yes. Which is why we now focus on sustainable development and reversing the damage that has been done in the past.'

He warmed to his theme, describing reforestation programmes to extend areas of native rainforest, which went hand in hand with developing ecotourism—an area he was investing in himself. Rafael could see her listening attentively, and she asked intelligent, penetrating questions.

Just as Madeline had used to.

Emotion flickered through him. He wanted Celeste to

be completely different from Madeline, yet in this she was proving similar.

Or was she?

He had come to realise that the superb grasp of economics that Madeline possessed, allowing her to soar in the business world, did not extend to being overly concerned about the very issues he was now talking about with Celeste. The shadow in Rafael's eyes changed to something harder—more critical. He could still hear Madeline arguing with him, refuting his enthusiasm for such projects as ecotourism and long-term sustainable development and natural resource conservation.

Her assured, confident voice sounded in his head now. *'Rainforests are a prime capital asset that have to be exploited to get anything useful out of them! You can't hold back economic growth by sentimentalising over a bunch of trees and the monkeys living in them! Get real, Rafe! It's a dog-eat-dog world out there, and we both know it! You and I both came from nowhere, and look at us now! We've made good by following the money—using our talents to get our share of it! Being sentimental would have got us nowhere!'*

He heard her vehement, scornful voice—knowing now, although he had once ignored it, that her callous attitude should have been a warning sign to him long before she had revealed her true character and finished their relationship for good.

Celeste's reaction to his environmental concerns was very different. Sympathetic, enthusiastic, approving. Sharing his values.

His eyes rested on her warmly, darkening momentarily with desire. He wanted to do more than share his environmental values with her…he wanted to share his bed… *Fold her to me, hold her in my arms, embrace and caress her…*

He felt frustration mingle with desire. She was so set on rejecting him—rejecting all men!

But then, he reasoned, if the kind of men she came across

were all of the same stamp as Karl Reiner, was that so surprising? Rafael's thoughts darkened. And if men like Karl Reiner were used to models sleeping their way into lucrative contracts, exploiting their beauty with rich and influential men to further their careers, no wonder Celeste did not want to run the slightest risk of being tainted by embarking on any kind of relationship with anyone who could be considered in that light.

Such as himself, Rafael acknowledged. His wealth, as he knew only too well, made him a target for just such women, and he also knew that it was precisely the fact that Madeline had already made her own money—huge amounts of it!—that had been a key factor in their relationship. There had been no question that Madeline had wanted him only in order to further her career!

But he didn't want to think about Madeline—he wanted to think about Celeste—

*Is she worrying that people might think she turned down Reiner for a man even richer? Is that the reason for her reluctance? Because it would show her to be no better than that other model who did have an affair with Reiner to advance her career?*

If so, it was a tribute to her character, demonstrating yet again how right he was to want her as deeply as he did! He could be confident that he could trust her not to be venal or corrupt—not to be the kind of woman who would trade herself for financial advantage!

His eyes shadowed. In his country of birth, still teeming with impoverished masses, there were women so abjectly poor they had no choice but to sell their bodies simply to survive. But here in the rich Western world there was seldom such desperate need. Here it would simply be a matter of making easy money...

In his head, the harsh sound of mocking laughter echoed viciously...

His mouth tightened to a whipped line and forcibly he

wiped his mind of all such tainted, toxic thoughts. Celeste was nothing like that—*nothing!* That was all he had to know. All he needed to know.

Apart from the most important thing of all—how to win her. How to allay her reluctance and wariness and get her, little by precious little, to relax with him. To enjoy his company as he was enjoying having hers this evening.

He put aside such troubling thoughts, focussing instead on making this a pleasant, easy meal to share together, without stress or strain.

He nodded at her with a slight smile. 'Sole OK?' he checked as they began to eat.

'Beautiful,' she assured him.

'And I can't tempt you to a modest spoonful of hollandaise sauce?' He indicated the silver jug containing the butter-rich sauce that went with his own salmon.

'You can tempt me,' she said lightly, 'but I won't succumb.'

Even as she spoke she realised it was a *double entendre*.

Long lashes dipped down over his obsidian eyes. 'I shall live in hope,' Rafael murmured, the now familiar humorous glint in his eyes.

She gave a resigned shake of her head even as her lips twitched with unconscious amusement. She was coming to appreciate that this uniquely disturbing man had a beguiling sense of humour that could tease gently—but not threateningly.

He might radiate the sense of powerful self-assurance that sat on many a wealthy man's shoulders, and beneath the hand-tailored suit there might be an innate underlying toughness that came, she suspected, from the struggles he had faced in his life to make himself what he now was, but for all that—perhaps *because* of that!—there was a chivalry about him that could only warrant her respect and her appreciation. She felt warmed by it. His intervention in that horrible, ugly scene with Karl Reiner was proof of that—as was the open contempt he displayed towards the man.

No, she acknowledged, with wrenching self-awareness, Rafael Sanguardo posed one threat to her only: he attracted her—attracted her as no other man had ever done!

*That is his threat to me! That! And that is why I cannot— must not!—let myself be beguiled by him! However much I want to be! I am not free to be beguiled by him! I am not free to want him as I do!*

It was impossible. Always impossible. Which was why this evening could not be the start of anything—only the end.

*And so I must make the most of it! Have it as a good memory for the future. The memory of what might have been but cannot be...*

That was all she could have. All she could *ever* have.

She took a breath, made some polite, praising comment about the quality of the food they were eating, and the conversation moved on. It was easy and yet mentally stimulating, too, as well as pleasant and enjoyable—let alone that it quickened her pulse so powerfully, so beguilingly, to talk to Rafael Sanguardo, whatever the subject.

The single glass of crisp white wine she'd allowed herself helped, she knew, and she sipped it carefully as she ate. Quite what they talked about she wasn't aware—only that they ranged over a variety of subjects. Rafael proved a skilful conversationalist, his wry comments infused with glinting humour, and yet when he was serious—as when they talked about his work and his country—she could see a clear sense of commitment and passion about him.

More and more Celeste found herself thinking well of him, even beyond the oh-so-potent physical attraction that so disturbed her senses. *He is an enlightened, upright man, with sound principles and a sense of the responsibility that comes with the kind of wealth he has made for himself—and made for others, too.*

A man she could respect. The little stab of anguish came

again. And a man she could easily, so dangerously easily, start to feel much more for than respect.

But that reaction must be quashed. She must not give in to her silent urge to hold his eyes, to let her own eyes dwell on the strongly planed features of his face that drew her gaze so much, to let herself feel that shimmer of response to his effortlessly compelling masculinity. She must restrict and restrain herself to being cool and composed and letting no emotion well up from the core of her being.

But as they neared the end of their meal Celeste's determined composure was overset by a quite different source. She had just made an interested reply to something Rafael had said about the new eco-friendly beachfront resort in Maragua that he was investing in when her eye was abruptly caught by a couple taking their place at a table at the far end of the room. They were almost concealed by the red velvet drapery—but not enough to stop her recognising, with a sudden tautening of her stomach, that the man was Karl Reiner.

Then another ripple of unpleasant recognition went through her. The woman he was with was Louise, the young model she'd met the day before.

'What is it?' Rafael asked quietly, seeing her expression.

Celeste swallowed. 'Karl Reiner's just turned up with a model I know is only a teenager and is totally new to modelling,' she said tightly.

She looked as if she was going to jump to her feet. Rafael stayed her, loosely cupping her wrist for a moment. 'Do you think she's underage?' he asked, in the same low voice.

Celeste shook her head. 'No, but she's made up to look my age—which she is not. I don't want—' She stopped.

'Just keep an eye on her,' Rafael advised. 'Has Karl Reiner seen you?'

'No, and now he's out of my vision—he's hidden behind that drape.'

'Well, he's not the important one—she is.'

They resumed eating and conversation returned, but

Celeste was constantly aware of Louise on the far side of the room.

As the waiter cleared their plates and she glanced again towards Louise she frowned. The expression on Louise's face had changed. She was looking vacant, and there was a slackness about her posture. She lifted the glass at her setting and drank from it. Water? thought Celeste. Or vodka? Then, as Louise bent her head to fork her food in a suspiciously slow-motion way, Celeste saw Karl Reiner's hand extend from behind the drape and drop something into Louise's glass.

She was on her feet in a second. Crossing the restaurant in moments. Standing in front of Louise.

'Hello, Louise,' she said. She kept her voice friendly.

Louise lifted her drooping head and smiled. 'Hi!' she slurred. Her eyes were glassy, but at least she'd recognised her, Celeste noted.

'What the hell are *you* doing here?' Karl Reiner leant forward belligerently.

Celeste's eyes lasered him. 'You've put something in Louise's drink. I saw you! And, looking at the state of her, it's not the first time this evening!'

Karl's face darkened. 'You make accusations like that and I'll see you in court!' he attacked belligerently.

A voice behind her spoke. Cool, but with an edge to it that cut like a blade. 'One moment—'

Rafael's hand cupped Celeste's tensed shoulder and he reached forward to pick up Louise's glass. It looked clear and pristine, but he raised it to his nose.

'Roofies don't smell and they don't taste—and they dissolve instantly!' Celeste ground out.

'There's no damn roofies in that!' Karl snarled angrily.

The bladed voice came again. 'Well, if there's nothing spiked about Louise's drink you won't object to drinking it yourself, will you?'

Wordlessly he held it out to Karl. Who did not take

it. It was all Celeste needed. She went round to Louise's banquette.

'Time to go home,' she said bracingly, and helped her to her feet.

'I'm fine,' said Louise, but as she tried to stand up she started to sway, and collapsed back down again.

The *maître d'* was there, having realised something untoward was going on.

Rafael turned to him. 'Bring a small, unopened bottle of mineral water,' he ordered. 'Mr Reiner's guest is feeling unwell, so we'll be seeing her home.'

As the *maître d'* clicked his fingers to a minion, who scurried up with the requisite bottle, Rafael turned back to Karl Reiner.

'We'll get this analysed, shall we?' he said. He took the bottle, emptied the water it contained into the jug on the table and carefully poured the contents of Louise's glass into the now empty bottle, screwing on the lid and putting the bottle in his jacket pocket.

'You can't do this!' Karl pushed to his feet.

'I just have,' said Rafael. 'Would you like me to call the police as well?'

The *maître d'* looked aghast, and Rafael relented.

He turned back to Celeste. 'Can she walk, do you think?'

Celeste drew Louise to her feet again. 'Come on, Louise— let's go.'

Carefully, they escorted her from the dining room. Rafael phoned for his car. As they passed the reception desk Rafael paused to instruct that his bill be sent to his office.

'Oh, and cancel Mr Reiner's room for the night,' he added. 'He won't be needing it after all.'

The expression on the receptionist's face told him that his assumption had been right.

'The upper floors are bedrooms,' Rafael elucidated to Celeste as he guided both her and the woozy Louise out to the pavement. 'And, no, I was *not* planning on availing myself of the hotel facility here tonight!' he added stringently. 'I leave that kind of crassness to the likes of Louise's druggist!'

He got them both into the car and helped Celeste strap in a supine Louise. Then, after Celeste's protracted extraction of Louise's address from her, he instructed his driver and the car moved off.

He turned back to Celeste. 'Did you definitely see him spike her drink?'

'*Yes!* And that analysis will prove positive!' she bit out vehemently.

He held up a hand. 'Celeste, I don't know the exact legal status of Rohypnol, or anything else it might be, but proving that you saw him do it, plus that it was non-consensual on Louise's part, is going to be very difficult—if not impossible.'

He saw the stormy expression in her eyes in the street lights and went on, 'So let's just get her home, shall we? You can read the Riot Act to her tomorrow. But you know…' His voice changed. 'You have to allow for the fact that she was there of her own free will, and might very well have been perfectly willing to go ahead with whatever it was that Karl Reiner had planned.' He took a breath. 'I know it's not anything you could possibly go along with yourself, but there are women who would.'

*Women who would do a lot more…*

He saw Celeste's face still. For a moment it was as if he could see the bones beneath her skin. Stark and skeletal. But maybe it was a trick of the strobing street lights.

Louise groaned. 'I feel sick,' she said.

Silently Rafael handed Celeste a clutch of paper tissues from the supply in the car. To his relief they were not needed, and some fifteen minutes later they were in Earls Court, pulling up outside the address Celeste had extracted. They got Louise up the steps, and eventually inside, into the hands of the flatmate who had come down to answer the door.

She stayed to explain, briefly, what had happened, sufficiently reassured by the concern of the flatmate, who seemed sensible and level-headed. 'Probably a roofie,' she said. 'Possibly vodka, too. Get her to phone me tomorrow,' she instructed. 'Celeste Philips—we're at the same agency. I have some ground rules to spell out to her if she's going to survive this modelling game!'

After handing over the woozy Louise, she returned with Rafael to his car. Back in the interior, she closed her eyes. Rafael settled in his seat and looked at her. Her face was tight and stark.

'I'll see you home,' he said quietly.

The car moved off and he found himself looking at her, at her pale, haunting beauty which moved him so. Her eyes stayed closed, her face averted, her taut expression not easing.

His thoughts were troubled. In his head he heard again her voice at the restaurant.

*'I don't date,'* she'd said. *'I don't date and I don't have relationships. Or romances. Or affairs. Or anything—whatever you want to call them. I just...don't.'*

The bald, blunt words echoed in his mind. Setting his thoughts running.

Had what had so nearly happened to the teenage model tonight happened to Celeste? Was that the explanation for the sad, bleak announcement she'd made? Had she been so badly scared—scarred?—that she'd played safe since then?

Does she see herself in that young, vulnerable girl? Was she once such a girl and there was no one to rescue her in time?

If that were so, no wonder she was now so wary of men!

But resolution seared through him. *Well, I must change that! I must show her that desire can be very, very different from lust! I must show her how desire should be between a man and a woman!*

His eyes rested on her where she sat, so close to him and yet locked in her lonely world, so apart, so separate. He felt emotion coursing through him. Desire—sweet and strong, yet tender, too. He felt his hand lift and almost grazed her silken hair, almost cupped the sculpted turn of her cheek, brushed the tip of his thumb across the alabaster satin of her eyelids…

With an effort he drew back, waited until the car had completed its journey back to Notting Hill and drawn up outside her flat. She opened her eyes as the engine was cut, automatically turning her head towards the kerbside.

Her gaze collided with Rafael's. For a moment her unguarded gaze poured into his. He felt his breath catch. Then, before he could stop himself, he was doing what he'd had to hold himself back from. His hand moved towards her, slid around the nape of her neck. His fingers shaped her jaw, lifting her face to his as he lowered his mouth.

As his lips grazed hers he felt her give a little gasp, almost a tremor. But it was too late. He could not stop himself. He could only give himself to the overriding impulse surging within him to move his mouth to enclose hers, to feel the silken brush of her lips against his, feel her hesitation, her uncertainty.

He wanted to sweep them away! To melt them away until she was soft and molten in his embrace! Willing and ardent!

And just for a moment he felt that melting that he sought from her! Felt her soften, yield, felt her tremulous lips start to part so that he could do what every fibre of his being was urging him to do—taste the sweetness of her honeyed mouth.

Triumph swept through him. Not the triumph of conquest but the triumph of trust bestowed, that she had chosen— *chosen!*—to let him kiss her.

And then she was withdrawing.

Instinctively he wanted to catch her to him again, to coax and persuade her silken lips to open to him again. But with a higher knowledge he knew he must not. He must relinquish her. For if he did not she would be scared away again, and what he had achieved would be lost already.

Yet even as she drew away from him his hand lingered at her cheek and the tips of his fingers threaded into her hair. His eyes poured into hers, lambent in the dim light of the interior of the car. Absently he was glad of the smoked glass between them and the driver, but even so he could not care. The whole world could have witnessed this moment! With his blessing!

For she was holding his ardent gaze, open and transparent, and he was seeing into her eyes, into the depths of her, with nothing between them.

'Celeste…' Her name was on his lips, husky and low, and his fingers stroked at the delicate bones of her cheek.

'Rafael—I…I…' She could say no more.

He did not want her to. 'Hush…' He spoke softly, intimately, to her alone. 'This is my promise to you, Celeste.' His eyes spoke with his voice, his gaze rich and full. 'My promise is that if you give yourself to me I will give myself to you in equal measure. With me all shall be well—I promise you. Whatever scarred you long ago will be undone.' He gave a wry smile, letting his hand fall from her while his eyes still held hers like precious pearls. 'We will take it slowly—as slowly as you need. I promise you.'

He drew back, straightening, holding her gaze for one last moment. Then he was opening the passenger door, stepping out, turning back to take her hand in his and help her out. He made no attempt to kiss her again. He would keep his word—take this as slowly as she needed.

But for all that he knew, with an absolute conviction that coursed through him like a strong, dark current as his eyes rested on her with a last, caressing glance, that 'slowly' did not mean that in the end they would not reach the destination that he sought…

Celeste in his arms…his embrace…his bed…

# CHAPTER SIX

IN A DAZE, Celeste walked upstairs to her flat. Her mind was reeling, her senses were reeling and the blood in her veins seemed to be alive with a spirit she could not quench or quell.

He had kissed her! Rafael had kissed her! And the touch of his lips was seared upon her own as if he were kissing her still—as if that coaxing, seductive velvet were still working its magic upon her.

Unconsciously she put her fingertips to her lips as she stepped inside her flat, leaning back breathless against the door, her vision blinking in the bright light, seeing not this light but the dim lamplight of the car's interior, the sculpted outline of Rafael's strong face, the dark light of his eyes as they held hers.

Her breath caught. How long—how emptily, achingly long?—had it been since she had been kissed? Years upon empty years!

And never, *never* like that!

*No one could create that touch—that softness, that magic!*

Only Rafael. Only him—

She pressed a hand to her breast. Beneath her ribs her heart was beating fast, not just from the stairs but from the hectic pulse in her throat.

*I should have stopped him! I should have said no. I can't do this—I must not!*

But even as she adjured herself she knew it would have

been impossible to have stopped him! Impossible to have resisted the velvet caress of his fingertips, his mouth. Impossible to resist the magic he had woven on her lips.

As if he'd broken a spell...

Freeing her from a prison that had held her for too long.

She gave a little cry. Half anguish, half disbelief. Lurching forward, she hurried into the kitchen, busied herself deliberately with filling the kettle, setting it to boil. Tea—that was what she needed! Tea—strong and hot and comforting and *normal*—that would scald away the last remnants of his touch upon her lips. Because scald it away she must—of course she must.

She closed her eyes. A great anguish filled her.

What he wanted she could not give.

And what she wanted she could not take.

Barred for ever...

Bleakly she made her tea, disposing of the teabag, rinsing the sink out with the remainder of the boiling water, scouring it as if she were scouring her skin, killing his touch.

It didn't matter—it didn't matter that he'd kissed her. How could it? It changed nothing...nothing at all. What she felt, what she wanted...longed for...did not matter.

With unseeing eyes she started to sip the scalding hot tea, sip after sip. Obliterating the taste of his mouth from hers. While, inside her, her heart ached with an unbearable anguish for what must not be—could not be.

Celeste was asleep and dreaming. Despite her fears that it would not, sleep had come immediately after she'd gone to bed, barely staying up long enough to take her make-up off before pulling her nightdress on and slipping under her duvet. She was asleep almost before her head hit the pillow.

And then she started to dream.

But not about Rafael's kiss.

*Hands—hands all over her. And she could not stop them. There was a voice, too, talking at her, and she had to hear*

*it, could not block her ears. She could feel her dress falling
off and she could not stop it. And then the touching started...
the stroking...and the hot breath on her skin. And she could
not stop that either.*

*She could not stop anything.*

*And there was one more thing she could not stop.*

*She could not stop remembering.*

Rafael replaced his phone in its cradle on his desk, a look
of grim satisfaction on his face. The conversation he'd just
had had been off the record, but it had confirmed that Karl
Reiner was not popular even on his own company's board.

Louise was the first teenage model he had plied with
what a lab analysis of the water Rafael had taken from him
last night had confirmed as Rohypnol. Reiner's unsavoury
reputation had become a liability, and his fellow directors
were going to take action—Karl Reiner was about to be removed from the board and sidelined from the running of
the company.

Wanting to pass on the good news, Rafael phoned Celeste.
As ever, it went to the answer machine, but he was unfazed
by it. He was used to it by now. He kept his tone casual and
conversational, with only an underlying trace of concern.

'How are you? Have you heard anything from Louise?
Let me know if there's anything I can do on that front. And
I have some welcome news about Karl Reiner. Give me a
call some time and I'll tell you about it.'

He had no very great expectation that she would do so,
and he was not disappointed. Instead, addressed to him at
his London office, there arrived a card adorned with a Dutch
still life from the National Gallery's collection on which she'd
handwritten, 'Thank you for your help the other evening. It
was very good of you'.

It was signed simply 'Celeste'.

The glint came to his eyes again. Then he picked up his
phone and called her number. Not her landline, her mobile.

She answered it promptly, simply saying, 'Hello?' in a businesslike tone.

'Celeste—I'm glad I've reached you.'

There was a choking sound at the other end. The mordant glint in Rafael's eyes intensified.

'How did you get this number?' Celeste demanded. She did not sound businesslike now. She sounded agitated.

'Louise. She was very helpful.'

*'Louise?'* Celeste expostulated.

'Yes. I called at her flat yesterday evening, asking how she was. She said you'd talked to her and had been "really sweet" and she said how sorry she was, and how grateful to us both, and how she'll never be such an idiot again. I took ruthless advantage of her gratitude and asked if she had your mobile number.' He paused. 'She was thrilled to give it to me, and said you were "really lovely" and "really friendly" and hoped we'd be "really happy" together.'

There was another choking sound.

He waited for it to subside, then continued smoothly. 'So, in order to fulfil her rose-tinted romantic expectations, I would therefore like to invite you to the theatre one evening. Will you come?'

There was a moment's silence at the other end. Then, 'It's very kind of you, but it isn't possible.'

She spoke with what, Rafael could tell she intended to be, an air of finality.

'Louise will be extremely disappointed,' he replied. 'How will you possibly explain to her that you turned me down? She's played cupid, and this is her reward?'

'If you hadn't conned her into giving you my number she wouldn't know anything about it!' Celeste bit back.

'What's done is done,' Rafael replied, unconcerned. 'What sort of theatre do you like? Drama? Musicals? Opera? Tragedy…comedy…kitchen sink—is that the right expression in English?'

Celeste shut her eyes. 'Please,' she said, 'I explained to

you—I don't do this. I just...*don't,* and you have to accept it. Please. It isn't...personal.'

She had to make herself speak. Her throat was narrowing and it was painful. More painful than it should be.

There was silence for a moment. Then Rafael spoke. The lightly teasing tone was gone. In its place was a quiet resolve. 'I'll give you time, Celeste, all the time you need. But I won't give you for ever. Take care of yourself for now.' Then he rang off.

She stared at the silent phone. Then slowly turned it off.

Her heart seemed to be thumping heavily in her chest.

Rafael kept himself busy. It made passing the time until he could get back in touch with Celeste easier. He wanted to give her the time he knew she needed, and didn't want to spook her by being too pushy about how much he wanted to get to know her more, wanted to woo her.

He habitually worked at a punishing rate, clocking up long hours, but now he upped his schedule, taking in a gruelling round of meetings with his existing companies, and with the prospective recipients of his investments, and with financial institutions that might co-fund them as appropriate. Then he flew to New York and did a similar round, heading back to the UK via Barcelona before arriving in London.

The time away had done nothing to lessen his resolve. In the non-stop schedule of meetings and socialising he'd undertaken, Celeste's image had hung perpetually in his mind. And more than her image. It was as if he could still taste the sweetness of her lips, feel the soft silk of her skin, the delicate structure of her cheekbones and jaw.

When, on the return flight, he chanced to be sitting next to a female passenger perusing a fashion magazine, his eyes dropped to one of the adverts for Blonde Visage. Celeste—in all her pale, pure, ethereal beauty! His breath caught and stilled, his eyes devouring her.

How hauntingly beautiful she was! And yet... His eyes shadowed. There was a hauntedness about her, too.

*What happened to her in that long-ago trauma that has set her on this isolated course she steers?*

Whatever it was—whether or not it was akin to the fate she had saved the young and naive Louise from—he would release her from its haunting! Because the promise of release was there—he had tasted it on her lips, in the sweetness of her mouth.

*I can free her from it! I can take her to the place she should be free to go to fulfil the desire that flares between us! I can lead her back from her lonely world, lead her at my side—so she no longer has to be apart, no longer has to keep the world at bay.*

Back in London he phoned her, leaving a message on her landline. He heard nothing, and the following morning he tried her mobile number. It went to voicemail. He instructed his PA to send flowers. But at the end of the day she told him the florist had been unable to deliver, and that the occupant of the ground-floor flat had told them she was away.

By noon the next day, courtesy of a call to a harassed-sounding individual at the agency he knew represented Celeste, Rafael knew exactly where she was. Not just away, but abroad. A glamorous shoot on a glamorous tropical island. It had been arranged at short notice, and it was about as far away from England as you could fly.

He leant back in his leather executive chair and stretched his legs under his desk, looking out into the middle distance. Turbulent emotion speared through him. He had thought—hoped!—that his kiss would tell her more than words ever could just what could be between them if only she would let him take her to the place he longed to take her—to the intimacy he knew would light them both. But yet again she had fled from him. Yet again she had disappeared—

He frowned, frustration biting at him. Had she taken

work abroad simply to get away from his attentions? It was likely—and he feared it was so.

Thoughts swirled within him. Should he simply accept, heavily, that what he wanted was impossible? Should he simply relinquish her to the sterile, lonely world she wanted to go on living in? That sad, isolated place she lived her life in—alone and solitary.

But every sentiment within him rebelled at such defeat.

*No! I can't let her do it to herself! I can't let her shut out the emotions, the physical joy, that should be hers! If she is haunted by her past I will exorcise it for her! I will rescue her from her isolation...her bleak, sad, self-imposed prison.*

And in doing so he knew he would find a joy that only she could give to him.

He sat forward energetically, with renewed vigour. He would not—*could* not—let Celeste languish without making one final attempt to reach her. Convince her that he could bring a joy to her that would free her from her lonely life.

He leant forward, picking up his phone to speak to his PA. Seeking out Celeste one last time would mean a long flight and clearing his diary ruthlessly.

But he would do it.

To win Celeste, Rafael was fast coming to realise, he would do a great deal.

# CHAPTER SEVEN

CELESTE CRANED HER neck to look out of the tiny porthole. The plane was banking, bringing into view plunging cliffs lapped by the deep cobalt of the Pacific, vividly contrasting with the verdant green of the island ahead. She felt a little rush of pleasurable anticipation. It was an extravagance, she knew, coming here for a fortnight's holiday to this tiny Hawaiian island after the hectic shoot on Oahu, but she didn't care.

The other models had chosen to stay on at the large, lively Oahu hotel, but Celeste had opted for this small—if fearsomely expensive!—luxury resort on an island so small its airstrip could only take propeller-powered planes. She didn't want nightlife and entertainment and crowds—she wanted peace and quiet and the awe-inspiring beauty of Hawaii.

And when the deluxe SUV delivered her and the other incoming guests to the hotel she knew she had made the right choice. Her breath caught as she walked into the wide, open-air atrium of the low hacienda-style green-roofed hotel. A refreshing fountain tinkled at its stone-tiled centre, and beyond, framed by sprays of vivid crimson bougainvillaea, was a fabulous vista of lush verdant gardens, leading down to the sea beyond. She stood entranced, the delicate blossoms of her welcoming *lei* around her neck, drinking it all in, her eyes alight with wonder and pleasure.

Half an hour later, checked in and unpacked in her room—which might have been the cheapest in the resort but was still absolutely beautiful, with its little balcony overlooking the gardens at the side of the hotel—and having anointed her pale skin with the sunblock that was obviously going to be essential when she was outdoors in daytime, she headed out.

Delight filled Celeste as she walked down towards the beach past the azure freeform swimming pool, through landscaped gardens. Little paths meandered past rivulets and miniature waterfalls, lush with verdure and foliage, and vivid white and pink and red flowers grew everywhere, with sweeping beds of birds of paradise and other exotic blooms she could only guess at. It was hot, but not oppressively so, with a light, fresh breeze off the ocean.

As she arrived at the silken-sanded beach an attendant glided forward to usher her to a parasol-shaded lounger, arranging the towels and headrest for her. Gratefully she settled herself down, accepting his offer of a refreshing fruit juice and iced water. Moments later she was sipping as she gazed, entranced, out over the dark blue ocean, which was lapping the soft sand with gentle waves. A sense of peace enveloped her. She was away from everything else in her life—away from the clatter and noise of London, away from her work, from the frenetic pace of the fashion world.

Away from the man who had intruded into her life even though she didn't want him to.

Into her head leapt his image—as potent and powerful as it always was, as vivid and as real. As disturbing...

And more than just his image.

Like a tactile brush against her mouth, it was as if she could feel the soft, seductive graze of his lips on hers, arousing in her such sweet, tempting sensations that even now she felt her body tremble with the recollection.

Her peace was shattered. She must not let herself think—remember—feel! She must not! She must only remind herself of the impossibility of what he wanted—how it could never, *never* happen!

Abruptly, she picked up the resort's activities guide and

started to peruse it. One activity in particular caught her attention. It was a stargazing expedition to the deserted side of the island—a nature reserve where there was no light pollution from the resort. There would be an astronomer to instruct them, and professional-level telescopes to view the heavens through. Early booking was recommended, owing to its popularity. The cost was high, but it would be worth it, Celeste knew.

As she made the decision to book the expedition she found herself remembering, yet again, how she'd gone out to look at the stars that evening of the charity show at the country house near Oxford. And how Rafael Sanguardo had simply strolled up to her and into her life...

She turned the page decisively. Well, he was out of her life now. And he had to stay that way. It was essential. She could not risk any further contact with him. His impact on her had been too powerful, urging her with every instinct of her being to respond to what she knew he sought from her.

Sadness haunted her eyes. She could not respond—must not respond. However much she might try and forget the past it controlled her still—dictated the terms on which she could now live her life. And that meant she had to abide by what she had told Rafael that evening in the restaurant.

*'I don't do relationships...'*

The stark, harsh truth was indelible. She had to stick to it—*had* to. And now she was nine thousand miles from him and it must stay that way! But even as she reminded herself of that, another thought slid into her head.

*It would have been good to watch the Hawaiian stars together...*

She snapped the guide shut. Put her drink back on the table. Got to her feet. She would go for a swim. Change the inside of her head, as it clearly urgently needed to be changed.

Carefully removing her *lei* and her sarong, Celeste stepped over the hot sand and down to the cooling waters of the ocean. She was here to relax, to indulge herself, to rest, to have 'me time' in a fabulously luxurious place.

And that was *all* she was going to do.

And for the next few days that was exactly what she did. She slid into the lazy routine of the resort, keeping to herself except for casual chats with other guests. She drew male eyes, as she always did, but the clientele here were not the kind to plague her with uninvited attentions. Most guests were couples, anyway, either young honeymooners or older couples enjoying a leisured retirement.

Yet although she kept to her customary solitude, sometimes, with a little pang, she felt a flicker of envy as she watched their companionship, their affection to each other, their togetherness...

Then she would look away again. That was not for her and she must accept it.

Must banish, too, the thoughts that followed—thoughts that saw, clearly and disturbingly, the tall, magnetic figure she must not let herself think about. For he had gone from her life now, as she had told him to.

She must be content with what she had. Which, right now, was this magical resort and all it offered.

She'd booked the stargazing expedition and enjoyed the facilities of the spa, had gone out on a courtesy outrigger ride, seen turtles swimming over the reefs and tried a little gentle bodysurfing. Other than that she had done absolutely nothing except laze and swim and pass the days in peace and quiet.

*I could stay here for ever,* she thought as she lay on her sunbed, half drifting off to sleep in the shaded warmth, soothed by the murmur of the breeze in the palm fronds, the lap of the waves on the sand. Other than that, there was silence all around her.

Until a voice spoke above her. Deep and accented.

'Hello, Celeste.'

She jackknifed to a sitting position, shock—more than shock—jagging through her.

Rafael Sanguardo, clad in a dark blue T-shirt and pale board shorts, reached out a hand to pull an adjacent empty sunbed closer, and lowered his long, lean body down on it.

'Before you ask—because I can see the question...or rather the outraged demand...is on your lips,' he informed her, 'you can blame your booker. I bullied him shamelessly to tell me where your shoot was, and then found your erst-while colleagues disporting themselves on Oahu. And I must say...' he glanced around '...you have made a wiser choice than they. *This,*' Rafael said appreciatively, 'is fabulous.'

He settled himself back on the sunbed. One of the beach staff came up, having seen a new arrival, and Rafael turned to Celeste, nodding at her empty glass of fruit juice.

'A refill on that?' He didn't wait for an answer, but made his own request, smiling at the young Hawaiian.

When he'd gone, Rafael turned to Celeste again. Emotion kicked in him. It was so *good* to see her again! To be able to let his eyes take in the incredible beauty of her body, her face, to drink it in like the sweetest nectar. The days since he'd last set eyes on her—handing her out of his car after they'd taken the hapless Louise home—had stretched to an endless age. But now he was seeing her again. She was here, so close to him, and it was good—oh, it was good!

She was staring at him. But not with the expression that he was gazing at her with.

'What are you doing here?' she said, her voice staccato with shock.

Dark lashes lowered over darker eyes. Then he spoke, his voice different from the tone he'd used just now. Sombre. Grave. 'This is my last attempt, Celeste. Allow me it—because if I fail now, then you have my word. I will let you be. I will leave you alone.'

*Alone in that sad, bleak, empty world you tell me you live in, bereft of all that romance can offer the human spirit—*

*denying yourself all that could be yours...all that I could give to you...*

Her eyes were troubled.

'I thought I was alone,' she heard herself say.

His gaze was level on her. 'As I've promised, we will take it as slowly as you need.' Rafael's eyes held hers. 'I ask only that you give me a chance.'

For an endless moment, it seemed to her, his eyes went on holding hers, asking a question to which she could give no answer. Had no answer to give.

She knew, with a hollowing of dismay, that the leap in her heart-rate had nothing to do with shock. And everything to do with Rafael Sanguardo walking back into her life.

She shut her eyes, willing herself, hopelessly, to banish his image—the image that had leapt into her retinas, burning with a vividness that was as shocking as recognising his voice.

'I can't stop you,' she said, her tone low. 'This is a hotel—if you want to stay here you can. But don't think you can just take it for granted that I'll—' She stopped.

'Celeste, about you I take nothing for granted, I assure you,' Rafael said dryly. 'Every step of the way with you is a minefield. Every moment of communication I achieve with you makes me feel I deserve a medal!'

His voice had changed again—she could hear it.

'I ask nothing from you except your time and...' he chose his words carefully '...your trust. Trust me and spend time with me. You may enjoy it. I'll make no demands on you other than keeping company with me. Spending easy time—leisured time—time out from our working lives, our busy lives. Time to lie here beneath the palm trees, time to enjoy this wonderfully beautiful place, time to savour the scent of flowers and the sight of the sea and the sound of the bird-song. Time,' he finished, 'to gaze up at the night sky filled with tropical stars.'

He paused.

'Will you give me your trust and spend that time with me?'

She did not answer. Did not accept or refuse.

He let his eyes rest on her a moment. Her features had stilled and she had closed her eyes against him. Letting her silence be her assent.

# CHAPTER EIGHT

'WHICH RESTAURANT WOULD you like to dine at?' Rafael's courteous enquiry came as they reached the foot of the steps leading back up into the atrium.

'I don't mind,' Celeste answered.

She was not *in* her right mind, she knew—because how could she be if she was allowing what was happening? What she had allowed to happen all afternoon.

She had allowed Rafael Sanguardo to say those things to her, to settle himself on the sunbed next to her, keeping her company, asking her about the hotel, what she had done so far. She had allowed him to suggest trying the sea together, which she had declined, and so she'd watched him peel off his T-shirt and run lithely down across the hot sand to plunge into the waves, ploughing out through them with a strong forearm stroke before returning to land eventually, dark hair wet like a glossy raven's wing, water droplets glistening off a bared torso that had been every bit as muscled as she'd known it must be, the shoulders just as broad, the back just as sculpted, his thighs just as steely...

She'd been unable to peel her eyes away from his lean, toned body, unable to stop the strange flush of heat that went through her as she had gazed as though the sun had gained an extra fierceness and started beating in her veins...

She'd allowed it all—allowed him to sit beside her on his sunbed, quiveringly aware of his presence, as they'd watched the sun turn to gold as it sank into the cobalt sea…allowed him to help gather her things and scoop up the used towels to drop them into the canvas box by the beach kiosk, to pad with her along the warm stone pathways across the dusky gardens, back towards the hotel.

Allowed him to stand here now and consider which restaurant to take their dinner in.

Together.

And she would allow that, too, she knew, because she didn't want to have to think about this any more. Didn't want to feel the pressure or the temptation to say no, to send him away, to banish him.

She knew, with the strangest feeling inside her, that she didn't want to do anything right now except go on allowing him to be with her.

She also knew, however reluctant she was to admit it, that she didn't want to try and reject that quivering awareness of him, that flush, that rush of heat in her veins that came just at his nearness to her…

'Then I'll choose,' he said. 'Why not meet at the terrace bar in an hour or so?'

He smiled, the lines around his mouth deepening, and watched her go along the pathway that led to her wing of the hotel. He was on the other side of the complex, in one of the cabana-villas that had their own secluded garden areas and their own private plunge pools.

Would he be taking her there one evening? Rafael found himself thinking. Would there be a time when they would not go their separate ways after lazing on the beach, but instead wander, arms entwined, to find a private hour together? The hour between sunset and moonrise…an hour filled with desire and passion and the fulfilment that he longed for—that had brought him here, across two oceans and a continent, to find her…woo her…win her…?

As he set off in his own direction he knew the answer was

still unspoken. However much he hoped for it and sensed that Celeste hoped for it, too.

Yet later, as he walked up to Celeste across the atrium towards the open-air loggia bar, Rafael knew his hopes were soaring higher than ever. She was poised by the balustrade, looking down over the tumbling water feature, and for a second he was back in that Oxfordshire mansion, seeing her at the head of the staircase there, remembering how his eyes had gone to her immediately, how he had taken in a vision of pale beauty, rare grace, and how he'd been struck by how... *alone*...she'd seemed. How apart from the rest of the world.

So beautiful. So alone.

*But now she is alone no longer! Now she is with me!*

Oh, it was the most tentative of achievements simply for her to accept his company as she was doing, but for all that he knew he had come a long way since that first sighting of her. She was no longer walking away from him, walking out on him, rejecting his overtures, his company. And that, he knew, was an achievement indeed!

But the way ahead—the way he so wanted to guide her towards, for both their sakes—was uncertain, and he had to move with care, with caution. For one rash, rushed move could send her fleeing from him again.

And he did not want that! Did not want it with an intensity that was almost palpable. This was, as he had promised, his very last attempt to win her—and he might lose her yet! Yet now, as he greeted her, he knew that his dominant emotion was pleasure—the pleasure of letting his eyes rest on her, on how lovely she looked, her pale beauty set off by a long, flowing dress in hibiscus-red, floral and graceful. It was gathered at the waist and the bodice was softly clinging, with a wide, low ruffle framing her shoulders. Her fair hair was loose, but drawn back from her face with pearl-edged combs, and her only jewellery was a mother-of-pearl pendant.

He came and stood beside her, not standing too close. He

did not want to crowd her at so tentative a stage of his careful, wary courtship. He looked out, as she was doing, over the lush gardens spreading below the cantilevered terrace, the verdant greenery hardly visible now in the gathering night except where the torches had been lit and at the faintest line of light from the far horizon.

'This really is just exceptionally beautiful,' he breathed, his eyes roaming the vista before him.

Celeste turned. 'Isn't it?' Her cautious, brief smile met his. Admiring the hotel and its grounds was safe. 'I just can't get over how idyllic it is.'

Idyllic it was, Rafael knew, but he also knew, with sombre recognition, that as in every paradise there was a serpent here. The serpent that lay coiled deep within Celeste, engendered by whatever dark trauma had wounded her so long ago, making her feel she had to keep apart...alone.

But as his eyes rested on her he felt the swell of emotion and resolve filled him.

*I will draw her to me so that she is no longer apart... alone! So that she can share with me what I so wish there to be between us!*

'What can I get you to drink?' His own voice penetrated his thoughts. He welcomed the question. He must keep the atmosphere between them light, easy—companionable. Nothing more than that for now. In order to let her come to feel comfortable with him.

As anticipated, she asked for mineral water, and he went off towards the bar. Behind him, Celeste's eyes followed him. Although the hotel was deluxe, formal dinnerwear was not required, and Rafael was wearing smart but casual trousers and an open-collared light blue shirt, the cuffs turned back. As he came back to her, a drink in either hand, she saw how lean and strong his wrists were, how the natural tan of his skin tone contrasted with the pale brushed cotton of his shirt.

He'd brought a beer for himself, and he sipped it thoughtfully as they stood in a silence that was not, she realised, strained, but which seemed—impossible though it must surely be—natural and easy... They looked out over the darkened gardens, letting the warm night air waft over them. Beyond the gardens the susurrating sound of the waves breaking on the shore was still audible.

As more guests gathered on the terrace, their conversations rising, Rafael turned to Celeste. 'Shall we go and eat?'

She nodded, setting down her glass beside his on the ledge of the balustrade to be cleared away.

'Which restaurant did you choose?' she asked.

'I played safe and went for the fine dining French cuisine one,' he answered. 'I wasn't sure how you were on other styles of cuisine.'

'I haven't been there yet,' she said.

It was the most expensive in the hotel, which was why she'd been avoiding it. A frown furrowed her brow. She would have to make it clear to Rafael that when they ate she would be paying her own share.

They had to walk a little way along a torch-lit pathway across the gardens to the restaurant, which was set apart from the main body of the hotel. The restaurant opened to its own private garden-level terrace, with a view out over the sea beyond the lawn, framed by palm trees. They took their places and perused the menu. Every gourmet item looked tempting to Celeste, and with a sense of sudden freedom she gave her order.

Rafael quirked an eyebrow. 'I suspect the sauce that comes with that has cream in it,' he warned.

'I don't care!' she answered defiantly. 'Every day of my working life I have to calorie-count! But I'm on holiday now—and that includes my diet, too!'

He smiled. 'That's the spirit,' he said. Inside, he felt another spurt of satisfaction.

He took extreme care, throughout the evening, to keep her in that zone. His tone was always light, with humour lurking in his eyes, a smile at his lips. Using every skill at his command, he strove to draw her out and yet keep the conversation sufficiently impersonal—things any two people together might chat about—so as not to scare her off yet again. He started by talking about the hotel and the amenities of the resort, about which she knew more than him, which made it good for getting her to talk more.

'Do you dive?' he asked at one point.

She shook her head.

'Then perhaps snorkelling would do? Will you come out some time? The hotel will provide the equipment, I know. And,' he went on, 'how are you on the sea? Apparently there's a bay around the headland where dolphins gather—we can take a catamaran to see them.'

Celeste's face lit. 'Oh, yes—I haven't done that yet and I want to!'

'Good.' He smiled. 'What else shall we do?'

Skilfully, he steered the conversation along, and as the courses passed he could see her finding it easier and easier to talk to him. In the same mood of calorific defiance that had made her order fish with a buttery sauce, she did not object when he refilled her wine glass.

By the time the waiter placed their coffee in front of them there was an air about her that he'd never seen—an air that was almost…well, *carefree*. That was the best word Rafael could think of.

Gladness filled him. And a sense of well-being. This was the right thing to have done—to have flown nine thousand miles to find her—to try one last time to persuade her to put behind her the ghosts from the past, to forget whatever it was that men like Karl Reiner had forced upon her. Whatever the ugly episode that had scarred her in the past—perhaps one such as she had saved the young model Louise from—he knew for certain it hadn't been one she had voluntarily engaged in. Others might choose to do so—and now his mind darkened, naming no names, but knowing well who he had in mind!—but not Celeste. Never Celeste!

He lifted his coffee cup, letting his eyes rest on her. His breath caught, as it did every time he looked at her anew. Now, with the night all around them, Celeste's so-beautiful face was underlit by the candles on the table, casting her features into luminous sculpture.

*How beautiful she is! How much she moves me!*

She picked up her own coffee cup, and as she did so her eyes met his.

Met and held.

Emotion washed through Celeste. Warm, vital…

In the flickering candlelight Rafael's face took on the planes of a dramatic *chiaroscuro*. Her pulse thickened—quickened.

*How right it seems to be here now! How right to sit here, with Rafael, in this place, at this time! To gaze at him and let him gaze at me, to feel the warm, strong current flow between us…*

The question she so badly wanted to answer shaped itself in her mind yet again.

*Could I really do what he so wants me to do? Is it possible? Is it really possible?*

Doubt and torment filled her mind. Until Rafael Sanguardo had walked into her life her resolve had been absolute. Romance could never be part of her life! *Never!* But he had overset her resolve, made her question all her bleak assumptions about what was no longer possible for her.

And now, as she gazed across at him, she felt that resolve weaken, that bleak determination erode. Longing swept through her—longing to accept, to take what he was offering to her! To take it with all her being! To give herself to him as she longed so much to do!

*Could I give myself to this time, this place, this moment? To this man? Could I truly give myself to him?*

That was the question that hung like a dazzling star in the heavens, waiting for the answer that only she could give…

* * *

Celeste could not sleep. She lay tossing and turning in the wide bed in which she'd slept soundly and uninterruptedly all the previous nights. She knew what had made the difference.

Rafael.

The man she desired as no other… With a desire that had leapt in her veins the moment her eyes had lit upon his tall, lean figure suddenly beside her on the beach that afternoon!

A desire that was tempting her to do what she had never done. To defy the past, and claim a present that was everything Rafael Sanguardo held out to her!

She gazed, sleepless, at the slowly turning fan over her head. She had never thought this day would come. Had thought that she would continue alone—must continue alone…always alone! Dragging the past behind her. The past that clung to her like a foul miasma, its tainted tendrils netting her. The past that she could never leave behind her. Never cut herself free from—

But never before had she so longed to be able to do so! To take with open heart and hands what Rafael was offering! To give herself to him fully and freely—

She pushed the bedclothes back, strode to the glass doors that opened to her balcony and slid them open, the mosquito mesh with them. She stepped out into the night, glanced upwards. Stars blazed overhead, burning through the golden floor of heaven. So far away—so far away…

Memory coiled in her head. How she had first gazed up all those years ago, when she was as young—as helpless!—as Louise…gazing up at the blaze of stars in a sky where clouds were unknown. Gazing up across the vast distance between where she'd stood and where the stars dwelt in the lofty, remote reaches of farthest space, freed from the mire of the world so far below them.

She had longed, then, to be drawn upwards into their distant reaches—to be taken up off the earth, far, far away from everything that had been happening to her, everything that had surrounded her there below, dragging her into the sordid mire of the world that she'd been so helplessly, hopelessly trapped in.

Yet now, as she tilted her head upwards and gazed at the jewelled sky, it was not the scintillation of the distant stars that was dominant in her senses but the warm, balmy air, the fragrant scent of the blooms upon the trees wafting towards her, the sound of the sea, the wash of the warm, breaking waves, their airy foam dispersed into the tropical night.

The profusion seemed to play upon her skin, lulling her, slowing her breathing. She felt her gaze slip from the distant stars, rest instead on the outline of palm trees, the pale shimmer of flowers in the gardens beyond her room. The warmth of the night enveloped her, the soft breeze whispering over her skin. And in her head the soft whispering of words was taking shape.

*You don't need to gaze up at the stars to find beauty and wonder, or to seek refuge in the heavens. You no longer need to long to escape the earth. This earth—here, now— this scented garden, this dark foliage, these velvet flowers it bears, all lapped by the moon-silvered sea—is good. It has blessings of its own.*

And beyond the gardens, in his cabana close to the sea's edge, across the smooth-cropped turf, was Rafael.

She felt her heart give a little lift. Rafael! A man who waited for her—waited for her to bestow upon him what she knew—*knew!*—was in her to bestow! Rafael! A man to whom she could give what she so longed to give. For he would cherish it—cherish her—respect her.

*Can I be free to do so? Finally free? Free to leave the past behind?*

She felt emotion swell within her.

*'We can make ourselves anew.'* Into her head came Rafael's voice, talking about how even the solid earth beneath their feet was constantly remaking itself. New land,

new continents…constantly forming, constantly remaking themselves.

Her gaze went out across the garden, glimmering in midnight beauty.

*These very islands are proof of that continual change! Each one has been formed from the liquid mantle deep beneath the ocean floor, each one formed and shaped and made anew, moving on, ever westwards, each island newborn—leaving its past behind them…*

Could she do likewise? If the very earth could change and leave its past behind could she not do so, too? Could she, too, be new-made like these emerald Hawaiian jewels? Finally leaving her past behind her?

*Surely I can do so!*

And surely that was the answer that she sought—she could leave her past behind and remake herself for the present that was offering itself to her. Give herself to the man who, alone of every man she had ever encountered, she longed to give herself to!

Slowly she returned to bed, shivering slightly in the air-conditioned cool as she shut the glass doors, slipped back under the coverlet.

And now, finally, she slept. Content, at last, with the answer she had found. The answer she had longed for so much…

# CHAPTER NINE

'THERE! THERE THEY ARE!' Rafael's voice rose over the rush of the wind in the huge sail of the catamaran as they clung to the tarpaulin with their hands and bare feet.

'I can't see!' cried Celeste. Then, with a gasp of excitement, she saw them.

A school of bottlenose dolphins, rising and plunging to starboard, leaping one after another, effortlessly keeping abreast of the wind-powered sail craft.

'Oh, they're wonderful!' she exclaimed joyously.

The helmsman grinned and shouted something to Rafael she could not catch, the wind whipping at his words.

'They'll surf our bow wave,' Rafael relayed.

She craned her neck, and sure enough she could see half a dozen dolphins rising and falling through the creaming bow wave and then the wake of the catamaran. Then, suddenly, she gave another cry.

'Rafael! Look—*look,* they're beneath us!'

She gazed down, enraptured, into the space between the twin hulls directly below the tarpaulin, as the dolphins swam beneath them.

'The currents bring the fish in,' the Hawaiian helmsman explained. 'Our wake stirs them up, too, and then the dolphins make the most of them. If you come to this bay in the morning you might be able to swim with them. But beware—they are wild creatures still.'

Rafael shook his head. 'This bay is theirs, not ours. We invade their world far too much.'

They were content with this exhilarating catamaran ride—even though it seemed to Celeste she was clinging to the tarpaulin for dear life.

When the boat tacked she slewed sideways, but Rafael was there, holding her firmly. Safely. Then they came about and he released her. But she could feel the imprint of his grip. Feel, too, the echo of the sense of security it had afforded her.

*I can be safe with him—safe in this wonderful, blissful present. Safe from the past.*

The words flitted through her mind.

All that morning she had felt different. As different as the stars that shone down on this azure water world of the mighty Pacific, in which the precious islands of the sea glittered like scattered emeralds, born from the ocean floor. How deep the ocean was, she thought, how drowning deep—*but here, with Rafael, I am safe.*

Safe in this bright new world, with Rafael at her side, the past seemed very far away.

When they got back to the little harbour and clambered ashore her legs felt like jelly. Rafael saw her wobble and caught her, his arm going around her waist. And once again Celeste felt his anchoring, felt his strength supporting her. She smiled up at him, her hair wind-tousled, fronding wildly out of the plait she'd woven it into to try and keep it tidy.

'OK now?' he said, and she nodded.

He let her go, turning to thank the helmsman. Then they climbed aboard the electric buggy to drive back up to the hotel.

'A good experience?' Rafael asked.

Celeste grinned, brushing back her unruly hair. 'Wonderful! I'll remember it all my life!'

He gazed, enthralled. Never yet had he seen her with so carefree an expression. He could not take his eyes from her. Only a smothered 'Rafael!' from her made him realise he was steering the buggy at the verge. He straightened it and concentrated on driving.

Back at the hotel, they headed for the pool. Diving into its cool depths was refreshing after the heat of the sun and the salty air at sea, and as Celeste surfaced it was to find Rafael beside her. His sable hair was slicked back off his face; strong, sinewed shoulders broke the surface. Effortlessly, he levered himself out of the pool in a single movement, then held down a hand to Celeste. She took it, feeling his strong fingers close around hers, and with similar effortless ease he lifted her clear. Then, refreshed, they settled back on their loungers.

A server cruised by and Celeste gratefully ordered iced water and coffee.

'No tea?' Rafael queried, echoing her order.

She gave a laugh and made a face. 'This is the USA— they don't do tea that's drinkable by the English! I stick to coffee here!'

'Have you travelled much in the States?' he asked.

She dried her face and started to apply more sunblock after her swim.

'Some,' she said. 'I've done a shoot at the Grand Canyon, which was breathtaking. And one in New Orleans—which is an amazing place. And then New England in the fall—also breathtaking. Plus, of course, I go to New York every year for the fashion shows.'

He nodded. 'I have offices there, but I spend less time there now. I prefer to visit the West Coast when I can. It's quicker to get back to Maragua from there.' He glanced at her again. 'Do you know California?'

Celeste shook her head. 'We stopped over in SF on our way out here, but only at the airport.'

'And what about Hawaii? Have you been here before?'

She gave another quick shake of her head. 'No, this is the first time. And it's as fabulous as its reputation says it is!'

Rafael smiled. 'And does it tempt you to go further across the Pacific? Down to Australia, perhaps?'

It was a casually voiced question, asked in the same friendly conversational tone as before, but as he asked her it was as if a shutter came down over her face. Just as he'd seen happen before, in London, when he'd asked her about how she'd become interested in astronomy.

'No,' he heard her say. The single word was negating and final.

He frowned. What had made her close down like that? 'You'd never care to go there?' he probed carefully.

She looked away, unwilling to meet his eyes. 'Not really,' she answered, making her voice as indifferent as she could. Hurriedly she sought to change the subject. 'Did you manage to get a place on the stargazing trip?' she asked.

He had—he'd made it a priority, knowing how much Celeste was looking forward to it.

The expedition did not disappoint.

With no moon, and no light pollution, the night sky was blazing with stars.

'OK, can anyone tell me what any of these constellations are?' The young astronomer, a postgrad from the University of Hawaii earning some extra money, waved a hand at the sky above them.

Immediately Celeste pointed north. 'The Great Bear and the two pointer stars pointing to Polaris, the Pole Star. Then over there…' She wheeled her arm around and proceeded to identify several more constellations.

'Great!' enthused their guide. 'Want to come and give me a hand?' he teased.

She laughed, shaking her head. 'Sorry!' she said.

'No, don't be! It's great that you're enthusiastic,' he said, and then helped others in the group see what she had indicated.

Rafael spoke over Celeste's shoulder. 'You know the

southern hemisphere constellations, too. Does that mean you've already been in that part of the world?'

But she didn't answer him, and appeared not to have heard him. He found himself frowning again.

*She is sensitive about it—why?*

Did she have bad memories? Was that it? Had whatever it was that had happened to her to make her withdraw from men, from love and romance, to make her so protective of naive young women like Louise, occurred somewhere like Australia? Was that why she was so evasive?

He felt the questions running through his head as he turned his attention back to the stargazing. Celeste, he could see, was clearly rapt, and he was glad. He wanted her to enjoy things—wanted her to enjoy things with him...

He enjoyed seeing with her the secrets of the heavens revealed to them through the powerful lenses of the telescopes—the stellar nurseries, where stars were born; the twin beacons of a binary system, with their different visual spectra; and, best of all, the galaxies revealed not as the blurry points they looked like from earth, but as populous as the Milky Way, teeming with a billion stars.

'To think that their light reaches us from so very, very far away!' she murmured wonderingly to Rafael as he stood back to let another guest take his place at the telescope.

'And from so very long ago,' he answered. 'Those stars have burnt out millennia ago, yet their light still reaches out to us. Their past becomes our present—'

She did not answer him. A shiver seemed to go through her. Rafael sensed it.

'Cold?' he asked. They were high up, on a terraced viewing platform cut into the side of the extinct volcanic peak that had formed the island long ago, and here the night air was cold, not balmy. They had been handed thick jackets to wear, to keep them warm as they stood under the stars.

Celeste did not answer him. It had not been the cold that had made her shiver. It had been the words he'd said.

*'Their past becomes our present—'*

They echoed again in her head, changing as they did.

*My past became my present...trapping me in my past...*

She shook her head. No, she would no longer let the past reach out to her. She would no longer let it isolate her, keep her away from what she knew, with every passing day, she wanted so much!

Rafael—Rafael to hold and be embraced by! Rafael to take her from the past, to set her free into a present that she wanted to embrace wholly and fully! Rafael to cradle her in his strong arms, kiss her with his warm lips...desire her with his body...

And she would let it happen! She would make herself anew—just like the continents and the islands did—leaving their past far, far behind.

She felt Rafael's warm, strong arm come around her shoulder, drawing her close to him against the chill of the starlit night. Her head tilted slightly, resting on his shoulder. His arm tightened around her. She pulled her gaze away from the distant stars and looked up into Rafael's eyes. He was looking down at her. His gaze was warm, and very close. And it glowed with a light that was only in the present, only in the time that was *now*.

By the time they got back to the hotel it was gone midnight. Celeste had drowsed as the SUV snaked its way slowly down the unmade roadway to the metalled coastal road that led back to the resort, and as they disembarked she was yawning.

'Off you go to bed,' Rafael said.

She smiled at him sleepily and headed off across the atrium to her wing of the hotel. Rafael watched her go until she was out of sight, then set off towards his cabana-villa in the other direction. As he walked through the night-scented gardens, with the stars burning above, his mood was strange.

He glanced upwards. He desired her so much, the woman whose name was as celestial as the pale, burning stars above.

But there was more than desire in what he felt—what he sought.

*What is happening to me?*

The question formed in his head, hanging there like a solitary star in his consciousness. Then he shook it aside and continued on his way.

But it hovered still, and in the morning he woke to its presence. It was with him as he set off on his daily run through the hotel grounds, and sprang stronger as he joined Celeste for breakfast. As it did every time, her beauty hit him. Today she was casually but beautifully dressed, as she always was, in a loosely shaped Grecian-style tunic sun-dress, her hair simply caught back at the nape of her head with a scarf. She had no make-up on, and her skin, despite her assiduous application of sunblock, had developed the glow of pale honey.

'Hi,' she greeted him. Her voice was warm. Her eyes warmer.

He felt emotion kick in him as he took his place. Desire, yes, and gladness that she was smiling at him—but there was more as well.

*What is happening to me?* The question hung again in his consciousness.

'Wasn't last night wonderful?' she was saying.

'Stars in your eyes?' He laughed.

'Oh, yes,' she answered. She speared another slice of the pineapple that was her breakfast staple.

'Mmm...' she murmured appreciatively as the incredible rich, ripe sweetness of its juice filled her senses. 'This is the best yet! Every morning I think this is the best Maui Gold pineapple in the entire universe—and then the next morning there's an even better one!'

He laughed, reaching forward with his unfurled linen napkin. There was a tiny drop of pineapple juice on her chin and he dabbed it away. An intimate gesture...

Their eyes met, mingled. Then she pulled hers away.

'What shall we do today?' she asked. There was the slightest hint of heightened colour in her cheeks.

'Your choice,' Rafael said expansively, pouring strong black coffee into his cup.

'After last night I'm feeling lazy,' she admitted.

'Then we'll have a lazy day. In fact, why don't we go the whole hog and indulge in a therapeutic massage? Every morning I run past the open-air massage beds by the edge of the sea and think I should book myself in!'

Celeste's eyes lit. 'Oh, yes—definitely! What a brilliant idea!'

His lashes dipped over his eyes. 'I'm full of good ideas, Celeste,' he said.

She felt heat flush through her and knew that he could see it, too. Knew, too, the truth of what he'd said. Resolve filled her. She would take everything that he was offering her, gladly and fully. No more questioning or torment or doubt or fear.

Rafael had reached out to her as no other man had done, had been able to. She did not know why, knew only that with him the past that chained her seemed so far away…so long ago. As far away as those distant stars that had burnt out long aeons ago.

Whose light no longer reached her.

The oceanside massage proved a wonderful idea, Celeste swiftly discovered. To lie in the sheltering shade of the open-sided cabana as the slow, relaxing, rhythmic kneading of a skilled masseuse worked its magic on her back and shoulders was blissful.

Afterwards they repaired to the oceanside bistro for lunch, taking a table dappled with the shade of fronded palm trees towering overhead. Beyond the ocean lapped the shore in gentle waves.

'Not much to surf on here,' Rafael observed.

'You have to go to the North Shore of the islands, in

winter, to get the big swells coming down from the Arctic,' Celeste replied. 'That's where all the best breaks are—like Banzai Pipeline, Jaws and Tunnels.'

Rafael glanced at her. 'You sound very knowledgeable. Is that from personal experience?' He cocked an eyebrow at her.

She gave a smiling, self-dismissive shake of her head. 'No. I've never done more than bodysurfing.'

Rafael kept his enquiring glance on her. Had it been a boyfriend, then, in years gone by, from whom she'd learnt about surfing? Someone from before whatever had traumatised her in her modelling career.

'Surfer boyfriend, then?' he asked laconically.

Like a shutter coming down, her face closed instantly. Just as it had when Australia had been mentioned.

Frustration bit at him. He had no wish to probe into what he knew must have been some trauma caused by the likes of Karl Reiner early in her modelling career, but he wanted to know a little of the ordinary things about her—did she have family still? Where had she been raised?—just as he had told her of his own background, and how he'd won a scholarship to an Ivy League university that had given him the opportunity to make his way in the world, and how his parents had been killed in an earthquake when he'd still been an undergraduate.

Yet she had told him so little!

But now she answered him. It was done reluctantly, he could see, because she did not quite meet his eyes as she spoke, but let them flicker away out to the sea beyond their table.

'My father,' she answered. 'My father surfed. My mother used to tell me tales about him when I was growing up.'

Rafael heard the past tense in her speech.

'What happened?' he asked quietly.

She looked at him. She bit her lip, her expression drawn. 'One day there was too rough a sea—'

She broke off. The server was at their table, depositing

their plates in front of them. Rafael could have cursed her, but it was too late. Celeste's expression had changed. The sadness in her eyes was gone. She made an appreciative murmur at the exotic seafood salad, smiling at the server to thank her.

'This looks delicious! Thank you!' she exclaimed.

The server smiled back. 'Enjoy,' she said, and headed off.

They started to eat, but Rafael's mind was racing. So she had lost her father young—how young he couldn't tell, but young enough for her mother to have been the one who had told her about her father's love of surfing. A love that had proved fatal?

Another thought struck him. Was *that* behind her clear reluctance—shown to him twice now—whenever Australia was mentioned? Was it because it had been while surfing in Australia that her father had died? He wanted to ask but felt it would be too intrusive, too inquisitive. Instead he chose another response. One that resonated with his empathy with her.

He looked across at her. 'I'm sorry,' he said quietly. 'It is hard—hideously hard—to lose a parent, whatever our age.' He took a breath. 'I can still remember the day when I heard that my parents had not survived the earthquake that had hit my home village. I was at university, almost a grown man, but I broke down and wept like a child—'

There was a catch in his voice. He could not stop it. Found himself blinking. Then there was the touch of a hand on his wrist. Fleeting, momentary, but there all the same.

'To be so far from them must have made it even harder for you,' Celeste said softly. 'But perhaps...' She chose her words carefully. 'Perhaps you can take a little comfort from knowing how proud they must surely have been of you for gaining entry to such a formidable, elite place of education, and how relieved they must have been to know that you were not caught up in the disaster yourself.'

He nodded, taking another breath. 'Yes, you are right.

And I owe it to them—to their endless encouragement of me
as a child to fulfil their dreams for me, which they worked
so hard to enable me to realise—'

Rafael's eyes rested on her. His parents had dreamed of
a better life for their son—a life free of the endless toil they
had spent their years enduring. But they had dreamed of
something even more important for him, he knew.

*They wanted me to find that special person—the one I
could make my life with, the one I could cherish and care for,
who would cherish me in return, with whom I would have
the grandchildren they never lived to see...*

His eyes drank her in, this beautiful, pale-haired woman
sitting opposite him to whom he was so drawn, whose beauty
was not just in her face, her graceful body, but was also in
her temperament, her sweetness of nature, her sensitivity
and kindness, in the determination he had witnessed when
she had got the hapless Louise out of the ruthless clutches
of Karl Reiner.

Emotion moved within him.

*Is she that one? Is she the one my parents dreamt I would
one day find? Is that why I am drawn to her as I have been
drawn to no other woman?*

Madeline, he thought bitingly, would never have been the
woman his parents would have wanted for him. She would
have half scared them, half repelled them. And, as for Madeline, she would have wanted him to discard them as she had
discarded her own lowly parents.

She had made no secret of the fact that she had bought her
working-class parents a luxury bungalow in Bournemouth,
then never gone near them again. She would have expected
him to do the same—to settle his parents comfortably, then
cut them out of his globetrotting, glitzy life to spend his time
exclusively with her, being a glittering, glamorous golden
couple, living in Manhattan, frequenting only the most fashionable and expensive restaurants, jaunting about the world

in a private plane, entertaining the rich and famous, making more and more and more money...

*That's not what I want! Not any more.*

Once he had enjoyed that lifestyle, with Madeline at his side. But since they had parted—since she had opened his eyes to what she truly was—his outlook on life had slowly changed. Now he knew with a deep inner resolve that what he wanted was right here in front of him, around him. A beautiful place to be, nature in all its cultivated bounty, and the company of a woman who wanted it, too.

*And who wanted him. Wanted him as he wanted her...*

Celeste. The only woman in the world he wanted...

His eyes rested on her, met her gaze which had returned to him. He smiled at her and drank her in.

And she smiled back at him...

There was sympathy in her smile, and kindness.

And intimacy.

And promise...

Rafael felt his heart lift—lift and sing.

# CHAPTER TEN

CELESTE DRESSED ESPECIALLY carefully that evening. Her body felt wonderful after the massage, and she seemed to have a glow about her. Her eyes looked more luminous to her tonight, her hair more lustrous. She'd left it loose completely, and it cascaded down her back in silken folds, feeling cool and sensuous on her skin. She slipped her dress over her head—layers of gauze-fine cotton in shades of blue…azure and cobalt and deepest turquoise in a haze of colour. It was worn off one shoulder, and fleetingly she remembered that the dress she'd worn that evening at the charity fashion show had been, too.

The first time she'd set eyes on Rafael.

A little tremor of emotion went through her.

*I never dreamt then that I would be here, with him— now, like this!*

Was it possible? Was it truly possible that she was here with him?

But as she joined him on the terrace for their customary pre-dinner drink she knew it was vividly true. The physical impact of his presence overwhelmed her, and his smile, as he saw her approaching, made her breath catch. He took her hands as she came up to him, stepping back from her to survey her.

He said something in Spanish she could not catch and

smiled down at her again. And though his smile was warm his eyes were warmer still...

Warm with desire...

She felt a little thrill go through her—a shimmer of awareness, of more than awareness. *Intimacy.* She had felt it earlier that day at lunch, when Rafael had told her of his parents just after she had told him about her father, his life cut short so young.

A sense of wonder came over her as she thought about that. She had been so reluctant to say anything at all of herself, even of the distant past and her childhood. The past was dangerous—all of it. Yet somehow she had found it possible to tell him something of her father's life, even if only that brief fragment. Tragedy had struck them both, she realised, losing their parents far too young, and perhaps that realisation was another thread that was drawing her to him.

Drawing her closer and closer yet.

*How close?*

The question hovered tantalisingly in her mind as they went down to dinner, her hand still loosely held in his.

It felt, she thought, with that little thrill again, the right place for her hand to be...the only place...

*This is right—it is the right thing to do. To be here with Rafael. To accept all that has happened, all that will happen...*

Certainty filled her. And a sense of peace. Rafael had been right all along. She could remake herself. She could leave the past behind.

She would give herself to what was between them wholly and fully, with no more reluctance or resistance.

*The past is gone—there is only the present. The wonderful, magical present that has Rafael in it.*

Happiness glowed within her, radiant in its power.

They ate, that evening, once again at the French cuisine restaurant by the shore. They had tried others, but this had proved their favourite. The setting was so spectacular, almost at the sea's edge, and the lights from the hotel were shaded by the palm trees and plants framing the restaurant's terrace.

After they had dined they walked along the pathway that led in the opposite direction from the beach, out onto a little headland beyond, where they paused.

'Look,' said Rafael.

Celeste followed where he was indicating.

A sliver of new moon was rising in the east—a slender crescent of silver. Rafael took her hand, nothing more than that, standing beside her as they stood in silence. His clasp was warm and strong.

She felt his fingers twine between hers. Felt her heart-rate quicken. Felt her head turn towards him. Felt the dark glow of his eyes holding hers. So rich, so full…

For one terrible moment she felt panic rising in her, clutching at her throat…then she felt it fading…fading in the warmth of his lambent gaze.

'Celeste,' he breathed, and then slowly, so very slowly, his mouth came down to hers.

His kiss was as soft as the breeze, as gentle as the caress of the new-risen moon. Moving slowly, sensuously, tenderly over her lips.

Wonder filled her, and as he drew back from her she could only gaze up at him, eyes wide, lips parted.

His free hand lifted to cup the side of her face. 'Will you come to me, Celeste? Will you give yourself to what there could be between us?'

His eyes were searching. His fingers tightened on hers.

He took a breath, speaking with more care than he'd known he possessed. 'I know that this has not been easy for you.' And now his voice changed, became both hesitant and more resolute. 'And I know you have scars on your soul.' He took another breath. 'I know that something bad happened to you a long time ago.'

He made himself go on, for this had to be dealt with—the buried poison in her had to be drawn out at last.

'Perhaps something similar to the fate you saved that *ingénue* Louise from. No!' he urged, for he had seen the flinching in her eyes, the pulling away of her hand, which he had to reclasp. 'I say this to you only to show you that I understand, that I wish with all my heart that you could leave all that behind you. I ask nothing—only that you trust me. Trust me to share with you what *should* be between a man and a woman…this precious gift that nature gives us.'

His fingers at her face splayed, spearing gently into her hair, stroking with sensitive tips. She felt warmth dissolve through her, felt the terrible fear that had knifed her at his words fade. Her eyes fluttered, her breath caught.

'This precious gift,' he said again, and now his mouth was dipping to hers.

His kiss was as slow, as careful as before, as tender and as sensuous. But now, as his lips moved over hers, he eased hers apart, deepening his kiss. His hand slid around her skull, shaping it, holding her head. His body stepped forward into her space. She felt a rushing of sensation, felt her eyes close, her free hand wind around his strong, muscled back.

His kiss deepened more.

Wonder filled her. To be held, embraced, kissed like this! By Rafael… Here, on this magic isle, beneath the moon and the stars…

As he released her to gaze down at her, his eyes lambent in the starlight, the moonlight, she felt her heart sing—felt it soar. Wildly, like a bird set free.

For one long moment more he gazed down at her. Seeing in her face all that he had longed to see.

He brushed her lips with tender brevity. 'Come,' he said to her.

And she went with him. Went with him along the winding paths, beside the little waterfalls and fountains, beneath the trees with their glowing white flowers heady with fragrance. Walked hand in hand with him, wordless, for no more needed to be spoken between them. Their bodies would speak now.

He led her inside his cabana-villa, turning on no lights, locking no doors, leading her into the room with the wide, waiting bed.

'How beautiful you are! Celeste...my Celeste!'

It was all he said before his hands reached to her, drew her into his arms, holding her wand-slim body against his. He was kissing her again, tenderly, softly, deeply.

For one last moment she thought she could feel the pain of the past seek to catch at her, to leave its slimy trail across her skin. Then it was gone. Replaced by the healing touch that was in Rafael's lips, in the tender, arousing caresses of his fingertips at the nape of her neck, in the strong, cherishing warmth of his body embracing hers.

A sense of wonder—of freedom—swept through her.

This—*this* was how it should be between a man and a woman! This was where desire and passion met—in tenderness and sweet, sensuous cherishing! Never again would the echo of a foul touch pollute her with its poisoned tendrils...

She was free—finally free of the past that had netted her in its prison of rank and fetid memories.

Rafael had freed her! Set her free with every touch, every caress, every sweet and nectared kiss.

Slowly, sensuously, his hand unfastened her dress, peeled its gauzy layers from her. She wore no bra—she needed none—only a wisp of lace around her hips, soon shed, just as his unnecessary clothing was swiftly shed.

His eyes feasted on her, and then, as he laid her gently, tenderly on the waiting bed, his mouth lowered to her. Her hands reached to him—she let her fingers graze wonderingly along the lean, muscled lines of his torso, fold around his back, outline each sculpted plane and curve. His lips were on her skin, arousing her with each soft and sensuous caress in whorls of sweetest pleasure, whorls that seemed to meld and join, until her whole body was a mesh of sensuous delight.

She could hear a moan in her throat, low and husky, feel a quickening of her pulse, a mounting restlessness in her limbs. Her hands pressed into his body, drawing him closer, wanting him closer, wanting to feel that lean, hard weight against her.

He felt her desire and answered it, covering her body with his, splaying over her as his mouth sought and found hers again. Her tender breasts peaked against his chest, her long legs winding with his. His pace quickened, became more urgent, and it drew from her a matching quickening, a matching urgency of desire that sought fulfilment.

A fulfilment he could feel her straining against him to attain. Fire filled him. With swift urgency his thigh parted hers and he felt her lift against him. His hands meshed in hers, pressing them down upon the pillows as he took her mouth again, seeking and melding even as their bodies sought and melded.

She cried out—he could hear her—and he gentled instantly, fearing to hurt her. But her hips lifted to him, drawing him deeper. Fire flamed between them, burning fiercer and more fiercely, glowing with the white heat of a passion he had never felt before, an intensity that possessed him, possessed him utterly. He felt her body changing beneath his, felt its heat, its molten fusion with his.

He cried out, deep in his throat, and heard an answering cry from her, and then the living flame enveloped them both, consuming them.

It burned away from her all that she had feared for so long. The purifying flame seared through her, through every atom of her body. And as it ebbed she knew with absolute certainty that everything had changed—for ever.

Wonder filled her—and more than wonder. She clung to Rafael, clung to his sweated body, warm and heavy on her. She could feel his heart racing beneath the hard wall of his chest. Feel hers racing, too. His arm folded around her back, hand splayed over her spine.

He kissed her, his breathing heavy, smoothing back her hair with his hand. His eyes poured into hers. He said something to her in Spanish, which she did not understand. His voice was warm, and rich with emotion.

And then his forehead drooped, his body slackened. The arm around her back loosened. She saw his eyelids close, felt her own grow heavy. And even as sleep swept over him, so it did her, too.

Bodies still entwined, still fused, they lay together.

'Ready?'

'Yes!'

'OK, let's go.'

They lowered themselves off the rear platform of the boat into the translucent waters. Adjusting the mouthpieces of their snorkelling gear, they dipped down their heads and started to flap lazily across the surface of the sea, their flippers making their motion almost effortless as they gazed down, entranced, into the ocean beneath them.

She could feel her T-shirt billowing in the water. Wearing it was essential for her pale skin—unlike Rafael, with his natural dark tan. Her gaze wandered from the fish, to him, feasting on his honed, sculpted body, clad only in a pair of hip-hugging swimming shorts.

Emotion speared her. Could she really be here with him, now, in this paradise time together? After all her lonely, solitary years, imprisoned by her past, was it really so simple... so easy?

And yet it was! That was the wonder of it—the miracle. That in his arms she had made herself anew, stepped free of the prison of the past.

So easy—in the end, so miraculously easy...

So easy to be with Rafael, by day and by night, to be with him all the time, separated by nothing—not even the gardens of the hotel. She had moved into his cabana-villa and, whilst she was still insisting on paying her own share for meals and any activities, such as this morning's snorkelling expedition, Rafael had refused to accept any contribution to his accommodation. It was costing him nothing to share it with her, he'd pointed out with irrefutable logic, and on that issue she'd had to concede.

And so she was here—here, as Rafael had said, for as long as they both could be. She, for her part, had emailed her agency, saying she would not be back yet, and Rafael had ruthlessly cleared his diary of anything other than remote interactions that he could conduct, if necessary, from the hotel's business centre.

Because Celeste was his priority. Nothing else. Disbelief still washed over him sometimes, to think that she had finally found the courage to trust him—trust him not just with companionship but with passion and desire. For it had taken courage, he knew that. Whatever it was—that 'something bad' that she had glossed over—it had scarred her badly, poisoned her badly. Kept her in that lonely state she had been in, separated from all that she should have been free to give herself to.

But she'd stepped out of the long shadow the past had cast over her. Taken the hand he'd held out to her, stepped back into life—warm and joyous and passionate. To share it with him.

Share it *all* with him.

All that their time together could give them...

After their snorkelling Rafael could hardly wait to get her back to the cabana. 'Time for a siesta,' he told her, the glint in his eyes also telling her that sleep would not be high on their agenda for a while...

Celeste threw him a teasing glance. 'Aren't we going to have lunch first?'

'No,' he said, and kissed her to prove his point. 'You are all I want to feast on,' he told her, as they gained the cool privacy of the villa and he took her in his impatient arms.

'And I you,' she said huskily, gazing up at him, her eyes full with desire.

The desire that was pouring through her. Desire that was

like *terra incognita*—a land she was exploring with a sense of wonder and release that she had never dreamt possible. A land she had thought barred to her for ever.

After so much fear, with Rafael she found there was *nothing* to fear! Only to embrace and accept and cherish. In this blissful, wondrous present the past had vanished like dark smoke on the wind—the clear, fresh wind that blew off the endless reaches of the vast Pacific here on these emerald isles, these precious jewels set in a cobalt sea.

How simple it had been—how easy! Wonder filled her—and gratitude…boundless gratitude. And desire—oh, rich, rich desire. The passion in her body so long starved now filled her every cell, set her eyes glowing with an ardent flame that fired her with a heat that set her ablaze.

She wound her hand into his hair, pulling his mouth down to hers, her body clinging to his as she kissed him deeply, arousingly.

And he responded. Responded with an urgency that only fuelled her own, that only made her hands fumble in their haste to free them of their clothes, to draw him down with her upon the waiting bed and sate her desire on his strong, sculpted body.

How beautiful that body was! How perfect in its form, its texture and its honed, vital masculinity! She let her hands roam across his muscled torso, knowing every contour, knowing, too, with a delight that enthralled her, just how the touch of his hands, his mouth, the skilfully skimming tips of his fingers, could draw from her sensations she had never dreamt of! And how his surging body could ignite her own, could fuse with hers, melding them as one single flame in which they were consumed.

And afterwards…ah, afterwards she would lie in his loosened embrace, her racing heart slowing, her hands limp on his chest, his hands slackening around her. They would lie together, limbs splayed and tangled, heated and exhausted by passion fulfilled, and she would be cradled against him and know a peace, a happiness, she had never known.

Happiness had set a glow about her, like an inner light within her, thought Rafael, gazing at her now, their heads upon the same pillow. He could see it, rejoice in it. It was there all the time—as they walked through the gardens, as they dined and lunched and breakfasted together, as they lay lazily on the beach or by the pool, even as they glanced at each other as they went out running together in the cool early hours of the newly minted mornings, as they talked and laughed and passed the long, easy days, the clinging, passionate nights.

It was a happiness he felt, too, he knew. Lifting his spirit so that this time with her here seemed to be a time out of the world—a garden of paradise found. But the world, he knew, was waiting beyond the running swell of the seas, and it must reclaim them in the end.

But not permanently. That much he knew. Knew for certain that this time with Celeste had changed him fundamentally.

*I want her so much to be the one! To be the woman I want to share my life with! But not the life I know—the one filled with buying and selling and making money and yet more money.*

No, he had enough money. His money-making days were over now—now was the time to slow down, take a different tack, move his life into a different orbit. Focus more on his work in his own country, improving the living standards of those he had once been one of.

That life would have Celeste in it—always.

But he had to hasten slowly. To declare himself to Celeste now might yet be too precipitate. She had come so far with him—so far from the prison of her lonely, solitary life—but she needed time. Time with him. Time to accept what he was to her—what she, he knew with every twining of their hands, every shared glance, every moment of companionship and intimacy, was to him. Time to be with him not just on holiday but to become part of his life, and for him to become part of hers.

But, however they arranged their lives together from now on, there were practical things to be attended to. They could not stay here on the island for ever. She probably had work commitments ahead of her, which she would want to honour—and he most certainly had his, which he could no longer postpone.

One above all was looming. One he welcomed. It would see justice achieved for someone who deserved it.

In his head he heard the memory of his own voice remonstrating with Madeline about her latest coup—taking over a struggling luxury brand fashion company but firing its founder. Rafael had argued strongly against such ruthless action.

*'You could pay him a royalty—just a small one—or make him an artistic consultant...keep his talent in the company,'* he'd suggested.

Madeline had not listened. *'Rafe, the man's a loser! A fool.'* Her voice had been scathing. *'He should have damn well put the design trademarks in a separate company and kept it private—and he should have looked after his cash flow. Not left himself vulnerable. Now he's paying for it.'*

*'He's an artist, Madeline, a creative,'* Rafael had pointed out. *'Naive, possibly, and not good at business, but you own his designs now, and his brand, and with your marketing and financing skills they'll make you a fortune—you can afford not to hammer him into the ground and take everything he values from him!'*

She'd only looked at him. Her deep-set eyes, which could blaze with scorching sexual desire, make him forget everything but sating himself on her lush, threshing body, had taken on a hard diamond brilliance. Her voice had been as hard as her eyes.

*'Sentiment is for losers—and I don't intend to lose, Rafe.*

Ever. *I've done whatever it took to get here, and I'll go on doing it to get further still. I always have and I always will!'*

Had that exchange finally opened his eyes to her? Made him realise that despite what they had in common—their shared talent for winning the good things in life, including each other—they were very different people at heart? Madeline's ambition drove her to the exclusion of everything else—all other values were cast aside.

Rafael's eyes steeled. When he had finally discovered just how utterly uncaring Madeline was of anything other than fulfilling her driving ambition for wealth—when he had learnt just what she was prepared to do to achieve those ambitions—it had only finished what had already been dying between them.

And all her scornful derision of his shock and revulsion at her revelations about herself had not been able to revive it! Finally he had seen Madeline without the gloss and allure of the passion that had once burned between them. Seen her for what she was—a woman he could never in a million years consider to be someone he could make his life with.

He would never make that mistake again!

And now his gaze came back to Celeste, nestled against his chest, her beautiful face tender in repose. Emotion welled through him.

With Celeste he was not making a mistake, he knew! With Celeste he was doing the right thing, making the right choice! Her difference from Madeline could not be more absolute!

He felt his heart glow as he gazed at her sleeping figure. Celeste was the woman he wanted in his life—for all his life! And to achieve that he was determined.

The first step was to persuade her to come back with him to New York. He made himself broach the subject later that day over dinner.

'I don't want to leave Hawaii,' he told her, his eyes lambent, 'but I can postpone my return no longer. I have people waiting for me whose enterprises and livelihoods depend on my input and decisions. I cannot, therefore, indulge myself here for ever.'

He took a breath, for he could see by the sudden shadow in her eyes that she was as loath to leave as he was. He reached across the table, taking her hand in his, pressing it closely.

'But that does not mean that we have to part.' He took another breath. 'Come with me to New York, Celeste! Stay with me there!' His voice lowered, became husky, and his eyes poured into hers. 'I want you so much, Celeste. I cannot do without you.'

There was a sudden caution in his eyes that she saw immediately.

'If I am presuming too much, forgive me...' he said.

She felt her heart lift—soar. Her fingers squeezed his. 'Do you mean it? Do you really mean it?' Her voice was a breath of hope in her throat. Her eyes widened with the same emotion.

He lifted her hand to his mouth and kissed it—the age-old gesture of homage and devotion to a woman from a man...a man to whom she knew, without a flicker of doubt, she could entrust herself, a man to hold and to cherish.

'*Yes!*' he breathed. 'What we have here I do not want to lose!'

'Nor I,' she answered. 'I want only you, Rafael. Only you!'

He kissed her hand again, his lips pressing to her knuckles in the sheer relief of hearing her answer. Then, with an intake of breath, he released her hand, picked up his wine glass and took a mouthful.

'We can be as flexible as you need in respect of your work commitments,' he assured her. 'It might get complicated, but I'm sure we can work something out.'

Celeste smiled back. Her heart was singing. Not to have to part from Rafael, as she had been increasingly dreading she must once this idyll here was over—for him to want her to go with him to New York—to be with him. Be part of his life!

*How much he has come to mean to me! I could not bear to leave him.*

Emotion welled within her.

'In the meantime,' he went on, his eyes pouring into hers, 'we're going to enjoy our very last days together here. And,' he finished, 'I think we should book our next visit before we leave! Coming back here again is most definitely on the agenda.'

He got to his feet, drawing her with him.

'And now...' He smiled down at her, familiar, intimate, making her heart lift as it always did. 'Let's take a walk along the beach and watch the moon set over the Pacific. And let's make our wish to come back.'

She went with him gladly, at his side—the one and only place she wanted to be...

# CHAPTER ELEVEN

NEW YORK WAS…well, New York, thought Celeste. As full-on and non-stop as ever. Rafael had had to plunge into work to catch up with all he'd postponed while they'd been in Hawaii, so Celeste had looked in on the New York branch of her agency and managed to get some short-term work. But her heart was no longer in her career. It was, she knew, with a warm, glowing wonder, with Rafael.

Rafael…who had set her free from her past so that it could never haunt or harm her again! She had made herself anew—the past was finally gone from her life. Now there was only this wonderful present! Being with Rafael, living with him, was all she wanted!

As his backlog cleared they were able to have more time together—either spending relaxed evenings in his apartment on the Upper East Side or going out to quiet, out-of-the-way restaurants. Then one afternoon he phoned her from his office downtown and asked whether she would come to a function with him.

'It's an informal initial launch party for a designer I'm backing—not clothes, but handbags,' he explained. 'He's had a bit of a rough time in the past year or so, but I want that to change now. If you're OK with it I'll have one of his evening bags sent round to you—if you could wear something that will show it off?'

'Of course,' she said at once. 'I'd be glad to.'

She was, too, when the bag was delivered. It was a beautifully made clutch, in vivid royal-blue silk, with an appliqué
swirl of what Celeste suspected were real sapphires. To show
it off to its best she opted for a white dress in silk plissé—
a simple design that would not compete with the exquisite
evening bag.

Rafael was changing into black tie at his office, so she set
off on her own for the small but ferociously elegant boutique
hotel at the edge of Central Park. In the lobby she paused by
the function board to see which room the function was in.

'I take it,' said a voice behind her, 'that you, too, are heading for the Leonardo Suite?'

She half turned. It was a female voice that had spoken,
with an accent that was decidedly English.

'Yes.' She smiled, glancing at the woman who had spoken to her.

Some years older than Celeste, she was not as tall—few
women were—but her looks were as eye-catching as her voluptuous figure, moulded by a vermilion gown that set off her
most striking feature: the rich auburn colouring of her hair.

She looked very faintly familiar. Celeste's brow furrowed
a moment. Actress? Socialite? The wife of someone famous?
But she couldn't place her—and it didn't matter anyway.

The woman was returning her regard, but it was a lot
more comprehensive than Celeste's quick glance. Dark hazel
eyes went to the clutch Celeste was carrying, and narrowed
very slightly.

'May I see?' she asked suddenly, and held her hand out.

Carefully, Celeste handed it over. The woman promptly
turned it around in her hands, and then opened it. 'You don't
mind, do you?' she said, without glancing at Celeste and certainly without expecting her to object. The woman looked
at the discreet label within and then, with a snap, closed the
bag and handed it back to Celeste.

'Interesting,' she said. There was the slightest bite in her voice. Then her expression cleared. 'Shall we go up together, since we're heading in the same direction?'

Celeste could hardly object, and they walked to the lift together.

'It's an effective choice,' the woman said as the elevator doors closed on them. Her glance indicated the white gown Celeste was wearing.

'Thank you,' she said, adding nothing more.

'Is it going to be a theme?' the woman asked.

'I'm sorry?' Celeste looked confused.

'Having all the models dressed in white, each with a different coloured bag. It would be very effective,' the woman said.

Celeste shook her head. 'Yes, I see that. But in fact, no—I'm just a one-off tonight,' she said lightly, with a social smile.

'Really?' the woman replied. 'Sounds like he's missed a trick. Which isn't surprising, of course. Tell me, out of curiosity, what's your fee for an evening like this?'

Again, Celeste looked confused. Then she realised the woman had, perhaps not surprisingly, assumed first that she was a model and second that she'd been hired to carry one of the designer's products.

'Oh, I'm not here professionally,' she said, again keeping her voice light. 'I'm just a guest.'

'Really?' said the woman, her eyes flicking again.

Probably, Celeste thought, because she could see that the necklace she was wearing with the white evening gown was nothing more valuable than freshwater pearls.

Fortunately the elevator opened at that point and they stepped out, seeing the entrance to the function suite just opposite.

'Let's go in together,' said the woman. 'We'll make quite a visual impact side by side, I think.'

Again, it was hard to object, so Celeste let her walk in beside her. They paused by the reception desk. Celeste gave her name, but said nothing more as a tick was put against it. Then the member of staff looked expectantly at the woman at her side.

'Oh, I'm her bodyguard,' said the woman with an insouciant air. Then she hooked her arm into Celeste's and moved forward.

Alarm bells started to ring, very decidedly, in her head. She looked hurriedly around for Rafael. To her relief she saw he was already there, on the far side of the room, in a group of people.

'Do excuse me, please,' she said politely to the auburn-haired woman she now suspected was gatecrashing a private party.

But the woman was already disengaging herself from her arm and striding forward. As she did so people made way for her. Celeste suspected she was the type of woman for whom people always made way. Whoever she was, she was either rich enough to buy a couture gown—and sport some very good rubies with it—or something dodgy was going on.

Whichever it was, she realised that Rafael had seen the woman walking so commandingly up to him. She also realised that the other guests were looking at her and very slightly drawing back. Celeste's antennae started to quiver. There was an air of nervous anticipation being generated. Something was going to happen.

It did. And it was pure theatre.

Rafael was standing stock-still as the woman sailed up to him. Every line of his body showed an immobility that made him look turned to stone.

So, too, did the expression on his face.

Celeste felt a little chill start deep inside her. Slowly she started to walk forward. Then the auburn-haired woman reached Rafael and stopped.

'Rafe, how *good* to see you again!' Her voice carried—a rich, vibrant purr—and its English accent made it distinctively audible.

Celeste watched as the woman leant forward to bestow an air kiss on his cheek, then stand back to look at him. Let him look at her.

Which he did. Celeste could see his eyes flicker very briefly. Then, almost unnoticeably, he nodded, acknowledging the woman's greeting.

'Hello, Madeline,' he said.

She gave a little laugh. 'You couldn't *possibly* think I'd stay away tonight!'

Long lashes dipped over obsidian eyes. 'No, I couldn't think that, Madeline.'

His voice was very dry.

And very cold.

Another laugh came from her—rich and throaty. Then Celeste saw her turn to one of the men in the group Rafael was with. He was slightly built, not tall, and he looked, she realised, as expressionless as Rafael. But in the other man, Celeste could see with disquiet, the lack of expression could not mask the dismay in his eyes—dismay and fear.

'I believe you know Lucien Fevre,' Rafael said. His voice was only dry now, with an edge to it that Celeste recognised—she had heard it before, when he'd spoken to Karl Reiner. 'He's the creative genius that *you,* Madeline—' he gave the slightest slashing smile, without a trace of humour in it '—were too stupid to realise was the core value of the company you bought.'

Celeste halted. Suddenly, with total clarity, she realised who the woman was. Realised that she should have known from the moment she'd heard Rafael call her by her name.

Madeline. Madeline Walters. Self-made multimillionairess and the woman Rafael Sanguardo had once been involved with. Belatedly, into Celeste's head came the thumbnail sketch of him that her fellow model Zoe had given her all that time ago at the charity fashion show...

The rich, carrying tones came again. 'The company, Rafael,' she riposted, 'that is now a global brand, with sales that are twenty times what they were, whose stock price has quadrupled, and whose product range is—'

'Is a travesty of what it once was,' he cut in.

Celeste saw Madeline's head go back.

'They *sell,* Rafael!'

Her voice was not a purr any more. There was a harsh note in it that sounded ugly to Celeste's ears. 'They sell in their thousands—their *tens* of thousands! And with the Chinese market opening up even more they'll sell in their *hundreds* of thousands!'

Without consciously realising it, Celeste felt her feet start forward again. She walked up to the group.

'I think this will sell,' she heard herself saying as she held up the sapphire-studded clutch with a little gesture of display. In the same movement she turned to Lucien Fevre— who was still looking terrified, she realised. '*I'd* buy it,' she said, speaking directly to him but knowing her words could be heard by everyone present—as she'd intended. 'It is, quite simply, one of the most beautiful and exquisitely crafted handbags I've ever been fortunate enough to carry.' She spoke sincerely, for what she said was true.

Lucien Fevre's stricken face broke into a smile, and she could see appreciation for her simple compliment in his face.

'I don't suppose,' Celeste asked him, 'they come in other colours as well, do they?'

Lucien Fevre lifted his hands, turning his attention exclusively to her. 'The spectrum of the rainbow!' he said, with enthusiasm in his accented voice. 'Every hue! But that is just one of my collection—over here…'

He started walking away and Celeste followed him to where he was going, which was to a large silk-swathed table with a lavish display of his designs.

'Here,' he went on, indicating with a flourish, 'I have tried to capture the sea. Look.' He picked up a blue-green clutch, made of silk shot with pale mauve. 'Here is the pearlescence of the ocean—and the ornamentation is nacre, which I have also used for the clasp, with Tahitian pearls to enhance it.'

'It's beautiful!' Celeste breathed.

'And here,' he went on, 'is fire! It is the elements, you see—'

She could see immediately, and listened and looked while the designer went through his designs with her. As he did so he became more animated, the stricken look gone completely.

Until, that was, two figures approached them. One was Rafael, and the other was Madeline Walters. As if a spell had been cast Lucien Fevre froze. But it was Rafael who spoke.

'Go on, Madeline, say it.'

He spoke pleasantly, but Celeste could hear the steel in it. She looked at Madeline Walters's expression. She could not read it. But she could hear what she said very clearly.

'I made a mistake,' she said. Her voice was clipped, and she addressed the designer directly. 'I did not understand the fashion design industry as well as I thought I did. And I...I regret the decision I took.'

'Well done,' said Rafael.

His voice was dry—as dry as the look he bestowed upon Madeline. For a moment Celeste could see her eyes glittering, as if she'd swallowed poison. Then it was gone.

She put her hand out to Rafael, resting it on his sleeve. 'There,' she said, 'may I come off the naughty step now, pretty please?' She spoke humorously, as though the toxic expression on her face had never been, and her glance at Rafael was teasing.

More than teasing, Celeste could see, and the realisation did not chill her—it froze her.

It was inviting.

Words formed in her head. Stark, sharp, and carved into her consciousness.

*She wants him back.*

\* \* \*

Rafael pulled his bow tie clear, dropping it down on the dresser, and slid the top button of his dress shirt open. He stretched his neck, loosening his muscles, profoundly glad to be back in his apartment. It hadn't been an easy evening...

Madeline's calculatedly dramatic entrance had not come as a complete surprise—she'd taunted him, and he'd half expected she would try something on. Her anger would have driven her to it.

Anger because he had sought out the broke and discarded Lucien Fevre and set him back on his feet again. Even more anger because what Lucien was now producing was even better than his earlier work—work that could have been hers had she not treated him so callously when she'd acquired his debt-ridden company.

But something good had come out of her *coup de théâtre*. He'd got Madeline to apologise to Lucien. It didn't matter that the apology had been insincere, as he knew very well that it had. Madeline made a point of never regretting her past actions.

He knew that better than anyone alive...

For a moment Rafael felt his skin crawl. He moved restlessly, picking up his discarded tie and hooking it inside his closet. From the *en suite* bathroom he could hear the sound of the shower running. His expression changed, lightened. Something even better had come out of the evening than just Madeline's apology to a man she had treated harshly.

Seeing Madeline with Celeste could not have emphasised to him more the complete difference between them! Even if Madeline had not been what she was, he would never, *never* prefer her to Celeste! It was Celeste who drew his eye, Celeste who made his pulse quicken, Celeste whose rare, pale beauty made his breath catch!

*How did I ever desire Madeline? How could I ever have thought her anything other than overblown and obvious? How was I ever enthralled by her?*

He shook his head, disposing of a comparison that was not needed. Madeline was nothing to him—less than nothing—and Celeste…ah, Celeste was everything!

Even as he thought it he realised the shower had stopped and the bathroom door was opening. She emerged, her hair pinned up on her head and a cotton bathrobe wrapped around her. Even in such unromantic garb she took his breath away!

He went up to her, his expression warm, and kissed her cheek, cupping her elbows with his hands.

'Thank you,' he said, his eyes as warm as his voice.

She looked at him questioningly.

He released her. 'Thank you,' he said, 'for getting through this evening as beautifully as you did. Thank you for behaving with grace and dignity—and kindness.' He looked at her. 'Kindness to Lucien. You saw instantly how unnerved he was, and you stepped in to help him through it.'

'I was glad to,' she said.

He nodded. Then took a breath. 'And thank you, too, Celeste, for something even more.' He paused, looked her in the eye. 'Thank you for coping with Madeline Walters.' He took another breath. 'Although I knew she wasn't going to be pleased with what I've done for Lucien—I'll fill you in on the whole sorry saga later—I hope you will believe that I didn't quite anticipate her showstopper.'

Celeste looked troubled. 'I'm so sorry I enabled her to get in like that—'

'Don't be. If it hadn't been you it would have been someone else. Madeline is unstoppable when she sets her mind to something.'

Celeste's gaze faltered.

*And if that something is you, Rafael, is she unstoppable then?*

But she did not say it. Could not.

Rafael was shrugging off his tuxedo jacket, followed by his dress shirt. Celeste sat down in front of the vanity unit and busied herself letting down her hair and starting to brush it out. Her thoughts were troubled, uneasy.

Wrapping himself in a black silk knee-length bathrobe, Rafael came up to her.

'Let me,' he said fondly, and took the brush from her. With slow, sensuous strokes he started to brush the long length of her hair.

Her eyes met his in the mirror of the vanity unit. His glowed with a familiar fire.

'You're worried about Madeline, aren't you?' he said. His voice was careful.

Celeste swallowed. 'Should I be?' It was hard to ask, but she had to.

He stopped brushing. 'No,' he said. He resumed his brushing, then a moment later spoke again. His voice was steady—decisive. 'Madeline is the past, Celeste. Yes, we were once an item, but we broke up some time ago, and that, I promise you, is that. Her only emotion when I ended it was anger.'

He paused, then went on. It was vital he make Celeste realise that Madeline was nothing to him now—nothing!

'I see her from time to time in public,' he went on. 'We are civil to each other. But that is all. I know she's had several liaisons since, and probably has one running now. I could not care less about that. I wish her neither ill nor well. I am completely indifferent to her.'

Celeste picked up her comb, then set it down again in a random gesture.

'Do you think she feels the same indifference?' she made herself ask. She tried to keep her voice neutral, as though she were asking a question about something entirely impersonal.

Rafael shrugged. 'I don't care, Celeste. I don't care what Madeline feels or wants or doesn't want. And right now...' He set down the brush and reached for her hand, drawing her to her feet. 'Right now the only thing I care about is taking you to bed.'

His voice was husky, his eyes washing over her, and the intimacy, the familiarity, sent a wave of warmth through her.

He kissed her. A kiss as tenderly arousing as it was sweetly sensuous. Meltingly, Celeste gave herself to it, gave herself to him, to everything he was—everything wonderful and wondrous and precious to her. Rafael! *Her* Rafael.

Her last conscious thought before bliss swept her away in his arms was, *Poor Madeline...poor, poor Madeline, to have lost him!*

Celeste was sitting in a pool of sunlight at the desk in Rafael's study. She was making notes and sketching, with Lucien's sapphire-blue evening bag in front of her. Excitement filled her. This morning—the morning after the Lucien Fevre party—Rafael had talked with her. Asked her to contribute her ideas, based on her long experience in the fashion world, to the advertising and marketing campaign that was being prepared for Lucien's relaunch.

She'd been delighted—thrilled. Now she was jotting down everything she could think of, and making little sketches, to bounce off Rafael when he got back later. Dimly she was aware of the apartment door opening. Rafael must have been able to get away early.

'I'm in your study!' she called out. 'Stealing your printer paper to draw on!'

The office door, ajar, opened fully.

'So,' said a voice behind her, 'when you said "just a guest" to me last night, what you really meant was, "just" Rafael's current squeeze!'

Celeste whipped round. Madeline Walters, looking stunning in a formidably well-cut navy blue business suit, which radiated 'power player' with every centimetre of fabric, was standing in the doorway.

Celeste's expression changed. 'How did you get in?' she asked blankly.

Madeline looked scornfully at her. 'I've kept sets of keys

for *all* Rafael's properties, though I've never made use of any of them till now,' she said. She shifted position. 'So, let's have a proper look at you.'

Dark, dramatically made-up eyes flicked up and down over Celeste, who stood there, recovering her composure. Whatever the hell was going on, she was going to stand her ground.

A slightly satisfied smile played on Madeline's vivid red lips.

'How gratifying,' she said, 'that Rafael consoles himself with women who are the antithesis of me! Even if it *does* mean he has to sleep with a stick insect!'

Celeste could hear the purr in her contralto voice and said nothing. Madeline wandered around the office, glancing around, and then down at the sketches Celeste had been making. She turned back to her. Eyebrows raised.

'My, my—multiple talents! Not just arm candy—or just good in bed, as I assume you must be, because Rafe...' the purr was back again '...is *so* very demanding in that respect!' She glanced again at the sketches. 'Are you going to run with my idea of white dresses to show off all the different colours of the bags?'

'It's a good idea,' agreed Celeste, because it was, and not giving credit where credit was due would be petty.

'Oh, I'm full of good ideas!' snapped Madeline.

*She wants to get a rise out of me,* thought Celeste. *She's come to check me out—scout out the opposition.*

Well, maybe it was time to provide some opposition...

'Not always,' she said, keeping her voice neutral.

Madeline's eyebrows arched interrogatively. 'Do you mean running off with Lucien Fevre's company but not him? Ancient history.'

Celeste shook her head. 'No,' she said pleasantly. 'The idea you've got that Rafael is available to you again.'

For an instant she knew her comment had hit home. Then Madeline laughed. Rich and full and throaty.

'Rafael is ancient history, too,' she said dismissively. She quirked an eyebrow. 'I thought models like you were always *au fait* with all the celebrity news? Haven't you seen that I'm busy with a senator who's tipped to be the running mate of the next presidential candidate? Mind you...'

Once again Madeline's voice changed, taking on that purring note, but edged with something underneath—something that sent a chill down Celeste's veins just like the one she'd felt when she'd realised last night just who the auburn-haired woman was.

'Between you and me, the venerable senator is a little too...venerable. He might make me the Second Lady in the USA one day, but he is, to put it frankly, too...*restrained*... for my tastes.'

She tilted her head, eyeing Celeste.

'So maybe, yes, it would be fun to have one last session with Rafael—something hot to remember while I'm enduring the missionary position for the millionth time! Not like Rafael,' she said, never taking her eyes off Celeste. 'As you must know by now, Rafael is so very, *very*...enthusiastic when it comes to bedtime!'

Her deep-set eyes flashed as she saw Celeste's reaction to her blatant jibe.

'My God, you've coloured up!'

In an instant, her expression had changed. That flash came again in her eyes, but now it was loaded with a venom that made Celeste's already frozen face freeze more.

'Well, well, well...' said Madeline, biting out each word. '*Now* I know what your appeal is! It's not just that he wanted a skinny whey-faced blonde who doesn't remind him of me. He wanted a nun, too! *Blushing* because I said the wicked word "bedtime"!'

She moved towards her and suddenly, Celeste felt Madeline's hand snake around her neck and stroke down the length of her loose hair.

'Such beautiful hair you've got,' she said, 'like silk...'

Her voice was a caress. Her touch soft.

Yet Celeste felt her skin crawl.

She stepped back. An instinctive movement of recoil.

'Whatever the purpose of your visit, Ms Walters,' she said, forcing herself to a composure she was far from feeling, 'you had better leave now.'

'My thoughts entirely.'

The deep, cold voice from the doorway made both heads turn. Rafael stepped into his study.

'Get out, Madeline,' he said.

He said it with an air of complete indifference, as if she were nothing more than a passing nuisance. Celeste saw her deep-set eyes flash with anger at such dismissal. Then a different expression filled them. She moved towards Rafael, who was standing motionless in the doorway, every line of his body showing tension.

'Why, Rafe, darling, you're looking dreadfully stressed out!' Madeline advanced purringly. 'Why don't you let me give you a massage? You know,' she said huskily, 'just how... *relaxed*...I could always make you with a massage.'

She was baiting him. It was obvious to Celeste. And just as obvious was Rafael's stone-faced lack of reaction. Madeline must have seen it, too, for she tilted her head of fiery auburn hair and found a new line of attack.

'No? Then maybe your lovely blushing nun here would welcome it? She looks very tense to me.' Her eyes moved across to Celeste, who stood as expressionless as if she were walking down a catwalk, then back to Rafael, equally blank-faced. 'So, what do you say, hmm?' she asked tauntingly. 'You could always just sit back and watch if you're too puritan to join us...' She laughed mockingly.

Rafael only stepped back out of the doorway, holding the door open for her pointedly. Madeline's eyes flashed fire again.

'No wonder you're stuck with Little Miss Pure here!' she bit out. 'Tell me, do you just sit chastely side by side, holding hands, and sigh at each other?' Her face twisted. 'God, Rafe, what a bore you are. To think I wasted time on you!'

'Out, Madeline' was all the response she got, in a tone that did not hide its note of impatience.

Celeste saw her snap, her temper flaring openly. Before she could stop her, the other woman had snatched up the blue evening bag from Rafael's desk and was pushing past her to the door.

'I'll take a souvenir with me, I think!' she exclaimed, and then, as she gained the large hallway, she halted and turned back. 'In fact...' She turned, and her eyes were gleaming with an expression of satisfaction. 'I'll even do you a favour—*and* your precious Lucien Fevre! I'll take this bag with me tomorrow night to the state reception at the White House! That should be good enough publicity for you! I might even get the senator to buy me some more of them! I could make the damn things fashionable all across Washington, if you like! Is *that* sufficient atonement?'

Celeste's eyes flew to Rafael. His stone-faced expression was gone.

'Senator?' His eyes pinioned Madeline.

She gave that laugh again, the satisfaction in her eyes blatant. 'You *are* out of touch, aren't you, Rafe? Too busy mooning over your pet nun! Yes,' she said, preeningly, 'Senator Roxburgh and I are most definitely an item now. And, since he's *so* likely to get picked as running mate in the next presidential election, you could, if you ask me nicely, soon be on the Capitol Hill guest list. I'll be the Second Lady in the land.'

She turned to go again, having shot her bow and saved her pride, Celeste could see. But Rafael's voice stayed her.

'Are you serious, Madeline?' His voice was different.

She whirled round, animation in her face. She was delighted.

'Oh, yes,' she purred. 'And the senator is so very, *very* devoted to me! Widowed, you know... It's so sad. And you know how expensive political campaigning is over here in the States—I'm *so* keen to help him on that front! Once we're married, of course!'

Rafael's hand brushed aside her preening.

'Then you're quite mad,' he said.

There was a bluntness in his voice that made Celeste stare at him. His attention was focussed only and entirely on Madeline.

'You will never,' he said to her, 'get away with it.' He took a step forward. There was an edge audible in his voice as he spoke. 'Madeline, drop him now. While you can.'

She was looking at him. Her face was different now, Celeste could see.

'You don't *really* think,' Madeline said slowly, 'that anything *you* put out about me will look like *anything* other than thwarted jealousy and open malice? You'll make a laughing stock of yourself!'

Rafael's eyes speared her. 'And you, Madeline, will get yourself crucified by the American press!' His expression changed. 'For God's sake, get real! Do you *really* think you won't get found out? If Roxburgh gets selected, the press will go through everything about you—absolutely and totally everything! And once you're on TV and campaigning, memories will be jogged, I promise you! Someone, somewhere, will recognise you, make the connection—and then they will cash in with the biggest political sex scandal they've ever found!'

Madeline had gone white, Celeste could see. White with fury.

'Don't you *dare* threaten me!'

'I'm not threatening you. I'm warning you!' he shot back. 'And if you imagine *I'd* say a word about it you're even more insane. Insane to think I would want to be caught in any sordid backwash!'

Madeline was twisting Lucien's bag in her hands, crushing it with the force of them. Her face working.

'I *will* get what I want—because I always do! I *always* do! Nothing's stopped me in my life—and it won't now! If I want to be Mrs Edward Roxburgh, wife of the next damn Vice President, I *shall!*'

Rafael took a breath. Hard and scissoring. His eyes were like bullets.

'Madeline,' he said, incising each word, 'you might be the world's most...*liberated*...woman, and you might be worth close to a billion dollars now...but you can never, *never* be the wife of the Vice President of the USA. Because there will never be a Vice President whose wife...' he took another breath, then said it '...once worked as a prostitute.'

# CHAPTER TWELVE

THERE WAS SILENCE—complete silence. Then into the silence came the sound of the sapphire clutch falling on the floor. Madeline had dropped it.

Rafael watched her turn, slowly, back to the front door. Saw her walk out of it. Saw her walk down the carpeted corridor to the elevators. Then he crossed to the door and closed it quietly. He turned back to Celeste.

She looked like a ghost.

Regret hit him—regret that she had heard what he had just said. Regret flooded through him that she'd had to endure Madeline at all.

He came up to her as she stood, as motionless as a statue. 'I am so, *so* sorry,' he said, looking her in the eyes. 'I am so sorry that you had to be subjected to that—to *any* of that!'

'She's still got keys to this apartment.'

Celeste heard her voice speaking. It didn't seem to be saying the most important thing, but it was saying the thing that seemed to be in her head right now. Keeping out everything else. Everything that *had* to be kept out.

Rafael swore, then simply said, 'The locks will be changed today.' He took another breath, steadying himself. 'I need a drink,' he said. 'And you look like you do, too.'

She didn't answer, just went to pick up the discarded bag, smoothing it out. She put it on a side table and then, since Rafael was looking at her with such concern on his face that it hurt, she nodded. She followed him through into the kitchen. He got out a bottle of malt whisky and downed a shot in one. She ran some water and started to sip it.

'You're in shock,' Rafael said. 'I can see you are. Look, come and sit down. I need to talk to you.'

He ran himself a glass of water as well, and they both went through into the lounge.

Rafael threw himself onto his usual place on the sofa and looked at Celeste. 'Please—sit down before you fall down.'

Carefully she lowered herself down at the other end of the sofa, her fingers curled around the cold water glass. She looked at Rafael. His face was shadowed, but not from the light outside. From the darkness within. Then, abruptly, he started to speak.

'I didn't know,' he said. 'I didn't know all through our affair, our relationship.' His voice hardened. 'And I wish to God I'd never found out. Except,' he said, and now his voice had the dryness of the desert in it, 'that it was Madeline herself who told me.'

He stared ahead for a moment, seeing nothing but the past, then spoke again.

'She'd been drinking, so maybe that made her rash—but then, Madeline always has had a reckless streak in her. It's the one she uses, gambles with, to make her fortunes. And, of course...' his voice changed again '...she doesn't see it as rashness. To her, it's simply no big deal.'

He turned to look at Celeste again.

'It came out of a conversation we were having—just after-dinner chat at her flat, nothing more drastic than that. We were talking about economics and the conditions required for economic growth in general, such as a financial system that can create reliable and relatively low-cost credit, and so on. And, on an individual basis, we talked about capital formation. That,' he explained, 'is the formal name for ac-cumulating sufficient surplus wealth, or capital, to use for investment. We started talking about how we'd both dealt with the problem ourselves. It's a real problem for budding entrepreneurs without pre-existing assets to serve as security for a loan.'

He paused, then went on.

'I said I'd built up my initial investment capital by working through university, living as frugally as I could. Then, when I graduated, I worked eighteen-hour days, non-stop, for over three years, doing the kind of work that paid a premium because it was so noxious or back-breaking or in godawful places...' He paused again, and then went on. 'When I'd finished telling her, Madeline laughed.'

He looked at Celeste.

'She laughed and said that what I'd endured made her glad she was a woman in business. Because she possessed a natural asset that gave her an ROT—Return on Time— that was orders of magnitude greater than anything *I'd* had to do to accumulate my capital for investment.' He took a breath. 'In six months, she boasted, she'd made three times as much as I had in three years of slaving non-stop. And the work, she told me, had been the most enjoyable she'd ever had. She'd even, at one point, considered making it her main line of business. Brothels, as she pointed out, are never loss-makers...'

He took a gulp of water, and then another, and another, draining the glass as though it might wash him out. Then he looked back at Celeste. There was no expression on her face still.

He got to his feet.

'I'm sorry,' he said. 'More sorry than I can say that you ever got touched by any of this! Let alone found out about Madeline!' His face tightened. 'I wish I'd had the damn self-control not to blurt it out in front of you, but it just came right out because she's being so incredibly blind to the risk she's running! What I warned her about is inevitable! When the electioneering starts, and the global TV coverage heats up, some former client or fellow call girl will recognise her—and will sell the story to the media!'

He took a breath, his face grim.

'If she doesn't find a graceful way to break up with Roxburgh I'll have no choice but to warn him myself, for his own sake, because it will finish his career otherwise. I don't want to—God knows I don't!' His eyes hardened. 'Madeline knew perfectly well when she told me about her past that I wouldn't publicise her method of capital formation! But where she miscalculated, of course—' and now his expression changed yet again, becoming for the first time clearer, as if a weight had stopped crushing down on him '—was in thinking that I would share her tolerance towards her method.'

He looked at Celeste again.

'I left her flat that evening—walked out on her. My decision to end our affair, and for that reason…annoyed…her. She did her best to get me back…'

Into his head sprang the image of Madeline, stretched naked and voluptuous on his bed, taunting him not to desire her any more…refusing to accept his rejection of her… of what she had done…what she was…

He spoke again, willing Celeste to believe him. 'I hope with all my heart you can believe that there is no power on earth that could ever, *ever* induce me to tolerate her again! I wouldn't touch Madeline with surgical gloves on!' he spelt out. His voice iced. 'Or any woman like her!'

She could hear the contempt in his voice, the disgust. The total revulsion.

She pulled her eyes away, her gaze going towards the wide windows that opened out to the terrace beyond. She opened her mouth to say something, then stopped.

Rafael's cell phone was ringing. With a curse, he glanced at the number, then answered it.

'No, I haven't forgotten. I'll be there.' He disconnected, reached out a hand to Celeste.

'I am really gutted to do this, but I've got to go,' he told her. 'That was my PA, reminding me I have to be downtown in half an hour. I'd get out of the meeting if I could, but this guy is flying out to SF this evening.'

He bent to drop a kiss on Celeste's head. She was still looking like a ghost, and he hated to leave her like this, but in a way, although the scene with Madeline had been ugly in the extreme, surely it must have convinced her that Madeline Walters was out of his life for ever.

'Are you going to be OK?' he asked, concerned. Celeste nodded, and he spoke reassuringly. 'I'll be back as soon as I can, but it probably won't be till about seven. Let's have a really easy night in—I think we both deserve it!'

He smiled encouragingly, squeezing her nerveless hand again.

'And, please, don't waste another single thought on Madeline. She isn't worth it. She isn't worth anything—no woman like her is.' He glanced at his watch and swore. 'Damn—I have to go.'

He crossed to the door. Looked back at her. Felt emotion pour through him.

*Thank God I've got Celeste! Thank God she is in my life—thank God!*

How much she meant to him! How very, very much…
*I never want to lose her…*

Then, tearing himself away, he left the apartment.

Behind him, on the sofa, Celeste went on sitting. Inside, knives with the sharpest blades were slicing her into pieces.

Though his meeting had gone well, Rafael had spent it itching for it to be over. He wanted to get shot of work, shot of his office and back to Celeste. He'd texted her when he'd got downtown—something warm and reassuring—but hadn't heard back. Now, as he finished running through his agenda for the following day, prior to finally getting out of his office to head home, he checked his mobile again.

His head lifted—there was a text from Celeste. He clicked

it open. As he read, his spirits nosedived. He read it twice through, but it was still the same.

She'd texted to tell him that her London agency had phoned and wanted her back urgently for an upcoming job she felt she could not turn down. She was booked on a flight out of JFK and en route to the airport.

Disbelievingly, Rafael stared at the words. Then, as if a blow had fallen, he took the full impact of her message. She was gone. Gone—just like that.

He felt winded, as if he'd been punched.

How could she just pick up and go like that? How *could* she?

Could she still be upset about Madeline, even after he'd assured her that there was nothing more between them—that all he felt for her was revulsion?

Urgency filled him. He had to go after Celeste right away!

*I have to go to her—do whatever it takes to convince her that Madeline is nothing to me!*

He called her number. He had to speak to her. But her phone went to voicemail. A crippling sense of *déjà vu* hit him.

His calls going to voicemail, answer machine...

Her abrupt disappearing acts...

The punch to his stomach came again.

With a razoring breath, he seized his laptop and minutes later had booked an evening flight to Heathrow, then he headed down to the pavement to his waiting car. 'JFK,' he instructed tersely, and got his phone out again, retrying Celeste's number, then texting her his flight details.

Then, as if the devil were driving him, he sat back, staring out with bottled frustration at the rush-hour traffic jamming the roadways out of Manhattan.

# CHAPTER THIRTEEN

THE LOW HUM of the jet engines vibrated through the fuselage as Celeste reclined in her seat. Outside the night was dark mid-Atlantic. She was trying not to think, trying not to feel—trying not to be conscious at all. Willing herself to sleep. But sleep would not come.

By the time the plane landed she was living up to its reputation as the red-eye. She looked haggard, she knew, and if she really *had* got an assignment she would have needed a ton of make-up to disguise the fact. But she wasn't going to a job—that had been her excuse for leaving New York.

Leaving Rafael.

No—she mustn't think that. Mustn't say it. Mustn't allow it into her head. She must block it totally, completely. Because if she didn't—

*Claws tearing at her, talons ripping her, knives slicing her—shredding her to pieces, into bloodied rags of flesh.*

She bit her lip, trying to stifle the pain. Forced herself to keep functioning even if she felt as if she was a walking corpse. A corpse coming through Immigration, walking out into the arrivals area. But not in Heathrow, nor any UK airport. The first plane leaving when she'd got to JFK the afternoon before had been for Frankfurt, and that was where she'd landed. And it was just as well. The unanswered—unanswerable—texts piling up on her mobile told her exactly what Rafael was doing.

Following her to London.

The pain came again. Pain for herself. Pain for him.

*I don't want to do this to him!* The cry came from deep within her. *I don't want to do this to him—but I must...I must!*

She knew with a sick dread that she could not flee for ever. Could not hide for ever. At some point, eventually, she would have to go back to London.

Face him.

An ordeal she would have given the world not to have to face. An ordeal she could not face yet.

*I need time—just a few days...*

A few days to accept what had happened.

To accept that everything between her and Rafael was over...

Rafael was in London. He hadn't moved from his apartment there since the morning he'd arrived. The morning he'd arrived to find that Celeste had not gone to her flat. Had not gone to her agency. That her agency thought she was still in New York. That there was no urgent assignment they'd called her back for. That they had no idea where she was.

So he'd stayed in London. Where else should he go? If she turned up back in New York he would be informed. If she turned up at her London flat he would be informed. If she contacted her agency he would be informed. He'd even contacted Louise and asked...*begged*...her to tell him if she heard any news about her. He knew of no one else in the modelling world she might know.

But for five endless days now she had simply disappeared off the planet.

He'd stopped phoning, stopped texting. She wasn't going to reply, it was clear. He could only wait until she reappeared out of the thin air she'd vanished into.

He reached sightlessly for the whisky bottle on the table beside the sofa, then stopped himself. He had to get a grip.

Had to control himself. Getting mindlessly drunk to numb himself would serve no purpose.

He set the bottle back with a clunk on the table. As he did so, his mobile suddenly buzzed into life. He fell on it like a drowning man.

'Ms Philips has just returned to her apartment,' said the operative set to watch her flat.

Rafael could feel relief flooding him. Drowning his senses. Gratitude poured through him. He was out of his apartment moments later, flinging himself into his waiting car, and within twenty minutes he was outside her flat in Notting Hill. Launching himself up the steps from the pavement, he pressed the buzzer to her flat.

How long would it take her to answer? Perhaps she was in the bathroom, the kitchen—somewhere it might delay her picking up the entry phone. Maybe, of course, she just wasn't going to answer her door at this hour of the night.

He flicked open his mobile, phoned her. But before it connected the front door was buzzed open. He was inside instantly, running up the stairs to her floor. Not caring if his rapid tread disturbed her neighbours. Not caring about anything in the entire universe except seeing her again—being with her again...

Celeste—*his* Celeste...

*Always my Celeste!*

Because he knew that now. Knew it with every fibre of his being. Knew it with every cell of his body. He could not do without her. Could not live his life without her. She was everything to him—everything!

Had he once truly, actually considered marrying Madeline? Had he ever been that deluded? It was impossible to believe now. Impossible to believe that he had felt anything for her.

Even desire...

But as he circled the stairwell, two steps at a time in his

haste, he pushed Madeline out of his head. Celeste was everything Madeline was not—and was everything to him.

He rounded the last corner of the stairs onto Celeste's landing. She was standing in the open doorway of her apartment. He'd never been there, he realised with a rush of surprise. Well, it was of no account. She wouldn't be needing it any longer.

His arms went around her, enveloping her in a hug. 'My God, where have you *been?*' he asked into her hair. He drew back, holding her shoulders, drinking her in like a man who had been in the desert for five punishing, killing, waterless days.

She was in a dressing gown. Nothing glamorous or stylish—just a plain, light blue, thin wool, ankle-length, waist-tied wrap. Her hair was in a ponytail, her face bare of make-up. But his eyes feasted on her. She was the most beautiful woman in the world. The most wonderful. The most precious…

He guided her inside so he could kiss her properly.

But she backed away from him. 'Rafael, no—'

Her voice was high-pitched, and there was something wrong with it. He looked at her, consternation in his face.

'Are you all right?' Concern was open in his voice. He wanted to put his arms around her again, hold her close.

'Um…' she said.

She was looking deathly pale, he realised suddenly. His expression changed.

'Are you ill?'

The question shot from him, infused with fear. God, was that it—was that why she'd suddenly rushed off? Nothing to do with Madeline at all! Images sprang in his head of her in hospital, having tests, being told nightmare news…

She gave a half shake of her head.

'Thank God!' he exclaimed. He looked around. They were in a tiny hall, and he could see a sitting room beyond, through the open doorway, with the large sash windows—curtained now—that he'd seen from the street below.

He went through into it and she followed numbly. He turned back to her, having taken in an impression of simple decor, soothing and tranquil, a soft, comfortable sofa in grey fabric, and a pale oak dining table and chairs. There was a pale grey carpet, landscape prints on the walls and books stashed in an open-front bookcase against the wall. An old-fashioned Victorian iron fireplace held fat candles on its hearth.

He looked at her. Words fell from him. 'I've been worried out of my mind.'

Two spots of colour started to burn in her cheeks. 'I'm sorry,' she said. 'I'm...sorry.' She paused. 'But I...I had to go...'

'To a non-existent modelling assignment?' His eyebrows rose.

She took a breath. 'No. You know that was just an excuse.'

He looked at her. Every antenna he possessed had gone on high alert.

'So why did you leave?' he asked. He kept his voice steady. He had to know! If it were because of Madeline then he must find a way to convince her that she meant nothing to him now!

Celeste looked away. Then back at him. 'Would you mind if I made myself some tea? It's been a long journey. I've just come back on Eurostar.'

*'Eurostar?'*

'I flew into Frankfurt,' she said, 'from JFK. And since then I've been...' She fell silent.

*I've been trying to find the strength to do what I must do now, and I don't know whether I can, though I know I have to. I have to because you've turned up now, like this, and I'm not ready... I'm just not ready. But I've got to do it because it has to end now...right now. I have to end it...*

She moved towards the kitchen that opened off the sitting room. It was compact, and Rafael came and stood in the doorway, making it seem smaller than ever. Making the air in it hard to breathe.

She filled up the kettle. 'Coffee?' she asked, trying to sound normal. 'It's only instant, I'm afraid. I don't have a machine.'

Into her mind's eye leapt the formidably complicated machine in the Manhattan apartment that only he knew how to use. That she would never learn to use now...

She tore her mind away, focussed only on putting the kettle on, getting out the coffee jar, her tea caddy. No China tea tonight—this needed strong Indian...Assam. With a strength to get her through the coming ordeal.

She busied herself with mugs, with tea and coffee and boiling water, milk out of the fridge—milk she'd bought at a late-night convenience store near the station before she'd got a taxi here. Her mind darted inconsequentially, trying to find an escape. An escape from what was going to happen.

But there was no escape. She knew that. Knew it with the certainty of a concrete weight crushing her. Crushing her in to the ground.

Burying her.

Anguish cried within her.

*I thought I was free! Free of the past! Free to make myself anew! Free to claim what was being given to me! Free to take Rafael's hand outstretched to me! Free to be with him—to hold him and kiss him and embrace him!*

*Free to love him...*

Because she *had* fallen in love with him. Of course she had. How could she not? Self-knowledge sliced through her, cleaving her in two. She had fallen in love with him somewhere along the way...some time when she had lain in his arms, cherished and safe...

But she hadn't been safe at all.

And she hadn't been free.

'I want you to tell me what's wrong!'

Rafael's voice penetrated her anguish. His accent was pronounced—a sign of the tension he was under—although he was keeping his voice rock-steady. He sat himself down on her sofa, waiting for her to sit beside him.

Her eyes went to him. Her heart leapt. Oh, how good it was to see him again! How good to let her gaze feast on him, to drink in every sculpted plane of his face, every feathered sable shaft of his hair, every lean, honed line of his body! How good it was to see him again…see him here.

*I have to make a memory of this moment! I have to imprint his image on the sofa, so that I can always see him there. Always have this moment…only this moment…*

She moved restlessly, hands cupping her mug of tea, going not to sit beside him but on the edge of the armchair by the fireplace. She saw his eyes flicker uncertainly as she took her place away from him.

She didn't want to—she wanted to set down her tea, take his coffee from him and then wrap her arms around him as if he were the life raft of her life.

But she could not do that. She could never do that now. She was adrift, alone on an endless sea that was carrying her far, far away on a current that had started long ago, trapped in it for ever…

'Why did you leave?' he asked.

He looked into her face and knew the answer. The answer he hadn't wanted to hear. The answer he'd thought needed no response from him. But it must, or why else would she have done what she had.

'It's because of Madeline, isn't it?' he said. His voice was quiet. Deadly.

Her eyelids dipped over her eyes. 'Yes,' she said.

He looked at her. The fumes from the coffee cup on the low table in front of him rose in a coil. Madeline had thrown *her* coil around them—he had thought he'd broken it, but it must be tightening still around Celeste or else why would she have run from him?

'She said something to you, didn't she?' he said, never taking his eyes from her. 'She dripped some vicious, toxic poison into your ears before I came, and that's why you left.'

That had to be it—it *had* to! But Celeste was shaking her head.

His face worked. 'Then why—in God's name, *why?* Didn't I make it crystal clear to you just why I would never in a thousand years have anything more to do with her? Do you think I would *ever* want anything to do with her—with anyone who's like her?'

He took a shuddering breath. Celeste was looking at him and her face was set.

His expression changed. Slowly, he spoke. 'You think I was too harsh, don't you?'

His words fell into silence.

He spoke again. 'You think I was too harsh, too condemning. Too pitiless—too *puritan!* Despising Madeline for what she did—how she earned her first money!'

He sat back, drawing a breath. Never taking his eyes from her. Then he spoke again.

'Celeste, I come from a country that is poor—with a level of poverty almost unthinkable in the pampered West, in the developed countries of Europe and North America and Australasia. I come from a region where *peones* toiled on the land, barely scraping a living by subsistence farming or working on the landlord's vast *estancias,* where those in the cities lived in shacks and shanty towns. Where children begged in streets with gutters running with sewage, where they slept in doorways at night and stole by day, and inhaled glue to numb their hunger and their fear.'

He looked relentlessly into her eyes.

'And where women, young and old, would sell their bodies for a meal, or for shelter, or to feed their children! *That,* to me, is poverty! *That,* to me, is need and desperation! And if you think—' His voice gritted with intensity, his eyes burning. 'If you think that I would ever, *ever* condemn a woman in those pitiless circumstances from surviving in any way she could, then you have misjudged me utterly!'

He leant forward now, infusing his body with urgency.

'Those women have no choice! Their only choice is prostitution or to go hungry—or to see their children hungry! They are driven to it by desperation!'

His expression changed. Hardened like steel.

'Madeline Walters never experienced anything like that! She was never going to starve in the gutter! Never going to go to bed hungry! She took to prostitution because it was easy money! That's all! She mocked me because I'd worked hard and long for what I'd saved! Mocked me for working non-stop at back-breaking work in bloody awful conditions when she could earn a thousand pounds a night on her back in a luxury hotel room! She *chose* to sell her body for sex! She *wanted* to do it! She wanted to make money fast—any way she could! And she wasn't fussy about how she did it! *That's* why I despise her. Condemn her. And I would condemn *any* woman who made the same choice—chasing easy money by whoring herself out!'

He fell silent. Celeste hadn't moved. Not a muscle. Then, with a little jerk, she lifted her mug to her lips and took a mouthful. The tea was too hot still, and scalded her mouth. But she did not feel the pain.

There was too much in the rest of her body.

Consuming her.

Slowly, she set aside her mug. Slowly, she got to her feet. Slowly, she looked back to Rafael. The time had come. The moment was here. The moment when she destroyed the happiness she had so briefly glimpsed.

*I thought I was free to be happy! But I can never be free—never!*

The slicing knives cut into her heart—her soul. Because the past had not gone. It had never gone. Could never be gone. It had become the very future that was now rushing in on her, forcing her throat to work, her words to be shaped, her mouth to open and her voice to sound.

*Any woman,* he had said… He would condemn and despise any woman.

*Say it—say what you must! What you cannot keep silent on any longer!*

She had thought she could keep silent. Thought she could silence the past—silence all that she had done. But to do so now was impossible.

She made herself speak. Forced herself.

'I have to tell you something,' she said. Her voice was as thin as a reed.

He was looking at her. Such a short distance away, but separated from her by a gulf so large it could never be bridged. Into her mind came a memory—a memory of standing on the lawns at that Oxfordshire mansion, gazing at the Milky Way. Of Rafael coming to her, telling her about the Chinese legend of lovers separated on either side of the galaxy.

*It was us all along…those lovers parted by an ocean of stars.*

Pain pierced her as the knives in her heart sliced again.

His face had changed expression. There was concern in it again, tenderness. The pain came again.

'I've upset you,' he said, 'and I'm sorry. I know it must be difficult for you—painful, even—to hear about women like Madeline. Women who *choose* to exploit their sexuality as she did! To use it to make money.' His mouth twisted in angry contempt. 'Easy money.'

He took a breath, his eyes holding hers.

'Celeste, I know you've had some trauma in your past. Some ugly experience that traumatised you—made you lock yourself away in a prison of celibacy because of what had been done to you! I've never asked—never probed. But I saw how you reacted to Karl Reiner when he said those foul words to you—and how you reacted to what he was intending for Louise. I've always thought that you must have been through something similar—and that there was no one to save you from it! So I can understand—I truly can—how distressing it must be to you when someone like Madeline flaunts what she's done and makes a calculated decision to use the likes of Karl Reiner for commercial gain. I *know*,' he said, and his voice was resonant, 'that whatever happened to you, you never intended it to happen! You never *chose* it! You are nothing, *nothing* like Madeline!'

A sound came from her. A sound like something breaking. Her face was stretched like brittle plastic over steel mesh beneath. Her eyes seared him to the bone. Her voice tore like talons.

'I am *exactly* like Madeline!'

He surged to his feet. 'You are *nothing* like her! How can you say that? You *saw* how Karl Reiner was getting Louise drunk, drugged—whatever it would take to get her into bed with him without her realising it was happening!'

A hand slashed in front of him. 'I am *not* Louise! Don't think of me as her, or anything like her! I knew *exactly* what I was doing! And I knew *exactly* how much money I was being paid for it!' Her eyes were slitted like a snake's. 'Because fixing a price for sex is the first and most important thing *any* prostitute does!'

He froze. His brain froze. Stopped working completely. He just stood there, immobile.

She was not, though. She was swaying, very slightly, and there was a look on her face that was entirely and totally blank. As though she were no longer inside her body.

Yet her voice was still speaking. He could hear it coming from a long way away. An endless distance.

'So now you know,' she was saying. 'I am exactly like Madeline. I made the same choice as she did. I wanted money—fast. And I did what she did.'

There was silence. An agonising silence that stretched for eternity. Then into the silence Rafael spoke.

'I don't believe you.' His voice was flat. His denial absolute.

She rounded on him. 'Believe it! *Believe* it, Rafael, because that's what it was! Prostitution! Nothing else—just that. Sex for money.'

'No—' There was horror in his voice.

'*Yes!* It was prostitution—exactly that!' Bitterness and self-accusation scored her words. 'Oh, I tried to tell myself it wasn't—but it was! It *was.*' She took a ravaged, heaving breath, making herself remember—making herself tell him what she had to tell him. What he had to know.

Her voice changed. Stretched thin, as if a wire was garrotting her.

'I'd only just started modelling, and there's very little money in it to begin with. It came as a shock, because I'd assumed—like so many other teenagers—that once I'd been scouted I'd be swanning around in luxury like a supermodel from then on. The reality was different.' She paused, swallowed. 'Sometimes we didn't even get paid—not in money, just in clothes from the collection we'd modelled. So I was... short of money.'

Her voice was flat now, with no emotion.

'But money was what I wanted. Badly. So—I made a decision. I found a way to make...easy money.'

She took a breath, like a razor in her throat. Her eyes were dead now—quite, quite dead.

She cast those eyes at Rafael, not seeing him, seeing only the past, seeing the choice she had made, the decision she had taken.

'Have you ever heard of something called "summer brides"?' she asked, her voice as dead and as expressionless as her eyes. She paused, her eyes still resting on Rafael.

Did he shake his head? He didn't know. He knew only that something was gripping his entrails, his heart, like pliers.

She went on in that calm, dead voice. 'They are quite common in the Middle East. In some places local culture bans all sexual contact between men and women outside marriage. So what they do…wealthy men…is buy themselves a bride. A summer bride. Temporary. Just to provide them with what they want.' Her voice was emptied now of all expression. 'They pay her a bride price. Enough to…to compensate her for the fact that the marriage won't last more than a few weeks at the most. That once the man has…finished with her she'll be…discarded.'

She was silent a moment. Her eyes slid past him, looking into a place that was very far away and yet as close to her as the agonising synapses in her memory. Then she went on, in the same expressionless voice.

'I got a modelling assignment out in the Middle East—an oil-rich city in the Gulf, where a new fashion mall was opening. They were doing publicity shots using European girls, especially blondes like me. It was good money for modelling at my level then, but it still wasn't as much as I wanted. So when one of the photographers' assistants asked me if I was interested in earning more money—a lot more—I said yes. He explained to me the custom in that part of the world. Said that as a "summer bride" I could make a lot of money—fast. That as a blonde I'd be at a premium…my bride price would be high.'

She looked at Rafael again, not seeing him, only letting her gaze rest somewhere in the desert that was the place where she was now.

Her voice changed. Twisted in her throat.

'He called it a bride price but I knew what it was. I knew what a summer bride was. I *knew* it. Knew what it would be called here in the West.' And now her eyes did see Rafael's face. Saw every stricken feature. 'Prostitution. What else? What else is it when a girl is given money in exchange for sex with a stranger? I was given money—a lot of money. And I know what that made me.' She paused. Swallowed. 'What it *makes* me…'

She met his eyes, forced herself to do so. They were blank. Blank with shock. With more than shock.

'There are no excuses for me. I wasn't tricked, or forced, or fooled. I knew what I was doing and I did it. Because I wanted to. Just like Madeline I *chose* to make easy money, fast. *Just like Madeline.*'

She closed her eyes a moment. Then opened them again.

'So now you know why I left New York that afternoon. And why what we had is over.'

A shudder seemed to go through her, as if something were shattering deep inside. Her voice changed.

'Rafael, I lied about myself by not telling you. I deceived you. Because I wanted you so, so much, I told myself that I could finally leave it behind me—ignore that it had ever happened—accept from you what I had come to feel I could never accept from a man. A normal, honest relationship! But when you told me about Madeline, how you despised and condemned her for what she did—what she chose to do— then I knew that all my hopes had been lies! I knew...*know*... that I can never escape the past, never put my past behind me! That by hiding it from you I've been lying to you right from the start! And when I saw the revulsion in your face as you told me about Madeline, I knew—' her voice choked '—knew that I could deceive you no longer. I could not look at you and know that you would condemn any woman who made a choice like hers. A woman like Madeline. A woman...' the breath razored her lungs '...like me.'

She paused, shutting her eyes for a moment, then forcing them open again in order to say what she still must.

'So I left. And now,' she said, swallowing, lowering her voice, 'you must leave, too. I am sorry—truly sorry, more sorry than you can ever know—that I have treated you so badly, both in my deception, my silence about what I did, and in the anxiety you have felt these past days, not knowing where I was.'

He was still standing there, frozen into immobility. She

drew breath and went on. She had to do this right to the bitter, nightmare end.

'I would tell you, Rafael, that my time with you has been the most precious time of my life—I would tell you that, but for you I have destroyed it all by telling you the truth about myself, about what I've done. But it remains true, for all that, and to my dying day, each and every moment of my time with you will be a jewel in my memory.'

Her voice was breaking. *She* was breaking. She could speak no longer.

She saw him start, saw his face work. Then he spoke.

'How old were you?' His voice was stark.

She looked away again, then back at him. 'I was seventeen. Over the age of consent. And I consented to what I did. No one forced me or tricked me!'

'You were little more than a child!' Anger bit in his voice. 'You were shamelessly taken advantage of! You had no idea what you were doing!'

Anger flashed in Celeste's eyes in retaliation. 'Rafael, my age is irrelevant! Of *course* I knew what it was I was doing—I was having sex with a stranger for money! I prostituted myself! And calling myself his "summer bride" didn't stop it being that! I told you—I wanted money fast, a lot of it, and I got it. I got what I wanted! Just like Madeline did!'

'I absolutely refuse to compare you to her!'

'Well, you must! I'm sorry—I'm desperately, desperately sorry to inflict this on you, but—'

He cut across her. 'Are you? *Are* you sorry?' He seized on her words, silencing her.

She looked at him. 'Of *course* I'm sorry for doing this to you—'

He cut across her again. 'But are you sorry for doing this to *you?* Now, with your adult eyes, surely to God you bitterly regret what you did? Because Madeline doesn't! Madeline does not think she did anything at all to rcgret! But do *you?*

Do you regret it, Celeste? Do you look back now and wish you had not done it? Do you regret what you did?'

Every word was loaded. Every word carried a weight he could hardly bear. Her answer would tell him everything he had to know.

Everything he had to hope.

She looked at him. Looked at him with eyes that saw his pain.

And then she inflicted more. The killing blow.

She shook her head. 'No,' she said. 'I don't. I don't regret it. It got me what I wanted. Easy money. Fast.' She paused a fraction of a second. 'So you see I am just like Madeline…'

For one long, last moment he looked at her. Into the space between them went everything that he had once held so dear.

Then, without a word, he turned and left.

The night sky was cloudy, with rain threatening. No stars were visible. He walked. He walked without stopping, without pausing. Somewhere behind him his car was trailing him, his driver probably thinking him mad, but he could not think about that now. He could not think about anything.

Least of all about Celeste.

Who was not Celeste at all. Who was not the woman he had seen and sought, whose trust he had so slowly won. The trust to give herself to him knowing he would never hurt her.

Savage pain lacerated him.

*I trusted her—trusted her. Believed in her—believed her to be nothing like Madeline…*

His face twisted. In his head he heard, over and over again, her voice crying out. *'I am just like Madeline!'*

And inside his head, all the things that Madeline had told him about herself forced their way in, in sickening, vivid detail. His revulsion had been instant—total. And her mockery of him for it had been virulent. She'd been incredulous at his reaction, refusing to believe he was shocked by her revelation. He could hear her voice now, inside his head, scornful and scathing.

*'Oh, for God's sake, Rafe, sex workers aren't some kind of "fallen women" any more! Sex is just a commodity—an industry like any other! There's a market for sex and people buy and sell in it! What the hell's wrong with that? I had natural assets to capitalise on and I sold what my customers wanted—and my profit margin was the best I've ever achieved! So don't look down your damn puritan nose at me and quote Victorian morality like you want me whipped in the stocks as a warning to other women!'*

He hadn't answered her—hadn't been able to—and his silence only infuriated her more. Her eyes had flashed with anger. Her voice with scorn.

*'What's your damn problem? Most men would think it a fantasy come true, what I've told you! Personal, private, on-tap professional sex! Which, I would point out, you've been enjoying with me for quite some time! I didn't hear you complain while we were in bed! But if you think I've got boring, darling, well, let me spice it up for you! Because I can do that—with pleasure. Pleasure and a great deal of experience!'*

He still had not spoken to her. Only his expression had shown his reaction. Then he'd turned to go. Her voice had screamed after him.

*'Don't you dare walk out on me! Don't you bloody dare! Women don't have to put up with your kind of attitude any more! We are strong, we are independent and we can make our own millions—and we can have sex any damn way we want it, without men like you looking down on us! Half a century of feminism has made us free of men like you and your condemnation!'*

He'd stopped then, turned back to look at her. Then he'd spoken to her. His voice flat. Bleak.

*'Half a century of feminism and all you've achieved, Madeline, is the oldest profession of all. You debase yourself,*

*and you debase sex. It should be a gift, freely given by each partner, not a commodity to be sold for a cash profit. And if you cannot see that, if you cannot regret what you did, then there can be nothing more between us.'*

He'd gone then—walked out of her flat and out of her life.

And now he'd done the same to Celeste. Walked away from her.

Inside, a voice was protesting. *Not Celeste—not Celeste! She can't be like that—she can't!*

Not the woman he'd held in his arms night after night. Not the woman he'd been sharing his life with. A blow landed on his heart. Not the woman he'd wanted to go on sharing his life with.

For the bitterest truth of all was that in the anguished days he'd spent not knowing where she was, one overwhelming realisation had hit him. He did not want to be without her. He wanted her to be with him—stay with him. Make her life with him.

The realisation had shone like a beacon, impossible for him to deny, impossible for him to do anything other than reel from the truth of it.

A beacon that she had extinguished with one fatal utterance.

Pain jagged through him.

He walked on into the night.

# CHAPTER FOURTEEN

CELESTE SHIVERED AS she stepped out of her front door onto the steps to the pavement. Though she was wearing a warm coat, the winter weather was cold. But it was more than the weather that chilled her. She was cold in her bones. Cold all the way through.

Sometimes, even though she tried desperately—despairingly—to keep them out, memories forced their way into her head, memories of when she had been warm...

*The balmy Hawaiian breeze from the ocean, the heat of the day rising up from the hot sand, the sun like a benediction on her.*

The memories mocked her. Mocked her just as all her memories mocked her. With cruel, jeering laughter. Mocking her for having dared to think that she could find happiness, that she could escape the past. Walk free of it.

*Of course you couldn't! You were a fool to think you could! A fool to think you could just ignore it, blank it out of your consciousness! A fool to think you could set it aside as though it had never happened—as though you'd never done what you did! A fool to think you could allow yourself to have what you knew from the start must be impossible!*

*Yet you thought you could have it—you thought you could finally take for yourself the happiness that was barred to you. And all you have achieved is to wound a good man—a man who cared for you and cherished you, a man you deceived by your silence. You betrayed his trust in you.*

Remorse filled her—remorse at what she had done to Rafael. At her culpable silence, her self-blinding foolish hope that she could take what he offered her—take the happiness she'd found with him.

Telling him the truth had been like stabbing him... And the knife had thrust into her as well. A lethal, deadly thrust to the heart.

*And you deserve it! You deserve to feel that pain, to feel it now, still and for ever! You deserve it for what you did to him! You deserve your broken heart.*

She had broken it herself. No one to blame but her. No one to rail against but her. No one to mock but her.

She hugged the coat around her, against the bitter arctic wind. There was no spare flesh on her to warm her. She was thinner than ever, for she had no appetite at all. But it was *good* that she was so thin. She'd done the autumn fashion shows, and now she was booked in for the round of shows that would take place before the spring.

She would be as gaunt and starved as even the most demanding designer wanted, she thought mockingly. It would be exhausting, non-stop, but she'd welcome it—just as she had welcomed the punishing pace of the autumn shows. For it would blot out the rest of the world for her. Not that she could do anything but just get through them. Tough them out until they were all over. And then... She took a lungful of freezing air. Then she would quit. Quit everything.

She could not face continuing with her career. Could not face the absurd triviality of fashion, the endless fuss and furore over what was so entirely pointless, so utterly unimportant. Who cared what hemlines and silhouettes and colours and fabrics were in or out? Who cared which designers were on a roll and which in decline? Who cared?

Where once she might have had a careless tolerance now she had none. Only a bleak, chill emptiness.

About everything.

What she would do when she no longer modelled she didn't know. Didn't care. Could not care. She would sell her flat, that much she knew, because she could not bear to be in London any more. Where she would go, though, she didn't know either. Somewhere far away. Remote. A Scottish glen, a Welsh hillside, a Yorkshire moor... It didn't matter where.

Because wherever she went she would be trapped in her past—the past she could never leave behind her. The past that had destroyed her happiness, broken her heart...condemned her to a future of perpetual loneliness.

Loveless and alone.

Without Rafael for ever...

The small podium was illuminated by light, which also pooled on the rainbow-hued display of clutch bags at the side of the man who was speaking.

'But my greatest gratitude,' Lucien Fevre was saying, 'must go to the man who had faith in me and whose generous support has enabled me to bring you this collection today.'

He turned towards Rafael, who was standing some way away, letting Lucien have the limelight. But he smiled and nodded in acknowledgement.

He did not feel like smiling. He never felt like smiling. There was a grimness on his features, and he knew his staff found his manner intimidating. He could not alter it. It was permanent, he knew. A kind of bleakness of the soul.

Lucien was speaking still, moving on to the others he wanted to thank for their support. It was the official launch of his new company, his new collection, and it was going well. The fashion editors and their ilk were praising the collection, welcoming his revival, and since Rafael had ensured that Lucien had a crack management team around him—everything from publicity to finance—all the signs were that this time around he would not hit the rocks as he had before.

He was glad for him—though he wished with grim endurance that he did not have to be here at this moment.

It was too close a reminder of the informal party held for Lucien when Madeline had arrived like the uninvited witch in a fairy tale. And the curse of her presence had borne its baleful fruit. As had his own denunciation of her.

*If I'd never warned her about her insanely unachievable political ambitions...! If I'd never thrown in her face just why they were so impossible...! Then Celeste would never have known why I ended it with Madeline...*

*And if she had never known then she would never have told me about herself.* The punishing logic tolled through his head. He felt his stomach clench. And if she hadn't—?

*I would have never walked out on her. And she would still be with me.*

Pain stabbed at him. He knew what he had lost.

But if she had never told him about herself—never confessed her past to him—then they would have been living a lie...a lie of silence by her. After wrenching Madeline out of his life, as he had made himself do, there had been times when he'd cursed her for telling him about what she had done—just as he was now so torn about Celeste's confession to him.

But what he had felt about Madeline, about ending everything with her, was nothing to what he felt now. How could it be?

For, whatever he had once felt about Madeline, never at any time had he felt anything at all of what he had come to feel for Celeste.

*I never fell in love with Madeline...*

The words formed and shaped and burned in his head. Burning through his flesh...burning through his heart.

Lucien had finished his speech and the audience was breaking up, the proceedings becoming informal now. Rafael watched Lucien being approached by two influential fashion directors who were smiling enthusiastically. Rafael started to mingle, doing his bit, but a few minutes later Lucien was at his side.

'I was so sorry to find that Celeste was not here,' he said. 'I had hoped she would be.'

Rafael gave a reply that he hoped was not too clipped—something about her working in Europe at the moment.

'I was hoping she would be here,' Lucien went on to say, 'so that she could take her pick from the collection. I wanted to give her whichever she liked best.' He looked at Rafael. 'I will not forget her kindness to me when Madeline Walters gatecrashed. It is so rare to find kindness and beauty together.'

'Yes,' said Rafael, 'it is.'

Saying more than that was not possible. He moved the conversation on—away from the dagger in his heart that was Celeste.

But as more people came up to Lucien, keen to speak to him, and Rafael stepped aside to let them, Lucien's words echoed in his head.

*'I will not forget her kindness...'*

In his memory he saw the scene again—Celeste going up to Lucien, intervening, diverting him from Madeline's scornful boasts of sales and profit. She'd seen his distress and taken action.

Another memory played inside his head. Just as she'd taken action when she'd seen the hapless Louise in Karl Reiner's toils. She hadn't hesitated—just marched straight up, got Louise out of the danger she was in. She'd cared enough about someone she hardly knew to risk making a scene, risk the anger of a powerful and influential man in her industry.

Madeline wouldn't have done that. Madeline would have laughed—found it amusing to see Louise's drink spiked. Or she would have simply shrugged and said the girl was an idiot. Rafael's eyes darkened. Or she'd have said she was smart—doing the right thing. Getting on the good side of a man who could help her career.

But she would no more have dreamt of intervening, of rescuing Louise, than she would have dreamt of caring a cent for the feelings of a man whose company she had bought out from under his nose, then trampled on his pride and kicked him scornfully into the dust.

Words sounded in his head. Celeste's voice...

*'I am just like Madeline!'*

His eyes blazed. Fists clenched suddenly. She was *nothing* like Madeline! He had hurled that at her and she'd refuted it, spewing out the sordid, unbearable reason for their alikeness...

His face contorted.

*And is that it? Is that all she has to prove their similarity?*

Memory of that hideous evening stabbed again—memory of him trying desperately to argue that she had been too young...that she'd been exploited and taken advantage of... that she must surely regret what she had done...

But she'd refuted that, too.

*'No—I don't regret it.'*

Her voice—so very clear, so very insistent.

His voice now, in his head, just as insistent.

*It doesn't make sense!*

The words forced themselves into his head, repeating themselves. *It doesn't make sense!*

Because it didn't. It couldn't. What Celeste had told him about what she had done—that she had just wanted quick, easy money and had no regrets about how she'd got it!— matched nothing else that he knew about her!

*She'd turned down renewing her lucrative contract with Reiner Visage because she'd refused to give Karl Reiner what he wanted—sex in exchange for another year's contract! She'd refused to prostitute herself for her career—for easy money...*

How did that match with what she had confessed to him?

Nothing he knew about her matched with her confession!

Memory blazed through him like a forest fire, igniting the undergrowth, ripping through his consciousness. Nothing in any memory of her until that last painful confession bore any indication at all that she could justify that insistence of hers! It was the one jarring note in everything he knew about her!

Making no sense at all.

He stilled. Like an unbearably slow gear wheel turning, his mind worked. The cogs of logic twisted, bringing up into his consciousness the one blazing truth that proved beyond all things just how much her insistence that she was like Madeline simply made no sense. How much it was a lie—*must* be a lie!

*If she has no regrets for what she did, then why was she living a celibate life? Why had she cut herself off from all relationships with men? Why was she so obviously haunted and traumatised by her past? Why was it so painfully hard for her to come to trust me—to give herself to me—to accept me in her life?*

He stood stock-still, feeling winded by the realisation. All around him people seemed to be moving like an inchoate sea, but he was alone in it. Slowly, clankingly, the wheels of logic turned again.

*Madeline had no regrets—and she lived a life that showed it! A life that gave her her fill of affairs, of revelling in her sexual appetites!*

Yet Celeste had withdrawn totally from that side of her existence. Shown extreme reluctance—every sign of trauma...

And that could mean only one thing—

*She must regret what she did! She must! Or she would be as brazen as Madeline!*

But why would she lie about it?

*It can't be the truth—it can't! If she had no regrets, if she didn't care about what she'd done, then she would not have lived the lonely, passionless life she has...*

Yet what reason could there be for lying about something that had destroyed everything they had together? Smashing to pieces all that was between them?

With infinite slowness the wheel inside his head made one last turn. If Celeste were not lying about regretting what she had done, even though what she had done had so clearly traumatised her, then there was only one other explanation for her insistence…

Only one.

Without conscious awareness he started to walk out of the crowded room. His hand slid inside his jacket pocket. Took out his mobile. He had calls to make. Urgent calls upon which his entire future happiness depended.

*I have to be right about this! I have to be!*

Desperation filled him. Mingled with the most precious quality in all the world. Hope—to which he clung with all his strength.


Celeste was packing. Not for another modelling assignment abroad, but to leave London. For good. She didn't know where she was going to go. She was just going. She'd let her flat, furnished, and tenants were moving in after the weekend. An agency would deal with them—deal with everything that came up. Her clothes and personal effects were locked away, and she'd cleaned the flat scrupulously. Now she just had to finish packing the case she was taking with her. Summer clothes, for somewhere warm, because she was cold to her very bones…

She wasn't going to stay in the UK—not even now that spring was finally approaching. She'd done the fashion weeks for this time of year and then had quit her agency.

Her last act had been to leave an encouraging card for Louise, to wish her luck in the career that was taking shape for her. Not that she needed any luck—she was doing well and, Celeste had been glad to see, was dating someone from outside the fashion world. Someone who was six foot two and played rugby—quite enough to take on the likes of Karl Reiner or similar, who might be intending to exploit Louise. Louise had wised up fast, and was pretty good at taking care of herself now.

She'd be OK from now on, Celeste knew.

*And so will I—somehow!*

How, she didn't know, because right now it was impossible to imagine being 'OK' by any definition of the word—unless it included 'functioning like an automaton'. But at least she *was* functioning, she thought. Functioning sufficiently to have done everything required to get to this point, where all she had to do was close her suitcase, pick up her handbag with her passport in it and head for the airport.

Where she would go precisely she wasn't yet sure. She might try Spain—it was cheap enough to live there prudently for a while, on her savings and the rental income from her flat, and it was warm. Then she frowned. No, of course she wouldn't go to Spain. She would hear Spanish spoken there, and that would remind her of Rafael…

There must be somewhere else. She ought to have thought about it earlier, but she hadn't wanted to. Thinking about it would have required planning, commitment, envisaging the future. And she couldn't do that. The future had stopped. Stopped when Rafael had turned his back on her and walked out through the door…

*So where else is warm this time of year? Warm and not Spanish-speaking?*

She made herself think, because thinking of somewhere warm to go at this time of year was better than thinking about Rafael turning his back on her and walking out of her life…

Where was it warm now? Where did people go to get away from the UK?

Dubai was popular—and very warm—everywhere in the Gulf was warm…

The guillotine slammed down in her head. She would be dead before she ever went to the Gulf again...

Frantically she thought of somewhere else. Where was it summer now?

*Australia?*

The guillotine slammed down again.

With a smothered cry, she seized up her bag. She would find somewhere warm to go when she got to the airport. Who cared where? She didn't. She would never care about anything again.

Or anyone...

Pain clamped around her heart, but she ignored it. She always ignored it. There was nothing else to do but ignore it. And keep functioning. That was important.

And finding somewhere warm, even though her bones were cold...so very cold...

The entry bell to the house sounded. Her taxi had arrived. She picked up her suitcase. Her keys. The agent already had keys to give to the tenants. She looked around her bedroom one last time but could feel nothing. She was too cold to feel anything. Carrying her suitcase, she went into her little hall-way and buzzed open the front door, to show the taxi driver she knew he was there. Then she put on her coat, busying herself doing it up because it would be chilly outside. Then she opened her flat door, casting one last look around, in case there was something she had missed.

But there was nothing. Nothing left of her.

Nothing left of her anywhere.

She stepped out onto the landing, moving to pull her flat door shut behind her.

And stopped dead.

Rafael was coming up the last flight of stairs towards her.

She couldn't move. Could not move a muscle. This wasn't real. This wasn't happening. It could not be happening...

Yet there he was, striding across the short outer landing

right up to her door, right up to *her*. She opened her mouth to protest. To protest that this could not be happening, that it was impossible. That he'd walked out of her flat long, night-mare months ago and could never return...

He took her shoulders and she saw by the sweep of his eyes that he'd seen her suitcase. A flashing frown showed on his brow, but he simply manoeuvred her back inside her hallway, picking up the suitcase as though it was a feather and depositing it inside, then turned to shut the flat door.

'I want to talk to you—'

His voice was deep, harsh. His eyes burned as they ground into hers.

She felt faint, dizzy. Heard him saying more.

'I *have* to talk to you!'

There was still harshness in his voice, but there was more, too—a powerful, urgent emotion that impelled him forward so that she had to step backwards, back into her living room. She took another stumbling step away from his grip, which was burning through the layer of her coat to the skin beneath.

His rapid, sweeping glance was traversing the room, see-ing its bareness—there was nothing of her there any more, no books or ornaments, only furniture and curtains. The flashing frown came again, and his eyes returned to her.

'Where are you going?' he demanded. 'The empty flat, the suitcase...'

She found her voice. Finally forced her strangled throat to open.

'I'm leaving,' she said. 'I've rented out my flat and I'm going abroad.'

Emotion knifed through him. She had so nearly disap-peared again!

*I got here just in time.*

'Where?' he heard his voice demanding.

'I don't know...' She spoke almost randomly, unable to force her mind into coherent thought. Because her mind was not working at all. It had been overwhelmed by emotion. Emotion that was pouring through her like scalding water.

*I can't bear to see him again—I can't bear it!*

To see him here again, in the flesh, in physical reality instead of just in the dreams that had tormented her, slain her, all these long months since he had gone, was unbearable.

'Well,' he said, and there was something different in his voice now, beneath the harshness that was still in it, 'how about Australia? After all...' and now his eyes had changed, too '...you have dual UK-Australian citizenship—'

She paled. 'How...how do you know?'

But that wasn't really the question she was asking.

*Why* did he know?

His eyes pinioned hers, as dark, as heavy as basalt. 'I know a lot about you, Celeste. A lot more than I did. Which is why...' he took a heavy, searing breath '...why I have to talk to you.'

She was shaking her head. 'No,' she said. *'No.'*

His hands came onto her shoulders again. 'Yes, Celeste,' he said. His voice was different again, and something in it made her throat constrict.

'Sit down,' he said.

He pressed her shoulders, not roughly but insistently, and her knees buckled. With a jerk she sat down on the sofa, indenting the cushions she'd lined up so neatly, ready for her tenant to find a pristine flat. He sat down heavily at the far end. There was empty space between them. Yet it seemed to her that there was a force field emanating from him that was holding her in a traction she could not escape. She had to try—

'I've got to go,' she said. 'I've got a taxi coming.'

Even as she spoke the entry phone went again. She tried to rise, but Rafael was before her. He strode out to her hallway and she heard him press the intercom, heard him dismiss the taxi, then stride back in again. He stood there a moment, looking down at her. So tall, so overpowering...

She couldn't breathe, but she had to. Had to go on breathing in and breathing out, even though her mind had left her body. She could not think or speak—could do nothing except sit there, like a bag of nerveless bones, on her sofa.

Slowly, deliberately, he sat himself back down. He looked at her as she sat, clutching her handbag as if it were a breathing aid.

'You're too thin,' he said abruptly, his eyes sweeping over her critically. 'Far too thin.'

She said nothing. What did it matter what she looked like? What did anything matter at all? What could it matter ever again?

He was speaking to her and she had to hear him—had to let the words reach her ears though she tried to block them. But it was impossible. They penetrated every last desperate layer of her defence.

His voice was sombre, carrying a weight in it that seemed to bow and bend his words.

'It took me a long, long time to realise something, Celeste. But eventually it dawned on me—I realised what it was that was wrong about what you said to me. You said…' he spoke with incised deliberation '…that you did not regret what you did when you were seventeen, that you had no regrets even now, as an adult.'

He took a breath. It was time to say what he had flown here to say. Time to stake all his future happiness, his very reason for being, on what he said next.

'There are only two reasons why someone would say that.' His eyes were on her, like a beam of laser light she could not escape. 'Either it's because, like Madeline, they're perfectly happy with their behaviour—see nothing wrong in it, nothing to object to, no big deal.' He paused. 'Or one other reason.'

His eyes shifted a moment, gazing out into nowhere, then came back to her. 'Tell me…how do you happen to have dual citizenship?'

She didn't answer, but she didn't need to.

'Your father was Australian,' Rafael said. 'You were born there. But your mother was English, and when your father died you came back to the UK, grew up here. When you were seventeen you went back again, and stayed there for several years, only returning when you were twenty.' He paused again—a longer pause. His eyes never left her.

She sat numb, her face drained of colour. Remorselessly he went on.

'It's an expensive journey, from the UK to Australia. And you were raised in a council flat, weren't you? So there wasn't any spare money around. Certainly not enough to fund not only getting to Australia but the lavish lifestyle you enjoyed there. Because you lived it up royally there, didn't you, Celeste? First-class hotels and resorts, travelling right across the continent, from Perth to the Great Barrier Reef. It must have cost thousands. Thousands upon thousands! Especially,' he finished, 'when there were two of you to pay for...'

Her hands were clenched on her bag, her knuckles white. She knew what was coming next—knew he must have discovered everything, since he had found out so much already.

He spoke gently. Quietly. And so, so carefully.

'I've seen her death certificate, Celeste. My researchers in Australia obtained an official copy and sent it to me. I've brought it with me.' He reached inside his jacket, took out a folded document, unfolded it slowly.

'I don't want to see it!' Her voice was high-pitched.

'And I have your father's, too,' he said, his eyes never leaving hers. But they were gentle now, like his voice. 'They were both signed at the same registrar's office in New South Wales—fifteen years apart.'

He paused again.

'You told me about your father, Celeste. You told me that he'd drowned in a rough sea. But you did *not* say that he drowned while he was rescuing another surfer who had got into difficulties. I've seen the newspaper clippings from when it happened—he was given a posthumous award. There's a photo of your mother receiving it on his behalf. You're holding her hand—you were two years old.'

'I've seen it!' she cried, her voice anguished. 'I've seen it so many times. My mother treasured it! And I can't bear to see it again! She cried every time she looked at it. Every time! She loved him so much!'

She felt her hand being taken. Loosened from her clenched grip on her bag.

'Loved him so much,' echoed Rafael, in that same gentle voice that was a torment to hear, 'that she wanted to go back to Australia to die in the same place he had.'

His eyes went to the death certificate for Celeste's mother. Forty-two years old. No age to die. His eyes shadowed. But then cancer found its victims at every stage of their lives. His eyes lifted to Celeste. There were tears in her eyes now.

Gently he squeezed her hand, and she could feel his warmth, his strength running into her. Giving her the strength to speak at last.

After so many years.

'She was diagnosed when she was already terminal,' she said. 'Ovarian cancer is like that—the silent killer, it's called, because its symptoms are so hard to spot. Especially if, like Mum, you ignore them.' She swallowed. 'It's the reason I have routine ultrasound scans every year—to spot it early if it starts in me, too. Mum made me promise—she dreaded the same thing happening to me as had to her.'

Her voice was low and halting, but she went on. Forcing herself to speak. To relive the fear and the anguish and the grief and the loss. 'She left Australia straight after my father's funeral. She couldn't bear to be there any more, without him. But after she was diagnosed, and knew she could not survive, she wanted to go back—to die in the place he'd loved so much that had killed him in the end. And she wanted to do what they'd done for their honeymoon—backpack all around Australia, seeing everything, thinking they had all the time in the world to live together for all the years to come. But all they got was a bare three years.'

'So you took her back there, didn't you?' said Rafael quietly. 'You took her back and went with her all around the country, retracing the journey she'd taken with your father. And then you went to the surf spot he loved so much, when she got weaker and weaker, and she died there. And you buried her next to him. And they lie there together, Celeste—side by side, at the sea's edge.'

She was weeping now, the tears running silently down her cheeks. He brushed them with his fingers and her face buckled more.

'It was to pay for all of that that you did what you did. That you became a summer bride.'

She was silent. She could not speak.

'You said...' He spoke carefully, for this was very, very important. 'You said that you did it because you wanted money fast. But what you did not say was why.'

She looked at him. 'What difference does it make?' she said, and her eyes had that deadened expression in them now. 'You asked if I regretted doing it—and I don't. I made the decision I needed to make, and I would do the same again. And I have no remorse, or regret—not a single shred! If I could have done it differently, I would have. But this was the only way.'

He dropped her hand. Got to his feet in a jerking movement. Stared down at her.

*What difference does it make?'* he echoed. 'How can you even think that, let alone believe it?' His eyes flashed. 'It makes all the difference in the world!'

'No, it *doesn't!'* Her own eyes flashed now, with hatred—hatred for herself and what she had done, for what she would do again without the slightest hesitation or remorse or regret. 'I still did it! I still sold myself for sex! A summer bride. I was driven out to some villa at the edge of the city and I went through a travesty of a ceremony, in a language I didn't understand and didn't need to, because all that was required of me was that I did what I had been paid to do—*paid to do!*'

She took a ragged, ravaging breath.

'And to ensure I was docile and submissive I was given something to drink every night—something like roofies, I suppose. It turned everything into a kind of fog and I was so, so grateful. Because it blurred everything…everything that was going on…everything that was done to me…'

Her voice changed, he could hear it, and her gaze now followed the long, dark tunnel leading back into her past.

'Sometimes,' she said, 'I had to wait. In a courtyard, on a terrace or a rooftop. I don't remember too well.' Her face furrowed. 'I just remember that it was cold, and I was given some kind of wrap. And I used to look up and see stars. Stars that were very far away. I liked that. I liked that they were so far away…so far away from everything that I was doing…'

She stopped, and yet again her voice changed, becoming a kind of harsh whisper.

'I wanted to be part of the heavens. I wanted to be taken up there—away from everything down here on the earth, away from everything that was happening to me. I wanted to be amongst the stars—as far away as they were. Because I could not *bear* what was happening.'

She swallowed. 'Except it *was* happening…and I had to let it happen…or else my mother would die without seeing again the one place in the world where she had been happy, without getting to the one place in the world where she wanted to die—'

She stopped again, and this time she did not continue.

Rafael reached his hands down to her, taking both of hers so that her handbag fell to the floor, unregarded. He drew her up, still holding her hands.

'I want you to understand something,' he said. 'Something that is very, very important for you to understand.' He spoke carefully, because what he said now was the most important thing he would say in all his life. 'We are judged,

Celeste, not only by our acts, but by our reasons for those acts. It is the deed *and* the intent for that deed. Do you understand me? Do you understand?'

His voice was shaking with the immensity of what he had to get across, what he *had* to make her comprehend, even though she was looking at him with a deadened blankness in her eyes that was like a knife in his body.

'It is because you did what you did not for yourself but for your dying mother that it is entirely and totally different! You forced yourself to do something that repelled you so much it traumatised you for years! It shut you in a prison of celibacy, cut you off from all normal relationships! That isn't the reaction of someone who has no regrets because they don't consider they did anything they didn't *want* to do!'

He took a ragged breath, clasped his hands around the cusps of her shoulders. 'To think that you stood here and compared yourself to Madeline! Insisted you were exactly the same! God Almighty—if you had only *told* me that night what you've told me now—what I had to find out for myself once my imbecilic brain had finally worked out what the *hell* was going on in your head! What had gone on in your life. Because if you had…'

His voice changed. Now it had a timbre in it that found its way into her nerveless body as she stood like a limp rag, scarcely able to keep standing without his hold on her.

'If you had, then I would have done what I will do now, my most precious Celeste,' he said.

And now his eyes were changing, too. The blaze of anger in them—anger at her silence, at his own unforgivable stupidity and blindness—was gone now, and in its place was not a fire, but a glow…a glow as warm as the palms of his hands curved over her shoulders.

'I would have begged your forgiveness for not trusting you, not trusting everything I knew about you, not trusting everything we had together. I would have begged you, implored you, to come back to me.'

His eyes poured down into hers, reaching to her heart.

'I would have begged you, implored you,' he said softly, 'to love me as I love you, as I always will love you, for your heart alone.'

He kissed her softly and cherishingly.

She looked up at him, not daring to believe. 'I saw the revulsion in your eyes.' Her voice was low, and shaken. 'I saw it when you told me about Madeline. When I told you about myself.'

He looked down at her. 'Do you see it now?' he asked. 'Do you see *anything* but love, Celeste?' He shook his head. 'You will never see it. Never see anything but love for all our days. What you did,' he said, 'took courage I doubt many could find, and I have for you, my most precious Celeste, only the deepest respect. I told you once, when I was condemning Madeline, that I would never condemn any woman who was driven into prostitution by desperation. Do you think you were different? Do you think you did it for any other reason than to give to your mother her dying wish?' His gaze poured into hers. 'What you did, you did as an act of love,' he said.

He did not wait for her to answer. Waited only to see the darkness in her eyes finally start to clear. Letting back in the light of life. Of love.

Then, and only then, did he sweep her into his arms and hold her close, so very close, against his heart. Where he would keep her for ever.

She was weeping now, he could tell. Her thin body shuddered as he wrapped her against him. He let her weep, holding her safe in his arms. And when she was done and she lifted her head, her cheeks stained with tears, her eyes clinging to his just as her body clung to his, he looked down at her.

'Shall we go now?' he said, his voice still soft, still cherishing. 'Shall we go together, as we shall be from now on—where we belong, with each other?'

He smoothed her hair, kissed her again, then loosed his arms and simply took her hand. He bent to pick up her handbag and gave it to her. Then he walked with her to the door and picked up her suitcase.

She looked at him, her heart beating...soaring... Soaring like a bird towards the heavens... Leaving the past behind—for ever, this time...

'Where?' she breathed.

Her eyes were wide—wide with hoping, with finally daring to believe. To believe everything he was telling her.

'Into our future,' he told her.

# EPILOGUE

THE WARM BREEZE lifted the fine netting of her veil. Through its misted folds Celeste could see the brilliant sunlit cobalt-blue of the Pacific. Feel the warmth of the sunshine on her face as she gazed towards the gazebo at the end of the pathway. Its position was perfect, framed by white bougainvillaea, enclosed in a little private glade from the rest of the gardens, and with the vista of the ocean behind it.

But it was not the gazebo that held her gaze. It was the man waiting for her.

Rafael—her beloved Rafael! Who had freed her with his love—freed her to love him as he, as she knew from every loving glance he gave her, loved her.

Her heart constricted. How much she loved him! How very, very much! He was looking back to her now, his dark eyes smiling with all the love in them that she had in hers for him. The priest was waiting for her and she started to walk forward, as tall and graceful as a lily in her wedding gown. Soft Hawaiian music played from hidden speakers and the scent of exotic blooms wafted to her.

She reached Rafael's side and stood beside him, her heart singing with happiness. They had eyes only for each other. When the service began she gave her responses clear and low, as his were clear and resonant. She could feel her heart swell.

Then, at last, as the priest raised his hand in blessing of them both, Rafael's mouth dipped to hers.

'Señora Sanguardo…' he whispered to her.

'For ever,' she whispered back.

Then, hand in hand, they walked back with the priest to the wedding breakfast that awaited them. And to the rest of their life together.

\* \* \* \* \*

# THE TAMING OF A
# WILD CHILD

## KIMBERLY LANG

To Jane, who swoops in to save my butt with everything from food to child care and only ever asks for a book to read in return. Here you go, Jane; this book is for you, with my heartfelt thanks for being a super friend.

And I owe another shout-out to the fantastic Cristina Lynn (CristinaLynn.com), who gave me the perfect song for the epilogue to Lorelei and Donovan's story.

# CHAPTER ONE

THE ONLY THING WORSE than waking up naked in a strange bed was realizing there was someone else sleeping in the bed, too.

Someone male.

The bright light on the other side of her eyelids sent pain streaking through Lorelei LaBlanc's head as she tried to piece together exactly what the hell was going on…and who she'd just spent the night with.

She forced herself to lie still; jumping right up might wake her companion, and she didn't want to get straight into a confrontation before she had a handle on things.

*Think, Lorelei, think.*

She had a hangover that would slay a mule, and it hurt to think. How much champagne had she consumed in the end?

Connor and Vivi's wedding had gone off without a hitch; all of the four hundred guests had had a fabulous time. The church had never looked better, and the hotel had outdone itself with both the decor and the food. She'd been at the head table for dinner, but once the dancing had begun and the champagne had really started flowing… Well, that was where things began to get a little fuzzy. She remembered having a small, good-natured disagreement with Donovan St. James over…

Her eyes flew open.

*Oh. My. God.*

Bits and pieces of the night before came rushing at her with distressing speed and clarity.

Carefully, so as not to aggravate her hangover, she rolled slowly to her other side. Sure enough, Donovan lay there on his back, bare-chested, with only a sheet covering his hips and one leg. His hands were stacked behind his head as he stared at the ceiling.

She swore under her breath.

"Right there with you, Princess."

The amused sigh in Donovan's voice put her nerves on edge. "What the hell happened last night?"

He had the gall to look pointedly at the tangled sheets— which she was currently trying to pull over herself in a belated attempt at modesty—and raise an eyebrow. She really wasn't ready to go to the whole *we had sex* bit just yet. She cleared her throat. "I mean, how? *Why?*"

"How? Buckets of champagne. And there were tequila shots involved. As for why…" He shrugged. "Beats the hell out of me."

Tequila explained a lot. Jose Cuervo was *not* her friend. *I've done some stupid stuff in my life, but this? With Donovan St. James? And now?* A chill ran down her spine. If she'd *publicly* done something… Oh, her family was really going to kill her this time. Her sister would be first in line.

"Please just tell me we didn't make a scene at the reception," she whispered.

"I don't think so. It's a little blurry, but I think the reception was pretty much over before…"

That alleviated a bit of her immediate worry; being stupid wasn't quite so bad as long as there wasn't an audience for the stupidity. Now, though, she had to face the fact she'd had sex with Donovan St. James.

No red-blooded woman would question her taste. Donovan had poster-boy good looks: deep green eyes, inky black hair with a slight wave that he wore long enough to look a little dangerous, and skin the color of the café au lait she desperately needed to combat this monster hangover. The high cheekbones and square jaw now shadowed with dark stubble spoke to a heritage as mixed as New Orleans itself—if one could pick the best bits and discard the rest.

Donovan definitely rated high on the *hummina* scale. Good looks, though, were pretty much all he had going for him, in her opinion. Why had he even been invited to the wedding? It must have been a professional or courtesy invite. At least a hundred of the guests had fallen into that category. But the St. James family was the worst kind of nouveau riche—using money to buy influence and respectability—and if Donovan had any class at all, he'd have RSVP'd *no* to what had obviously only been a polite gesture.

But money couldn't buy class, that was for sure.

And she'd *slept* with him. She must have reached an astonishingly new level of intoxication to completely lose all her self-respect. *I am never drinking again.*

"Oh, don't look at me like that, Lorelei. I'm not real keen on this new development, either."

Donovan sat up—slowly, she noted, implying his hangover was equally as miserable as hers—and reached for his clothes. Lorelei averted her eyes, but not before she got a good long look at broad shoulders, a trim waist and a very nice, very firm butt. Donovan ticked up another notch on that *hummina* scale before she noticed the red claw marks marring his back.

She'd enjoyed herself, it seemed. Pity she didn't have a better recollection of what had led to those marks. Although she felt like hell, underneath the hangover was a pleasant muscle soreness that spoke to a good time.

The silence felt awkward and uncomfortable. Despite her reputation, Lorelei wasn't an expert on morning-after protocols, but she'd brazen through this somehow. Clutching the sheet to her breasts, she let it trail behind her as she grabbed her dress off the floor and headed for the bathroom. She thought she might have heard a sigh as the door closed behind her.

The sight in the mirror was not pretty. Lorelei splashed water on her face and tried to wipe away the worst of the mascara circles under her eyes. Then she finger-combed her hair until it didn't look quite so wild and made use of the mini-bottle of mouthwash provided by the hotel. Feeling marginally human, she righted her dress and slipped into it.

She could only hope that no one would see her heading back to her room as nothing said *night of debauchery* quite like wearing a cocktail dress before breakfast. Six months of very hard work could be shot all to hell.

Of course she had a much more pressing—and disturbing—problem right outside that door which she had to deal with first.

"Okay," she said to her reflection, "you need a dignified exit." Taking a deep breath, she opened the bathroom door.

Donovan stood by the window, looking out over Canal Street, but he turned once he heard the door open. He'd pulled on a pair of jeans—ending up in your own hotel room instead of someone else's had perks, like clothes—but he'd stopped before adding a shirt. Lorelei had a hard time keeping her eyes from wandering as he wordlessly handed her a bottle of water. She nodded her thanks.

"There's aspirin, too," he said, dodging past her into the bathroom and returning with a bottle. "Care for a couple?"

He shook the bottle, causing her head to throb, and she was pleased to see him wince at the noise, as well.

Lorelei felt like she was in a bad movie. "Look, I think we would both agree that last night should not have happened."

"That's for sure."

She stamped down the remark she wanted to make at that insult. *Dignity.* "So we'll just pretend it didn't happen. I won't mention it to anyone and you won't write about it, okay?"

From the look on Donovan's face, he didn't like the implication, and Lorelei worried that she might have made a tactical error. Donovan had turned his high-school hobby of flaying people alive for sport into a profitable career. He destroyed careers, lives, families. Rumor had it that he was looking for another big story. People tried to avoid pinging onto his radar screen; no one with a shred of self-preservation would bait him intentionally.

"I limit myself to topics of public interest, and even if this fit the definition—which it doesn't—it's not something—*wasn't* anything—to brag about."

Dignity be damned. She was *not* letting that slide by unchallenged. "I wouldn't know. Must not have been that memorable an experience."

"Then forgetting it happened at all won't be a problem for you."

"No, it won't." That was a lie, but Donovan had no way of knowing better, so it was a safe lie. And it allowed her to hold her head up as she gathered the rest of her things.

Her small purse was upside down by the door, her phone, lipstick and room key spilling out. Not far from that was one of her shoes, then Donovan's tie and shoes, then her other shoe. It was a breadcrumb trail of shame that led straight to the king-size bed.

*Lord, was there anything less dignified than searching for your underwear?* She picked up Donovan's jacket and gave it a shake. Nothing. Dropping to her knees, she looked under the bed. She found an empty condom wrapper, alleviating one of her fears, but finding two more had her cringing.

No sign of her underwear, though.

"If you're looking for these…" Donovan drawled. She looked up to see him dangling her panties from one finger. She bit her tongue and settled for shooting him a dirty look as she jerked them from his hand and tucked them into her purse. The addition of the undergarment, as tiny as it was, was too much for the little bag, and it refused to close. Heat flushing her face, Lorelei had no choice but to take the extra time to put them on.

Funnily enough, she felt a little less flustered once she had. *Underwear was a form of armor, it seemed.*

Squaring her shoulders, she went to the door and examined the fire-safety map posted there. According to the red *X* marking her location as room 712, she could easily get to the fire stairs, go down one floor and she'd come out only a few doors away from her own room. *Excellent.* The chances of running into someone she knew had just decreased exponentially. *Something* might actually go her way this morning.

"Planning your escape route?"

She turned to see Donovan stacking the pillows on the bed into a comfortable back-prop, and then reclining, remote control in hand. He wasn't even looking at her, and, if anything, he now sounded bored. Obviously this was not an out-of-the-ordinary morning for him. *Why am I not surprised?*

"Exactly. Goodbye, Donovan. I hope I don't see you again for a very long time."

She didn't wait for his reply. Cracking the door, she peeked into the hall and found it empty. With at least a hundred of last night's guests having taken advantage of the location to enjoy Connor and Vivi's open bar, she just needed her luck to hold for a few minutes. The quick dash to the stairwell was no problem, and her stiletto heels clacked on the stairs as she moved as fast as possible in the tight skirt. At the door to the sixth floor she paused, took out her room key, and took a deep breath. Another peek showed two people in the hall, but neither of them looked familiar. Just to be safe, she waited until they were at the elevators before making the last break for her door.

Only to find that her stupid key didn't work.

Donovan was relieved Lorelei had left in a huff. He'd been awake for about fifteen minutes before her, and he'd spent that time anticipating a number of equally horrific and awkward scenarios.

But Lorelei had gone straight to indignation and huff—which, in this case, had been more than he'd dared hope for.

Of all the women who'd attended what was arguably the biggest society wedding of the decade, he'd managed to hook up with Lorelei LaBlanc. He'd known both Connor and Vivi at least tangentially since high school and, while they might not be close friends or anything, they were business associates and often traveled in the same social circles now.

He might be considered an interloper by some in those social circles, since his blood wasn't quite as blue as theirs, but no one had the courage to say that to his face anymore. And, while he might not have generations of Old South manners ingrained into him, even *he* knew it was bad form to bed the sister of the bride after the reception.

Yeah, pretending it had never happened was an excellent idea.

Another excellent idea was liberal quantities of aspirin and coffee until he felt human again. That might take days.

The little two-cup coffeemaker on the desk didn't have the best quality coffee included, but it would do for now. He set it to start and the smell of coffee soon filled the room.

The jackhammering behind his eyes had been honestly earned. He'd lost count of the tequila shots, but there might have been a bet involved about who could drink who under the table. He and Lorelei had never been friends, never hung out together, so how they'd got to that point last night was a mystery.

Lorelei had been a couple of years or so behind him in school—and they certainly hadn't traveled in the same circles in those days. St. Katharine's Prep was the school of choice for New Orleans's best families. A safe haven for their precious children from the riff-raff of society, with only a couple of charity-case scholarship students as a nod to "diversity." The Lorelei he remembered had been spoiled, narcissistic and stuck up. Even when he'd morphed from one of those scholarship students to the son of a major donor by his senior year, Lorelei hadn't deigned to give him the time of day.

Oddly, he respected her for *that*. She might be shallow, but she'd proved herself to have slightly more depth than most of her socialite friends when the sudden influx of money into his family's bank account hadn't changed her attitude toward him at all.

Tequila had, though.

He had a few hours before checkout, and the need for a nap was nearly overwhelming, but if he headed on home he could nap in his own bed—a bed that did not now carry the scent of Lorelei's perfume. He might not remember exactly everything that happened last night, but he remembered enough that the light fragrance sent a stab of pure desire through him and made the scratch marks on his back burn. Lorelei certainly had stamina.

He turned on the TV for background noise and picked a news station to listen to while he waited on the coffee. He still had to decide on a topic for Monday's column, and...

The phone rang. Not his phone, but the hotel's phone. Who would be calling him here? "Hello?"

"Open your door and let me back in." The voice was quiet, whispery.

"Who *is* this?"

"Oh, for the love of... How many other women would need to get *back* into your room this morning?"

"Why aren't you in your own room?"

"Because my key won't work." It sounded as if Lorelei was spitting the words through clenched teeth. "I'm now stuck in the stairwell, so will you please open your door and let me in?"

The image of Lorelei hiding in a stairwell caused him to laugh—which then made his head hurt. He heard her sharp intake of breath, followed by some muttering that probably wasn't very flattering to him. It was tempting to leave her there, just for the amusement factor and a much-needed ego-check. But Connor and Vivi might not be happy to hear about that.

He relented. "Come on."

He returned the phone to its cradle and crossed the room. Opening the door, he stuck his head out. A few doors down, he saw Lorelei's dark head do the same. After seeing that the hallway was empty, she sprinted for his door, nearly mowing him down in her haste to get inside. "You could have just knocked, you know."

Lorelei didn't seem to appreciate that statement, shooting him the pissiest look he'd ever seen. "This is a nightmare."

"Just go down to the front desk and they'll recode your key."

It seemed Lorelei had an even pissier look—and this one called him all kinds of names, as well. "I am trying to avoid seeing people." She gestured to her dress. "It's rather obvious that I didn't spend the night in my own room, and I don't want people wondering where I *did* spend it. Or who with."

"Since when do you care?" Lorelei was a LaBlanc. One of the benefits of being a LaBlanc was complete certainty of your place in the food chain. Lorelei could do pretty much whatever she wanted with almost complete impunity. And she had.

"I care. Let's just leave it at that. Just call Housekeeping and ask for towels or something. Whoever brings them will have a master key and can let me into my room."

"That's a lot of assumptions."

"What?"

"I sincerely doubt that any hotel employee who wanted to keep their job would just let you in without a way to verify that you are the registered occupant of the room. And there's no way to do that without going through the front desk."

She looked as if she wanted to argue that point. Did the woman seriously not understand what she was asking?

Lorelei cursed an unladylike blue streak and flopped dramatically on the bed. Then she bounced right back up like the bed was on fire, cheeks flaming.

Honestly, he had to admit it was a good look for Lorelei. The pink tint offset her fair skin and dark hair and called attention to her high cheekbones. Of course he'd be hard-pressed to decide what *wouldn't* be a good look for Lorelei. Even nursing what had to be a massive hangover, she could still stop traffic. There were shadows under those big blue eyes—eyes that were currently shooting daggers at him—but they only emphasized her ethereal, almost fragile-looking bone structure.

That same structure gave her a willowy look, all long and lean, that made her seem taller than she actually was, and the slightly wrinkled cocktail dress she'd worn to the reception last night only made her legs look longer. The memory of those legs wrapped around him…

Lorelei was stronger than she looked. The look of fragile elegance was misleading. There was *nothing* fragile about the personality behind those looks, and Lorelei was pacing now with anger and frustration.

"What the hell am I going to do?"

He sighed and reached for his phone. "Let me call Dave."

"And this Dave can help how?"

"Dave is the head of security here. He'll be able to sort this out. Discreetly, of course."

That stopped her pacing. "You just *happen* to know the head of security for this hotel?"

"Yes." He paused in scrolling for Dave's number and looked up to see her staring at him suspiciously. "Is that a problem?"

"It just seems convenient." She shrugged. "Considering."

"Considering what?"

"Your job. Having an in with security here just seems… Well, *convenient.*"

The insult, while not unexpected considering the source, and certainly not the worst he'd heard, still rankled. His columns and commentary were syndicated in newspapers around the country, and he'd built his platform and audience the old-fashioned way. She might not like his style, but he'd earned his place in the national discourse. He didn't need an "in" with anyone to get his leads—hell, these days he had people falling over themselves to provide all the information he needed and then some.

He tossed the phone on the bed. "You know, I don't *have* to do you any favors, and I find myself quickly losing the inclination altogether."

Lorelei's lips pressed together until they disappeared. He could practically see the way she was fighting back a snappy, snarky comeback, but she finally nodded. "You're right. My apologies. Please call your friend."

It was terse, and not completely sincere, but he'd be the bigger person. Accepting the apology at face value, he called Dave. He glossed over the situation as much as he could, trying to avoid mention of Lorelei's name, how she came to be in his room and why she just couldn't go to the front desk like a normal person would in this situation. After some laughter and speculation on Dave's part that Donovan didn't dare relay to Lorelei, he hung up. "Someone from Security will be up with a key to your room shortly. You'll just need to hang out here a little while longer."

"Well, it's not like I have anyplace else to go." She walked over to the small coffeepot and asked, "Do you mind? I feel near death."

"Help yourself."

She did, and then sat in the leather chair. Legs crossed at the ankle, she held the cup with both hands and sipped gratefully. It was an incongruous picture: a disheveled Lorelei, hair rioting around her face and shoulders, in an obviously expensive, though slightly-the-worse-for-wear dress and stiletto heels, sitting primly in his hotel room as if they were politely having tea in the parlor.

And he knew exactly what kind of underwear she had on.

Somehow this was even more awkward than the wake-up-naked-and-get-dressed part. Were they supposed to make small talk now or something? What would an appropriate topic be?

There was small comfort in the fact that Lorelei seemed equally at a loss. He'd bet this situation was not covered in cotillion classes. She studied the art on the wall like it was an Old Master, pondered her coffee like it held the meaning of life, then finally turned her attention to her fingernails. He kept one eye on the TV and feigned interest in the talking heads on the morning show. He'd made his living by always having something to say, but this time his vaunted golden tongue failed him.

Lorelei cleared her throat. "So, will you be writing about the wedding?"

Lord, she really had no idea what he did for a living. "I don't do society news, Lorelei. I came as a guest to the wedding, nothing more."

"I had no idea you'd become such good friends with Connor and Vivi."

"I sit on two boards with Vivi. We share an interest in the arts. Connor and I have several mutual friends. I wouldn't exactly call us close, but I probably know them at least as well as a third of that guest list."

"They are a popular couple."

"Indeed."

"And it was an amazing event, start to finish."

It had been a star-studded event, thanks to Connor's fame, and the entire ranks of the New Orleans elite had been there, traveling in their usual pack. "I expected nothing less."

Lorelei nodded, and he realized that topic had now run its course. Well, that had killed a couple of minutes. How long would it take Security to bring Lorelei a key?

She seemed to be wondering the same thing. "I wish they'd hurry."

"Me, too. I have things I need to do."

"Well, don't let me stop you."

His three options were to take a shower, take a nap or go home—none of which he could do while Lorelei was parked in his room. "I'm sure they'll be here shortly."

Hard on those words there was a knock at the door, and Lorelei jumped up as he went to answer it. Her sigh of relief when the man identified himself as the assistant head of security was audible from across the room. He asked to see her ID, verified her as the occupant of the room, then handed her a key. "Would you like me to escort you to your room, miss?"

"No!" she practically shouted, before she caught herself and lowered her voice. "I'll be fine, thank you."

The man nodded, then left without question, and Donovan wondered exactly what Dave had told him about his assignment. Of course it probably wasn't the oddest thing Security had ever done: this hotel catered to an elite crowd, and that elite had probably made far more questionable requests of Security in the past. He'd moved more toward analysis and away from the "shocking exposé" camp of journalism himself, but he'd bet there were all kinds of stories to be told from this hotel.

Lorelei cleared her throat, bringing him back to his own little drama. "Goodbye. Again. Thank you for your assistance, and, um, have a nice life."

The re-do of her exit lacked the dramatic huff this time,

but it retained its silliness as Lorelei once again checked the hall and slipped out like a bumbling spy in a bad movie.

At least he knew she wouldn't be back this time. Oddly, that seemed to be a little of a letdown. Lorelei certainly had entertainment value.

Although he'd been thinking more about the events of the morning, not last night, another particularly *entertaining* visual flashed across his mind.

And that quickly answered his question about what he'd do now: a cold shower was calling his name.

# CHAPTER TWO

A GUILTY CONSCIENCE was a terrible thing. It wasn't something Lorelei was overly familiar with, as she intentionally kept away from situations that might lead to one. She had regrets, sure, but she'd always lived—well, until recently—by the philosophy that she'd rather regret the things she'd done than regret that she'd never done them at all. So why did this thing with Donovan seem to be haunting her?

It wasn't even worry over what people might say. As far as she could tell, no one knew. Vivi and Connor had left for their honeymoon and Vivi hadn't said a word. She'd waited on pins and needles for the news to circulate, but it seemed she was going to get away with it. She'd gotten lucky by not screwing the whole plan up at the eleventh hour.

So the worry had to be over Donovan himself.

Over the last three days, more of her memory had returned—but not the parts she'd have liked. If she *had* to carry around the knowledge that she'd had sex with Donovan St. James, she'd like to be in possession of memories of the good stuff, too. She had all the knowledge she needed to know that she'd enjoyed herself, but she lacked the memory of the proof. It seemed like a shame.

She rolled over and punched her pillow into shape.

Vague, incomplete dreams were leaving her tired and grouchy in the mornings and, even worse, leaving her with a ghostly, frustrated feeling.

Maybe that was why she couldn't quite shake the whole situation off: she wanted that memory and her brain was determined to wring out the tequila and find it. Maybe she wasn't feeling guilty; maybe she was just confusing one nagging feeling with another.

And now she had to be hallucinating, because she could *hear* Donovan's voice. She sat up. That wasn't a hallucination; that really was Donovan's voice, coming from her living room. *What the hell?* Shock rocketed through her as she heaved herself out of bed, covers flying. She was in the hallway before she caught herself in the middle of the ridiculous thought.

It was coming from the TV.

"Morning." Callie sat on the couch, hugging a cup of coffee and watching the morning news. She was dressed already, her backpack on the coffee table, ready to go.

Although this was technically still Vivi's house, Vivi had moved out six months ago, after news of her engagement to Connor hit the press. The little house on Frenchman Street just couldn't provide the privacy and security Connor and Vivi needed. Lorelei had enjoyed the solitude for about two weeks, but had then offered Vivi's old room to a friend-of-a-friend just so she'd have some company.

It hadn't quite worked. Between Callie's schedule and her latest romance with some guy she'd met at the library, she was rarely home. It was only slightly better than living alone.

Callie was a news junkie—the serious stuff, not the pop-culture and human-interest fluff—and now Donovan's face filled the screen as he droned on about something being unconstitutional. Callie was rapturously hanging on every word, and Lorelei wondered if it was because anything unconstitutional was catnip for Loyola Law students or because the words were coming out of Donovan's pretty face.

Lorelei wished she'd purchased a smaller, lower-quality TV, because the sight of Donovan in HD sent a jolt through her. She tried to brush it away and act casual as she continued to the kitchen and the coffeepot. She moved in slow motion, killing time, but Donovan was *still* talking—no surprise there, really; the man truly loved to hear himself talk. Finally she couldn't stall any longer and had to go back out into the living room.

"No class today?" she asked as she took the other corner of the couch and settled in.

"The air-conditioning in the building is broken. They had to cancel classes."

Lorelei nodded. The older buildings in New Orleans—those built before the invention of air-conditioning and designed for the heat—could sometimes be habitable, if not comfortable, in August, but not the newer buildings, with their low ceilings and windowless rooms.

"I'm meeting my study group at the library instead. What about you? Not going to the studio?"

"With Connor away, things are pretty slow at the moment. I'll go in later and check messages and things, but a vacation for the boss is a vacation for the minions, as well."

People might think that Connor had hired her as assistant and office manager for ConMan Studios out of pure nepotism—and that did have a little to do with it—but the truth was she was good at the job, much to everyone's surprise. She'd finally started to earn a little respect; somehow her working for her brother-in-law impressed people more than just working for her father, even though the positions were very similar.

And she liked it, too. Who wouldn't want to be part of a rock star's entourage? It was exciting, and the high-profile nature of the job meant people knew she was actually earning her keep.

"I'm kind of glad things will be slow. Being Vivi for the next three weeks is going to be crazy enough."

Callie nodded, but she wasn't really listening. She still had most of her attention on the TV—where, thankfully, Donovan was wrapping up. "Donovan St. James is right. The city is just asking for a major lawsuit."

Lorelei didn't bother to ask about what. "I've always wondered how someone becomes a pundit," she said in what she hoped sounded like idle curiosity. "Is there a degree program for that? A Bachelor's in Talking Headism?"

Callie shrugged. "I think you just have to make a name for yourself in politics or journalism to prove that you're smart enough to have something sensible to say, and then show that you're articulate enough to say it on TV."

"Then how did Donovan St. James get anointed?"

Callie looked at her like she was crazy. "Because he's freaking *brilliant.*"

"So *you* say."

"No, so says the world. Haven't you ever read his column?"

"Not since he destroyed the DuBois and Dillard families."

"They brought that on themselves. Corruption tends to bite you in the butt like that when it's uncovered."

Lorelei had sympathy for her friends' families. It had rocked everyone's world. "But Donovan seemed to *enjoy* it. He certainly got a lot of attention out of their misery."

"That *is* what got him attention initially. But in the

last three years that attention has grown because of his insightful analysis and dogged chasing of facts. When he comments on politics and issues, people listen. He's syndicated in newspapers and on websites all over the country. That's why he's on TV all the time."

"Oh. I didn't know that." Hmm, it seemed she should have.

"Now you do. Should you decide to get more up-to-date on the rest of the world, his columns wouldn't be a bad place to start. There's an archive on his website. Good stuff there. I've even quoted him in some of my papers."

Well, it seemed that Donovan had been out making a name for himself over the years and she'd been ignorant of the whole thing. Callie didn't need to look so darn surprised. Just because she used to go to school with Donovan, it didn't mean she was an expert on his life—or that she wanted to be.

Politics—and the blow-hard talking heads that covered it—gave her a headache. The news depressed her. She heard enough from Callie to keep her feeling at least as well-informed as the average citizen; she didn't need to go looking for more than that.

Callie tossed the remote her way and grabbed her backpack. "I'm gone. Some of us might go grab some drinks after we're done with study group. Want to come?"

"Thanks, but not tonight." Her personal prohibition was still in place—the memory of Sunday morning was still too fresh even to consider breaking it.

"Call me if you change your mind. Bye."

"Bye."

A second later Callie reappeared. "Today's paper." She tossed it on the coffee table. "By the way, Donovan's column runs in the editorial section—if you're interested, that is."

Once Callie had left, Lorelei unrolled the paper, flipped to the middle and pulled out what her grandmother and mother still called the "Wednesday Pages," even though it was now a glossy, magazine-style insert about society's doings. There, on the cover, was a full-color picture of Vivi and Connor on their way out of the cathedral. The caption promised a full write-up and more pictures inside. Lorelei flipped to the pages. There were some great shots of the guests going into the church, and a few from the reception. Most of them focused on the star-studded guest list of Connor's friends in the music business, but there were a few photos of New Orleans' business and society leaders. She had made the cut, too, in a photo of the bridesmaids and Mom and Dad with Vivi, right before they went into the church. Donovan was in a picture as well, standing in a group with some city councilmen and the heads of three charitable organizations Vivi worked with.

The picture of Donovan made her think of Callie's parting shot, and she flipped to the editorial section to find his opinion of a bill being argued in Congress this week. It seemed well-written and impressive in its commentary, but she'd need a primer about the bill itself before she could form a cogent opinion.

Lord, even his writing had that condescending, sarcastic tone. Donovan had a hell of a chip on his shoulder.

She folded the newspaper decisively. Time to shake off this whole Donovan thing and move on. Forget it ever happened. She'd go to the studio, get some work done, maybe meet Callie for dinner, if not drinks. She needed to look over Vivi's schedule, start preparing herself and firm up her plan of action. She would take center stage tomorrow. Her first big appearance in her new temporary role.

Butterflies battered her insides. It was stage fright—but not because she would be center stage. This was make or break time. If she screwed this up, she'd only prove to everyone that she really was a flaky screw-up, an airhead with only her trust fund going for her. But if it went well... She sighed. If it went well she'd be on her way—not just "the other LaBlanc girl" anymore. The last six months had been building toward this moment, and the pressure was doing bad things to her.

It was just one more reason why she needed to forget about what happened with Donovan and focus on what was important. Staying busy was a very good idea; it would give her mind something to think about other than Donovan, and soon enough she'd be past this whole embarrassing situation.

She picked up her coffee cup and the society section again, intending to set it aside for Vivi, when her own name caught her eye.

> *Several of the younger guests continued the celebrations long into the night, keeping the bar open and the staff hopping. Lorelei LaBlanc, sister of the bride and Maid of Honor, swapped her bridesmaid's dress for a flirty, sparkly number and danced the night away with some of the city's most eligible bachelors. Interestingly, she and the most eligible bachelor of all, journalist and TV commentator Donovan St. James, seemed to be quite friendly—much to the dismay of the other eligible bachelors and bachelorettes.*

Lorelei nearly dropped her coffee.
*Oh, merde.*

St. James Media looked like any average office building from the outside, but within the company the building was called "Whiz Castle." It had been built on the success of an infomercial for the unfortunately named Toilet Whiz, which had taken the company from struggling to superstar nearly overnight and made them the largest direct response and infomercial production company in the South. His father had an original Toilet Whiz framed and hanging outside Studio One in a place of honor.

The sight still made Donovan laugh every time he passed it. Part of Donovan's success as a TV personality came from the fact he always seemed to be amused about something when the cameras rolled; only a few people knew it was because he'd just passed a framed Toilet Whiz.

Donovan had an office right down the hall from his father's, but he rarely used it. He wasn't a part of the business—infomercials had given him a comfortable checking-account balance and paid his college tuition, but he wasn't interested in the actual production of them—but since his siblings had offices in the building Dad had given him one, too.

He could have used it, but he far preferred to work in his own space, where there were fewer distractions and his tendency to work odd hours went unquestioned. Because he was so rarely there, his office had a sterile, unlived-in feeling. It was expertly and expensively decorated, and it gave him a place to hang plaques and pictures and things, but he couldn't actually work in there.

He was using the studios more often these days, though, as his TV appearance schedule picked up. Their facilities and staff were truly top-notch, and he'd found he rather liked using the family's home field. His brothers had even expanded the studio's capabilities, and St. James Media was getting traffic from a lot of famous faces these days.

Maybe he *had* contributed something to the family business, after all.

However, it was proving quite handy to have the office to use as a place to drop off his stuff and put on a tie before he went on air. Unknotting the noose around his neck, he headed back toward his office, ready to go home.

His father's secretary followed him down the long hallway, talking a mile a minute, and he listened with half an ear. As he opened his office door and saw Lorelei sitting on the low sofa under the window, he wished he'd paid a bit more attention.

*How had she known he'd be here?*

He closed the door behind him. "Lorelei. This is… unexpected."

She crossed her arms over her chest. "Oh, really?" Sarcasm dripped off her words.

"Yeah. Your 'have a nice life' statement kind of implied you wouldn't be dropping by to chat."

"That was before we made the newspaper."

"We?"

"Yes, *we*." She sounded downright irritated about it.

"When? For what?"

"This morning. In the write-up about the wedding."

"And you came by to tell me about it?"

"I rather assumed you'd already know."

This was obviously going to take more than just a minute. He sat on the edge of his desk. "Uh, no. I usually skip that part of the paper."

"Well, it might not be as far-reaching as that transportation bill, but it certainly rocks *this* little part of the world."

The mention of his column caught him off-guard. He wouldn't have thought Lorelei read the editorial section of *any* newspaper. And normally he'd be surprised that the mention of something two private citizens possibly did at a private function could be considered earth-rocking in *any* part of the world, but he'd humor her for the moment. "What did it say?"

In response, Lorelei pulled a torn page out of her purse and shoved it at him. It took a second for him to get through a rundown of the guest list, what everyone was wearing and a description of the ice sculptures, but finally he found Lorelei's name and his. He turned the paper over, looking for more, but on the back was an advertisement for a casino. "That's it?"

Lorelei's jaw dropped. "You don't think that's *enough?*"

"I don't actually see the problem, Lorelei."

She looked on the edge of a sputter. "My mother reads the Wednesday Pages like the Bible."

"As does mine. So?"

This time Lorelei did sputter. "*So?* That's all you have to say?"

"Well, I don't see a reason to freak out."

"Obviously *your* mother hasn't been texting you all morning, looking for an explanation because half the city is asking *her* for an explanation."

So *that* was what had her panties in a twist. *Damn it. I shouldn't have thought about her panties.* Especially since he knew for a fact that her taste in undergarments ran to the tiny and lacy. "Definitely not."

"Well, that figures."

He could hear the sour *that must be nice* tone under those words. "Look, Lorelei. We don't owe anyone an explanation for anything—much less some busybody's baseless speculation in what is little more than a gossip column."

Lorelei's eyes widened. "'Baseless speculations?'"

"Well, it was baseless—at least until your little freak-out gave it credence. The very fact you came running down here makes it look like there really *is* something going on. Something more than what was publicly witnessed. Someone went fishing and you took the bait. You've pretty much told the world we had sex."

Her eyes widened. "For the love of…" Lorelei obviously hadn't thought it through until now, and the realization set her pacing in frustration. She started muttering to herself, and he caught the occasional phrase about her mother or Vivi killing her. Even Connor's name came up once. Finally she stopped pacing and turned to him. "What do you suggest we do?"

He didn't see the big deal. "*We* don't do anything. *I'm* going to go about my business as always. *You* can do whatever you think best."

"Donovan, I'm asking for your help here. You may not care that there's gossip in the paper, but I do."

"Since when?" There was certain information a person couldn't avoid, no matter how uninterested they might be. That included news of the adventures of the young, wealthy, beautiful and fabulous. Lorelei had made the papers plenty of times with far more descriptive rundowns on her activities.

"I know I haven't cared in the past, but things are different now."

Her voice lost the impatience and the snark, and for a moment she sounded almost vulnerable. But she was completely overreacting. This was not nearly the catastrophe Lorelei seemed to think it was, and, left alone, it would all blow over soon enough.

"I know I've never been a saint like Vivi. Never will be, either." She smiled weakly, and he realized that it had to be tough to live up to an example like Vivi. "The thing is, with Vivi and Connor on their honeymoon, I'm going to be making appearances on their behalf—for the charities they represent and the organizations they support. I don't need—and can't have—this kind of gossip hanging over my head and coloring everyone's thoughts." Lorelei's blue eyes were wide and earnest. She was serious. "It's not just about me. It's about them and their reputations and the organizations they do so much for. There's a lot more at stake than just a little public embarrassment for me."

He normally didn't have any patience for the troubles of the children of the city's elite. Connor and Vivi had been the exceptions that had slowly brought him around to a different view. They hadn't sat on their trust funds or relied on family connections to coast through in a perfect life. They'd worked hard: Connor with his music career and Vivi with her art gallery and work with every non-profit organization in the parish. *That* he respected.

If Lorelei had hit him with anything else...

*Damn.* He felt himself buckling. When had he become such a sucker for a damsel in distress?

"Who did the write-up?"

Lorelei looked relieved as he relented. She glanced at the article for its byline. "Evelyn Jones."

He knew Evelyn slightly through the newspaper. Her true calling was in tabloid gossip, and the New Orleans society pages were the closest she'd gotten. "Was she a guest at the wedding?"

Lorelei seemed to be thinking. "She was *there*. I'm pretty sure she left after the cake-cutting, though."

"Then she's reporting hearsay. Everyone in the bar that night was just as far gone as we were."

"Except for the servers—"

"And the one who gave up *that* little tidbit probably got a nice fat tip for the story."

"That's a terrible—"

He shrugged off her outrage. "That's the way it works.

For a hundred bucks I could get a source to swear they once saw Mother Theresa doing keg stands. Times are tough all around. Money talks."

Lorelei looked outraged. "That's dishonest."

"That's tabloid journalism for you."

"And you wonder why—"

"I don't wonder anything, Lorelei. It is what it is."

"So *you'd* sell someone's reputation out just for money?" She looked worried. He assumed she'd only just now realized that he now had quite the story about her to sell. He wouldn't even have to lie or embellish it, either.

"Calm down. I see no need to spread the news, and I certainly don't need the money."

Lorelei shot him a look he couldn't decipher. Then she sighed and sank back onto the couch. "So how do I disprove something when I don't know how much of it is true? I'm not a very good liar." The corners of her mouth turned down as she confessed that like it was a character flaw.

"We did not engage in any PDA at the bar. It was later that…" He trailed off as Lorelei flushed that rosy color. "We laugh it off. That's it. We and the others were just having a good time—as one does at a party—and any other claims have been exaggerated for effect."

Lorelei started to nod, but caught herself. "Wait a second…" A suspicious look began to pull her eyebrows together. "How are you so certain that there was no PDA in the bar? You told me it was all fuzzy from the tequila."

*Damn.* She'd caught that. "Fuzzy, yes. Total blackout… no."

"So you do…remember?" The suspicion on her face turned to horror, and then that rosy embarrassed color she'd had since he'd brought up PDA deepened to an amazing shade of red. She crossed her arms over her chest again, but this time it was more a gesture of modesty, like he could see through her clothes. "Oh, my *God*. It was bad enough to know it happened even though I didn't remember it. But to know that you do and I don't…"

Now he felt like some kind of pervert, which made absolutely no sense at all. And he had no idea what he should say to take that vulnerable, disgusted-with-herself look off her face.

"Did I—? Did we…?" Lorelei pushed to her feet and picked up her purse. "Oh, God. I have to leave now."

"It was just sex, Lorelei."

"Oh, well, *that* completely alleviates my mind. Thank you."

"You want a rundown? A play-by-play?"

Her eyes widened. "You could provide that?"

He let his silence answer her question.

She swallowed hard and cleared her throat. "Oh, this just keeps getting better and better."

Now he felt like a *twisted* pervert. "Lorelei…"

She squared her shoulders. "I think you're right, Donovan. We should just ignore the innuendo and laugh it off if anyone has the bad manners to bring it up. Forgetting it ever happened doesn't seem to be an option anymore—at least for *you*—but we'll go with pretending it didn't." Lorelei grabbed her purse from the couch and a bitter laugh escaped. "I mean, who's really going to believe it, right? Me and you? Please. *I* can barely believe it. It's absurd."

The more she tried to convince herself, the more insulted he got. He wasn't a leper, for God's sake, and most women wouldn't be acting as if they'd committed some gross, shameful, unforgivable sin like Lorelei was. Most *normal* women—women who weren't like Lorelei and her ilk—considered him a pretty good catch and would be trying to capitalize on this instead of flagellating them-

selves over it. Their hook-up might have been insane, but
it certainly hadn't crossed over into the absurd. They were
both of the same species, whether Lorelei wanted to admit
that or not.

She might not remember it, but she'd enjoyed herself.
It wasn't as if he'd forced her into his bed, either. She'd
been a willing, active participant who'd gone to sleep with
a smile on her face.

His ego had had just about enough of the martyr act,
and when Lorelei tried to brush past him, heading for the
door, still muttering about absurdity, he grabbed her elbow
and turned her to face him.

"*I* won't have the 'bad manners' to bring this up the
next time we meet, Princess, but at least let me leave you
with the truth. It was hot, sweaty, athletic sex, and you
enjoyed it. You're quite flexible, you know."

Lorelei swallowed hard. He had to give her credit,
though. She met his eyes and never wavered as he described, in graphic detail, the way she'd ridden him like
a polo pony and begged for more. Her pupils dilated until
only a small ring of blue remained, and her breathing
turned shallow. But as his skin heated with the memory
and his erection pressed painfully against his zipper, he
cursed the fact he'd let his ego and pride take it this far.
Being this close to Lorelei allowed the scent of her perfume to fill his nose with each breath, sending sharp pangs
through his belly. Even the soft skin of her arm where he
held it seemed to sear his fingers. When her tongue snaked
out to moisten her lips he could practically feel it moving
over his skin instead.

The air around them felt charged and heavy, and time
slowed to a standstill as he let his eyes wander down to
her lips and then to the pink flush climbing out of her
cleavage. He had so much more to throw at her, but the

words seemed trapped in his chest under the desire to do something entirely different.

Lorelei closed her eyes and took a deep but unsteady breath. When her eyes met his again he saw regret there. "You know, the worst part of this isn't what other people might think."

He braced himself.

"What really kills me is that you remember it and I don't."

The words were out there before Lorelei could stop them, and Donovan's sharp intake of breath had her regretting them instantly. The moment he'd touched her, though, every nerve in her body had cried out, wanting more of what her mind couldn't quite remember but her skin obviously did.

And his *words*... Crude as they were, they had spoken to something inside her, awakening that same feeling of frustration she'd faced every morning this week. The achy need in her core, the shivers in her belly... She wanted to find the cause and the cure.

*Donovan is both,* her mind whispered.

Lorelei gritted her teeth. That wasn't an option. The last thing she needed right now was to get involved with anybody. This was a time to focus on her professional life, not her personal life. Hell, it was probably that focus that had led her to Donovan's bed in the first place; she hadn't had the time for a social life—and hadn't wanted the scrutiny, either—and celibacy must not sit well with her. If she gave in to that little whisper, it could torpedo everything.

She stepped back quickly, breaking the web of heat and electricity that had snared her and led to that embarrassing admission. The air felt cooler immediately, and rationality returned. At least until she looked at Donovan. His eyes were hot, his body tense. It awoke something primal in her that was almost impossible to ignore.

She swallowed hard. Once again she needed a dignified exit. "I've got to go."

She didn't wait for a response, and focused instead on looking casual and carefree as she left Donovan's office. Donovan was right: coming here had just given that one sentence legs to stand on, so she forced herself to look unbothered. Normal.

She pasted a false smile on her face and kept her head up as she exited the building and crossed to the lot across the street where she'd parked. Once safely inside, with the doors locked and the AC running full-blast, the pride that had buoyed her out of there deflated.

Not only was she never drinking again, she was going to go online today and order herself a chastity belt. Maybe she should just drive straight to the convent and beg to be taken in for her own protection. There had to be something really disturbingly wrong in her brain for her to be in this position.

To be honest, one line in a newspaper was nothing. She'd had far more accurate and damaging reports printed about her before. Her mother's garden club might be twittering about it—but, honestly, it would pass. It wouldn't be the first time she'd downplayed something until it went away. No, she had to face the fact that she'd grabbed on to to the flimsiest of excuses to go and see Donovan and ended up having her worst suspicions confirmed.

It was one thing to have no shame; it was another thing entirely to realize she had no pride, either.

*That's not true.* She did have her pride. The fact she'd gotten the information she wanted and was currently sitting in her car *alone* was proof she possessed a spine *and* self-control. Her dignity might be a little dented, but her pride was intact.

If feeling a little shaky.

In a way, she should be glad that Donovan was at the center of this debacle. It wasn't as if their paths crossed often—they traveled in different circles—so she wouldn't have to face him repeatedly, knowing the whole time that he was able to picture her... *Ugh.*

Time would work its magic, and probably by the time she saw him again this would be an even fuzzier memory—and hopefully she'd be past the chemical reaction he seemed to cause.

Her mom's ringtone sounded again, and this time she answered. "I'm sorry I haven't had the chance to call you back. I've had a busy morning." That was true; panic had kept her quite busy.

"Where *are* you?"

"I'm on my way to Connor's studio." That wasn't a lie, either; the St. James Media building was sort of on her way. "I've got some work to catch up on."

"And are you going to tell me what that comment about you and Donovan St. James is about?"

Lorelei forced herself to laugh. It sounded fake and hollow to her ears, but her mother didn't seem to notice. "There was an after-party and we were both there, but... me and Donovan St. James? That's insane."

That wasn't a lie, either.

# CHAPTER THREE

"BUT YOU SAID YOU'D stand in for Vivienne while she was on her honeymoon. They're expecting you to be there."

*That was before I knew what I was getting myself into.*

Standing in for Vivi had sounded like a good idea—it would give her a chance to show that her sister wasn't the only one with saintly, service-oriented tendencies *and* get her out there as Connor's representative—but she hadn't had a full understanding of what Vivi's life was really like when she'd hatched that plan. Oh, she knew in *theory* that Vivi was busy and involved in everything, but actually inheriting even part of that schedule had left her wondering how Vivi had time to do anything else. Like sleep. She sighed into the phone. "I know, Mom, but I think I'm getting a migraine."

"You've never had a migraine in your life."

*I never had Donovan St. James turning up everywhere like a bad penny before, either.*

She'd finally read the emails from Vivi about her schedule. After her shock at how dense that schedule actually was had passed, she'd nearly choked when her preparations for those events had informed her that Donovan was also all over that schedule. Somehow she'd missed the memo that outlined how he'd gotten neck-deep into the city's business. No wonder Vivi and Connor had invited him to the wedding. If nothing else, it was professional courtesy.

"Well, it's a killer headache, regardless."

"Your father and I have tickets for the ballet with the Allisons. You'll have to solider through. It will be a challenge, but—"

"LaBlancs love a challenge," Lorelei finished for her. "I know."

"You'll do fine, darling. Even with a headache."

Her mom's words brought a smile to her face even in her misery. *Finally she was getting somewhere.*

"Just be friendly and gracious. Stick to club soda and remember to think before you speak."

*And there was the dig.* Lord, it was hard to live down a reputation.

Eventually, though, she'd live it down. Even if it killed her in the process.

Her mother hung up and Lorelei leaned her head back against the couch. In reality she was pretty much ready to go—and early, at that—but panic had set in, causing her to call her mom for a way out of this mess.

The headache, while not as debilitating as she'd claimed, *was* real—and it was named Donovan. She thought longingly of the bottle of Chardonnay in the fridge as a solution. But even if she hadn't sworn off drinking, hadn't she already proved beyond a shadow of a doubt that she, Donovan and alcohol were a bad, bad mix?

Of course she probably shouldn't worry about Donovan's part in that cocktail. Her personal humiliation was bad enough, but Donovan had to be wondering who'd given her a day pass from the asylum. Just the thought of facing him again... And so soon after the last debacle...

*Suck it up, kiddo.* The third time *had* to be a charm. She was a LaBlanc, for God's sake; she needed to start acting like one. If she had to channel Vivi, or her mother, or even the Queen of England to get through this with poise and class, she would.

She knew what she had to do; she knew she could do it. Her plan was solid—even if the execution wasn't a sure thing.

Her dress hung on the closet door: a deep blue to match her eyes, with a modest but not matronly neckline, and a hem that hit just above the knee. It was age-appropriate— youthful without being trashy—and stylish without falling into the "trendy" trap.

It was also Vivi's. But she'd told herself that if she was going to do Vivi's job she needed Vivi's wardrobe. Right now it looked like a suit of armor, ready to protect her from herself.

Yes, the dress was completely appropriate, and Lorelei suddenly hated it. She might need to channel her sister, her mother and the freakin' queen to do this right, but she wasn't going to betray herself, either. She was letting Donovan have way too much control of her mind, letting him shake her already shaky confidence in herself.

She wasn't stupid, and she wasn't *that* much of a screw-up. She had the manners and the experience to get through this, but if she tried too hard to be something— or someone—she wasn't, everyone would know she was faking it.

And she didn't want to fake it. She didn't *need* to fake it. She could do so much more than anyone assumed; she just needed the chance to show them that. She wanted to be accepted on her own terms and for her own merits— not just because she was a LaBlanc. She had an uphill climb, though. She'd broken or flaunted every rule and edict ever laid down, and the old guard was not exactly forgiving. She couldn't just reclaim her birthright—she was going to have to earn it back.

But she could. She just needed to find that happy medium.

And it started with a different dress.

Donovan had never quite outgrown the sick kick he got out of attending events like this.

As much as they might try to deny it publicly, New Orleans society was an old, established hierarchy, and it galled many members of that hierarchy to open its ranks even the tiniest bit. But Old Money wasn't quite what it had used to be so, like it or not, those ranks had had to make exceptions. Even for a family like his that many still considered to be only a step above carpetbaggers. Oh, they had to respect his money, and his money bought influence—even if they didn't like it one little bit.

The truth was—and it had taken him a while to figure it out— that the Old Guard were scared of that influence, scared they were losing their monopoly to upstarts and the trashy nouveau riche. If anything, they were closing the ranks even tighter and drawing very clear lines in the sand.

For him, though, it was more than just his New Money and lower-class roots that they disliked. With him, it was personal. He'd brought down some of their own. He was a social pariah—but not one who could be ignored. And they didn't like that at all.

He'd admit he still got a bit of immature glee sometimes over the situation, but the reality was that he really did support the mission of the Children's Music Project and was more than happy to sit on the board. "Nouveau riche" might not be a title he'd shake anytime soon, but he and his nouveau riche friends were the prime check-writers these days. Times really were tough all around—especially for those who'd lost a bundle in the market crash. Genteel poverty in the upper classes was a New Orleans tradition that dated back to Reconstruction—which only underscored the fact that the right DNA was more important than a healthy bank balance, and the lack of that DNA would forever keep certain doors locked tight.

He went to the bar to refill his drink as the CMP's executive director took to the small stage that normally contained the house band. There were general thanks, a rundown of the year's successes, plans for the future...

Jack Morgan, a partner in the law firm that represented St. James Media and an occasional racketball partner when no one else was available, joined him at the bar and signaled for a refill, as well. "How long do you think the speeches will last?"

"Why? Got a hot date?"

"Would that get me out of here?" Jack slid a bill across the bar and then rested against it with a sigh.

"Make a run for it. No one will notice you're gone."

"My mother will."

Donovan snorted. Mrs. Morgan was a true dragon of the old order. "Sucks to be you."

"Tonight it does."

"...Lorelei LaBlanc," the director announced.

*That* got his attention, snapping his head toward the stage so fast his neck cramped. His first thought—*What the hell is Lorelei doing here?*—was rebutted by remembering the remark she'd made Wednesday about stepping in for Vivi and Connor while they were on their honeymoon. Still...he'd seen her more in the last week than he had in the last five years.

Then Lorelei emerged from the crowd to climb the

steps to the stage, and he nearly dropped the drink he held in his hand.

Wrapped in a curve-hugging deep purple dress, she looked like a princess addressing the motley masses. Lorelei was the epitome of elegance, style and class, a product of extremely good breeding. She wore it easily, confidently. That black hair curled around creamy shoulders and tendrils snaked over her breast like a caress. Want streaked through him like a flash, and the low whistle he heard from beside him proved he wasn't the only one feeling it.

*"Damn,"* Jack muttered. "Little sis grew up nicely."

He considered Jack more of an acquaintance than a friend, so it was tough to allow him to keep his teeth as the compliments continued.

Lorelei's smile was blinding as she took the microphone from the director. "Vivienne hasn't missed one of these events in years, and she didn't want to miss this one, either, but she hopes you'll forgive her since it's her honeymoon." Lorelei paused as polite applause moved through the crowd. "And before you ask…yes, I do know where they are. But, no, I won't tell you where they went. You'll just have trust me when I tell you it's fabulous and they're having a wonderful time."

A laugh rippled through the crowd. He had to admit Lorelei knew how to command a crowd's attention.

"I'm not just here tonight on behalf of my sister. I'm here for Connor and ConMan Studios, as well."

At the mention of Connor's name the low rumble of conversation in the crowd died instantly.

"As you can imagine, music and music education is a cause very close to Connor's heart. CMP has focused, by necessity, on in-school programs for younger children…"

Lorelei looked comfortable up there, and if public

speaking was one of her fears it certainly didn't show in her speech or body language. She had that same presence that Donovan had seen in her sister—that confidence that could only come from the security of knowing exactly who she was. Unlike her sister, though, Lorelei had a low, hypnotic timbre in her voice that sounded like pure sex to him.

It did bad things to his equilibrium.

"It's my great privilege to announce tonight that Con-Man Studios is partnering with the CMP to expand its summer programs for the area's youth by providing not only funding, but space and access to some of the city's best musical talent." She paused for the applause, and then said with a laugh, "We have big plans in the works, so rest assured you'll all be hearing from me very soon. And often."

There was shock that Lorelei was going to be so involved with whatever plans Connor had cooked up with Vivi for his project, but it didn't cancel out the slice of desire that cut him at the sound of that husky laugh.

In broad strokes Lorelei outlined the basics of the plan, preparing folks to open their checkbooks. It took a moment for him to realize she kept saying "me" and "I." She'd started this speech as a Vivi substitute, but it was now becoming clear that Lorelei would be playing an active role. *That* was new. Lorelei hadn't had much involvement with anything beyond the periphery until now. And she seemed genuinely excited about it, as well. The universe was slightly askew.

To more applause, Lorelei handed back the microphone and left the stage, quickly being swallowed into the crowd.

Jack let out another low whistle, jerking Donovan's attention back since he'd long since forgotten Jack was even standing there. "I never had a thing for either of the

LaBlanc girls back in high school, but I'm rethinking that now." He pushed away from the bar and patted Donovan on the shoulder. "See ya."

"Where are you going?"

Jack grinned. "To gather my thoughts, of course."

There was that need to punch Jack again. It made no sense whatsoever, but he was starting to get used to the feeling.

*Why do I care?*

"Well, hello there."

He turned and found Jessica Reynald flashing a broad smile and ample cleavage. He did not need this now. After listening to Lorelei's straight-sex voice he was primed—but not for Jess Reynald. He'd been caught by her smile and her cleavage in a brief moment of insanity six months ago, and it had been nothing short of disastrous. Jess's family had made their money in commercial properties, and they'd initially bonded over their similar still-not-good-enough circumstances. But Jess was desperate to eventually break into those circles that excluded her, and that desperation to be accepted had turned him off. Jess, though, wasn't one to give up. She was looking to marry into the upper class—he wondered how long it would be before she realized that just wasn't going to happen—but until then she was willing to make do with him.

"I was hoping to find you here, Donovan. It's been a long time."

*Now the universe is just screwing with me.* "Not really. Only a couple of months."

"Where've you been hiding?"

"In plain sight. I've been really busy."

"But all work and no play is not good," she purred as she stepped closer. The heavy rose scent of her perfume nearly choked him. "I heard there's a great new jazz club that just opened over off Tchoupitoulas Street at Poydras. This is getting boring. Why don't we go check it out?"

"Not tonight, Jess."

She pouted and moved even closer, letting her breasts rest heavily on his arm. After his salivating over Lorelei's elegance and class, Jessica seemed overblown. "So when, then? I've missed you."

He heard a snort—quickly covered by a cough—and when he looked up he saw Jack and Lorelei at the bar, close enough to have heard Jess's purr and invitation. That snort had come from her.

"Well, Donovan?" Jess rose up on to her tiptoes, her lips only inches from his ear. "Haven't you missed me even a little bit?"

Lorelei rolled her eyes before turning back to Jack with a smile and letting him lead her away.

*Damn it.*

Lorelei smiled at the doorman as he opened the door and offered to call for a taxi, but the smile felt stiff on her face. She'd done nothing but smile all night, whether she wanted to or not. Her cheeks might never recover.

She *should* be happy, she reminded herself. She'd done well in there, and though she'd officially been standing in for Vivi and Connor, she'd talked to enough people to get the word spreading that she was stepping up to the plate in her own right, as well. She had several commitments of support for next summer's workshops, and when Connor got back they'd have lots to follow up on. She'd seen and been seen, shaken all the right hands, and she hadn't done anything that would even raise an eyebrow.

And Jack Morgan, who'd never so much as given her the time of day in high school—or since, for that matter—

had spent the last forty-five minutes flirting with her. In front of his mother, no less.

Tonight could be chalked up as a success all the way around. She'd done it. She'd pat herself on the back if she could, but that headache named Donovan had only gotten worse. A couple of people had mentioned the comment in the paper to her, but she'd laughed it off—and the people who'd mentioned it were exactly the kind who'd spread anything remotely gossiplike, so hopefully her response would shut down any other speculation.

The cause of her headache had ignored her all evening. That fact hadn't really bothered her—much—until she'd seen Jessica Reynald resting her impressive bosom on Donovan's arm and making cow's eyes at him. And Donovan hadn't exactly been fighting her off. The man was nothing more than a hound dog. And if last Saturday night hadn't felt cheap and tawdry enough, that just pushed it right over the edge into sordid.

*It's none of my business who he sleeps with. I'm just another notch in his bedpost.* It was downright embarrassing.

"Leaving already?"

She spun so fast at the sound of the last voice on earth she wanted to hear right then that her heel caught in a sidewalk crack, causing her to wobble dangerously. Quickly righting herself, she snapped, "Are you *following* me now?"

Donovan stepped back. "Whoa, you've got one hell of an ego there, Princess."

There was something so snide in the way he called her Princess that it put her teeth on edge. "Why *are* you here?"

A look of complete confused innocence crossed his face. "Because I'm leaving and this is the way out."

The reasonableness of the statement left her feeling a

bit silly. That feeling caused her to snark, "Alone? What happened to Jessica?"

"I could ask you what happened to Jack."

"That's absolutely none of your business."

An eyebrow went up. "But Jess is yours?"

*Damn it.* She squared he shoulders and looked around, determined to limit their conversation since ignoring him was going to be difficult. "Why are there no taxis?"

"To annoy you, I'm sure."

The doorman returned, thankfully forestalling the comeback she desperately wanted to make but shouldn't. "Dispatch says it's going to be about twenty minutes. Lot of things letting out right now."

She tried to keep the frustration out of her voice. This wasn't his fault. "Thank you."

"Why don't you ask Jack to give you a ride home?"

There was an edge to Donovan's voice that she didn't like. "You know, I'm actually thinking a short walk might be nice."

"Do you have a death wish?"

"How patronising of you. I'm an adult, and more than capable of taking care of myself. It's not even ten o'clock, and it's a populated area. I'll be perfectly safe."

"I meant your shoes. You'll kill yourself in those things."

"They're quite comfortable." That wasn't exactly a lie. They *were* quite comfortable—provided she was indoors and able to sit occasionally. An eight-block hike down Esplanade was a different situation entirely. That was why she'd asked for a cab in the first place. "I'll be fine. Good night, Donovan."

Proud of herself, she began the trek home. This would be good for her, she told herself. It would give her a chance to clear her mind, enjoy the sights. This part of Esplanade was heavily residential—folks out with their dogs, tourists exploring… It would be nice. And good exercise.

Within seconds, though, she began to rethink the idea: the temperature had dropped to a reasonable degree, but the humidity was still high and her skin felt damp already. She'd barely gone a block before her heel caught in another crack and nearly sent her sprawling.

She groaned as she righted herself. Pride and stubbornness would be her downfall one day.

Donovan's laugh floated down the street to her ears. "That was graceful."

*Don't take the bait,* her brain warned, but she was already turning around. "And you're obnoxious and immature." She held on to a streetlight and wiggled her ankle experimentally.

*Note to self: Buy some of those little foldable flats and keep them in your purse.*

*Better note to self: Next time ignore him and wait for a cab.*

*Even better note to self: Don't let there be a next time. Avoid him at all costs.*

She looked up from her mental lecture to see Donovan closing in. "Are you all right?"

So much for 'no next time.' Or maybe she could consider this the same time as earlier. "I'm fine."

"I was just being polite, Princess—making sure you hadn't hurt yourself."

"That's very kind of you. However…" *time to be brutally honest* "…in case you haven't noticed, I'm trying very hard to ignore you."

"I thought we were pretending it never happened?"

"We are."

"Then why the need to ignore me?"

*God, why was he being so difficult?* "Because it would

be much easier for me to actually do the pretending if you weren't around."

"You're overreacting. We're adults. It was consensual—if not intentional. It's not half as big a deal as you're making it out to be."

A man walking his dog slowed his steps as he passed, the look on his face a mixture of concern and interest. Lorelei bit back the words on the tip of her tongue. Reaching for Donovan's arm, she dragged him a few feet away from the street into the shadows. "Believe it or not, I'm not in the habit of sleeping with random men. I find this situation to be awkward and quite disturbing."

"Which part?"

That was not at all the response she'd expected, and when coupled with the fact that his voice lacked any mockery at all... She looked up and froze. Donovan was mostly in shadow, but his stance was relaxed, hands in his pockets. What she could see of his face looked genuine, with no trace of the usual smirk.

It took another second for her to register that she'd pulled him into a secluded spot—one that might be considered romantic due to the lush greenery that draped over the courtyard wall, creating a mini-bower. Donovan's white shirt stood out in the partial gloom, and he'd opened the top few buttons against the heat. He was so tall and broad-chested that even in her stilettos she was at eye-level with the hollow of his throat. The humidity had created a fine sheen of moisture across his skin, releasing the scent of his aftershave to mix with the fragrance of the hibiscus. The sounds of the Quarter were muffled, and the houses around them quiet. It felt...intimate—sultry, even—and it threw her off her game.

She swallowed hard, completely forgetting what she'd

planned to say—or even what he'd asked. "I'm sorry—what?"

"The situation is awkward and disturbing. I asked which part."

Was it her imagination, or was Donovan's voice lower and huskier than normal? The embers that had smoldered in her belly for nearly a week flared to life, the sounds and the scents around her kindling a feeling that her body remembered even if her mind didn't.

And she wanted to know.

*Don't make this even worse.*

But her legs felt wobbly and weak, and her hand was already reaching for him. She was setting herself up for disaster, but the draw was almost too painful to fight. Her hand landed on his chest, and she could feel the rapid beat of his heart under her palm and the jump of the muscle under the skin. Donovan wasn't immune to her, and that knowledge gave her the courage to meet his eyes. What she saw there nearly took her breath away, and the heat that flooded her had nothing to do with the weather.

"Lorelei…"

It was now or never. If she walked away now she'd regret it. But this was a huge risk; if Donovan turned her down, her humiliation would be everlasting.

Rising up on her toes until only inches separated them, she dug deep and let the ache inside her force the words out. "I want to know."

She felt the shock ripple through his body as she closed the space and let her lips meet his.

There was a pause, then everything exploded.

The sensations hit her with the force of a hurricane, cancelling out her higher brain functions. The feel and taste of Donovan was both new and familiar at the same time, giving reality to what had only been a vague craving before.

His mouth was hot and demanding, each stroke of his tongue licking her like fire and sending the sensation searing through her entire body. The solid bulk of his chest pressed against hers, anchoring her to the brick wall at her back and trapping her in a cage of warm male flesh.

It was divine.

She felt a tug on her hair and let her head fall back, allowing Donovan to press hot kisses down her neck to the sensitive skin at her collarbone. She arched against him, getting contact from breast to knee, and his hands wrapped around her waist to hold her there.

*This* was what she'd been trying to remember. *This* was what her body knew, what her skin had been trying to tell her about. Memories of the sensations butted at her brain, allowing her to savor the anticipation of the next touch, the next taste, while somehow knowing how good it would be at the same time.

Her fingers tightened in his hair, dragging his mouth back to hers. She melted under the onslaught.

"Lorelei…"

The sound of her name, whispered huskily next to her ear, sent goose bumps over her skin, but she heard the reluctant *this isn't a good idea* echoing underneath.

"I know." She could force herself *not* to think about all the reasons why this was a really bad idea, but they were still on a public street, only a block from the restaurant, and the shadows and the hibiscus blooms were far from the adequate privacy needed. She pressed a kiss against his neck, tasted the salt and felt the thrumming of his pulse under her lips. "I just don't—" The words were stopped as she gave in to the urge for another taste. She tightened her fingers around the collar of his jacket, unwilling to let this moment, this feeling go. "My house is seven blocks from here."

She felt Donovan smile against her temple as his hands splayed across the small of her back to pull her even closer. "Mine's four."

Her decision had been made the moment she touched him, but when he didn't move, she realized Donovan must be waiting for a response. "Sounds good."

The feel of Lorelei pressed against him was mind-scrambling, and the orders from his brain to his feet seemed to be getting lost.

Rationally, he knew this shouldn't be happening, but somehow it felt inevitable, as well. He hadn't followed her with this intent, but now he didn't know why he hadn't.

The four blocks to his house seemed ridiculously far when his body was screaming for him to take her right here, right now.

*Move.*

He reached for her hand and twined his fingers through hers. He realized Lorelei's hand was shaking. She wore a dazed look, her lips swollen and moist, and her breath was uneven and shallow. The woman was lust incarnate, and pure want cut deep into his belly.

Lorelei trailed slightly behind as he led her quickly across Esplanade and down Dauphine into the Quarter. When he felt resistance in her arm, he glanced over his shoulder to see Lorelei's gaze firmly on her feet and wondered if she was having second thoughts. Belatedly he realized it was those impossibly sexy shoes. The ancient and uneven sidewalks of the Quarter were treacherous, and he was practically dragging her like a caveman back to his den.

He shortened his stride and slowed his steps. Lorelei squeezed his hand in thanks without looking up.

Dauphine Street was primarily residential, and the few people out on the street didn't give them a second glance—even though Donovan felt like his erection was leading the way and their intent was obvious.

One block up St. Phillip to Burgundy and the redbrick of his house appeared like a lighthouse. The knowledge they were that close sent blood rushing to his groin so fast he had difficulty finding his keys and remembering how to make them work.

A rush of air-conditioning cooled the sweat on his skin as he pulled Lorelei inside and slammed the door behind her. The light from the hall showed a faint glistening of sweat around Lorelei's hairline and a pink flush to her cheeks that could either be from exertion or arousal.

*Arousal,* he decided, as Lorelei threw herself into his arms again with a force that nearly knocked him off his feet. Her arms twined around his neck, pulling his mouth to hers. In response he picked her up and headed for the stairs.

Lorelei's fingers worked on the buttons of his shirt and a hand slipped inside. The tease of her fingers over his nipple nearly caused him to miss a step. He sucked in his breath, trying to focus on remembering where his bedroom was.

*Finally.* It took every ounce of control he had not to fling her onto the bed and bury himself in her. Instead he set her carefully on her feet. She'd kicked off her shoes somewhere along the way, and now the top of Lorelei's head was even with his chest. She opened his shirt farther and placed a kiss on the bare skin.

He'd thought the burning, clawing need he remembered had been a byproduct of too much tequila and a trick of his mind, but as it swept through him in a fierce wave, he realized the memory was dull in comparison with the reality. Lorelei was as hypnotic and drugging as her namesake—and probably just as dangerous.

Her hands were busy, untucking his shirt and pushing it and his jacket off. Then, with an appreciative sigh, she ran her fingers from his collarbones to his belt buckle. She looked up and gave him a small smile, before turning around and lifting her hair over her shoulder to expose the zipper down the back of her dress. A second later the purple silk was in a puddle at her feet, and she was facing him wearing only a scrap of black lace.

Dear God, she was even more beautiful than he remembered. He hadn't realized he'd voiced the thought until Lorelei placed a hand on his chest and said, "I'm glad there's still some element of surprise for you."

How they got to the bed he didn't quite know, but a second later Lorelei was flat on her back, that jet-black hair tangling around her face, and he was on top of her, savoring the feel of her skin against his.

*Oh, mercy,* Lorelei thought. This was… It… This was… *Mercy.* She just couldn't grab hold of a thought for very long.

Donovan had amazingly soft skin draped over hard muscle, and the crisp hair on his chest left her nipples tingling. His hips moved tantalizingly as his lips mapped her skin, and she wasn't sure if she was melting or going up in flames. Hands shaking with desire, she fumbled with his belt until Donovan finally took over.

Then it was just hot skin and hands that seemed to know exactly where to touch, driving her insane and right to the very edge. Donovan's mouth… *Oh, dear God, his mouth…* She arched against him, her hands searching for purchase on the sheets as she realized the cries she heard were coming from her.

And then the wave she was on broke, her mind going blank as violent tremors shook her to her bones. She heard Donovan's growl as his mouth found hers, and he ate the scream that came when he drove into her in one hot, thrilling thrust.

Her orgasm just went on and on, and she anchored herself to Donovan's heaving torso as she rode out the waves of pleasure until she saw fireworks and the world went black.

# CHAPTER FOUR

LORELEI'S EYES WERE CLOSED, but she wasn't sleeping. Even if he hadn't slept next to her before he'd know; her breath didn't have that deep, even quality of sleep. The cool sophisticate she'd been hours ago was gone. There were dark smudges under her eyes and a slight stubble burn around her mouth and jaw. That jet-black hair ran riot around her shoulders, the tangles sticking to her damp skin.

She looked earthy and sensual and far too tempting to be real.

But she was also uncharacteristically silent. Lorelei was not the quiet type, and while he really didn't care for idle pillow talk, the fact she wasn't saying anything at all bordered on unnerving. Lorelei *always* had something to say. About everything. But not right now. She faced him, but from her side of the king-size bed, leaving plenty of distance between them. So while there wasn't exactly a wall running down the middle of his bed, there was a very respectable fence.

And it was probably electrified.

That realization kept his hands to himself when they itched to reach for her again. Instead, Donovan stacked his hands behind his head and stared at the ceiling. In reality, the only thing more insane than hooking up with Lorelei was hooking up with her twice. He'd known it, but he'd let his little head do all the thinking.

What was it about Lorelei that turned him into a teenage boy who'd never laid hands on a real woman before? The lack of self-control or higher brain function was just embarrassing even to think about. Wouldn't *that* be a surprise to all those people who liked to write those "Most Eligible" articles that painted him as some sort of Creole Casanova?

"Something funny?" Lorelei's voice was husky— probably a side effect of all that screaming—and he turned toward her to see that her eyes were open and watching him. "You've got a little smile on your face."

"Why? Are you thinking you're the one who put it there?"

Her lips twitched. "If it were anyone other than you… maybe."

"*Now* who's wearing a smile?"

"Oh, I don't doubt it. *That* was pretty damn amazing."

The honesty of that purred statement floored him— figuratively speaking, at least. He was glad he was already lying down. Then Lorelei stretched, catlike, her back arching off the bed and drawing his eyes to her small but perfectly shaped breasts. The sensual movement caused his brain to short-circuit. Her skin seemed luminescent in the half light, the curves begging to be traced again. He knew how that skin felt under his hands, and how it would respond to his touch.

She laughed quietly. "I feel like I should thank you."

That got his attention. He looked at her and grinned. "Well, you're quite welcome," he answered formally.

She shot him an exasperated look, but there was humor behind it, not irritation. "I *meant* for appeasing my curiosity."

"And is it appeased?"

Lorelei stretched again—probably just to torture him—before collapsing back on to the bed with a sigh. "Definitely appeased." She grinned and rolled to her side, propping her head on her fist. "I knew it was a pity I couldn't remember last time. High marks across the board, by the way."

This was a different Lorelei. Relaxed. Not biting his head off. *How novel.* "Oh, good. I was worried."

She snorted. "Somehow I doubt that."

"And somehow I'm not surprised that you do."

The sheet across her legs shifted as she wiggled her legs. "As soon as I get full feeling back in my legs I'll get dressed and call a cab."

The casual statement did something bad to him that he couldn't quite name. Trying to keep it out of his voice, he tried for a lecherous smile. "So soon?"

"I think it's probably a wise idea." She bit her bottom lip as she looked at the sheets tangled around her. "And I'm due for one, don't you think?"

A second taste of Lorelei had only whetted his appetite for more. There were several inches of her skin he had yet to explore and, no matter how insane it was, he very much wanted Lorelei to stay exactly where she was.

Well, not *exactly* where she was; she needed to move about two feet closer. Or all the way back on top of him. That would be good.

Good Lord, when had he completely lost the big brain/little brain battle? Lorelei was offering him an easy out of this situation; he should be jumping on it, helping her into her dress and straight into a cab. Hell, he hadn't brought a woman back to his place in years for the very reason that he didn't know how to get them to leave. It was much easier to claim an early meeting or an important deadline and make a graceful exit while everyone still had a smile on their faces.

It seemed that getting Lorelei to leave wasn't going to be a problem, though. She was already pushing herself up and swinging her legs off the bed. Her movements seemed a little stiff, though, and her smile had lost its humor, becoming more forced. The casualness from just a few minutes earlier seemed to evaporate.

She reached for her dress, avoiding eye contact. "I've got to get up really early in the morning—for a breakfast meeting—so I should probably get on home."

The irony slammed into him, causing him to laugh and earning him a questioning look from Lorelei. "I never knew until right now how utterly lame that excuse actually sounds."

Shock crossed her face, but then her lips twisted in amusement. She knew she was busted, but he had to give her points for not denying it.

Lorelei stepped into her dress and began struggling with her zipper, twisting herself like a contortionist and making his shoulder hurt just watching her. Walking up behind her, he moved her hands away and they fell to her sides. She stilled, and he felt her sway slightly toward him before she straightened.

He wanted to slide his hands inside the dress, around the indentation of her waist, but he settled for just resting them on the flare of her hips, letting his thumbs stroke lightly over the bare skin of her lower back. He felt the small tremor that ran over her skin and heard her breath catch.

Neither of them moved, but the pull was real, palpable, like an iron filing trying to resist a magnet, and the small space between their bodies vibrated from it.

*Zip the dress. Call her a cab.*

*But why?*

The *why* caught him off-guard. Why should he bustle her out the door like she was some kind of bad bar hook-up? He'd been working under the assumption that this was insane. Crazy. A bad idea.

But now he couldn't quite articulate why.

They weren't kids anymore; all that foolishness had to have a statute of limitations that had long since passed. Lorelei was smart, articulate, challenging—not to mention absolutely gorgeous. So why, then, was this such an insane idea? He didn't want to marry her; he just wanted to get her back to bed. Why couldn't they just enjoy this?

No reasons came immediately to mind.

What *did* come to mind was the sincere wish that she'd lean back just an inch or two... "At least let me offer you a drink or something."

"The time to buy me a drink is *before* we..." She glanced at the bed, giving him a view of her profile, and swallowed hard. "Well, it's not really necessary now."

"Lorelei—"

"Look, Donovan—" She turned as she spoke, stepping back another foot and snapping that electric strand between them. "Sorry. Go ahead."

"No, ladies first."

She ran her fingers through her hair, taming the tangles and pushing it back from her face. "I don't want you to think that this... I mean, that *I'm*..." She sighed and cursed softly. "And here I didn't think anything could be more awkward than last Sunday morning."

"Just spit it out, then."

"I just don't want *you* to think that *I* think that this—that—was...um...*anything.*"

His surprise must have shown on his face, because Lorelei hurried on.

"It was great—really great—I just don't…*expect* anything from you, okay? It just…*was*. It's not—well, it's not… Well, you know?"

Lorelei couldn't keep eye contact, and Donovan found his temper rising as she muddled through her speech. "No, I don't know. I'm not sure that was even English."

She sighed. "I'm just trying to say that it's all good now. I don't expect this to be anything other than what it was. Or that it's supposed to become anything."

"I have to give you credit for honesty."

Her smile was weak. "Thanks."

"But that doesn't make what you're saying sound any less insulting and tawdry."

She shook her head. "Oh, don't be so thin-skinned. It's not tawdry, and there's no need to take it personally. I'm just trying to move past this."

"Dare I ask why?"

"Because I think it's pretty clear that's the best idea. For both of us." She shrugged. "It's not like this can go anywhere."

"I don't recall saying I wanted it to."

"Then what's the problem?"

That was an excellent question. He only wished he had an answer for it. He leaned against the foot of the bed. "Not quite a week ago you told me to forget it ever happened, yet here you are."

Lorelei's mouth twisted. "I know."

"Am I supposed to believe that this time you really, *really* mean it?"

"That would be nice." She sighed, but then caught herself and crossed her arms over her chest. "You were pretty adamant about the whole forget-it-happened-thing yourself, yet here we are again."

"Hey, *you* kissed *me*."

"You weren't exactly fighting me off," she fired back.

*There was that.* "I'm only human, Lorelei."

"As am I." She sighed. "I'll be honest with you. You're a good-looking guy, and there's obviously chemistry between us. But we're adults, and it looks like we're going to be running into each other now. These chemistry experiments have to stop."

"Because God forbid two healthy, consenting adults have sex just because they want to?"

He watched her swallow and then lift her chin. "Something like that."

*Whatever.* Lorelei should carry a warning label because, as a whole, she could drive a man right off the edge. And since he valued his sanity, he should probably just let this go. She had a point about chemistry: it was a great thing, but it could also be very dangerous and blow up in your face.

*So why were they both still standing here?*

"Then go."

Donovan's words dropped like a gauntlet and Lorelei felt like a fool. An idiot. The right thing to do would be to breeze right out of here, head held high.

But her feet felt nailed to the floor.

It didn't help that Donovan was stark naked—and seemingly completely unselfconscious about it—and the evidence of what she'd be walking away from was impossible to ignore. She tried keeping her eyes on his face, but he looked like a freakin' sex god, all tousled and sexy, and her mouth watered at the *acres* of skin and muscle to be explored and appreciated. And even though he was basically telling her to get lost, it was also *very* clear that he was interested in something else entirely...

Donovan cleared his throat and she snapped her eyes up, finding a focus spot on the wall above the headboard.

"If you're going—go. Just lock the door behind you."

Really, the only thing this lacked was him tossing cab fare at her. She didn't know she could feel humiliated and irate at the same time. "There's no need to be a complete ass about it."

"You got what you wanted. Your curiosity has been appeased. And you don't want to be too tired for that breakfast meeting."

Donovan sounded downright annoyed about the whole thing. Which, coming from someone like him, seemed implausible enough to be amusing. The idea that she might have *offended* him was just…well, impossible.

Now she was standing here in Donovan's bedroom, barefoot, her dress gaping at the front because it still wasn't zipped, with a naked and *damn* pretty man who a few minutes ago had asked her to stay practically throwing her out onto the street while her legs were still wobbly from the most mind-blowing orgasm of her entire life. And she was ready to leave—*should* leave—but she didn't really want to now.

Her life had turned into a farce. An X-rated farce.

*Make a decision. Any decision. Do something other than just stand here.* Leaving was obviously the best option, but she hesitated. Why *shouldn't* she take what he was offering? There were no strings attached: just a chance to relax and burn some sexual energy without anything being messy and complicated later. It seemed so simple, so easy…and so tempting.

She took a deep breath. "Actually, I'm kind of thirsty."

Both of Donovan's eyebrows went up.

"I'll, um, call and reschedule that meeting."

When Donovan didn't move Lorelei wanted to die.

She'd read the whole thing wrong. He'd been messing with her. She should have pried her feet off the floor, not gotten pulled into a conversation. Now she'd have to kill him.

Then Donovan held out a hand. Relief rushed through her—only to be quickly swamped by a wave of desire once she touched him and his fingers curled around hers. He pulled her the few steps toward him until she stood between his thighs. Without breaking eye contact, he moved his hands to the straps of her dress, sliding them down her arms until the dress puddled on the floor again.

His hands splayed over her hips, sliding down over the outside of her thighs, then up to her waist. Strong fingers traced her ribs, then her breasts and her collarbones. Hooded eyes followed the path of his hands in an inspection that should have left her blushing and feeling exposed, but left her sizzling silently instead. She felt powerful, sexy, worshiped.

When Donovan began to retrace his path with his lips, her muscles began to melt. She swayed and reached for his shoulders for support. When his tongue slipped into her navel, her knees buckled, and only his hands on her hips kept her on her feet.

*Mercy.*

*Curiosity killed the cat.*

But the cat would die happy.

A loud, embarrassing growl from her stomach had Donovan tossing her a Saints jersey that hung nearly to her knees and leading her down to the kitchen a couple of hours later. He produced a bottle of wine and poured her a large glass. "A drink. As promised."

She laughed. "Finally."

"Now for food…" Donovan opened the fridge door and stared inside.

Donovan's house had barely registered in her brain when she'd arrived, but now she couldn't help but notice. The bedroom had been gorgeous—sumptuous and relaxing, without being overdone or competing with the view from the balcony doors—and that sumptuous, tasteful feel extended through the rest of the house. The interior renovations were very modern, with clean lines and a masculine décor that complemented the exposed brick walls and high ceilings of the original architecture. So many people renovated the charm and personality out of these older homes, and it pleased her to see that wasn't the case here.

"Your house is gorgeous. Did you do the renovations?"

He looked over his shoulder at her and grinned. "Not personally."

"But you approved the design?"

"Yep. Feel free to look around while I get us something to eat."

Honestly, watching Donovan prepare food wearing nothing but a pair of jeans had more appeal. *Mercy,* she could happily stare at him all night long, but staring *was* a little rude. She picked up her glass and wandered into the living room.

The fireplace and mantel looked to be original to the house, but it was the attention to detail that impressed her. Either Donovan or his designer had an excellent eye and a love for the historic bones of the house.

There was the requisite enormous television stationed across from a leather recliner that looked buttery soft, and a wall full of CDs and DVDs. A quick glance at the alphabetized titles told her that Donovan was both very organized and extremely eclectic in his tastes. There was a bit of everything from jazz to punk and *Casablanca* to *Shaun of the Dead.*

French doors led from that room to a courtyard behind

the house. She opened the door and stepped outside onto the patio, where the bricks still radiated warmth captured from the summer sun. Lights flipped on at her movement and she caught her breath.

High walls and lush plants provided privacy and created a feeling of seclusion in the middle of one of the busiest neighborhoods on earth. Iron benches provided seating to her right, and to her left was what looked like a large round pond. On closer inspection it proved to be a whirlpool. Dipping in a toe, she noticed it was cool water, not hot, just perfect for warm, muggy summer nights. Lorelei sat, letting her feet dangle into the pool as she listened to the night sounds.

The house, the garden—both were beautiful. But not at all the kind of place she'd thought Donovan would live. He seemed more like a high-rise condo or urban loft type of person: all brushed nickel and glass and—

She stopped the thought. *Why* had she assumed that? And when had she come to that conclusion, for that matter? She barely knew him—at least not in a way that would have given her insights into his natural habitat.

It was shocking and a little disconcerting how little she actually knew about him—beyond his award-worthy skills in that decadent bed upstairs. What did *that* say about her?

"There you are. Aren't you hot out here?"

Donovan was coming out of the house, juggling a tray with the bottle of wine tucked under his arm and the other wineglass held upside down by the stem.

"I like being outside on summer nights—even if it is muggy. There's just something real and grounding about a warm night…" She trailed off at his amusement. "I just like it. But if you don't, we can go back inside."

"No. It's why I have a garden." He put down the tray

and sat cross-legged next to her on the apron of the pool.
"As promised—food."

Lorelei eyeballed the tray and stifled a laugh. Baby
carrots and dip, a bag of potato chips, and a heaping plate
of pizza rolls. She didn't know what she'd expected him
to produce, but it hadn't been this. "You eat like a college student."

"No, I *cook* like a college student. That's why I normally eat out."

"I haven't had pizza rolls in years. They're so bad for
you."

"So many of the best things in life are."

She wondered if she should include Donovan in that
list. Or if he was including her in his.

Shaking the thought away, she reached for one. They
were hot, fresh from the microwave, with cheese and
sauce oozing out of the seams. She popped it into her
mouth and closed her eyes as she chewed. Over-processed,
fat-laden, high-sodium bliss exploded over her tongue.
She groaned quietly as she savored it. When she opened
her eyes, Donovan was staring at her, his glass halfway
to his mouth.

He cleared his throat and shifted slightly. "Damn, they
must be good. That's the face you make when—"

She frowned at him and he stopped. Nodding thanks
at his belated discretion, she sipped at her wine. Chasing
a pizza roll with a glass of excellent wine—and very expensive, based on the label—was almost surreal. But it
fit with the situation somehow.

Tonight, as a whole, seemed outside the bounds of reality. The fund-raiser seemed like ancient history. Even
taking the stage on Vivi and Connor's behalf no longer
seemed like a monumental achievement etched in time.
Time, for all intents and purposes, had stopped. It was

very late—or possibly very early; she had no idea—she'd had a long, stressful day and a longer evening of down-right gymnastic sex that would test anyone's stamina. She should be exhausted.

But she wasn't. And she was having a good time. It didn't bear close scrutiny, but she was, nonetheless.

They ate in silence for a while, but it wasn't an uncom-fortable one.

"I meant to tell you that you did a good job tonight. At the fund-raiser," he clarified.

The compliment wasn't the most effusive ever, but coming from Donovan it seemed like very high praise. "Thanks."

"You're a natural when it comes to working a crowd."

*Wow. Really high praise.*

"How much money did you get commitments for?"

"Some," she hedged, "but not as much as I'd like. How much can I put *you* down for?"

Donovan laughed. "See—a natural."

"Thank you." She gave him a regal nod. "But I'd still like a firm commitment on a dollar amount. I'm constantly amazed at how cheap rich people can be. The population of that room tonight probably has over half the wealth of the entire city, but you'd think I was taking food straight out of their children's mouths."

Donovan laughed. "Very true."

Too late she realized she'd opened a door, and braced herself for Donovan to come back with one of his scathing remarks about "elites" and "class." But he didn't go there. Instead he reached for one of the pizza rolls.

"I'm sure Jack will write you a fat check, though. He seemed keen on impressing you."

If anyone other than Donovan had said that she'd think that odd tone was jealousy. "Here's a newsflash: Jack Morgan will pinch a nickel until the buffalo burps. He promised me a contribution, but it's practically pocket change. If he's trying to impress me with his largesse, he's failed pretty miserably."

That earned her another laugh from Donovan. Then he casually tossed out a figure that nearly had her choking on her carrot. The St. James family—or maybe just Donovan—certainly put the riche in nouveau riche. When she could breathe again, she tried to sound just as casual. "Let's say I'm starting to feel impressed."

Donovan's white smile flashed in the moonlight. "Good."

"Now I've got to come up with another speech for tomorrow night. A similar yet different way to get a different set of people to open *their* checkbooks."

"Which group?"

"I'd have to check. The homeless shelter, maybe? It's at the convention center."

He shook his head. "That would be the Arts Association awards dinner. Not a fund-raiser for the homeless shelter."

*Damn it. How did Vivi keep up with all of this?* "Are you sure?"

"Quite. I'm supposed to be there."

Then when *was* the homeless-shelter event? She tried to picture Vivi's schedule… *Wait. Another* event where they'd both be there? That added a whole new dimension of conflict. It would be much easier to come to terms with her attraction to Donovan and the ramifications of that if she didn't have to face him.

"I guess I might see you there, then." *And sometime between now and then I'll figure out how I'm going to handle that.*

Donovan nodded before tossing a pizza roll into the air and catching it in his mouth. He looked at her expectantly.

It was the escape route she needed from confusing thoughts back into the fun surrealism of the evening. She applauded politely. "Nice trick. Now I am *really* impressed. You should have done that before you pledged money."

He picked up another. "Open your mouth," he said as he took aim.

"No way."

"Come on," he coaxed. "I'm trying to impress you, remember?"

Something about this seemed almost charming—which meant she either needed to get her head examined or else afterglow was even better than beer goggles. If anyone had tried to tell her that snide, pontificating pundit Donovan St. James would casually pledge an amount equal to an endowed chair at a university just seconds before trying to convince a woman to let him throw food at her, she'd have laughed in their face. But she hadn't seen the snide, pontificating pundit tonight. She didn't even really recognize the man in front of her as the Donovan she'd hated since high school.

*No.* Not hated. Just ignored and dismissed.

"Come on, Lorelei. Open up."

She shook her head. "If you miss I'll end up with sauce all over me."

"I never miss. Although I just might have to this time."

"Because...?"

He gave her a look that clearly said he'd be happy to lick her clean. It sent a naughty tingle all the way down to her toes. *Oh, why not?* Her proper upbringing frowned upon playing with one's food—much less tossing it at another human being—but hadn't she decided that tonight was outside the bounds anyway? Feeling foolish, she opened her mouth.

"Close your eyes."

"Why?"

"Because you'll flinch from it if you see it coming."

"Fine." She sighed and closed her eyes, then opened her mouth again.

"Tuck your chin in a little… Tilt your head a little to the left…"

She followed along like a puppet.

"Not that much… Okay, good."

It was amazingly quiet—quiet enough for her to hear the bubbles of the water in the pool. When nothing happened she started to get a little nervous. She kept her eyes closed, though, not wanting to end up with a pizza roll in them, but it was getting just a little awkward now.

A second later Donovan's mouth closed over hers. He caught her gasp of surprise, then his tongue swept in to tease hers.

"Sorry. Couldn't resist," he mumbled as he moved to her neck.

There was a small splash, and then Donovan was pulling her into the pool. The night was warm and muggy, and the water felt delicious lapping against her stomach. Somehow in those moments when she'd been waiting awkwardly, Donovan had lost his jeans, and she no longer minded being left to wait like that. The borrowed jersey floated up to her waist, allowing her bare skin contact with Donovan below the water's surface.

The contrast of warm skin and cool water, the tickle of hair against her thighs and stomach, and the heavy air above the refreshing water all combined with Donovan's kiss to send her senses into overload.

Oh, *yeah*. She was definitely impressed.

\* \* \*

Once again Lorelei woke in a strange bed with a man sleeping beside her. Her brain was faster this time in making sense of the situation—and she lacked the massive hangover from last week—but the feeling of déjà vu couldn't be shaken.

Weak daylight peeked in around the curtains, telling her it was early yet. She could hear Donovan's deep, even breaths beside her, and one heavy leg had hers pinned to the bed. She was very glad Donovan was still asleep, otherwise this morning would end up being equally as awkward—but hopefully not as hostile—as the last time.

At least this time she remembered all the details—even if she was still a little fuzzy on the "why" part. Well, not completely fuzzy. She knew why she'd had sex with him: because she'd wanted to. Why she'd *wanted* to was a bit trickier to nail down.

It was all very confusing. And not something she really wanted to deal with right now.

Slowly and carefully, she slid her legs out from under his. Donovan mumbled and rolled over, but didn't wake, so she slipped out of the bed and took her clothing to the hallway to dress.

Once again she'd be going home in evening wear, but the chances of her being noticed were pretty slim, actually, since she knew which streets to avoid to keep accidental encounters to a minimum. Tiptoeing down the stairs, she grabbed the rest of her things. The sight of the alarm keypad next to the front door gave her pause. Had Donovan set the alarm last night?

Cringing the whole time, she opened the door and waited for sirens to blare and announce her exit. Nothing. With a sigh of relief she stepped outside, pulling the door closed and making sure it locked behind her. Cursing her footwear, she started the trek home.

It was early enough not to be miserable, but the day was already promising to be a scorcher, and the humidity was already high enough to have her hair sticking to her neck. She couldn't say the Quarter was waking up, since it never actually slept, but there were few people on the streets, and some of them looked worse than she did.

Normally the walk home wouldn't have taken more than fifteen minutes, tops, but her shoes slowed her down and that gave her more time to think. Pretty soon she was starting to wonder if bolting had been the best idea—and not just because her feet hurt.

Sneaking out like that made her feel as if she had done something wrong, something she regretted, and that really wasn't the case. But she was darned sure she didn't want to do the morning-after bit. Not with Donovan, at least. They'd agreed it was just about the sex, and she was okay with that, because she wasn't looking for anything more. She had too much on her plate at the moment to get involved with anyone beyond a physical thing. She needed to focus—not look for distractions—but she had to admit Donovan had been an excellent stress-reliever.

Even sweaty and sore-footed, she felt better than she had in quite a while. She'd needed last night, needed that release.

Her feet were dying as she got to the sidewalk in front of her house, and she slipped the shoes off before climbing the stairs to her porch. The blast of air-conditioning that greeted her felt even better. Dropping her stuff, she headed straight for the shower and then into bed.

As she closed her eyes she realized the stress relief hadn't been just physical. Last night's surrealism, that step outside of the norm, had been exactly what she needed. And that was all Donovan.

*How very disturbing.*

Yeah, she'd done the right thing by getting out of there. She really didn't need the complication.

# CHAPTER FIVE

LORELEI SMILED ALL THE way through the awards dinner, applauded politely as the names were called, and gave a simple yet heartfelt speech on Vivi's behalf as she received a plaque for her gallery's support of young and upcoming artists. Where Vivi would find room to hang the plaque was an excellent question, as the walls of her office were already lined with dozens of other awards of appreciation.

She ran her fingers over Vivi's name and felt a small twinge of regret. If only she could send a message back in time to her younger self, explaining how not all attention was good attention, that infamy was not the same as respect, and that there was such a thing as a permanent record—at least in people's minds—it might be her name on that plaque instead of Vivi's. *One day...*

She'd accepted the fact she'd never be the saint Vivi was a long time ago, but she was slowly making inroads, repairing the damage. This insane schedule had its benefits. She would have met pretty much every single important person in New Orleans by the time Vivi returned. Not that she didn't know them already, but there was a difference in knowing someone socially and seeing them as a professional. *That* was her goal.

They'd know her face—know her interest and her desire to serve.

She set Vivi's latest dust-catcher on the table in front of her and stifled a yawn. Functioning on about five hours of sleep was not easy—especially when that five hours hadn't been consecutive. She'd barely lain down for a much-needed nap this morning before her phone had started ringing. After running to the studio to sort out a problem, she'd barely gotten home in time to shower and come here. She could do Vivi's life or she could do hers. Doing both just might kill her.

Ten more days. She could make it ten more days.

Of course, she needed to make it through the next ten *minutes* without falling asleep first. Snoring on the table would make *such* a good impression, practically advertising to the world that she'd been out all night.

*And, oh, what a night...*

She felt herself starting to smirk and quickly reschooled her face into an expression of polite interest. Out of the corner of her eye, she scanned the ballroom. Donovan had said he might come, but she hadn't seen him yet.

That was probably a good thing. She wasn't a very good actress, and her little secret would be obvious to everyone. Since she was trying to live down a reputation—not enforce her old one—that would not be good. Plus she was still feeling a bit bad about sneaking out this morning without saying goodbye, and she still hadn't figured out how she was supposed to interact with Donovan now. They weren't friends, but they were certainly more than casual acquaintances. Who would have thought that things could get *more* awkward?

Yeah, she was very glad he wasn't here. She had a job to do, and thinking about last night would not make it any easier.

The awards and speeches finally ended, giving her the opportunity to get up and walk around. The movement helped wake her up, and shaking hands and making small talk proved boring but kept her alert. At the bar, she ordered a club soda.

Tipping the bartender, she turned to find Julie Cochran, who'd only recently moved back to town as she fought through a bitter and nasty divorce, right behind her.

"I'm fine," Julie insisted when Lorelei offered condolences—and alcohol, if needed.

When Julie exhaled, the Scotch on her breath told Lorelei she was a little late for that.

"The lying, cheating bastard is going to pay dearly for his inability to keep his pants on. My lawyer won't settle for less than a damn nice settlement and nearly half of his salary for my humiliation and pain."

She and Julie had never been particularly close, so this seemed like information she shouldn't be privy to. She wasn't quite sure how to respond. "Wow. Amazing. Remind me to call you if I ever need a recommendation for an attorney."

"Three words, sweetie. *Prenuptial agreement.* Make sure there's a penalty for adultery."

Lorelei wasn't sure if *prenuptial agreement* counted as three words or two, but she nodded anyway.

"Let me give you some more advice. Learn from my mistake. If a man is marrying up by marrying you, *run.* Dump him. He'll never truly respect you, and will only come to resent you for it."

*That was a little more than expected.* "I'll keep that in mind."

"Good." Julie patted her arm. "You're probably the exact person I needed to run into tonight. Now that I'm back home, I really need some help."

"Okay." This was normally the kind of thing people

went to her sister for, but Lorelei was pleased to step up. *Inroads, indeed.* "How can I help?"

"Point me toward the single men."

"Oh. Um…" That was unexpected. She glanced around the room. It wasn't as if the eligible bachelors traveled in packs or anything, to make them easier to hunt. "Anyone in particular?"

"I don't really care as long as he's young, handsome and rich. Preferably good in bed, too."

Lorelei nearly choked. To think Vivi was always accusing *her* of being too blunt or outrageous. Vivi would faint at Julie's words. *No, Vivi would handle it with aplomb.* "The first three are easier to deduce than the last, Julie."

"We'll start with the ones I know. Mike Devereaux?"

"Sorry, he's married."

"John Howard?"

"Married."

"Seth Ryland?"

"Gay."

Julie's eyebrows pulled together. "Really?"

Lorelei nodded.

"Well, that's a pity."

"Yeah."

"Kyle Hamilton?"

"The Hamiltons lost all their money in the last crash."

"Well, damn. Who *is* eligible?"

Lorelei scrambled for words as Julie ran through names like she was reading from the phonebook. This was getting quite uncomfortable. Even if she did have a viable suggestion, she'd feel dirty setting Julie loose on some unsuspecting man. Before she could come up with an answer, Julie grabbed her arm.

"Well, hel-*lo*, yummy goodness… Wait—is that Donovan St. James?"

Her head snapped to follow Julie's line of sight. He had come after all. The fluttery sinking of her stomach at seeing him was complicated by a stab of possessiveness at the open lust on Julie's face. She tried to keep her voice even. "Yes, it is."

"He's moving up nicely in the world. Who'd have thought it?"

*Did Julie actually expect an answer?*

The answer seemed to be no, as Julie moved on. "I've seen him on TV. He's much hotter in person and he ticks all my boxes nicely."

Now there was an uncomfortable stab of jealousy she didn't care to examine. "Julie…"

"Lord, I'm not going to marry him. I just want to—"

She coughed, not wanting to hear the details. Donovan was the one guy on Julie's list whose prowess Lorelei could attest to, and Julie was now drooling over him as if he was a tasty morsel she was ready to gobble up. Belatedly, she remembered Vivi saying Julie had always been a viperous bitch, but before she could extricate herself from the conversation and Julie's clutches gracefully, Julie was dragging her across the ballroom.

"Introduce us."

"You went to school with him for four years, Julie. You don't really need an introduction."

"But he wasn't Donovan St. James back then."

She dug her heels in and forced Julie to stop. "What?"

"Oh, you know what I mean."

Lorelei had the sneaking suspicion that she did. It was tacky and calculating on Julie's part. She didn't have time to mull about it, though, as they were now just feet from Donovan and she was not ready to face him just yet. She didn't have a plan in place. If there was ever a time to simply brazen through, now would be it.

To make things worse, Donovan was standing with Jack Morgan—possibly the only man Julie hadn't had on her list. But then, there was some kind of bad blood between Julie and Jack that went back to their prom as far as she could tell. That was just going to make this even more fun.

She plastered a smile on her face. "Jack. Donovan. Good to see you both tonight."

Donovan nodded at her, a short, sharp motion that implied complete uninterest in her, and her hackles went up a bit.

"That was a nice speech. Pass along my congratulations to your sister."

Jack was giving the same short, uncomfortable nod in Julie's direction, which she returned. *Well, this was just awkward all the way around.* Then he leaned in to kiss *her* cheek in greeting.

"Hi, there."

There was something a little too intimate in Jack's voice, and Lorelei felt like he was making a very premature claim with that kiss. She peeked at Donovan, but his face didn't so much as move. Granted, it would be strange if she and Donovan suddenly seemed all chummy, but still… It was just *wrong.*

Julie cleared her throat, and Lorelei remembered why she was standing here. "Sorry. Donovan—do you remember Julie Cochran?"

"Hebert," Julie corrected smoothly, extending her hand. "I've already taken back my name."

Donovan shot Lorelei a look that she didn't fully understand, but then turned to Julie. "From St. Katharine's. Of course."

Julie's smile turned downright lustful, and Lorelei tried to swallow the urge to snatch those blond extensions right off her head.

*Where did that come from?* It wasn't as if she had dibs on Donovan or something. And Donovan was pretty much treating her like a complete stranger. It was more than a little galling, but not exactly something she could call him on in the middle of a ballroom. *Especially* since Julie had stepped between them, effectively removing both Lorelei and Jack from the conversation.

Jack didn't seem to mind, though. He was now leaning in a little too close. "I tried to call you after you left last night."

She forced her attention away from Donovan and Julie. Speaking to Jack last night seemed so very long ago. "I know. Sorry. I was so exhausted by the time I got home I just crashed. I didn't get your message until this afternoon." That wasn't a flat-out lie: Jack didn't need to know that it had taken her over ten hours to go approximately ten blocks.

"So, when can I take you out to dinner?"

Okay, Jack was asking her out on a date while she was close enough to Donovan to smell his aftershave. The smell alone was sending little tremors down her inner thighs. Her life really was a farce.

"I'm pretty much totally booked up until Vivi and Connor get back from their honeymoon. It's a really crazy time."

"Then as soon as they get back, I want on your calendar."

Lorelei tried to smile and nod in a way that was polite without being committal.

"It must be tough for you. Stepping into Vivi's shoes like that."

Was that a jab? Or was she just oversensitive? *Damn, Donovan's scent was driving her insane.* "Vivi has fabulous shoes, and thankfully we wear the same size."

Julie threw her head back and laughed at something Donovan had said, and Lorelei was able to direct her attention to their conversation without seeming over-interested. She and Jack were being roundly excluded. In just a few minutes, Julie had moved in like an aircraft carrier, creating a no-fly zone around Donovan that said she'd shoot down any woman who dared come too close. Last night Jess; Julie tonight. Lorelei amended that list—first it had been Jess, then her, and now Julie. It seemed Donovan was a prime commodity these days. *He should get one of those "take a number" things.*

"Why don't we go refresh your drink?" Jack said. "I think these two have some catching up to do."

Lorelei nearly snorted. But Donovan wasn't exactly fighting off Julie's advances, and nor did he seem overly concerned with Jack's rather proprietary hovering.

*Fine.* She'd said last night that she didn't expect anything from him, and he seemed to be taking that at face value. Rationally, she had no real cause to be irritated about it. They were nothing at all to each other. Repeating that fact to herself, she let Jack guide her away.

She spent the next hour making polite conversation with all the right people, and playing slightly dumb to Jack's attempts to charm her straight into his bed. A week ago this would have been exactly what she wanted: the powerful and influential of New Orleans treating her as an equal player and a guy like Jack Morgan playing arm candy.

Jack Morgan: grandson of a former mayor, lawyer in his father's firm. She'd known him—or at least his family—her entire life. His mother and her mother were in several clubs together. Handsome, stable, well-liked, from a good family...Jack was *exactly* the kind of man everyone had expected her to pair up with. Just like every other girl she'd grown up with.

Vivi had almost bucked the rules by marrying a musician, but the Mansfields were literally the family next door—as old and established and respected as every other family in their social circle. No one had batted an eyelid when they'd ended up together.

She, though, had always dated outside her expected peer group—but she hadn't strayed too far, because she didn't want to give her grandmother a heart attack. She'd carefully chosen men just acceptable enough to protect her grandmother's heart, but also unacceptable enough to keep people from expecting her to get serious with any of them. It had been a careful balancing act designed to let her have the most amount of fun with the minimum amount of hassle. It was just easier that way.

And now there was Jack Morgan. Her mother would be thrilled.

Why wasn't *she* more thrilled?

Even examining him with a critical eye, she couldn't come up with a complaint. Jack was a good catch. But there was no tingle, no excitement at the thought.

Mentally she ran through Julie's recent list of eligible males, and found that none of them gave her even the slightest tingle.

Once again, the "right" thing held little or no interest for her. Hadn't that been the story of her life? And wasn't that exactly how she'd ended up here, hovering on the outskirts of her own society, trying to get back in like some high schooler who wanted to hang with the popular kids?

It was just downright depressing to contemplate.

Donovan revved her engines, but he was like tequila: not a good idea unless she wanted to make a fool of herself. As if she hadn't already made a big enough fool of herself by throwing herself at him last night.

And look what that had gotten her.

She looked over at Jack. Jack was exactly what she needed, tingle be damned.

The expectations of the right thing to do were ingrained into her: she was *supposed* to marry a man from the right family, have a couple of children to raise the right way, and settle into the society niche that had been carved for her at birth.

She'd tried, but she'd never quite measured up. And as Vivi had become the paragon of all the right virtues, she'd finally just given up even trying to live up to that standard and had become a bit of a rebel just out of a need for self-protection. She'd even convinced herself that she *wanted* to be the horrible warning instead of the good example.

Now, after years of not caring—or merely doing the minimum required of her—she found herself fighting for her place. She had a hell of a lot to prove to a hell of a lot of people, and the only way to accomplish that was by playing by their rules.

She sneaked a peek to her left. Donovan St. James was not in the playbook at all. *Pity.*

The problem with rebelling was that, while it was liberating and exciting, it painted her as an irresponsible flake who didn't respect the traditions she'd been taught her entire life. She'd been both an embarrassment and a disappointment to her family, because after failing to live up to Vivi's example she'd simply quit trying. If she harbored any hope of changing that now she not only had to live by the rules, she needed to embrace them and live them.

Vivi's honeymoon had handed her the perfect opportunity to show that she wasn't that girl anymore. This was a

crucial time for her; she couldn't afford a potentially embarrassing affair with Donovan.

Not that it seemed to be an option now, since Julie
seemed to have made her claim without a peep of protest from Donovan. She should probably be happy Julie
had derailed that train before it could crash spectacularly.

A Lorelei-Donovan coupling—however brief and
non-permanent—would probably kill her grandmother.
Regardless of anything else he had going for him,
nothing—not the St. James family money, not even the
respect Donovan had earned in his profession—would
ever give Donovan St. James membership to the club as
long as the old guard were in power. And he probably still
wouldn't get an invite after they all died off, either. Some
lines just couldn't be crossed.

She might not fully agree with the attitude, but she was
so tired of being the family disappointment that she was
willing to do practically anything to change that. She'd
never be a pillar of that society, but she could at least be
a functioning member of it.

Damn. Now she was *really* depressed.

She signaled for a server and ordered a large glass of
wine.

*I should not be chasing after Lorelei LaBlanc.* It had been
an ordeal to get out of Julie Hebert's clutches—into which
Lorelei had delivered him in the first damn place, before
swanning off to spend the evening with Jack Morgan—
only to find out that Lorelei had left long ago, claiming
a headache.

Without saying goodbye. *Again.* Twice in one day was
just too much.

Honestly, he'd been a bit relieved when he'd woken to
an empty bed, as he had no idea how this morning would

have played out otherwise. Even though he could assume that Lorelei would have been much less huffy and antagonistic this time, there was no such thing as an *un*-awkward morning after. He was actually grateful that Lorelei had been so accommodating as to leave before the awkwardness set in and ruined the memory of a very pleasant night. Based on how adamant she'd been about leaving immediately last night, he rather assumed she felt the same way.

He had both respect for and experience with the fine art of the pre-dawn exit—so why, then, did he have a nagging irritation about Lorelei's? He'd done his fair share of bolting, but he'd at least tried *not* to make it look as if that was exactly what he was doing. And he never left without saying goodbye, even if he had to wake the woman up to do so, because not to would just be disrespectful. He liked to think he had better manners than *that*.

That was what ticked him off. And as the day had progressed it had only got worse. By the time he'd got to the awards dinner and seen Lorelei up on that stage...

Then, to make matters worse, she'd honed in on Jack Morgan like a heat-seeking missile—as if she hadn't been naked in *his* arms less than twelve hours earlier.

He'd known hooking up with Lorelei was insanity.

Yet here he was, navigating his way through the pedestrians that spilled out of the clubs on Frenchman Street on his way to her house. He hadn't phoned first—even after two nights spent tangled in her arms he still didn't have her number—but he knew exactly where she lived thanks to Connor and Vivi's press.

The one thing he didn't know yet was exactly *why* he had this need to track her down tonight. It could backfire spectacularly in his face, but even that knowledge didn't have him turning around. Damn, he was a glutton for punishment.

He found a spot on the street about a block from her house and parked. The streets weren't well lit, and jazz from one of the clubs floated on the air, broken only by the occasional laugh or shout of party-goers down the street.

Lorelei's house sat close to the road, with only a small strip of grass separating the sidewalk from a wide, screened-in wraparound porch. Most of the house was dark: only one light inside and one on the porch glowed against the night. He remembered Lorelei saying something about a roommate who was never home, and hoped that would be the case tonight.

As he turned up the walk he wasn't surprised to see Lorelei reclined lengthwise across a large wooden swing, head back against a cushion. She held a tablet in one hand, the steady movement of one finger scrolling through whatever was on the screen. One bare foot touched the wood planks, keeping the swing gently in motion.

When Lorelei heard his steps, she sat up and stopped the swing. The sparkly cocktail dress had been replaced with a pair of cut-offs that exposed the long sleek lines of her thighs and a tank top that clearly outlined her breasts—and advertised the fact she wasn't wearing a bra. That mass of hair was pulled up and clipped to the back of her head to keep her cool. She'd looked glamorous and sexy-as-hell earlier, but somehow the simplicity of this outfit had a powerful effect on him. His blood rushed south so fast he got a little light-headed. Even if his brain wasn't sure why he was here, his body damn sure was.

"Well, this is a surprise. What brings you by?" Lorelei didn't move from the swing, so he was left standing on the other side of the screen door.

He shrugged. "You left rather suddenly. People were concerned."

Lorelei set the tablet aside and reached for the beer bottle on the table beside her. "And so you decided to come check on me?"

"Seemed like I should. Hasty or stealthy exits usually mean something isn't right."

She nodded. "*Uh-hmm*. Well, my business was finished. No sense sticking around."

"Obviously."

Lorelei shook her head. "So *that's* the bee in your bonnet? Seriously?"

"Excuse me?"

"Let's not play games."

"That would be refreshing."

"You told me to lock the door behind me when I left. I did. You were still asleep, and I saw no reason to wake you and go through a weird morning-after pantomime. It wasn't some kind of statement." She laughed. "I had no idea your ego was so fragile."

God, she had the most amazing ability to twist everything. "My ego is *not* fragile."

An eyebrow went up, mocking him. "Really? Then why are you here?"

That caught him off guard, and he realized he was acting *exactly* as if that was the problem. It was just as ridiculous as it sounded, and while his earlier irritation wouldn't quite go away, it no longer seemed like a big deal. With that knowledge, the *other* reason driving him came rushing back to the forefront, causing his zipper to dig into his skin.

"This is the one place Julie Hebert won't think to look for me."

Lorelei bit her bottom lip, but he could tell she was trying not to laugh. She finally got off the swing and came to unlatch the screen door.

"You should be flattered. Julie has a list of requirements, and you were the only one who met all the criteria."

"Upright and breathing?"

If she bit her lip any harder she would draw blood. "They were a little more stringent than that."

"Fat checkbook?"

She shrugged. "That might have been on the list."

"Then spare me the rest of her criteria. I don't want to know."

She reached under the table and he heard ice rattling. "Beer?" She had one out and was holding it in his direction before he could even answer.

That was a good sign. He accepted the bottle and sat in the wicker rocker on the other side of the table as she went back to the swing. "Well, if you struck out tonight it's your own fault. Julie was certainly willing."

Was that jealousy he heard in her voice? "Did you not hear the part about me finding a place where Julie wouldn't look?"

"Well, this would be the right place. Julie Hebert and I aren't exactly friends."

"So you set her loose on *me?* Gee, thanks."

Lorelei might have smiled as she curled one leg up into the swing with her and used the other foot to put it in motion again. He liked how easily Lorelei seemed to get past things, without holding grudges or needing to discuss it to death. She might flare up easily, but once it was done, it was done, it seemed. It made things…comfortable.

Beside her, the glowing screen of the tablet went dark.

"Working?"

"The event for the homeless shelter is on Monday, as it turns out. I'm trying to prepare. Vivi's assistant sent over some notes, but…"

"Vivi had better watch out. Little sis will be showing her up, taking her title."

"Oh, I don't want her title. One saint is enough for any family."

"You're probably right."

Her head fell back. "I'll be so glad when they're back from their honeymoon. Her schedule is insane."

"Vivi makes it look easy."

"I know. It's been a humbling experience, to say the least."

"But I bet Vivi doesn't have time to sit on the porch and enjoy a beer on a summer night."

Lorelei conceded that with a nod. "She doesn't. But then porch-sitting and beer-drinking aren't the best use of my education or a productive use of my time. Privilege entails us to responsibility. I should be setting a good example."

Well, *that* was a loaded statement if ever he'd heard one, but Lorelei had delivered it without bitterness or sarcasm. She sounded more resigned than anything else. He watched her closely and decided the beer in her hand was not her first one of the evening. She wasn't drunk, but she was certainly unguarded.

He heard a ping and Lorelei reached for her phone. A glance at the screen had her snorting. "Julie may not think to look for you here, but she's definitely looking for you. She's texted me to see if I know how to get in touch with you."

"Please say no."

She frowned at the screen. "I'm trying to figure out how she got *my* number."

"I imagine it was quite easy for her. You both know all the same people."

"But I actually don't have your number, so it's not a lie

if I tell her that." Lorelei put the phone down and leaned back again. "You know she just wants you for sex?"

"That was made very clear, yes."

"And that doesn't bother you?"

There was a certain irony in her question, considering their situation. "Not really." He caught her eyes and held them. "As long as both parties are clear on the rules, I don't see the harm."

Lorelei seemed to think about that. "Maybe," she said, in the most non-committal tone he'd ever heard.

"I will admit that I'm rather surprised to be on her list, though."

"Why?"

"After listening to her tirade against her low-class, social-climbing ex-husband, I would have thought she'd limit her rebound choices to someone with a better pedigree."

"Charming. You make us sound like we're registered with the kennel club."

"Honestly, you sort of *are*. Got to protect those bloodlines."

Lorelei leveled a look at him. "I'll admit there's some of that going on."

"Just 'some'?"

Lorelei made a face. "I don't know quite how to say this nicely…but you do know that it's you *personally* that's the problem, right?"

At least she was willing to be honest about it. "There's a problem?" he joked.

"Oh, please. You destroyed two families—"

"I didn't destroy anyone or anything. I just happened to be the one who found out and exposed the whole dirty mess."

"Oh, *I* know that. But, say what you like about pedigrees, we are a loyal bunch. We protect and defend our own."

"Closed ranks?"

"Exactly. You're looking at families, businesses and relationships that go back generations, so we're all tied together. I know these people—have known them my entire life. I can't help but feel for them."

"It's not that I don't feel for those families, but Lincoln DuBois made his family vulnerable by the choices he made."

"No one believes that what Mr. DuBois was doing was right, but it still sent a shock wave through our community. And *you* were the cause of that shock wave."

"You think I did those articles with an ulterior motive?"

She gave a half shrug, half nod that said an awful lot.

"What motive could I possibly have?"

"A search for glory and fame, maybe? You certainly got both of those. Then there's the possibility of spite or jealousy? A chance to bring down people you envy?" Lorelei shrugged. "I'll admit I thought that way for a while."

He didn't know what to say to that.

"I'm just telling you that, right or wrong, you brought this on yourself. You can't take on the big dogs and not expect to get bitten. Like I said, the pack is loyal."

Just as she dropped that bomb her phone pinged again, cutting off his chance to respond as she grabbed it and read the text. Once again, her attitude changed completely as she laughed at whatever was on the screen.

"Sorry."

Before he would question her apology, his own phone started to ring.

As he fished it out of his pocket Lorelei said, "I wouldn't answer that if I were you. Not if you want to remain unfound tonight."

"Really? Julie got my number *that* quickly?"

"Never underestimate what a woman will do—especially when she's horny. I'd be careful with Julie Hebert, though. Even Vivi doesn't like her, and Vivi likes everybody."

He sent the call to voice mail. "I don't understand you at all, Lorelei."

"So few do." She chuckled. "But then that makes us even. I don't get you, either."

"I'm not exactly a mystery. What you see is what you get."

She looked at him closely, then shook her head. "No. I don't think so."

"What makes you say that?"

"The fact you're on my porch."

Once again the quick change in topic had him scrambling to catch up. *Boy, Lorelei really didn't want to play games.* "Think about it for a second. That's not really a great mystery, either."

She gave him a smile that made him want to take her right there, on the swing, without giving a single damn about who might see. "At least you're honest about it."

"Do you want me to lie?"

"Nah. If I want sunshine blown up my skirt I'll call Jack." She raised an eyebrow at him. "Do you know I'm the most *fascinating* woman he's ever met?"

There was that strange need to punch Jack again. "Actually, I would agree."

"Oh, so you *can* do empty flattery?"

"No, it's just I've met most of the same women. The competition isn't that stiff."

"Ouch." She shook her head. "If that's your pickup line, no wonder you're still single."

"So are you."

"*That* took careful planning on my part, my friend. The kennel club is all about selective breeding, you know, so I stay far away from the prize studs."

It was his turn to laugh at her. "The mutts are much more interesting anyway."

She grinned back and took another drink. They sat there in silence for a few moments, but it wasn't an uncomfortable silence. And that was kind of odd.

But it was nice, too.

Then Lorelei sighed. "Don't take this personally, but I think you should go."

"What?" How was he *not* supposed to take that personally?

"If you stay, I'm probably going to invite you inside."

He didn't actually see the problem with that, but Lorelei's voice was so heavy, *she* obviously did. "And here I was kind of hoping you would."

She sighed. "Two hook-ups make a fling. Three hook-ups… Well, then it starts to become something. And this isn't supposed to *be* something."

*And he was a mutt.* "'Something' is a mighty big category. Lots of room for interpretation."

Her chin lifted as she considered that. "True. Something doesn't have to be anything. I'm just not sure what, if anything, *this* something could be. Everything is so complicated right now that a something that's not anything might be a good thing. Or nothing. Or something like that."

He'd lost the thread of this conversation pretty quickly, causing him to rethink his earlier assessment of her sobriety. "How much have you had to drink, Lorelei?"

She laughed and ran a hand over her face. "That didn't make much sense, did it? But it's not alcohol. I'm more tired than anything else. I didn't get much sleep last night."

"Neither did I, now that you mention it."

"Can I ask you something?"

"Sure."

"I know why you're here, but I want to know why you're here instead of at Julie Hebert's. Or Jess Reynald's, for that matter."

"You're prettier, for one thing."

She frowned at him. "Honestly, now."

He'd had another flippant answer, but at that qualifier he swallowed it. "Jess and Julie have agendas. I don't like being an item on an agenda. Or a means to an end, either."

"I thought we were clear that Julie was just wanting to use you for sex?"

"If she were just looking for a good time, that would be one thing. But Julie's on the rebound and angry with it. I'm not about to get pulled into that. She'd just be using me to get back at her soon-to-be-ex. Jess's agenda is a bit more complex, but both of them are playing games and I don't play."

"So you assume I don't have an agenda?"

"Oh, you have an agenda, too. Whatever you're out to prove right now by taking over for Vivi." The look that passed over her face told him he'd hit a nerve there and confirmed his suspicions. "I'm obviously not a part of the plan. You wouldn't be so worried about 'everything' otherwise."

"How astute of you." Although it was politely enough said, a barrier dropped between them at that moment. "In fact, you would be—*are,*" she corrected, "a big old monkey wrench in my plans. Which is why this can't be something."

"I respect the fact you're honest enough with your-self—and me—to say that. Of course that also means that you're honest enough to take this for what it is—*without* it becoming something or anything beyond that."

"Wow." She blew out her breath and shook her head. "I'm not sure if I should be flattered or insulted."

"Neither, actually. You asked for honesty."

"And it seems like I got it."

With another deep sigh, Lorelei stood and stretched. Maybe honesty hadn't been the best policy. Maybe he'd read this situation wrong. Of course if he had, and Lorelei had been looking for some other answer, it was probably a good thing he'd found out now, instead of later. It was disappointing, but...

"I'm going to bed." Lorelei picked up the tablet from the swing and grabbed her beer from the table.

Well, he had his answer. "Good night."

Lorelei paused with her hand on the door. "Are you coming?"

# CHAPTER SIX

"LORELEI, HONEY, PLEASE sit up straight. I hate it when you slouch."

Mom hated so many things: slouching, chewing gum, Lorelei's hair in her face, white shoes after Labor Day... Lorelei pushed herself upright and wrapped another pink ribbon around the top of the prize bag she was making for one of her mother's friend's daughter's baby showers. "Sorry, Mom. I'm just a little tired today."

"I'm not surprised. The way you've been kept running between Connor's studio and Vivi's gallery and all of those meetings and things...I've barely seen you all week."

It was true that she'd been busy, and if her mom wanted to assume it was just because Connor and Vivi were out of town that was all for the good. Lorelei saw no need to enlighten her to anything different. Mom did not need to know about her extracurricular activities. That was a little secret she was keeping totally to herself. It was the only thing keeping her sane. Donovan was an excellent stress-reliever—not only physically, but mentally, as well. He made a good sounding board and a sympathetic ear. He was also pretty damn good for her ego, and her ego needed all the boosting it could get these days.

"Sarah Jenson told me about the speech you gave at the

Women's Leadership lunch. I'm sorry I couldn't be there to hear it myself. She said it was very good."

"Thanks. Vivi gave me the theme, but I was pretty pleased with how it turned out."

"Well, I couldn't be prouder. I knew you had it in you. It just took you a little longer to settle in."

Lord, it was like being handed a long-stemmed rose and being expected to smile while the thorns shredded your skin. Lorelei just nodded and unspooled another eighteen inches of pink ribbon. Five more to make and then she could probably escape, while still remaining in her mother's good graces for the help.

"Speaking of…"

Mom started in a casual tone, and Lorelei's antennae twitched. Her mom's casual tone meant the topic was anything but casual.

"I hear that Jack Morgan asked you to dinner."

The connection between Sarah Jenson, the Women's Leadership luncheon and Jack Morgan was as clear as mud, but she'd let it pass. "How'd you hear that?"

"Jack mentioned it to his mother, and Dorothy told me."

Why on earth would Jack tell his mother? "He did, actually."

"And…?"

"And I told him that I was completely booked until Vivi got back into town, but that we'd talk about it then."

"You'll 'talk about it?' Lorelei…"

"Mom, you just said yourself how busy I am. It's not like I turned him down flat or anything. I just want to focus on what I've already got on my plate. There'll be plenty of time for dinners after Vivi gets back and I've had a chance to recuperate."

"Fine. I just wanted you to know that I think it's a wonderful idea. Jack is an excellent catch."

"What does Mrs. Morgan think?" She couldn't keep the sarcasm out of her voice, but her mom didn't call her on it.

"Dorothy's willing to move past all of that now."

"I should hope so. It's been almost ten years." Mrs. Morgan had been president of the St. Katharine's parent-teacher association when Lorelei's freshman class had disagreed with an edict regarding the winter formal. While official blame had never been cast, and nothing had ever been proved, Mrs. Morgan still gave Lorelei that *look* every time she saw her. "It's not like her garden didn't benefit in the long run," Lorelei added quietly. "Manure is an excellent fertilizer."

Her mom frowned and shook her head, effectively changing the subject. "So, when you 'talk about' dinner with Jack, are you going to say yes?"

Damn it. She was losing brownie points now with this conversation. "I don't know, Mom. We'll see."

"Why, honey? What's wrong with Jack?"

"Nothing that I know of." That much was true. Jack was perfect on paper, but while there was nothing *wrong* with him, she was coming up with few reasons why he would be *right.* There was no good way to say that to her mother, though, because she really doubted Mom wanted to hear about tingling or the lack thereof where Jack was concerned. "I mean, I don't really know him all that well."

"And that's what first dates are for."

Mom had stayed out of her love life for the most part, but Vivi's engagement and wedding had her hyperaware at the moment. Maybe it would pass soon.

"I just wish that tacky woman hadn't started that rumor about you in the paper."

"It's not even a rumor, Mom. It was an observation—and it's not false. I *did* hang out in the bar until the wee hours of the morning."

That earned her a frown for her behavior. "But she made it sound tawdry. Which was not the best—"

"Yet I seem to be doing just fine regardless. The rumor didn't stick, and no one has brought it up in over a week." In an attempt to change the subject before Donovan's name actually came up, Lorelei said, "And did you see the write-up in yesterday's paper about the Children's Music Project?"

"Yes, and what a good picture. That purple dress was a good choice. It looked very nice on you."

Donovan had said almost the same thing late last night, when they'd sat in the pool in his courtyard. Only he'd added, "It looked even better on my bedroom floor..." with a grin and a leer. Lorelei kept her eyes on the slippery ribbons, hoping Mom would think she was concentrating on the prize bag and not notice the smirk she was trying to keep in check.

"In fact I'm thinking about looking for something for me in a similar color for your father's retirement dinner. What do you think?"

Since Lorelei had inherited her mother's looks—looking at Mom was the next best thing to a mirror with a portal to the future—any color that worked on her would work on her mother, too. "I think you'd look fabulous."

"Your father and I are going to the Delacroixes' for dinner tonight. You've been invited to join us if you're not busy."

"I don't know, Mom. There's nothing on the schedule for tonight, and I think I should probably leave it that way. Maybe have a quiet night and go to bed early."

"That's a good idea. A night in every now and then is good for your mental health. Take a long, hot bath and curl up with a good book."

"That certainly sounds like a good plan." *Her* plan,

though, was much better: she was picking up Thai food on her way to Donovan's, and while she'd go to bed early it would be not be to sleep, and she certainly wasn't curling up with a book. The bath idea held promise, though…

She tied the last ribbon and fluffed the bow. "Anything else you need, Mom, before I go?"

"Already?"

"I've got some phone calls to make and emails to sort through."

"I almost miss the days when you weren't so busy."

"Ah, but in those days you were after me to do something productive. Now I am."

"And I'm so pleased. Enjoy your night. Will Callie be joining you? A girls' night in?"

Lorelei coughed. "No. Callie is really busy with exams and things." And she was quite thankful for that. It made Lorelei's coming and goings at odd hours less noticeable.

Leaving her mom's with a sigh of relief—and one of exasperation, too—she went straight to the studio on Julia Street. The receptionist was reading a magazine. She wasn't the only one with a lighter workload while Connor was gone. Lorelei sent her home early, saying that she would watch the phones while she worked.

ConMan was normally a hive of activity, with musicians coming in and out of the recording studios while their entourages milled around the reception area and the phones rang off the hook, so the silence and stillness felt eerie.

That was a blessing, though, because she really did have a ton of emails and phone calls to deal with—including another one from Vivi, who wanted an update on how things were going. Vivi just couldn't let go. Instead of the detailed report she knew Vivi wanted, she chuckled and just typed, *All is well. Enjoy your honeymoon.*

The other emails and phone calls were easily dispatched, except for a couple that Connor would have to deal with, but Lorelei still hadn't received a text from Donovan, telling her he was home from today's round of televised punditry. She paid a few bills, did a little busy work around Connor's office, even shopped online for a wedding gift for Vivi since she hadn't found time to get one before.

Still no text from Donovan. It was now an hour past the time he'd said he'd be done, and she didn't know if she should be worried or just plain angry. Where the hell was he? Technically, where he was when he wasn't with her wasn't her business, but they'd made plans, and common courtesy required that Donovan contact her to let her know if the plans had changed. An hour wasn't just "a little late." An hour crossed into "stood up" territory. She called his phone, but it rolled straight to voice mail. She hung up without leaving a message.

*Screw it.* This was just plain rude and she wasn't going to put up with that.

She turned off the lights in the studio offices as she gathered her things, safe in the knowledge that she had every right to be angry and the steam coming out of her ears was completely justifiable.

What didn't make sense was that she felt a little hurt. Shrugging that off, she focused on being mad instead.

She checked her watch in disgust. She'd waited so long to hear from Donovan she'd now have to sit in rush-hour traffic and fume. By the time she was three blocks from home she was really good and mad—and of course that was the moment Donovan finally decided to call.

She was half tempted to ignore his call, but decided she'd rather give him a piece of her mind instead.

Donovan opened with an apology. "So sorry."

"For what?" she asked with as much innocence as she could. She was *not* going to give Donovan the idea that she actually cared one way or the other.

"Did you not hear about the scandal breaking in Baton Rouge today?"

"No, I've been really busy today." That wasn't a lie; she'd accomplished quite a bit.

"I was already in the studio when the news broke, and suddenly every network needed a talking head. It was insane. By the time I could catch my breath my battery was dead—"

She parked, turned off the ignition and climbed out. The sweltering heat hit her like a wall and didn't help her mood any. "Sounds like you were quite busy."

"I am sorry, though. I saw you called, but—"

The lame apologies were not going to work. "Your battery was dead. I know."

"Well, I'm finally done and I'm starving. You ready?"

"Sorry, Donovan." She tried to inject just the right note of insincere disappointment into her voice. "When I didn't hear from you I made other plans for tonight."

"I see." The words were clipped.

Where did he get off, acting like this? *She* was the one who had the right to be annoyed about this. She didn't need this kind of crap from him. "Good." She opened the door and stepped into the cool air of her house.

There was a brief silence before Donovan sighed. "You're mad at me."

There was no reason to lie. "Yeah."

"I apologized."

"And I appreciate that. Doesn't change things, though. It's simply good manners to call when you're going to be late."

"My battery was dead."

"And no one else had a phone? There wasn't a single phone in the entire building? Wow, that changes everything."

"Lorelei…"

"Don't. Look, I'm not your mother, so I'm not asking for an accounting of your time. I just expect a little respect for mine."

"Duly noted."

"Good. Now, I'm going to let you go and get on with my night. Bye, Donovan." Disgusted, she dropped her phone back into her purse and flopped onto the couch.

That hadn't been her best, most mature moment ever— but, damn it, she had the right to expect basic levels of human respect. She wasn't some booty call he got to make when it suited him.

Of course she now felt as if she'd cut off her nose to spite her face. Her stand for principle meant she was now going to spend the evening alone.

Yeah, her pride was a problem. She'd meant to draw a boundary and might have burned the bridge instead. She should have just let it go.

Bath, book, bed. It wouldn't kill her. She'd start with a glass of wine.

Donovan stared at his phone. Had she really just hung up on him? Because he was late and hadn't had time to call? He'd been *working,* for God's sake, not just playing around. Some people had *actual* jobs, *real* responsibilities that took precedence over a social calendar. Did she expect him just to stop in the middle of what he was doing to call her? It wasn't as if he'd blown her off completely; he'd called as soon as he could.

But it seemed that wasn't good enough. Good Lord, Lorelei needed a taste of life outside her little bubble before she got all high-and-mighty about tardiness.

Rush-hour traffic only increased his temper, and by the time he got home his mood was downright foul. He turned on the TV, grabbed a drink and settled in to watch a race, but it bored him pretty quickly. Eyeballing his laptop, he decided he would work a little, but for the first time ever, work didn't hold any appeal, either.

Mainly because deep down he'd rather be doing something else. And the realization that he wanted to do that something else with Lorelei was a bit of a shocker.

*I'm not asking for an accounting of your time. I just expect a little respect for mine.*

*It's simply good manners.*

Lorelei did have a point, he admitted. This was new territory for him. He preferred casual relationships for that exact reason: casual was easier. Lorelei was—or was supposed to be—even *more* casual, but for some reason he couldn't dismiss her words.

Which also meant he couldn't dismiss her anger, and he had to admit it was justified. Which put him in the wrong—a place he wasn't used to being.

Why did it bother him so much?

With a sigh, he reached for the phone and called in a favor.

To his relief, his phone rang forty-five minutes later.

"How on earth did you manage to get flowers delivered at this time of night?"

At least she wasn't mad enough to ignore the delivery. "I know people."

"I know people, too, you know."

"Yes, but *I* know the kind of people who own flower shops and owe me favors."

He heard her snort. "Seems like a waste of a perfectly good favor."

"Not really. I'm pretty sure flowers are the standard opening salvo for making amends."

"Well, they're lovely. But you're still in trouble."

He reminded himself that Lorelei wasn't one to hold a grudge. He just needed to get her past *this*. The fact she was talking to him, even giving him flak over the flowers, was actually a pretty good sign.

"So I'll apologize again. You were right. I was being very rude. I assure you I was raised better than that." When Lorelei stayed silent on her end, he added, "I'm not used to being accountable for my whereabouts to anyone else. At least not since I moved out of my parents' house."

"Well, that's quite a proper apology."

He could hear her giving in. "Nothing's more irritating than a non-apology apology, and I've ripped enough of those apart to make me a hypocrite if I tried it."

"You're assuming I'd fall for a lame non-apology apology?"

"Not at all. I respect you too much for that."

"Really?" She sounded skeptical.

"Of course. We couldn't be friends otherwise."

There was a pause. "Is that what we are? Friends?"

He hadn't really thought about it until now, but it had a nice ring to it. "I'd like to think so."

"I'm good with that, actually. Your apology is accepted."

He couldn't quite name the feeling that settled in his chest. There was relief, but there was something else, too. "So, are you ready for dinner now?"

"Yeah."

He was already reaching for his shoes. "I'll pick you up in about fifteen minutes."

"That's not necessary."

Before he could question that his doorbell rang. "Hang on for a second."

Opening the door, he found Lorelei on his stoop.

She smiled and put her phone back in her purse. "Hey."

He leaned against the doorframe. "So all of that was just to string me along?"

"No. I was willing to accept your apology even before the flowers arrived. I figured I'd save some time."

"So we're good now?"

"Yeah, I think we are."

He stepped back to let her in, and she smiled as she passed. She dropped her bag as he closed the door. "Are you really hungry? Like starving?"

"I can probably hang on for a little while longer."

"Good." Lorelei put her hands on his waist and rose up to her tiptoes until her mouth was just inches from his. "I think we need to kiss and make up first."

"What is up with the male fascination with gadgetry?" Lorelei scowled at his remote control. "This thing has more buttons than the cockpit of the space shuttle."

Donovan was replying to an email from his editor as Lorelei cursed at the remote. He looked up long enough to see her make a face at it and said, "The five buttons at the top are pretty much all you need."

"Then why does it have five-hundred buttons?"

He hit Send and laid the phone on the table. "I said those five at the top were the only ones *you'd* need. *I* know what the other four hundred and ninety-five do."

"Never mind. I've now forgotten what I wanted to watch." She tossed the remote to the other end of the couch. Remnants of Thai delivery food covered the coffee table, and Lorelei was nursing a glass of wine.

All in all it was a very casual, very comfortable, very laid-back evening—not something he was normally accustomed to. That should make the situation *un*comfortable, but for some reason it didn't. Over the last couple of days they'd settled into…well, not a routine, but a zone. An easy, comfortable zone. They spent their days doing their own thing, and their evenings doing something else. But it wasn't just All Sex, All The Time; they'd spent most of tonight on separate laptops, him working on an op-ed piece and her sending emails or something.

"I thought you had a big meeting to prepare for?"

"I do. But it's not like I have to cram for it."

"Why?"

"I'm starting to get the hang of this—finally. Fifty percent of it is just showing up, smiling and listening. That doesn't require much prep on my part. I'm very good at showing up and smiling."

He patted her leg. "It's good that you've found your true talent."

She stuck out her tongue at him. "You know, I've found that no one really likes it when someone just shows up and just starts bloviating endlessly, subjecting everyone to their opinion whether they want to hear it or not."

"I'm paid to bloviate, thank you very much."

She snorted. "Doesn't mean it will win you friends and help you influence people."

"I've got all the friends I need," he countered.

"God, you're cocky."

He just shrugged as Lorelei settled herself into the corner of the couch with her glass of wine and draped her legs over his. She had on jeans and another tank top, and her bare feet rested on his thigh. Her toenails were painted an electric shade of blue.

"Blue?" he asked.

She wiggled her toes in response. "I like it."

"It's just a little unexpected."

She shot him a grin. "I'm a rebel, don't you know?"

"With those toes? Of course you are. Everyone better watch out."

"Hey, I quietly rebel in my own way." The grin turned conspiratorial. "It's easier to look like I'm playing by the rules when I know that secretly I'm really not. It keeps me sane."

The differences between the new-and-improved public Lorelei LaBlanc and the private woman on his couch were getting starker each day. "I knew you hadn't turned over a completely new leaf."

"I'm just picking my battles more carefully these days."

"Why?"

She shrugged. "Everyone has to grow up sometime."

"I'm not seeing the connection."

She thought for a moment and sighed. "Have you never gotten tired of fighting something and decided it was easier to give in?"

It seemed he'd spent years not giving in. Not personally, not professionally. He wouldn't be here now if he had. Fighting the odds and succeeding was his heritage; his family tree consisted of sharecroppers and madams in Storyville, and now they were one of the wealthiest families in New Orleans. Backing down wasn't an option. "Not if the battle is worth it."

"And that's why I'm choosier with my battles these days. Some things will never change, so if I can't beat them I might as well join them."

"Such a cynical attitude from one so young."

Lorelei lifted her chin. "It's working, though. After my speech at that Women's Leadership luncheon, one of the Mayor's aides asked me to serve on a new task force."

"What kind of task force?"

"Honestly, I'm not sure. Something with schools, maybe?"

"And you agreed without knowing for sure?"

She nodded. "I was just so pleased she'd asked, yeah."

"My sister told me you gave a great speech. Obviously she wasn't the only one who thought that."

Lorelei pulled her legs in towards her chest and leaned forward. "I didn't know you had a sister."

"Caroline. And two brothers. David and Matt."

"Why didn't I know that?" Her eyebrows pulled together as if she was confused. "Did they go to St. Katharine's?"

"No. I'm the youngest by several years, so even if they had you probably wouldn't have known them." He was going to leave it there, but something had him saying, "Back then my parents couldn't afford the tuition for fancy prep schools. I was only at St. Katharine's because of a partial scholarship."

Understanding crossed her face. "Things changed quickly for you, though?"

"That they did." That was when he'd learned that being poor was far more acceptable than suddenly coming into money. The poor were treated with pity, but the nouveau riche were treated with suspicion and scorn. It had been a rude awakening.

Lorelei nodded. "I remember."

"Really?"

"Of course. Everyone was talking about it."

He'd known, of course, that people had talked—not to him, of course, because that wasn't the way it was done— but he didn't like being reminded of it.

"Didn't your father endow something shortly after that?"

He nodded. "A scholarship fund for other students." It had been too late for Donovan's siblings to benefit scholastically from their new wealth, and his folks had always regretted that fact. "Actually, we have scholarship funds in place at all the area private schools."

"Need or merit?"

"Both."

She smiled approvingly. "That's really great."

"You sound surprised."

"Not surprised," she corrected. "Pleased. People often forget to give back."

"Listen to you. Two weeks as the mini-Vivi and you know all the right things to say."

A frown crossed her face.

"What?"

"I'm not a mini-Vivi, and I don't want to be."

He hadn't meant it as an insult, but he'd hit a nerve nonetheless. "Isn't that what you're doing?"

"No. I'm just taking advantage of Vivi being out of the country. I score higher when she's not around for comparison."

"You sound bitter."

"I'm not."

Disbelief must have shown on his face, because Lorelei became emphatic.

"I'm *not.* Vivi is amazing, and I truly respect and admire her. It's just that she's set the bar so darn high it's impossible for anyone to measure up when she's around."

So many things made sense now. "And that's what you're trying to do?"

"It's what I *am* doing," she said, sitting up straighter. A note of pride entered her voice. "And it's working. I filled in for Vivi at the Women's Leadership luncheon, but it was *my* speech. *I* got offered the place on the task force. I don't think they offered it only because Vivi wasn't available. It's just that everyone in this town is so accustomed to going straight to Vivi that they don't think about asking someone else. Someone else who might be able to do just as good a job. Maybe even a *better* job because her time isn't as parceled out already."

She had a point, but… "That's what you want? To end up like Vivi eventually?"

"You say that like it's a bad thing," she said with a laugh.

"It's not the best."

The laugh died and the smile disappeared. "Vivi is loved and respected by everybody." Her hackles were up in defense of her sister.

"Nothing against your sister—you know I think she's great—but this city is doing its very best to suck her dry. Everyone loves a workhorse because they don't want to be the one doing the work, and everyone respects those who serve others. It's like nuns."

She'd been nodding in agreement until that last sentence. "Nuns?"

"You respect nuns, right?"

"Of course. Who doesn't?"

"Care to join a convent?"

Lorelei choked on her wine and coughed hard.

"I'll take that as a no. But if you're after respectability you should probably consider it. It might be easier for you in the long run."

She leaned back against the arm of the couch in a provocative pose. "Do you think I'm nun material?"

He let his eyes roam slowly over her. "No."

Lorelei returned the appraisal. "Good."

"But as far as I can tell there's very little you can actually do to change people's minds about you."

The femme fatale disappeared as Lorelei huffed in exasperation. "I disagree. You only have to prove them wrong."

"Oh, because that *always* works."

"*Now* who sounds bitter?" she challenged.

"Resigned, not bitter. There's a difference."

"Not really. I will concede that it's hard to do—"

"Exactly—"

"*But,*" she continued, talking over him, "it's not impossible. Case in point—I thought you were a conceited, blow-hard jerk."

He liked sparring with her. "And you still do."

"Because it's mostly true," she countered.

"I am not a blow-hard. I'm a respected pundit and journalist."

"Whatever." She waved a hand. "But since that's what you show the world, what do you expect? I speak from personal experience here. Act like a flaky rebel—be treated like a flaky rebel. It's hard to live down a reputation, but it's not impossible."

"Um…hate to break it to you, but your reputation is 'spoiled brat with a wild streak,' not 'flaky rebel.'"

Her jaw dropped. "Not true."

"True."

A snort escaped before she caught herself and re-schooled her face into a picture of dismay. "Then I'm screwed, because that's actually the truth."

"You don't say?"

"I might actually have to join a convent if I want to counter *that* label."

"That would be a shame. A waste of talent."

Lorelei sat up, swung a leg over his, and then settled into his lap. "Jerk."

"Brat."

Her bottom lip stuck out in a pout. "I thought we were friends."

"We are."

"Wow. I'd hate to see how you treat your enemies, then."

"I call 'em as I see 'em."

Lorelei grabbed her shirt and pulled it over her head. Then her hands moved to the clasp of her bra and she shrugged it off her shoulders.

His hands were already moving to her waist. "And that's just beautiful."

Lorelei purred as his fingers slid over her ribs to the soft curve of her breast. Then she was pushing the buttons of his shirt through their holes. "I may be a brat, but I do have good manners. Thank you for dinner. And thanks in advance for the hot sex."

"The sex is my pleasure. The dinner was nothing."

"I know." A sexy smile tugged at her lips as she spread the two halves of his shirt open and slid her palms over his chest with a hum of appreciation. She leaned closer, her nipples barely brushing against his skin. "That's why I appreciate it."

Later, though, as Lorelei sprawled on top of him with a groan, her heartbeat thundering against his chest, Donovan wondered if it might have been something after all.

# CHAPTER SEVEN

"LORELEI, COULD YOU BRING the rolls through?"

"Sure." She added a winking smiley face to Donovan's text and hit Send, then put the phone back in her purse and grabbed the bread basket. She took her seat in the same place she'd sat at for every meal at home for the last twenty-five years as Mom and Dad took their places. One day she was going to sit in Vivi's chair, just to see what the view was like from there. Maybe she'd even rearrange the furniture.

*Oh, she really was a rebel.* She could almost hear Donovan laughing now. She wiggled her toes inside her shoes. She'd run by the salon this morning and had them painted bright green. Then she'd had a small skull painted onto each big toe. She'd only be able to keep the design for a little while; she was planning on wearing her silver sandals to her dad's party, and green toes with skulls would *not* go over well. She'd been tempted to send Donovan a picture, but she'd rather see the look on Donovan's face when he saw them.

*Which would probably not be tonight.* They both had family things and lives, and they couldn't be—*shouldn't* be—in each other's pockets all the time. She tamped down the disappointment brought on by simple horniness. She would survive.

"It looks delicious, Mom." A tiny sniff set her stomach growling. Plump, perfect shrimp...the aroma of garlic and lemon wafting out of a sea of butter... Suspicion set in. Mom's scampi was her favorite, but it had fallen victim to the dietary restrictions of Dad's cardiologist. Butter—much less oceans of melted *real* butter—hadn't been in their diets for over a year now. "Is there something I should know?"

Her mother looked surprised. "What do you mean?"

"You don't eat butter anymore, so I can't help but wonder what I'm being buttered up for. You're not getting a divorce, are you?"

Dad laughed. "Of course not."

"I was just in the mood, and you being here was a perfect excuse for cheating just a little," Mom added.

"Good. I was worried there for a minute." Satisfied, she stabbed a shrimp. *Fantastic.*

"Although there *is* something we'd like to ask you. Well, something your father would like to ask you."

Dad put down his fork. Lorelei braced herself. Favorite food coupled with a serious "we'd like to ask you" didn't bode well. She braced herself before realizing that if it were really bad they'd wait until Vivi was home and tell them both at the same time. That knowledge relaxed her a small bit. "Okay. Ask away."

"My secretary wants to finalize the agenda for my retirement party—all the little details."

Dad was talking, but Mom was grinning. *Surreal.*

"I've talked Jim Nelson out of a full-fledged roast, but there will be speeches."

"Of course there will be. You've run that place for almost forty years. The speeches will probably be pleas for you not to go."

"In the interests of time," Mom interjected, "we've decided to put a limit on the number of toasts made. Your dad has narrowed the list of possibles."

"I know you'll have to let Mr. Nelson speak, but keep the microphone away from Mr. Delacroix. He rambles."

Dad nodded. "We know, Lorelei. But I've also decided I'd like a personal touch. I wanted to ask you if you'd be willing."

"To do what?"

They both laughed, adding to her confusion. Mom finally reached across the table to pat her hand.

"To make a toast for your father, darling."

She waited for the punchline. Her parents just looked at her expectantly. "Me? *Seriously?*"

"You sound surprised, dear."

*Because I am completely floored by this.* She gave herself a strong mental shake. "I'd be honored." At her father's smile, a warm, happy glow spread through her chest. "I promise not to roast you. Or ramble. Or get all weepy."

"Vivi said you could be counted on not to weep into the microphone."

"You asked—I mean, you've talked to Vivi?" The warm, happy glow cooled and shrank into a rather painful knot. She hadn't been Dad's first choice. She tried not to let that bother her. Much.

"She called this morning to say hi. I think she's getting a little antsy to come home. I asked her if she thought you'd like to do it, and if it would hurt her feelings if we asked you instead of her. I was afraid that you wouldn't want to do it after being 'on' so much recently."

The happy glow came racing back. *This* meant more to her than anything else. Not because she'd been asked and Vivi hadn't—it wasn't sibling rivalry—but because her parents hadn't automatically defaulted to Vivi. She'd just proved her own thesis: it was difficult, but not impossible to change people's minds. *Lorelei—one. Donovan—zip.* Oh, she couldn't wait to rub that in.

"And this is why I get shrimp scampi for dinner?" The second bite tasted even better than the first.

"It's not all about you, darling. Scampi is your dad's favorite, too."

After that dinner proceeded with the usual small talk, but mentally Lorelei was only half there. She was practically wiggling in her seat. The only thing that kept her still was years of *not* wiggling in her seat at dinner. Finally she couldn't stand it anymore and asked to be excused.

In the kitchen, she gave in to her need to do a small happy dance. She only had a minute or two before Mom would wonder why she hadn't returned, but she dug through her purse anyway. She sent a quick text to Donovan: *Can you meet me tonight around ten? Your place? I've got big news!*

She didn't have time to wait for his response, but either he could or he couldn't. She dropped her phone into her purse and went back to the table. Mom and Dad were now discussing the guest list for the party.

Her mother smiled at her a little too broadly and Lorelei braced herself. "I was thinking that you should invite Jack Morgan."

Damn. *Play dumb.* "Is he not on the list already?"

"I meant *you* should invite him. As your escort."

Dumb was not going to work. She switched to vague. "Oh…um… I don't know."

"Why not?"

"This is…" She scrambled for a good reason. "This is a family thing for us and a business thing for everyone else. I'd rather keep the focus on Dad."

"Most people there will have a plus-one. It would probably be less noticeable if you did, too," Mom countered.

"But this is a special night. I won't be able to enjoy myself if there's all that first-date pressure and jitters."

"I would think the jitters would be easier to overcome if the date itself was not the central aspect of the evening. It would take the pressure *off.*"

Oh, she hated it when her mom got all reasonable like that. She felt as if she was caught in a glue trap: good and stuck but with just enough wiggle room to get stuck even worse. Dumb and vague were not going to work; she might as well face facts.

She put her fork down and leveled a look at her mother across the table. "You're not going to let this go, are you?"

Completely unrepentant, Mom shook her head. "Probably not."

"I appreciate the honesty. *But,*" she stressed as her mom started to nod, "I really don't need you setting me up on a date—much less when I know for a fact that you brainstormed this idea with Mrs. Morgan. Neither Jack nor I need a fix-up. Not with other people, and certainly not with each other."

"You said you were just waiting for Vivi to get back to town."

"I said *we*—and by *we* I meant me and Jack, not you and Mrs. Morgan—would *talk* about it after Vivi got home. It wasn't a done deal."

"I just thought this would fit the bill nicely."

Lorelei looked to her father for help, but he gave her a *you're on your own here* shrug and focused his attention closely on his plate.

"Mom, I know that you and Mrs. Mansfield are just tickled pink that Connor and Vivi ended up together after all and made you related by marriage. The whole town knows you would have betrothed them in the cradle if that had been possible. I also know that you and Mrs. Morgan are good friends, too, and you're probably thinking it would be very nice if it happened twice."

Mom didn't deny that. "It's not impossible. You and Jack might be perfect for each other."

"Maybe. But I prefer to make my own dates. Unless you think there's something wrong with me…?" she challenged.

"Of course not, honey. It's just that the pickings are starting to get rather slim."

"*Slim?* Mom, there are over a million people in the greater metro area. At least half of them have to be male. Chances are pretty good *one* of them will suit my needs."

"You know you haven't always been as choosy as you might have been with the men you've dated."

A headache began forming behind her eyes. "Oh, Lord. We're going to go *there?* Really?"

"We don't *have* to."

"Thank goodness." She speared another shrimp.

"But…"

She should have known that Mom wouldn't just drop the topic like that.

"Have you met anyone *else* you like recently?"

The shrimp got stuck in her throat. She had to grab her water glass and wash it down. *"What?"*

"You've hit every cocktail party, fund-raiser and luncheon over the past couple of weeks. I think you've met every eligible male. Maybe one of them was more to your liking."

"I was kind of busy at those events. The atmosphere wasn't exactly right for that kind of socializing." That wasn't entirely true—some people *could* do that kind of socializing at an only semi-social event. But it hadn't crossed her mind. She'd been very focused and very careful. Lord, you'd think her mom would have been *pleased*

to find out she could be über-responsible and above re-
proach. Of course it probably helped that she'd hooked
up with Donovan right before. A memory of Julie Hebert using the guest list as a dating service flashed in her
mind. *Ugh.* The thought that it could have been *her* acting like that...

"That doesn't mean that you couldn't have met someone."

She could put a stop to this very easily. It was very
tempting. But the knowledge of the storm that would land
on her head kept her mouth firmly closed on that topic.
*Gee, thinking before you speak really is a good idea.*

She leveled a look across the table. "I tried to keep it all
very professional. It seems kind of inappropriate to prowl
for men while at an event in a professional capacity." Her
use of the word *inappropriate* was intentional. Mom had
strong stands on what was appropriate and what wasn't.
She laid it on a little thicker, going for Mom's most vulnerable spots. "It never occurred to me that I should be
interviewing men for dates while I was there representing
Connor and the studio. Standing in for Vivi. Representing
the LaBlanc family..."

Mom's lips tightened. "You've made your point, Lorelei."

"Thank you."

"But just think about it for a day or so. That's all I ask."

She didn't have to ask what "it" was. "And if I decide
in a day or so that I don't want to take Jack to the party
as my date?"

"Think about it first. Keep an open mind."

She didn't have to think about it. She couldn't be less
interested in Jack if he grew an extra head and started
rooting for the Falcons over her beloved Saints. She was
happy right now with Donovan: there was no pressure,

no games, no worrying about the future. It was just easy. And fun. She was enjoying herself, enjoying having a friend, and she wanted to continue enjoying it for as long as she could. A little knot formed in her stomach at the idea that it couldn't last indefinitely and she'd have to go back to "appropriate" men her mother approved of who already had their own membership at the Club. But that was at some point in the future, and she'd worry about that once she got there.

It was all she could do to keep her face neutral as her mom finally changed the subject. Mom wanted her to keep an open mind? The openness of her mind wasn't the issue.

A family business usually meant that family dinners turned into board meetings at some point before dessert. Why, Donovan didn't quite know—it wasn't as if his father and brothers didn't see each other every day at the office, where conversations of this sort would be more appropriate. And more productive. There was a reason why small children were not normally welcome at business meals; they tended to lose interest in the conversation and devolve to surreptitiously flinging peas and kicking each other under the table.

Donovan fully admitted he was probably not helping the situation any as he thumb-wrestled with his nephew and simultaneously oversaw the construction of a mashed-potato mountain by his niece at their end of the table. He didn't have much to add to the discussion anyway, and eventually his mom would put a stop to it and insist on a different topic of conversation. So he amused himself with his nieces and nephews for the time being.

As each of his siblings had produced at least two offspring—sometimes three—every family meal bordered on chaos. It was not a place for the faint of heart or those overly concerned with proper etiquette; it was just home and family—something Donovan looked forward to mainly because it came in small doses.

His phone vibrated in his pocket as a text came in, and he pulled it out for a quick peek: *If you're going to quote me, I expect a royalty.*

Lorelei must have read today's column, where he'd addressed how hard it was to squelch rumors once they started and how damaging those rumors could be to the reputations of not only the public figures in question, but also the integrity of their legislation and legacy.

Lorelei *had* inspired the central idea: that it was difficult but not impossible to reshape people's thinking. All you had to do was prove them wrong, but that was the hard part.

*Not a quote. A paraphrase. And fair use=no cash.*

"Donovan's texting at the table!"

"You're supposed to be setting an example, Donovan," his mother scolded.

"Sorry, Mom." He hit Send as he put the phone back in his pocket. Then he turned to his niece and said quietly, "It's not wise to rat out an uncle who is bigger than you. *Especially* when he knows exactly how the whole 'The Paint, The Puppy and The Living Room Carpet' debacle actually went down."

Sarah, who was only seven but nobody's fool, nodded soberly. "Sorry." Eyes wide, she turned to her mother, Matt's wife Tara, and whispered, "Can I be excused now?"

"Yes, go." Tara sighed. "In fact, why don't you all go play now?"

Children bolted from the table, and the noise level in the room dropped several decibels.

Tara moved to a now-empty chair next to him and leaned back with a smile. "Ah, that's much better. By the way, she's seven. She probably doesn't know the meaning of the word *debacle*."

"She got my point, though."

"And that threat will only work until she gets old enough to figure out that I also know how it *actually* happened." Tara took a sip of her water, then grinned at him in a way that put him instantly on alert. "Speaking of things that I know—"

"That you *think* you know," he corrected. There was no way she knew the true origin of that paint.

"I was with some friends at that coffee house down from your place the other night. As we were leaving, I saw you letting a woman into your house. Normally I'd assume it was a new assistant, or the cleaning lady or something, but it was pretty late for that. And you seemed to greet her rather *un*professionally."

The rest of the St. James bloodline at the other end of the table was in animated discussion about the cost-effectiveness of longer internet spots, so there was no escape there. *Non-committal is always a safe bet.* "Hmm."

Tara leaned forward and braced her arms on the table. "Oh, come on. Who is she? It was dark, so I couldn't see her face."

"A friend."

"And does this friend have a name?"

"Of course."

"Do you *know* it?" she challenged.

"First, middle *and* last."

That earned him a frown. "But you don't want to tell me any of them?"

"Not really, no."

Tara sat back with a huff. "Anyone ever tell you that you can be a jerk sometimes?"

He wanted to laugh, but kept it in. "Now that you mention it, yes." *And a conceited blow-hard, too.*

"Are you ashamed to be seen with her or something?"

"Not at all. I just prefer keeping this private for the moment."

Tara shot a look down the table. "I won't tell your mother, if that's what you're worried about."

"Mom is quite happy with the grandchildren she has at the moment. She's not on my back to settle down and procreate anytime soon."

*"Wow..."* Tara managed to stretch the word into four syllables.

"What?"

"Are you implying that this is the type of woman that you'd *want* to settle down and procreate with?"

*Good Lord.* "I'm not implying anything. *You* are jumping way ahead."

"Well, you're not giving me much to go on. I *have* to make jumps."

"I have made a friend whose company I enjoy. She seems to enjoy mine. That's all."

Tara's eyes narrowed suspiciously. "You're not *paying* for her time and companionship, are you?"

He laughed. Lorelei would *not* like to hear she'd been accused of prostitution. "She's not a call girl, Tara. She's a friend."

"Sorry. It had to be asked."

"Why?"

"Because you normally don't have female friends. You have dates. *Rendezvous.* Affairs. Maybe the occasional fling. But a 'friend?' I'm not buying that. Anyway, if she really were *just* a friend you wouldn't be acting like this."

Tara was right—or at least partially right. How had Matt ended up with a woman that astute? "Just give me some time. See how it shapes up. If it's nothing, then there's no reason to bring anyone else into it." Tara did not look satisfied, so he threw out a promise to make her happy. "I promise that if the situation changes, you'll be one of the very first to know."

"You could just bring her to dinner soon so we can all meet her. Just as a friend. No pressure." At his look, she added primly, "Friends very often meet each other's families, you know. And a meal is quite a friendly thing."

*That might not go over as well as one would hope.* "I don't think Lorelei's quite ready for the full-frontal impact of a St. James family dinner."

"*Lorelei,* huh?" Tara smiled. "That's a pretty name." *Damn.*

"It's unusual, too. You don't hear it all that often. I did go to school with a Lorelei years ago... Wait... No, she was a Lora Lee. Of course there's Lorelei LaBlanc—"

"More wine?" he interrupted.

Tara waved the offer away. "I'm good, thanks. I've never met her—Lorelei LaBlanc, that is—but I talked to her on the phone sometime back in the spring, when my company submitted a proposal to do the refurb on Connor Mansfield's new studio. Really nice person. But you've met her, of course. At the wed—" Tara stopped suddenly and her eyes grew wide. *"Oh..."* Once again one small word was stretched out into multiple syllables.

"What?"

Tara leaned in and dropped her voice. "Lorelei LaBlanc was the woman I saw at your house, wasn't it? I couldn't see her face, but size and hair and such all match up."

He didn't want to flat-out lie with a denial, but distraction and distortion might work. "I don't—"

"Oh. My. *God.* That reporter was right. We just all kind of laughed it off, even after she came by the offices, but..."

Thankfully no one else at the table had keyed in on their conversation yet. "Please let it go."

Tara dropped her voice to a whisper. "How long has this been going on?"

"Really, now. Do I have to beg?"

Her lips twitched. "Now that you mention it, that might be fun to watch. No wonder you're trying to keep it quiet. Her mother must be having a cow."

That would be the kindest of responses. "I don't think her family is any more aware of me than mine is—or *was* and hopefully will *continue* to be—of her."

"People are bound to find out, you know. Why the big secret?"

"Because it's nobody's business."

Tara nodded. "Fine. My lips are sealed. You like her, though, don't you?"

"I told you, she's a friend."

He was not doing a good job of selling Tara on the "friend" point. She wasn't even trying to hold back her grin. "Okay. Whatever. I just never pegged you as a social climber." She reached for her glass. "Planning on world domination now?"

He couldn't make the jump. "Excuse me?"

"I think it's called 'marrying well.' The LaBlancs are one of the oldest families in New Orleans. They have serious clout. You have money." Tara's son Jacob had toddled back into the room and skirted the table to his mother. Without even pausing, she settled him into her lap. "And you're famous already. You have some influence. But if you marry a LaBlanc you'll be simply unstoppable."

"First, I had no idea you were so Machiavellian—but you forget that I'm persona non grata in those circles, money or not."

"Why is that?"

"Between my lack of pedigree and the fact I brought down not one but two of the most powerful families in New Orleans, I'd think you'd see the problem."

Tara just waved that away. "One is not your fault and has no bearing on the kind of man you are and the other was no less than they deserved."

"Regardless, you've jumped way ahead again."

Tara grinned. "But it got you thinking, didn't it?" Tara turned to the small child tugging at her arm. "What, sweetheart?"

He whispered something behind a small, chubby hand and Tara nodded. "Excuse me." She scooped him up and sat him on her hip as she went into the next room.

Small children were quite useful as interruptions of conversations, and Donovan exhaled with relief at the reprieve. Pity Jacob hadn't had better timing. He could have saved Donovan a few uncomfortable moments.

*So much for being discreet.* If his sister-in-law had seen Lorelei at his house, how many other people had, too? Lorelei wasn't exactly low-profile. Half the people in the city could probably recognize her on sight; Lorelei made the papers because she was always where the cameras were. Plus, Lorelei had been in the papers a lot in the last six months or so: Vivi had become paparazzi bait the moment she'd hooked up with Connor, and Lorelei was often where they were—the Pippa to Vivi's Kate.

Honestly, he'd kind of forgotten why they were being so discreet. The one-night stand had been extended into a longer thing, but they'd stayed with the general premise of keeping their one-night stand under the radar. But why? They were both adults. It wasn't as if they had anything to hide. The local papers might have a bit of fun with another local celebrity-ish couple, but neither he nor Lorelei were nearly as high-profile as Connor and Vivi—or any of the dozen other celebrities that called New Orleans home.

His phone vibrated again. Lorelei had finally texted him back: *Who said I wanted cash? We can work it out in trade. ;-)*

That caused him to laugh. The status quo was serving him—and Lorelei, too—quite nicely at the moment. Lorelei was making the most of her time out of Vivi's shadow. She didn't need gossip or speculation on her love life becoming *another* shadow.

And him? He had no real plans for world domination—at least not plans that required Lorelei's influence for him to achieve them. He was climbing that hill quite nicely on his own. And he rather liked it that way.

Lorelei seemed okay with that, too.

Why mess with something that was working just fine?

As a kid he'd seen the LaBlanc family and others like them—the Morgans, the Mansfields and the Allisons—as golden and lucky. He'd thought that money was the only key needed for entry into that enclave, but he'd been proven wrong very quickly. His family's money had taken him from zero to hero overnight—but it hadn't brought membership into that particular circle of society. Eventually he'd convinced himself that it didn't matter and that he didn't want it. Tara's words had brought the remembrance of that feeling back.

But things were different now. He wasn't some kid just realizing his place on the food chain for the first time. He didn't care what the Morgans, the Mansfields, the Allisons or the LaBlancs thought about him. Well, except for one LaBlanc.

Lorelei was different. This situation was different. He didn't know why or how, but it was. And while it probably would never be more than just this, he was fine with that.

Tara kept giving him knowing looks the rest of the evening, and he'd swear at one point his other sister-in-law, Mary, was giving him one, too. He hoped it was paranoia and not that Tara was sharing her new-found information.

His phone vibrated again.

*Can you meet me tonight around ten? Your place? I've got big news!*

When Lorelei had left last night she'd said she probably wouldn't be able to see him tonight as she needed to put in some quality time with her parents. Whatever this big news was, she was obviously excited about it. He glanced at the time and texted her back that he would.

When Matt asked if he wanted to do a brotherly night out to a local club where a friend of theirs was playing, Donovan claimed he had an early meeting the next day. He caught Tara's smirk out of the corner of his eye.

Tara was probably right. If he and Lorelei kept this up eventually someone would see them. It would get out.

And Lorelei's mother would not be the only person in New Orleans to have a cow when *that* happened.

Lorelei navigated the tiny alley behind Donovan's house and pulled in behind his car. She was late, but she just hadn't been able to escape her mother gracefully, having to finally resort to a claim of a headache in order to get out of there. She must be getting better at lying, though, because her mother hadn't batted an eyelash about it.

She rang the bell, but instead of releasing the lock, Donovan spoke over the intercom. "Can I help you?"

"It's me."

"You're late, you know."

*Cheeky thing.* "If you check your phone," she said carefully, "you'll see that I at least sent you a text letting you know."

A second later the lock on the gate was released. Donovan was waiting for her by the French doors.

"You big jerk."

"Couldn't resist."

Lorelei shook her head. He was just too cute to stay peevish at, and she was just a sucker. When he stepped back to let her in she noticed that there was a champagne bucket and two glasses on the coffee table. "Wow."

"Well, you said it was big news. I figured we might need it."

"You're so sweet."

"I thought I was a big jerk?"

"You're that, too."

Donovan popped the cork and poured two glasses. "Whatever it is, congratulations," he toasted. After she drank, he motioned her to the couch. "So, what's the big news?"

"You know my dad is retiring, right?" She waited for him to nod. "His partners and some other folks he's done business with over the years are throwing him this huge retirement bash. They've been working on the plans for like a month. So, tonight Mom and Dad tell me that they need to get the agenda finalized and, long story short, Dad asks me to make a toast."

"That's great. Congratulations."

Her grin felt as if it was about to split her face. "Thanks. I mean, I've had so many great things happen recently—new opportunities opening up and all—but this… This is actually probably the best thing of all. There are so many people that he could have asked, but he asked *me*. Me! Can you believe that?"

"Actually, I can. I've seen you in action, remember?"

Donovan seemed totally sincere, and that meant more to her than she'd expected.

"I don't know why you're *so* surprised, though. You made a toast at the wedding."

"Yes, but that was Vivi's choice. *I* was under very strict supervision by my mother the whole time." She rolled her eyes at the memory. "Not only did Mom oversee the writing of it, but I'd been threatened to within an inch of my life if I mucked it up. That toast was the first sip of alcohol that crossed my lips that night."

He waggled his eyebrows at her. "You certainly made up for it later."

"Very funny."

"Is your mom going to supervise this one, as well?"

"Believe it or not, I don't think so. It seems I've proven myself now and don't need maternal speechwriting tips anymore."

"And you haven't been threatened within an inch of your life either, I take it?"

"Amazingly, no. Six months of good behavior was all it took."

"Six months? I thought this was all just while Vivi was out of town."

"God, no." She sighed. "*That* would have been *so* much easier. But as you quoted me—"

"Paraphrased you," he corrected.

She raised an eyebrow but said nothing. "It's not been an easy task to get to this point. I had to lay the groundwork first. Go low-profile, behave myself, show proper atonement for the sins of my youth. If I hadn't done that, then I wouldn't have been able to 'prove myself' these past few weeks."

"I had no idea you'd put so much thought into this plan." Understanding crossed his face. "No wonder you were so worried about that mention in the paper. Or getting caught leaving my hotel room."

"Exactly."

He lifted his glass again. "Well, it seems you formed a worthy plan and that it worked out exactly like you hoped. Cheers."

"I'll drink to that."

Donovan refilled her glass. "Now that you've accomplished those parts of the plan, what's next?"

"Do I have plans for world domination, you mean? Plans to stage a coup and steal Vivi's place as the saint of New Orleans?" She leaned back against the cushions and got comfortable.

"Something like that."

She shook her head. "I don't want Vivi's life. I now know that for a fact. All that love comes with a price tag I'm not willing to pay. I'll never be a pillar of society, but that's not really me anyway."

He sat at the other end. "I agree."

"I'm not sure that's a compliment."

"I'd be very disappointed to see you end up exactly like your mother."

Lorelei pushed herself up. "Hey, careful now…"

"It's not an insult against your mother, so there's no need to get your back up."

Temporarily mollified, she let him continue.

"I just don't see you as the matron and patron of social and civic clubs who lunches more than anything else."

That gave her pause. "You know, I don't see me there either—although I think my mother is already ordering me white gloves and filling out my paperwork for junior membership in the Ladies' Auxiliary Guild as we speak. I just have to find the happy medium before it gets out of hand."

Donovan looked surprised. "Do you not *want* to be in the Ladies' Auxiliary Guild?

"Not really."

"Isn't that some kind of status symbol, though?"

"Yes, but they don't *really* do anything other than lunch. They used to, but it's kind of lost its focus. I think I'd rather spend my time a bit more productively." She hadn't really thought it through before, so the realization was new to her, too. "There are so many worthy causes where I could really make a difference. I need to use my time effectively to make the most impact and do the most good." The look on Donovan's face had her laughing. "Yes, I know. It's a bit surprising to me, too. Look at me—I'm growing as a person. I'm no Vivi, but I'm rather liking this Lorelei."

"I rather like Lorelei, too," he said with a quiet laugh.

Her heart flopped over in her chest at his words, and the air felt really heavy all of a sudden. The silence was deafening as *something* shifted between them.

Then Donovan cleared his throat. "Uh…more champagne?"

"Yes! Please." She still had almost half a glass, and she stuck it out so fast the contents sloshed over the rim. Donovan reached for her hand and slowly licked the drops of liquid away. The feel of his tongue on her skin brought a different and far more familiar tension into the air, and Lorelei grabbed the shift in mood gratefully. Donovan looked up and that sexy grin sent little tingles all over her skin in anticipation.

"This gives me ideas."

"I think I'm quite interested in these ideas."

With a leer, Donovan pulled her to her feet and grabbed the champagne bucket off the table. She followed him quickly up the stairs, glad to leave whatever that disturbing moment was behind.

# CHAPTER EIGHT

ON DAYS LIKE TODAY even the locals were allowed to complain about the weather. The heat hit Lorelei like a wall the minute she stepped onto her porch, and the humidity was so high she could almost see the moisture in the air.

Today was the kind of day that should be spent sitting very still with a cold drink, but of course today was the day she had a million things to do. Post office, bank, drop off paychecks at the studio and the art gallery…all the minutiae of her life. Thankfully Vivi would be home the day after tomorrow and would take back her own errands and minutiae.

A frantic, panicked search for her iPad hadn't exactly gotten her day off to a great start, but she'd called Donovan—waking him up—and he'd found it under the couch, where it had slid out of her bag. Although he'd grumbled about it, he had agreed to meet her to return it.

After listening to the weather report this morning she'd skipped make-up altogether—it wouldn't have stayed on anyway—and pulled her hair up into a clip off her neck. She was wearing as little clothing as decency and good taste allowed, but sweat still rolled down her spine as she crossed one errand after the other off her list. Now she was running a little late to meet Donovan, but *actually* running was out of the question. Not in this heat. She had too much to do today to take time out for heatstroke.

Red-faced, sunburned, equally sweaty tourists meandered in the streets, going into shops primarily for the air-conditioning. Lorelei resisted that urge, since she only had two blocks to go, but she opened the door to the little coffee shop on Magazine Street gratefully and stood there for a moment enjoying the cool air.

Donovan was at a table over in the corner, reading something on his phone. He, too, was dressed in deference to the weather, and Lorelei fought back a grin. He looked much younger and not at all serious and punditlike in a grey T-shirt, khaki shorts and running shoes. *Wow, great calves.* How had she not noticed that before?

He was unshaven, hair slightly mussed, managing to hit that sweet spot between adorable and yummy perfectly. He looked up as she approached, and his smile tipped the scale in favor of yummy.

"Hey," he said, putting away his phone. "You look…" his lips twitched "…really hot."

"Hush. It's the armpit of hell out there." She dropped her bag on the chair and caught the server's eye.

"Yes, it is. Tell me again why I had to come out in it?"

"Because I still have to go to Vivi's to water the plants and drop off paychecks at the studio and then go back out to Mom's. I wasn't about to go all the way to your place, too." When the server came around, she ordered a large iced tea and got settled into the seat across from Donovan.

"Aw, so you just wanted to see me? How sweet."

He said it teasingly, but it hit a chord inside her. She *did* miss seeing him. But, looking at the smirk on his face, she knew she'd be able to ice skate on the sidewalk out front before she'd admit it. "I'm organized. This is a natural breaking point to my errands today."

"Why do you have to go back out to your parents'?" His eyebrows drew together in concern. "Is everything okay?"

The show of concern touched her. "Just party stuff. That's why I need my iPad."

He slid it across the table with a grin. "Maybe you're not so organized after all."

"Well, if you hadn't distracted me last night I might not have—"

"Lorelei?"

She turned, looking for the voice, and froze. *Awkward.* "Cynthia. Wow, this is a surprise." She finally got herself moving to stand and accept Cynthia's hug. "I haven't seen you in ages." When Cynthia's father had gone to jail, most of their assets had been seized, and the DuBois family had been forced to move to Chalmette. Shamed, they'd all but disappeared.

Cynthia's voice was cold and stilted. "This *is* a surprise." She looked pointedly at Donovan. "Quite a big one."

Oh, yeah, *really* awkward. *What to do?* Good manners said one thing; common sense said something else entirely. But since Cynthia didn't seem willing just to move on and let this pass without comment, she fell back on good manners to try to control it. "Cyn, I don't know if you've ever actually *met* Donovan St. James before?"

"No, I haven't." Each excruciatingly polite word could cut glass. Lorelei was giving Cynthia the opportunity to walk away, but Cynthia wasn't taking it. "Please do introduce us."

Donovan shot her a questioning look as he stood, obviously aware that there was something going on, but still acting as if this would be a somewhat normal introduction. "Awkward" quickly morphed into "downright uncomfortable."

"Donovan, this is Cynthia DuBois." Donovan didn't seem to make the connection, but DuBois was a common enough name. "Lincoln DuBois's daughter," she clarified.

The name dropped like a gauntlet. Donovan finally twigged to the problem and the hand he'd begun to extend fell back to his side. "I see. I'd say nice to meet you, but I, too, will go with this is a surprise."

Cynthia shot Donovan a look of pure hate, then dismissed him rudely, pulling Lorelei a few feet away and turning her back on him completely. "What the sweet hell are you doing with Donovan St. James?"

"Well...I..."

"Good God, Lorelei. Have you lost your mind?"

"No, I—"

Cynthia wasn't waiting for explanations. Her head might explode if she didn't calm down. "After what he *did,* you and he are—?"

Oh, God, this was going to be ugly. Lorelei lowered her voice in the hope Cynthia would do the same. "Cyn, calm down."

"I will *not* calm down. He destroyed my family, my *life.*"

Even Lorelei knew that Lincoln DuBois and his cronies were completely responsible for their own destruction; the fallout on their families was also their own fault. But she understood the feelings of Cynthia and the others, too. And, if she was honest with herself, a few weeks ago she'd *shared* them.

"Do your parents know about this?"

Ice slid down her spine. "What?"

"That you're all chummy with him? Are you dating him or something?"

Cynthia was practically shouting, and they now had the attention of everyone in the shop. Thankfully it wasn't that many people, but an audience only made this worse. "Cyn, it's not worth the outrage."

"Then what are you doing, exactly?"

"Donovan is…" She couldn't bring herself to look in his direction as she searched for an excuse. "Donovan is a major donor to one of Connor's projects. I'm Connor's assistant, remember?"

"So this is a business meeting?"

"Yes, business." Lorelei was surprised at how easily the lie came off her tongue. Self-preservation had obviously improved her acting ability.

Her eyes narrowed. "Here? Dressed like *that?*"

Cynthia had at least one good point. Not only was she not dressed particularly businesslike—even for the lackadaisical dress code of the music business—the powerful air-conditioning had cooled her enough that her nipples were now showing through her shirt. She certainly didn't look very professional.

"Cyn—"

"Well, don't let me interrupt your 'meeting.' Just make sure you get as much money out of him as you can. Since he made quite a bit of it from destroying my family, consider it a donation from me, as well. At least his ill-gotten gains will serve some good."

Cynthia needed a reality check, but this was neither the time nor the place. Her family's money was the ill-gotten gains; Donovan had just been the one to call them on it.

Their server, who must have somehow missed hearing Cynthia's tirade, returned with Lorelei's drink and set it on the table. Then she turned to Cynthia and asked innocently, "Will you be joining them?"

Cynthia's laugh was sharp and brittle. "Not even if you paid me."

"Oh…um…okay, then." The server looked around uncomfortably, and Lorelei mentally doubled the poor girl's tip. Finally she asked, "Well, can I get you anything?"

"No, I'm leaving."

The server scurried away, relief written on her face, and Cynthia turned back to Lorelei, anger and disappointment etched equally across her face.

"Lorelei, I just don't know what to say."

Desperate to smooth things, Lorelei said the first thing that came to mind. "Call me soon, okay? We'll go to lunch."

Cynthia gave her the tiniest of nods. Then, turning to Donovan, Cynthia twisted her mouth into a snarl. "You can just go to hell." On that note, she picked up Lorelei's tea and dumped it into Donovan's lap. Then she stormed out.

"Oh, my God." Lorelei called over to the server to bring towels as Donovan picked the ice cubes out of his lap. "Sorry about that."

Donovan waved away the apology. "I guess I should be glad you ordered iced tea and not hot. I just hope it wasn't sweet tea. I'd hate to be wet *and* sticky."

Relieved Donovan wasn't going to be angry, Lorelei took the towels from the server—whose tip had just been quadrupled—and tried to help clean up. "I think that's what they call a classic case of misplaced anger."

"I've heard worse." He held up a hand. "I've got this, Lorelei." After using the towels to mop up the worst of it, Donovan left cash on the table and headed toward the door. Lorelei added another twenty to the pile as an apology to the server and followed him.

"Did you drive?" When he shook his head, she said, "Neither did I. It's a long walk in wet pants, though. Want to see if we can find a cab?"

"It's fine. In a few minutes I'm sure the wet fabric will feel refreshing in this heat. I'll talk to you later."

"Wait, I'll go with you."

Donovan might not be angry, per se, but he certainly wasn't finding this funny, either. "Not necessary. Go finish your errands."

Something was *very* wrong. "Okay. I'll see you tonight?"

Donovan merely nodded.

She watched him leave. That had not gone well. She never would have thought Cynthia DuBois the type to make a big public scene like that. Obviously the last few years had changed her and made her bitter.

Lorelei was feeling a little bitter herself. In her anger at Donovan, Cynthia had ruined Lorelei's day, as well. *What a spoiled brat.*

And, while it wasn't her fault, Lorelei still felt as if she owed Donovan an apology.

He should have recognized Cynthia DuBois—she'd stared him down the entire time he'd been on the witness stand at the trial that had sent her father to jail—but the intervening years hadn't been kind to her. The DuBois family had not been sent into poverty, but they'd lost most of their money, and without that, Cynthia had lost her expensive shine.

He had to give her credit; her honest reaction was a nice change from the cold shoulders and avoidance by the other families involved and their friends. While it hadn't been personal—at least not for him—he wasn't stupid or naive enough to believe that she hadn't taken it personally. Honestly, he should be glad Cynthia had only dumped a drink into his lap. Lanelle DuBois, Cynthia's mother, had slapped him in front of a full press conference, in addition to questioning his ethics, his intelligence, his heritage and his legitimacy. At least Cynthia had restrained herself more than her mother had.

But neither Cynthia's insults nor his wet pants were what was bothering him hours after the fact. It was Lorelei.

The look that had crossed her face when she'd heard her name...

He couldn't quite describe it. The closest he'd come was an adolescent "oh-God-I'm-so-busted" look—one that encompassed guilt and shame and worry about repercussions.

And it had crossed her face *before* she'd turned—*before* she'd seen that it was Cynthia DuBois.

The only explanation was that she'd considered herself "busted" no matter *who* it had been.

Even worse, though, was the echo of it he'd seen when Cynthia had asked if her parents "knew."

If he hadn't known already, that look would have answered the question with a big fat "no." The fact that Lorelei didn't want her social life overshadowing her attempts at redemption in Vivi's absence was a fair enough reason to keep their association quiet, but that had been *horror* at the thought of her parents finding out.

He pulled a beer from the fridge and leaned against the counter, not sure what to make of today's events. He wasn't happy, but he couldn't put his finger on exactly why...

The bell on the back gate chimed, announcing Lorelei's arrival, and he reached for the button to release the lock. A minute later Lorelei was at the French doors.

She was still in the tank top and shorts she'd worn earlier, and carried a leather bag strapped across her chest.

"Hey." She rose up on tiptoes to for a quick kiss. "Careful—I'm all sweaty."

"Did you walk here?"

"Of course I walked. I try not to drive in the Quarter unless I have to—much less on a Saturday night. It's too easy to get frustrated and decide to take out a pedestrian or two." She removed the bag and set it on the counter, flashing a cheeky smile. "I figured if I got too sweaty you wouldn't object to a shower." She motioned to his beer. "Can I have one of those?"

He got another one, and she took a long swallow before digging into her bag and producing a small blue gift bag tied with a white ribbon. She handed it over almost shyly.

"What's this?"

"A present, silly. Open it."

He did, to find a generic CD with *Monty Jones/Connor Mansfield* and a date written in her handwriting across the front. He looked at her in confusion.

"I saw you had some Monty Jones in your collection, and he was at the studio about a month ago, jamming with Connor. I made a few phone calls this afternoon and got the okay to burn you a disk. It was a casual thing for them, and none of it has been through post-production, but it's pretty good."

It was a personal and thoughtful gift. He was oddly touched. "Thanks, Lorelei."

He could tell she'd been worried when she broke into a smile. "Well, you didn't seem like a flowers kind of guy and I needed an opening salvo."

"For an apology?"

"Yeah, because I owe you one this time. This afternoon was just…*bad*. I'm sorry. I really should have handled that better. It caught me off-guard, though."

Maybe he'd been overthinking it. Looking for insult when none was intended. He'd never done that before. But this was Lorelei, and it seemed he was a little touchy on that subject. "Me, too."

"So you're not mad at me?"

"You're not the one who dumped a drink on me."

"I know, but…" She sighed. "As you said, at least it was cold. Although I imagine that's not very nice, either."

She moved her eyes toward his zipper, and his body reacted even if his mind was still at odds.

She chuckled. "I was about to ask if you were fully recovered, but I think I have my answer." She winked at him. "I've got to admit, though, you handled that much better than I would have."

"Really?"

"Oh, yeah." Lorelei boosted herself up onto the counter. "I'd have probably totally freaked and there would have been hair-pulling and cat-scratching and a trip to the police station involved."

Tough talk, but he couldn't imagine Lorelei doing any such thing. He doubted the LaBlanc women ever got physical in an argument. It wouldn't be very ladylike. But he nodded anyway. "Thereby totally destroying that image you've been so carefully crafting?"

"Oh, definitely. That's why I'm glad it was you and not me. Can you see me trying to explain to my parents that I got arrested?"

"I'd have bailed you out."

"I appreciate the sentiment, but that might have only made it worse." She laughed. "Oh, I can see me explaining *that*."

Maybe it was just the fact that the look on Lorelei's face earlier was still fresh in his mind, but this conversation was making warning bells clang in his head. "Me bailing you out would be worse than you getting arrested?"

"Hmm, that's a hard one. Don't know." She laughed again. "I don't really want to find out, either."

Okay, he really didn't like this conversation. And he didn't like the fact he didn't like this conversation, either. "An arrest record might keep you out of the Junior Ladies' Whatever."

"I hadn't thought of it that way... The idea holds merit. I'll keep it in mind for the future. Actually, it might solve several problems. How does one go about getting arrested?"

"I've never been arrested, but I assume one breaks the law." He took another drink, and when Lorelei stayed silent he asked, "What problems?"

"Excuse me?"

"You said there were several problems an arrest would solve. I'm wondering exactly what those might be."

Lorelei's sigh held resignation and frustration, with a bit of exasperated humor, as well. "Just my mother's general insanity."

"Worse than white gloves and the Junior Ladies' Whatever?"

She seemed to weigh that. "Maybe. But it's nothing I can't handle. Did you do anything interesting this afternoon?"

"Okay, now I'm *really* curious."

Her mouth twisted. "Jack Morgan asked me out. Did you know that?"

That need to punch Jack in the mouth came roaring back. "It was rather obvious he was gearing up for it. What did you tell him?"

"That I was really superbusy right now and totally booked until Vivi gets back to town."

That wasn't exactly the flat denial he'd have liked to

hear. "So now that Vivi's return is imminent he's ready to take you at your word?"

"Obviously Jack is not familiar with the polite brush-off."

That mollified him a little. But only a little. "Most men are completely blind and deaf in that area of social inter-action. You have to be direct." There were several direct and obvious ways for Lorelei to respond to Jack's offer, but they hadn't seemed to occur to her. Why?

"I can't. Not now."

"Because…?"

Another eye roll from Lorelei. "Because now my mom and his mom have this great plan of breeding us or some-thing. Let's just say it's a good thing I can't be married off without my permission in this century."

"You're exaggerating."

"Not by much." She took another drink and sighed. "It's the only thing putting a damper on my anticipation of Dad's party."

"Not following you."

"Oh, did I skip that part? Mom has this really great idea that I should ask Jack to be my date for Dad's party."

"What did she say when you told her no?"

"I didn't exactly say that," she hedged.

He didn't like where this was going. "You told her you *would?*"

"No. She's knows I'm not keen on the idea, and we left it at 'I'll think about it.'"

He must have looked at her funny because Lorelei went on the defensive.

"It was in the middle of dinner. I was trapped. I couldn't think of a more graceful way out."

"You tell her you don't need to be fixed up on a date."

"I tried that, but without a really good reason to back

it up it rings a little hollow. She can't understand why I'd rather go stag and mess up the seating chart than go with eligible and good-catch Jack Morgan."

He simply could not hold his suspicions at bay any longer. He'd ignored the alarm bells as long as he could. Casually, belying the acidic taste in his mouth, he offered, "I could be your date for the evening."

Lorelei stilled, her beer halfway to her mouth, and shot him an *Are you insane?* look. "After what happened today with Cynthia DuBois, do you really think that's a good idea? People are still very touchy about that issue. And the ones who are the touchiest are on the guest list already."

"I can handle it." The question was, could *she?* Donovan was pretty sure he knew the answer to that.

"That's very brave of you, but party-etiquette rule number one prohibits me from intentionally inciting a riot among the guests. When possible, it's best to make sure that the presence of one guest won't cause embarrassment or distress for the other guests."

"Including you?" he challenged.

Confusion wrinkled her brow. "A riot would certainly distress me. It's my father's party and I don't want anything to ruin that."

At that, Donovan was done with this game. "Like his precious daughter showing up with Donovan St. James?"

Guilt streaked across her face so fast he nearly missed it. "I don't know what you mean."

"Don't play dumb. It's beneath you—and insulting to us both. There's a real easy way out of your mom's matchmaking. You tell her you're seeing me."

She shook her head. "It wouldn't matter. Here's a newsflash—my mom's not real crazy about you. She'd still try to match me up with Jack."

"And you can't be seen with someone your parents wouldn't approve of?"

He waited for a denial. It didn't come and he wasn't surprised.

"It's complicated, Donovan."

Strangely, he was disappointed that he wasn't surprised. But he was more disappointed than he liked to admit at her words. He stood. "Not really. The simple fact is that you don't want *anyone* to know you've been sleeping with me."

"Of course I don't."

That cut deeper than he'd expected. "At least now you're being honest."

He recognized the set of her jaw.

"I don't want *anyone* to know who I'm sleeping with because my sex life is none of anyone else's business. It's not something I feel I have to advertize."

"You're ashamed of yourself."

She sat up straight. "What?"

"Not of what you're doing, but *who* you're doing it with. At a certain point people who are seen in each other's company often enough are generally assumed to be sleeping together, as well. So it's not *what* people will think about what you're doing that you're worried about. It's the fact they'll know you're doing it with *me*. You're ashamed to be seen with *me*."

She shook her head. "That's not true. Not entirely true," she corrected. "There's a lot more going on."

He didn't really care. He just wanted to cut to the facts. "Why'd you tell Cynthia DuBois that we were having a business meeting today?"

"To protect her feelings. Her reasons may not be completely valid, but I understand why she feels the way she does. And she considers me a friend, so I was trying to make her feel a little better. I didn't realize your ego was so damn fragile."

He wasn't going to take that bait. "This isn't about my ego. It's about yours. The easiest way out of a date with Jack is to show up with me. But you can't do that because then everyone will know you've gone slumming."

Lorelei's jaw dropped but she didn't say anything, telling him with her silence that he'd hit the target with that jab.

"At least it's safe slumming," he continued. "I've got my own money and my own connections, so it's not like you're sleeping with a bartender or pool boy or someone *really* beneath you. You're not brave enough to date someone just to spite your family and your friends because you desperately want their approval."

At that, Lorelei's mouth slammed shut and her lips pressed into a thin line. Oh, yeah, he was definitely on target. He wished he'd had this insight weeks ago. He'd just been too caught up in Lorelei's spell to see the obvious. For someone who made his living going past the obvious, digging into the layers and finding out the truth… Well, it was a little humbling to find out he'd been so blind. He blamed the humbling and the disappointment for the feeling in his chest, since he didn't know how to describe it otherwise. He didn't like it, though.

"So you've gotten to do your little rebellion—sneaking around, banging the one guy guaranteed to horrify everyone you know and getting your kicks because you're getting away with it. Well, I'm done playing. You know the way out." He tossed the bottle toward the bin and walked away, leaving her sitting there on the counter before he said something he'd really regret.

"What the hell, Donovan?" She actually looked shocked and confused.

"I'm not interested in being your dirty little secret, Princess."

Her mouth snapped closed.

*A dirty little secret.* He'd been made brutally aware of the concept in high school. And he really resented the fact that Lorelei had him—a fully grown, successful adult—reliving high-school dramas.

Penny Richards. Daughter of a city councilman and cocaptain of the cheerleading squad. She'd cornered him under the bleachers after homecoming his junior year, and they'd snuck around for months like something out of a teenage movie. After a year of being only slightly better off than an outcast—he'd been good at sports, so he hadn't been completely ignored, but he hadn't been "one of them," either—it had been almost romantic, the two of them from different worlds. Hell, he'd been young, and just happy to be getting laid at all, so he hadn't really questioned it.

Then the news that his family's company had hit the Forbes list had spread through New Orleans like water from a broken levee. Figuring he was about to break through some invisible wall, he'd asked Penny to prom—only to be turned down flat and unceremoniously dumped.

All because she was too good for some "tacky *nouveau riche* social-climber." It was the first time he'd heard the term, and he'd had to look it up. With that knowledge, his entire understanding of the world had shifted. Nothing would change the fact he wasn't one of them. That invisible wall could not be broken through, and nor could it be climbed. It was actually better to be poor than nouveau riche.

It had been a hard-learned lesson, and one he'd been sure he would never forget.

Of course now it seemed he *had* forgotten that lesson,

or else he'd have steered far and wide of Lorelei LaBlanc. And he probably would have except for large amounts of alcohol. The ramifications of that had shown him a bit of Lorelei he hadn't expected.

And he'd lost sight of the obvious.

# CHAPTER NINE

IT TOOK A SECOND for Donovan's words to register fully, and by then he was out of the room. Lorelei had been wavering between anger and shame and guilt, but "Princess" took her straight into anger.

She hopped down off the counter and followed him into the living room. "You don't get to throw a grenade like that and then walk away."

"I just did, Lorelei. I'm done talking."

A red haze clouded her vision and she forced herself not to yell. "Well, I'm not. You know, you're not wrong—but you're pretty damn far from right, too. *Yes,* I'm sneaking around, sleeping with a guy simply because the sex is good. *No,* my family and my friends would not approve of that. *Yes,* their approval is very important to me. I'm really freakin' sorry that you don't see that."

"Oh, I see it. I just think you're shallow for caring that much."

*"Shallow?"* Oh, now she wanted to hit something. Namely him. "Wanting to spare the feelings of the people I love and respect makes me shallow? Showing respect for the society I was raised in, the traditions and the culture and the values that I was taught makes me *shallow?*"

"I'm well aware of the 'traditions and the culture' and

the so-called 'values' you were taught. They *are* pretty damn shallow."

"And you know this how, exactly?"

"Because they are. And the truth is *you* don't actually think they're important enough to really care about, either—you just want people to *think* you care."

Something about that nagged at her. "I'm trying to build something here, trying to make something out of my life, and that's not been easy."

"Making something out of your life is an admirable thing."

*Finally.* "Then why are you giving me grief over it?

"As I said, because you're more worried about what people think of you than what you actually are."

That nasty tone had her digging her nails into her palms as she forced her hands to stay at her sides. "So I should be like you and not give a damn at all what people think?"

Donovan shot her a look. "It works."

She shot him one back. "Not as well as you think."

"What the hell that mean?"

"Being involved with you will horrify everyone I know. But it's not because I'm 'slumming,' as you so tactlessly put it. I could bang the pool boy if I wanted to, and while everyone would *tsk* and shake their heads they'd get over it. It would just show poor judgment on my part, but that's not a crime. The problem is you. Specifically. Not your family or your finances. *You.* You're so damn smug. If anyone thinks they're better than somebody else, it's you."

"You're the one riding on the LaBlanc name."

"And your name is sitting like a chip on your shoulder. You've figured out that your money can't buy you class and respectability in some people's eyes, so you just mock what you can't have."

Donovan's eyes narrowed. She might be on to something here. Julie's speech about "marrying up" came rushing back to her.

"That's what bugs you about this, isn't it? Even if you bag one of the LaBlanc girls, you still can't get into the country club. Is that the problem? That even if I were willing to let you try, you couldn't ride on my name for your gain? Feeling a bit resentful, are we?"

There was a tiny twitch that might have been guilt, but his voice was cold and sarcastic. "Join the rest of us in twenty-first century America, Lorelei. You aren't some kind of European aristocrat."

"Then don't pretend that your 'humble' roots make you some kind of hero with an all-American success story, either. Let me remind you that you got your start on your daddy's money, too."

Donovan's jaw tightened. "I've made quite a bit on my own. Built my own reputation. Can't say the same for you, though."

"You know, you're right. I've realized recently that I still have a lot of work to do. I've got a lot to live up to. But I've got my own plans, too. I've been tying myself in knots over you, but for all the wrong reasons. You're not the right kind of guy, but it's not why you think."

She turned her back on him with every intention of leaving before this got any uglier—not that she could see how it could sink any lower.

"And you're an expert on what I think now?"

It was a cold drawl—one she recognized from years past as well as from his TV interviews as the warning note that Donovan was about to rip someone to shreds.

But she wasn't really worried. "I'm getting there. You've decided that I'm an elitist snob. A princess who thinks she's too good for the likes of you. And you're right. I *am* too good to waste my time with someone who disdains everything about me and everything I care about. My shame is that I thought it mattered."

She stomped into the kitchen, grabbed her bag and exited through the door she'd entered just a little while earlier with such excitement. She let her anger carry her a full block before she leaned against a building to gather herself.

*Where did Donovan get off with that holier-than-thou attitude?* Slumming, indeed. If anyone thought they were slumming, it was Donovan. She was glad to be proved right—at least in her desire to keep things between them on the down-low. Any guilt she'd felt about keeping him her "dirty little secret" was quickly being assuaged. Honestly, if she'd dealt with the fallout of seeing him and then realized how deep his disdain for her went... *That* would have been humiliating.

Oh, to turn back the calendar three weeks and fight that curiosity that had led her into Donovan's bed a second time. She hadn't done well in chemistry in high school—and she'd failed it miserably this time.

At least no one knew. There would be no awkward questions, no shaking of heads or I-told-you-sos. She'd had a fling. It was done now, and she'd go back to her regularly scheduled life.

*Why did it hurt?* She didn't know what was worse: the fact he'd said those things, or the fact he believed them. No, the fact that she cared that he'd said them was the worst.

Sighing, she pushed off the wall and started the trek home. The streets of the Quarter were busier now. With the sun down, the bars and clubs were gearing up. Sunburned tourists in T-shirts were now about equally balanced by the club crowd: the young and beautiful and dressed up, out to enjoy themselves.

Not long ago she probably would have been one of them. There was a small sigh of regret for what she'd given up. Suddenly she felt very old for twenty-five.

It wasn't as if she couldn't have that life back. She could be one of the local socialites—it wasn't as if there wasn't acceptance for that. Expectations were very low, but as long as her behavior stayed within legal boundaries and a certain level of decorum she could easily go back. While her parents would be disappointed, they wouldn't disown her or anything.

At the same time she was very proud of what she'd accomplished and didn't want to give that up. She was rather liking the fact that people wanted to talk to her about more than superficial things. That they cared about her opinion and wanted her as a representative for their mission. Her whole life she'd been accepted because she was someone's daughter, granddaughter or, more recently, sister. It was nice actually to have her own name, her own place, her own slice of respect that didn't come only because she was a LaBlanc.

If Donovan couldn't understand that…

And *had* he been hoping that he'd benefit through their association? She'd seen that quick flash. Maybe he'd been planning on making connections through *her* connections. He had his own money and influence, and his friendship with Connor and Vivi had him traveling in new circles. Had he hoped to expand those circles? Was that why he'd suddenly changed his tune when she showed interest?

She now understood one of the mantras she'd heard her whole life. When you dated inside your own circle you didn't have to worry about things like that. It was why like married like. Julie had just put it a bit more bluntly. It had as much to do with self-preservation as anything else. She wouldn't have these questons if she'd just remembered that one simple fact that had been pounded into her psyche her entire life.

She'd chalk this up as a learning experience. She'd know better next time.

It wasn't anything. She'd known that going in.

*Then why did it hurt?*

Lorelei stroked the silk sarong almost reverently. She'd never felt anything quite as luxurious in her life. "It's beautiful, Vivi. Thanks."

"I've got a necklace for you in here somewhere that matches it nicely..." Vivi frowned at the luggage exploding over the bed.

Even after a ridiculously long flight from the Seychelles, when any normal person would look like hell on toast from jet lag and dehydration, Vivi looked perfect. As always. In fact she looked rested and refreshed, her skin lightly tanned and highlights from the sun in her hair. Lorelei had always questioned the wisdom of highlights since her hair was so dark, but they certainly looked good on Vivi. Maybe she'd reconsider.

Both Connor and Vivi had tons to catch up on—she knew this for a fact since she'd been holding down the fort while they lounged on a beach—and Connor had headed straight for the studio this morning. But she and Vivi had gone to brunch instead, and Lorelei was now curled up on the chaise in Vivi's bedroom, scrolling through their pictures while Vivi made her jealous with details from her vacation.

"It all sounds amazing. And the beach looks gorgeous. I'm *so* ready to go someplace other than here. It's been nasty hot for weeks and, honestly, your life is not that much fun."

"I'm glad to hear you think that, because I'm ready to

take it back. Being away from it all was nice for about a week. Then I started to get bored."

"Only you."

"But I hear you've done quite well in my place."

"You've been home for twelve hours. How could you possibly know that?"

Vivi looked downright smug. "Just because you ignore my emails, don't assume others do."

"You were on your honeymoon. You're not supposed to email people while you're on your honeymoon. You're supposed to relax and have fun."

"I did. But now I'm done. Do we need to go over anything to bring me up to speed?"

Lorelei shook her head. "I typed up notes from everything—all the people I talked to, what you need to follow up on—and emailed the files to you this morning. Just let me know if you have any questions." She sighed and leaned back. She felt as if she'd just passed on a very heavy mantle, and the relief felt divine.

She'd done the same gathering and organizing for Connor, but that was her job. Connor was probably in his office right now, going through those files and making more work for her to do. And she looked forward to it, because she did love what she did, but Vivi's stuff...that wasn't hers. She'd been wearing borrowed shoes for almost a month, and it felt good to be back in her own.

"Those are some pretty deep sighs. Everything okay?"

"Yeah. Just tired. Oh, and now that you're back *you* can deal with Mom. She's wigging over Dad's party, and she's not even the hostess."

"I'll sort her out. We're meeting them for dinner tonight." There was that smug look again. "Want me to start with the Jack Morgan situation?"

*Unbelievable.* "How do you know there's a situation?"

"I told you—other people respond to my emails. Mom's right, though. Jack's a good catch. And he's a nice guy."

Lorelei just hummed a non-committal response.

"But I also agree with you that Dad's party is not the best time or place for a first date."

"Thank you. At least someone agrees with me. Finally."

"Are you planning on taking a date other than Jack?"

Lorelei shot Vivi a look, but Vivi just shrugged.

"It's a fair question. Seating charts do need to be made."

*Argh.* Lorelei closed her eyes and rubbed her temples. "I'm going stag. You'll just have to entertain me during dinner."

"Are you sure there's no one else you'd like to invite?"

*What a loaded question.* "Nah."

"'Nah?' That's your answer?"

Lorelei nodded and stroked the silk sarong again.

Vivi arched an eyebrow at her. "You are a really bad liar. You know that, right?"

She should have known better than to try. "There's a guy, but…"

That got her sister's attention. Vivi nudged Lorelei's feet until she curled them up and sat on the other end of the chaise. "My sources here must be falling down on the job. How'd I not know this? How long has this been going on?"

The brief spark of satisfaction that she'd gotten *something* by her sister was muted by the situation itself. "A few weeks. We kept it very quiet and very casual. Which turned out to be a good thing, because it didn't work out. So even if I wanted to ask him I can't."

"Hang on. Back this up. Start with his name."

She could trust Vivi, she knew that, but it was still difficult. Unfortunately it wouldn't get any easier, because she knew Vivi, and the chances of her getting out of this room without divulging the information were slim to none.

She took a deep breath and blew it out. "Donovan St. James."

Even Vivi, who had a game face like no other, couldn't hide her shock. "Whoa! *Really?*"

"Really." She shrugged. "Hard to believe, huh?"

"I would not have ever thought to put you two together, but—"

"I know. I was crazy. But, like I said, it's over."

"Why?"

"Donovan decided that I was ashamed to be seen with him and refused to be my 'dirty little secret' any longer."

"Why would he think you were ashamed of him?"

It was the issue she'd been arguing with herself over for days now. She had to admit the truth. "'Cause I was."

Vivi's jaw dropped in horror. "Lorelei Lucienne LaBlanc, tell me you are kidding."

"I wish I could." She dropped her head back and pulled a pillow over her face. "It's a big mess."

Vivi pulled the pillow away. She did not look happy, either. "Obviously. Now, please continue."

"I got totally hammered at your reception." Vivi's eyes narrowed in disapproval. "And spent the night with him. It just kind of went from there. A little fling."

"Keep talking. You're still not to the 'ashamed of him' part."

Lorelei hated being put on the defensive like this. "You can't deny that if I suddenly announced I was dating Donovan St. James heads all over the Garden District wouldn't explode."

"I won't deny that. But that doesn't make the exploding heads right, either."

"I worked so hard for months, trying to get people to take me seriously—"

"What for?"

Lorelei sighed. "Vivi, *cherie,* I love you, but being your sister really sucks sometimes."

Vivi nodded in understanding and reached out to squeeze her knee. "I know. And I'm sorry."

"I just wanted people to see *me* for once, to take me seriously, and you being gone was the perfect opportunity for that. I've been working toward a goal, and it was finally in reach. Everyone was so happy that I was finally acting like a LaBlanc. Mom and Dad were so proud, new opportunities were coming my way…there's no way I could drop the Donovan bombshell on all of that. I had too much at risk, too much to lose. So, no, I didn't want anyone to know. I was ashamed of myself, of him, of what we were doing…" She dropped her head back again. "It doesn't really matter. It wouldn't have worked out anyway."

"I don't know. Like I said, I never would have thought to put you two together, but now that I do think about it I can totally see it."

That had her sitting upright again. "What?"

"I, too, had my reservations about Donovan, but after I got to know him a little I got past all that. Connor's done work with him, I've sat with him on boards—hell, we invited him to the wedding. You don't see people's heads exploding, do you?"

"They are—just not where you can see. You and Connor can do whatever you want. You're established and way too powerful to mess with. No one would ever risk taking you two on. Now, me? I may be a LaBlanc, but I'm not… Well, that's just a whole different story."

Vivi was shaking her head. "You are not just a LaBlanc. You're Lorelei LaBlanc. Unique, fantastic and the envy of many. Including me, sometimes. Nothing will change that, and I never knew you thought there was some standard to meet or mold to fit in order to be judged worthy of something. I'm glad you're feeling stronger and more sure of yourself. I'm glad that others are finally starting to realize how awesome you are. But you should never distrust yourself or deny your own happiness because you're worried about what others think of you."

It was an impassioned speech, one that made her feel proud and loved, but Vivi wasn't exactly the audience she sought to impress. "Thanks. I'll keep that in mind for next time."

"Why wait until next time? It's obvious you really like Donovan. You wouldn't be so miserable otherwise."

"At first it was just hormones and chemistry and sex, but, then… Yeah." She'd been refusing to admit it to herself, but she couldn't deny it any longer. Good God, she was such a bad liar she couldn't even lie to herself. "I'm crazy about him. I just didn't realize that until after."

"And you haven't talked to him? Apologized and tried to explain?"

"No. I'm not a glutton for punishment."

"And you think it's too late now?"

"I guess it's never too late for an apology, but I don't think it can be fixed. It started off in the wrong place and just kind of stayed there. And I did say some really mean things. So did he, of course. Not all of which were untrue. But it leads me to believe that while he may want me, he doesn't really like me all that much. I'm not the only one who considered this a dirty little secret." That hurt to admit, but if she were going to be really honest with herself, she needed to face all the facts. "Maybe it's better to just let it go."

It was Vivi's turn to sigh. "I wish you'd told me about your grand plan sooner. I could have made things a lot simpler for you."

"I know, but I wanted to do this myself."

"And Donovan?"

"I think that was just doomed from the beginning."

"I don't think it was or is necessarily doomed, but I will respect your decision. Just know that whatever you decide, I've totally got your back. Nobody messes with my little sister."

It was a strong, comforting statement from someone she loved and respected. But she didn't need—didn't *want*—Vivi to fight her battles for her.

Especially since the battle seemed lost already.

The following Wednesday, Donovan picked up a newspaper on the way home. His oldest niece had placed second in the city-wide spelling bee and, according to the excited text he'd received that morning, a picture of the top three with their trophies was in the "Wednesday Pages."

He got himself a drink and unfolded the paper. The glossy society magazine slid out. On the front there was a picture of Michael LaBlanc, Lorelei's father, and a headline about his retirement. *The big bash,* he thought. *Lorelei's big moment.*

He flipped through, scanning, looking for the spelling bee, and ran straight into the write-up of the LaBlanc party with full-color pictures. A group picture of Lorelei's parents, two other older couples he assumed were business partners, Connor and Vivi—and Lorelei. Lorelei looked regal in a silver and black cocktail dress, her hair pulled up to show off her elegant features—the image hit him hard.

So hard, in fact, he didn't see Jack Morgan hovering over Lorelei's shoulder like the Hindenburg at first. It seemed Lorelei had buckled under the pressure after all and let herself be paired off with her mother's Mr. Right selection.

"Way to stand strong, Princess."

He turned the page. They deserved each other. As he located the picture of his niece he thought of the invitation that had arrived yesterday, inviting him to a party at ConMan Studios exclusively for the donors to Connor's pet charities like the Children's Music Project.

That was going to be awkward. Connor and Vivi must not know about his and Lorelei's little fling or else he wouldn't have received an invitation, donor or not. He knew he wouldn't extend an invite if the roles were reversed.

He had to assume Jack would be there—even if, as Lorelei claimed, he'd donated pocket change. It had been bad enough watching Jack hover over her previously, but now…?

Even as angry as he was, he still felt the loss of Lorelei like a knife in his gut. The one thing he'd come to realize recently was that the hurt ran deep because he'd allowed himself to get used to her. The anger was much easier to deal with than the betrayal and hurt, so he focused on that.

Lorelei's complete disappearance from his life only proved his accusations correct. And she'd very obviously moved on; he hadn't heard anything from her since the night she'd left. Based on that picture, she wasn't exactly suffering from the loss.

He'd wanted to call her; he nearly had a dozen times. But he'd finally deleted her number from his phone to remove the temptation altogether. He wanted her. He missed her. No one made him laugh—or jerked his chain—quite like Lorelei. He hadn't realized how used he'd become to having her around until she wasn't there, and his house felt a little empty. So did his bed.

There was also an empty, hollow place in his stomach.

He might as well accept the facts. Lorelei lived in a different world, and that world had no place and no tolerance for him. And since she wasn't willing to jeopardize her place in that world for him… Yeah, he just needed to accept that. Acceptance would help him move on. Move past Lorelei. His brain was on board for that, but getting his heart and body to agree was tough.

*Lesson learned. Move on.*

He thought about that for a minute, then grabbed his phone and called Jess.

# CHAPTER TEN

LORELEI WAS ABOUT to pull her hair out. Someone needed to explain to Connor that the title "rock god" was not literal. He could *not* simply decide to throw a major party for over a hundred people and assume it would simply come to pass because he wanted it to.

Obviously Connor thought that catering just *happened*.

She was in the uncomfortable position of being both family and employee. The employee wanted to quit in a fully deserved huff, but as family, she hadn't quite ruled out strangling him in his sleep. The only thing keeping her from doing either was her pride and the fact that Vivi would probably be mad at her. *LaBlancs love a challenge. This is just a challenge.*

This event was going to happen one way or the other, by God—even if Lorelei had to call in every favor she'd ever been owed. Pride was definitely driving her. She was a LaBlanc, and party planning and hostessing were in her DNA. She'd peel the crawfish herself before she let this event be anything but perfect.

However, deep down she was rather glad she had plenty to focus on and frustrate her. She'd been thinking about calling Donovan, going to see him—*something*—just to see if there was a way to repair the damage, but she'd chickened out every time. It had been a tough couple of weeks. Callie's romance had flamed out and she was around a lot more, alternating between feeling sorry for herself and cursing her ex's name. Since Callie had no idea that Lorelei had ever been with Donovan in the first place, Lorelei had to suck it up and pretend everything was just fine instead of joining her in misery.

Pretending was very hard to do, since she missed Donovan like crazy. She kept picking up her phone to call or text him random things, but then she'd remember that look on Donovan's face and remember she couldn't do that anymore. And it made her sad. He'd been the one person who'd been there for her through all of this, and now that she had accomplished her goal she didn't really have anyone to share it with who could really appreciate it.

So the party was a good thing. Focusing on it, however frustrating, was actually keeping her sane. Or sane-ish.

But tonight would definitely be a test. She'd designed and ordered the invitations, but the receptionist had been the one to get the guest list, mail the invitations and record the RSVPs. She hadn't even thought to look at the list until yesterday.

She'd been prepared to see Donovan's name on the list. She hadn't been prepared to see him RSVP in the positive, though. And she'd *really* been unprepared to see that he'd included a plus-one.

That had been a bit of a blow.

Obviously she'd left and he'd simply called, "Next!" She told herself she shouldn't be surprised, but it still hurt. The fling that wasn't supposed to be anything had turned into something. At least for her. She'd just realized it a little too late. After all that time worrying about what other people would think, she now only cared what one person thought.

It didn't seem as if he was thinking about *her* much at

all. She wished she could say the same. It had been the sight of "and guest" that had driven a hard piece of knowledge home: she was in love with Donovan St. James.

Unfortunately she'd come to that realization only after it was too late.

And now she'd have to face him—and the woman he'd replaced her with so quickly—and not let that knowledge show. It was a challenge she was not looking forward to.

Lorelei made one last check of the studio's reception area. The scent of fresh flowers filled the room. Caterers were setting up appetizer stations, and bartenders in matching uniforms looked ready to go. A loop of recordings made here, at ConMan, over the last few months played softly over the speakers. Security was already watching the doors, and Connor and Vivi were sneaking in one last canoodle in the sound booth before the guests began arriving.

Everything was as ready as it could be.

Except for her. She still needed to change and gather herself.

Upstairs, in Connor and Vivi's bedroom, Lorelei slipped into her new dress. It was a beautiful deep scarlet that showed plenty of leg and quite a bit of cleavage. It would be totally inappropriate in most settings, but tonight she was here as Connor's assistant, not Vivi's stand-in. She could go a *little* wilder, and after weeks of guarding herself, it felt quite good to let a little bit of her back out.

And it gave her confidence. Confidence she was really going to need if Donovan was going to be here. With a date.

That knowledge made her take a few extra minutes touching up her make-up and hair. After slipping on her shoes, she stood in front of the mirror and examined herself critically from every angle. It would have to do. She took a deep breath and braced herself.

The elevator had to be turned off during the party, so Lorelei came down the back stairs through Connor's office and into the crowded reception area. *Wow.* How long had she been gone? Hadn't these people ever heard of being fashionably late? A quick look around told her that everything seemed to be under control, so now she needed to mingle and make nice with the guests.

She felt a hand at her elbow. Vivi was pulling her back into Connor's office.

"I need to tell you something."

"What?" she said as Vivi shut the door behind them.

"Donovan's here—"

"I know. I can—"

"With Jessica Reynald."

That was a real blow to her ego. She swallowed hard. Somehow that seemed personal, although rationally she knew it couldn't be. "Thanks for the heads up."

"It gets better." Vivi's tone did not match her words, and Lorelei braced herself. "Jack just arrived."

"I knew he would. I can't seem to shake him off."

"You're going to have to be clear and direct."

*That was the same thing Donovan had said.* "But just not here, not tonight, in front of all these people."

Vivi frowned. "I'm pretty sure he's doing it on purpose. On the other hand..." She paused and brushed Lorelei's hair back over her shoulders. "Having Jack around might counterbalance Donovan and his date."

"I'm okay, really. He's moved on. I get that. I'm an adult and I can handle it."

"I know you can." Vivi squeezed her shoulders in support, then opened the door. Music and conversation rushed in to fill the silence.

For the next forty-five minutes Lorelei worked the crowd with every ounce of energy and personality she possessed. Connor had three pet projects, all music-related, and this crowd was the money that funded them and the talent that supported them. The energy in the room was amazing. So much talent, a shared love of music—and, of course, the money that supported these and other projects. Lorelei couldn't quite quell the rather hollow feeling in her stomach and the dread that sat on her shoulders, but she was able to hold it at bay and put on a good game face.

Then she turned and found herself face-to-face with Donovan. Her stomach tied itself into a knot, but she forced the smile to stay steady and even. Donovan wasn't alone, and she would not make a scene. Even if it killed her.

"Glad you could come, Donovan."

"I wouldn't have missed it for the world."

He introduced her to the people in his group: the front man of a zydeco band whose Cajun accent was so thick he was barely understandable, a white-haired blues guitarist who looked to be about a hundred years old, and a tall, sultry jazz singer who made her feel downright dowdy. Jessica, she noted, was nowhere around.

The presence of the others made it a little easier, but every time she looked at Donovan, her heart ached a little. When he laughed, it made the knot in her stomach tighten. She concentrated on being a good hostess, participating in the conversation, but she was dying a bit inside. Donovan's eyes were uninterested; they flicked over her and then dismissed her. There was no special, knowing smirk on his face.

She'd been right not to call him. It was bad enough coming to terms with that here, where he couldn't actually say anything to make her feel worse.

*Was that even possible?*

"Could you all excuse me? I need to check on a few things." It was a perfectly normal excuse for someone in her position to make, but she felt like a coward as she retreated. A relieved coward, and one who needed a break, but a coward nonetheless.

Just in case anyone was watching, Lorelei gave a cursory glance over the food and made sure that there were no empty dishes or dirty glassware sitting about, but the catering staff were on top of things and there was nothing really for her to do. She got a club soda from the bartender and stepped back near the fichus tree, out of sight, for a small breather.

There was a couple on the other side. The woman had her back turned, so Lorelei couldn't tell who she was, but Troy, one of the sound engineers, was definitely flirting.

She silently wished Troy luck as she started to move away and give them some privacy, but the name "Donovan" froze her feet in place. A split-second later she recognized the woman's voice: Jessica.

"I'm just arm candy. When Donovan called, he said he needed company. I wasn't about to turn down a chance to come to this party."

Feeling silly, Lorelei took a step back to hear better.

"I do *not* want to get on Donovan St. James's bad side," Troy said.

*Smart man.*

"All he has is a bad side right now. He's grumpy and angry at something."

*That might be my fault.*

"Even if he hadn't made it very clear I was just here to look pretty," Jessica continued, "he's so foul-tempered I nearly backed out."

"I'm glad you didn't." Troy was definitely moving in, hoping to score.

"Me, too."

Troy lowered his voice then, and Lorelei couldn't hear what he said next, but she'd lost interest anyway. That changed *everything.* Donovan hadn't turned straight to Jessica to replace her; he hadn't brought her as anything more than a showpiece.

To make her jealous, maybe?

That knot in her stomach released a tiny bit.

The foul mood was probably her fault, but it could easily mean he was just still angry over the whole mess. She could hold out the hope that maybe, *maybe,* he was a little miserable, too. That maybe he felt the same way about her that she felt about him.

That gave her hope.

And since Jessica wasn't really in the picture she had no ethical reason not to suck it up and apologize. She wouldn't be poaching on anyone else's turf.

With all these people around Donovan wouldn't— or *probably* wouldn't—make a stink if she told him she wanted to speak with him privately, and Connor's office would be private enough…

*I'm going to do it.* She had no idea what she was going to say, but she'd think on her feet, make it up as she went along. As long as she was honest, she had to believe the right words would come.

It was a big risk, but it was a risk worth taking. She had no idea what Donovan would say, but she had no problem groveling if she had to. She just wanted him, and she'd suffer whatever humiliation he wanted to dish out as her penance.

And if it was too late? The damage too extensive? She

didn't want to think about that. It would make this harder, but LaBlancs didn't back down from a challenge.

She actually felt better than she had in days. Her chest felt lighter, her head clearer. Quietly easing out from behind the fichus, she handed her glass to the surprised-looking bartender and scanned the room, looking for Donovan.

She thought she heard his voice and spun around—right into the waiting hands of Jack.

"Hey, sweetheart, I've been looking all over for you."

Oh, *merde*.


Donovan regretted giving in to the impulse to bring Jess. After less than an hour, she'd informed him that his attitude sucked, and if he was going to be grumpy and evil, he would have to do it without her on his arm. *She* was going to go and find people who actually wanted to enjoy themselves. He hadn't seen her since, but he really couldn't blame her.

He really had no reason to be at a party. Even a good party like this one. *Especially* this party. It might be Connor's name on the invitation, but this had Lorelei's stamp all over it, which only added to his already evil mood.

He shouldn't have come at all. He could have declined. He just hadn't realized how petty he actually was. He'd known Lorelei would be here, and with all the maturity of a ten-year-old, had decided he'd show her how little it had all meant by showing up at her party and being just damn fine. Bringing Jess had been to rub it in.

He hadn't counted on the plan backfiring on him. He might be putting on the face of being fine, but Lorelei was reveling in it. She circulated like a social butterfly, a huge smile on her face. That smile had been muted slightly when she'd put in her appearance in front of him, as required by the rules of etiquette, but no one, not even him, would be able to tell that they'd ever been more than polite acquaintances.

That had only made his bad mood worse. That red dress had every one of her curves on tasteful display, and the sound of her voice had stoked him like a furnace. He'd been soaking up her presence like a thirsty plant in a rainstorm as she charmed everyone in the crowd, then been left unsatisfied as she moved on.

And it wasn't as if he could ignore her. Whether it was that dress, or the sound of her voice or something more intangible, he could feel her in the room, and he found himself looking for her out of the corner of his eye.

This time when he located her, she was in Jack's arms. The feeling he now recognized as jealousy clawed at his guts. He was going to have to recommend that St. James Media find a new law firm to represent them, because he was *not* going to be gracious about this.

Jess could stay if she wanted to; *he* would probably be better served by getting the hell out of here. He scanned the crowd to see where Jess was, and his eyes landed on Lorelei and Jack again. Only this time Jack was wearing a frown instead of that possessive, smug smile. Lorelei also looked peeved, and her eyes kept darting around as if she was trying to make sure no one was watching them. It was definitely one of those whispering-type fights. *Trouble in paradise already.* He couldn't dredge up much sympathy, though.

Jack reached for her hand and Lorelei snatched it back. "Damn it, Jack, *no.*"

The fact Lorelei was shouting was almost as shocking as her words. Heads started to turn in her direction.

"You're not listening to me. I'm in love with someone else!"

All conversation in the room stopped. Every eye in the room focused on Lorelei, who went from angry to horrified in under three seconds. Her face turned the color of her dress as she realized what she'd done.

Donovan's shock at Lorelei's shout had delayed his brain in the processing of her words. When they finally registered, he thought his heart might have stopped beating. *Love.* That happy, content feeling he'd had was love—and the hollow, achy feeling in his stomach now was him suffering because she didn't love him and had left him. The feelings were so alien and strange he hadn't realized what they were, but now he did. The big question was whether the "someone else" was him…

Someone coughed in the silence.

Jack looked caught at the apex of anger, humiliation and disappointment. When he felt the attention of the room on him, he quickly tried to reschool his face into something more blasé and amused. He failed. Donovan had no pity for him.

There was movement in the crowd, and he saw Vivi dodging between people into the clearing that had opened around Lorelei and Jack.

Then, as if someone had sent out a signal, the conversation started again—not at its previous volume, but everyone seemed to be trying to pretend the last endless minute hadn't happened.

"Wait."

Eyes focused inward, Lorelei spoke softly. He'd have missed it if he hadn't been frozen in place himself, watching her.

She inhaled and tried again. "Excuse me."

This time her voice carried and that total silence cloaked the room again.

Lorelei swallowed hard. "First, let me apologize for that

outburst. I really do try to avoid making a scene and embarrassing people. Especially myself." She smiled weakly. "But, since I brought everyone into this, you deserve to hear the rest of it."

She turned to Jack. "I'm sorry, Jack, but you just weren't taking the hint. I didn't mean to break it to you quite like that."

Jack shrugged, obviously wishing he was anywhere but here. Lorelei addressed the crowd again.

"And, again, I apologize to y'all for interrupting your evening. But, since Vivi is probably going to kill me for making a scene tonight," she joked, "I have something I need to say before she does."

Lorelei's eyes found Donovan's in the crowd.

"I've been a real brat. And my priorities have been way out of whack. I have no excuse other than that I had my sights set on a goal and I totally forgot to look around me at anything else."

Others had noticed Lorelei's stare and followed it. A path began to open between them as people stepped back, and Donovan could feel the weight of their eyes on him. But Lorelei had him hypnotized again, and he couldn't break free.

"I wanted respect. I wanted people to see me as not just Vivi's little sister. The first person who did, though..." She sighed. "I didn't quite see *him*. And that was wrong. Even when he pointed it out to me I still missed it. He had—and has—every right to be angry with me. I should have said this already, but I didn't have the guts. I'm so sorry, Donovan."

He managed a nod.

Lorelei's lips stretched into a shaky smile. "And I realize it was probably kind of sudden and, um, not *quite* the way one is supposed to announce those kinds of things, but it's true. I'm in love...with you."

His heart felt as if it would burst in his chest, and it was hard to breathe.

There was an audible *"aww"* around him, as if someone had cued up a sound effect, and every single person in the room looked at him. It was obviously his move, but he didn't quite have full motor control yet.

As the silence stretched out, he saw Lorelei's smile start to waver.

Once again, Lorelei was able to tie his tongue, but he was able to get his feet moving. Lorelei's smile grew a bit stronger once he moved toward her, but it was still wary. Standing in front of her, he couldn't figure out what he wanted to say. He did the only thing he could do, the thing he'd been wanting to do: pulled her into his arms. She came willingly, easily, and her mouth landed on his with a power and promise that weakened his knees.

Vaguely he heard cheers and applause, but the only thing that registered was the feel of Lorelei melting into him, making him feel whole. He knew what that speech had cost her, and he loved her all the more for making it anyway.

Someone cleared her throat. "Might I suggest you finish your conversation somewhere private?" Vivi asked. "Connor's office is available."

Lorelei flushed and looked embarrassed, but she nodded at her sister. Twining her fingers through his, she tugged gently. "This way."

In the quiet semi-darkness of Connor's office, he finally found his voice again. "You made a bit of a scene there."

"I know."

"What are all those people going to think?"

She grabbed the lapels of his jacket and walked backward, towing him toward Connor's desk. She boosted herself up and pulled him close. "I honestly do not care."

His hands went to her waist as he stepped between her legs. The hem of her dress slid dangerously up her thighs. "Really?"

She tipped her face up for another kiss. "Really."

"Surely you care just a little bit?" he teased.

She shook her head. "I set out to prove people wrong, and I've accomplished that. I wanted to change their minds, and though you say that's not possible—and you might be right—I finally realized I honestly don't care. What can they do to me that's worse than what I've already done to myself?"

"And what *did* you do to yourself?"

"I drove you away." She shrugged. "I know that's technically considered something done to you, but I've been pretty miserable about it. I don't even *want* to be a junior member of the Women's Auxiliary Guild, so it hardly seemed right that I'd have to sacrifice you to gain it." Her hands rested on his shoulders, her fingers idly caressing the back of his neck as she spoke. Then her fingers stilled. "I am really sorry."

"Me, too. I changed the rules in the middle of the game and expected you to play. And then I got mad when you didn't. You were right about me. I am a pompous, blowhard jerk."

That earned him a grin. "And I'm just the bratty princess to handle you."

An eyebrow went up in challenge.

"If you're willing to give this another shot, that is. A proper one this time."

He inhaled, letting her scent curl through him. Meeting her eyes evenly, he said the one thing he'd been trying to deny this whole time. "I love you, Lorelei." Saying it out loud made it real—and a little scary. But he wasn't worried that he might have the emotion wrong: his whole body felt better and his mind felt clearer once he said it.

"And I love you."

All the things he'd set out to accomplish and prove in his life paled in comparison to knowing that Lorelei loved him. "I just wish you'd told me *before* you told the rest of New Orleans."

She pretended to think. "There are a *few* people who still don't know. I'll work on that tomorrow."

"There's a reporter for the paper out there."

"I know. Evelyn Jones. The same woman who speculated about my bad behavior with you before. She must be feeling quite vindicated at the moment." Lorelei bit her lip and let her hands slide down his chest toward his belt buckle. "Maybe we should *really* give her something to talk about…"

# EPILOGUE

IT WAS A SMALL crowd—just their families and a few friends. Less than fifty people, total. Lorelei had been to bigger children's birthday parties.

She wore white, because that was what brides wore, but the dress was neither pouffy nor big—just a simple sheath. Vivi was her only attendant, and she looked elegant and ethereal in silvery-blue. Both Donovan's brothers had stood up with him, making the numbers uneven, but it didn't really matter to anyone except the photographer, who kept grumbling that the pictures would be asymmetrical.

Connor had laughed when she'd asked to use the studio for her wedding, but she'd thrown enough parties here that it was where she felt most comfortable. It had taken a while for her family to get over the fact that Lorelei didn't want to get married in the cathedral with half of the city in attendance—especially since she would have had to invite a bunch of people who would be *tsk*ing under their breath the whole time because she was marrying outside of the fold.

Not that she cared what they thought or what they said, but she wasn't going to feed them while they shook their heads and whispered about her.

Plus, she was sentimental enough to want to make it

permanent in the same space where she'd admitted to Donovan that she loved him for the first time.

So this wedding was exactly what she wanted—from the small guest list to the simple flowers and all of Donovan's favorite foods. Food had been the only thing Donovan expressed a preference on—he'd wanted to elope to Vegas, and when she nixed that idea he'd taken over the menu. It wasn't your normal wedding reception food, but she didn't care.

Lorelei's cheeks hurt from smiling so much, but they weren't fake smiles worn for the crowd. She was just happy.

Donovan was on one of the sofas, talking to his brother, but when she joined them, Matt excused himself. She leaned against Donovan's broad chest and sighed.

"Everything okay?"

"Everything's perfect. Just resting my feet for a second."

"When will you learn not to wear shoes that kill your feet?"

She extended one leg to examine her shoes. She'd painted her toenails the same silvery-blue as Vivi's dress. "But they're so pretty." When Donovan raised an eyebrow at her, she confessed, "I have flats in my bag if I need them. I've learned my lesson well."

He took her hand and twined his fingers through hers. "Your grandmother is not happy."

"I'm the first LaBlanc not to marry in the cathedral in like a hundred years. Of course she's not happy about that. She's not convinced this is truly legit."

Donovan sighed. "We're going to have to go see the priest and get this blessed or something, aren't we?"

"Only if I hope to be in the will." The background

music stopped at the same time the buzz of conversation did, and Lorelei looked around. "What's going on?"

In answer to her question, she saw Connor seated at the piano.

Donovan stood and held out a hand. "How badly do your feet hurt?"

"They're okay."

"Good. Because we're supposed to dance now."

She let Donovan lead her to the middle of the room as Connor played the opening bars of one of his songs. It seemed it was rather handy having a brother-in-law who was a rock star.

As always, it felt good—and right—to be held against Donovan's chest. She could feel the beat of his heart, and that special smell of him filled her lungs as she inhaled.

*"Always remember..."* Connor sang, and Lorelei couldn't imagine a more perfect moment. *"You and me, and the magic of this day."*

The hand on her lower back moved gently in time with the music, keeping her close, making her feel safe.

*"Today I'm giving you my heart."*

She looked up at Donovan. "I did that a while ago."

His smile made her heart flip over. "I know. This just makes it legal."

*"Today I'm giving you my love.*
*Today I'm giving you my all.*
*Promise me, you'll save me..."*

"I love you, Lorelei St. James."

"Lorelei St. James." It still felt a little funny to say it, but... "I kinda like the sound of that."

*"Today I'm giving you my hand.*
*Today we'll say 'I do.'*
*So always remember..."*

She chuckled and Donovan looked at her. "What?"

"It still bums me out a little that I don't remember our first night together."

"You'll have to trust me when I tell you that it wasn't our best effort. All the nights you do remember are *way* better."

"What about tonight?"

The look Donovan gave her should have melted her on the spot. "Oh, tonight's going to be amazing. Definitely one to remember. Are you up to it?"

"Are you kidding me? I may be a St. James now, but I'm still a LaBlanc. And LaBlancs *love* a challenge." She rose up on her tiptoes. "But more than any challenge, I love *you*."

* * * * *

# MILLS & BOON

## THE HEART OF ROMANCE

---

## A ROMANCE FOR EVERY KIND OF READER

---

### MODERN

Prepare to be swept off your feet by sophisticated, sexy and seductive heroes, in some of the world's most glamourous and romantic locations, where power and passion collide.
**8 stories per month.**

### HISTORICAL

Escape with historical heroes from time gone by. Whether your passion is for wicked Regency Rakes, muscled Vikings or rugged Highlanders, awaken the romance of the past.
**6 stories per month.**

### MEDICAL

Set your pulse racing with dedicated, delectable doctors in the high-pressure world of medicine, where emotions run high and passion, comfort and love are the best medicine.
**6 stories per month.**

### *True Love*

Celebrate true love with tender stories of heartfelt romance, from the rush of falling in love to the joy a new baby can bring, and a focus on the emotional heart of a relationship.
**8 stories per month.**

### *Desire*

Indulge in secrets and scandal, intense drama and plenty of sizzlin hot action with powerful and passionate heroes who have it all: wealth, status, good looks…everything but the right woman.
**6 stories per month.**

### HEROES

Experience all the excitement of a gripping thriller, with an intens romance at its heart. Resourceful, true-to-life women and strong, fearless men face danger and desire - a killer combination!
**8 stories per month.**

### DARE

Sensual love stories featuring smart, sassy heroines you'd want as a best friend, and compelling intense heroes who are worthy of the
**4 stories per month.**

---

To see which titles are coming soon, please visit

## millsandboon.co.uk/nextmonth

# JOIN US ON SOCIAL MEDIA!

Stay up to date with our latest releases, author
news and gossip, special offers and discounts, and
all the behind-the-scenes action
from Mills & Boon...

 millsandboon

 millsandboonuk

 millsandboon

*It might just be true love...*

# MILLS & BOON

### MODERN

# Power and Passion

Prepare to be swept off your feet by sophisticated, sexy and seductive heroes, in some of the world's most glamourous and romantic locations, where power and passion collide.

Eight Modern stories published every month, find them all at:

## millsandboon.co.uk/Modern